The critics on Victoria Clayton

'A delicious teasing love story' Elizabeth Buchan

'Told with tremendous affection and care, this is an engrossing yarn that encompasses a range of endearing, sometimes eccentric characters and a not entirely predictable ending' *Ideal Home*

'[*Past Mischief*] is an excellent story told with dash and verve; and the characters leap out of the page to greet one . . . a lovely summer read'
Publishing News

'The charm and vivacity with which the author presents her scenario and the precision with which she describes character and setting make this a very enjoyable read. Social comedy is a difficult thing to do well, but Clayton shows herself an adept practitioner' *The Times*

'Clayton is unsentimental, and there is nothing sugary about her account of love, sex, friendship and manipulation' *Times Literary Supplement*

Victoria Clayton published two children's novels when in her early twenties. She then read English at Cambridge as a mature undergraduate, married and had two children before returning to writing fiction.

By the same author

Out of Love
Dance With Me

PAST MISCHIEF

Victoria Clayton

ORION

An Orion Paperback
First published in Great Britain in 1998 by Orion
This paperback edition published in 1999 by
Orion Books Ltd,
Orion House, 5 Upper St Martin's Lane,
London WC2H 9EA

A CIP catalogue record for this book
is available from the British Library.

Typeset at The Spartan Press Ltd,
Lymington, Hants.
Printed and bound in Great Britain by
Clays Ltd, St Ives plc

CHAPTER I

'I've always said this is a very dark room,' said Dorothy, as we entered the crowded drawing room together.

This was true. It was exactly what my mother-in-law had said the last time she had visited us, five years ago, and on every other occasion before then. I suppose it is the panelling that gives her this impression, for the room has three large windows that face south-west and one that looks north-east, and even on a day like this, when rain was dashing in vicious spurts against the panes, the light is good. The north-east window looks down the drive, which cuts a path through the woods, and on a fine day you can see the seething silver bar that is the sea.

'That looks a nice comfy settee.' Dorothy eyed the sofa by the fire. 'I'll go and have a chat with your mother. I haven't seen her since Henry was christened. I don't think the new vicar's much of an improvement.'

I watched her as she sat down by my mother and began to talk. Dorothy had cried a little during the funeral but now she seemed composed. She never had people to stay, as it 'put her out' and she didn't like staying with us because she was a 'martyr to draughts' and this accounted for the fact that five years had passed since she had seen Jack, who was my husband and her elder son. She much preferred Jeremy, her 'baby' as she referred to him, though he was in his thirties.

Dorothy was talking away with great animation. My mother, Fabia, was sitting very upright with one elegantly shod foot crossed over the other, and staring out of the window with an expression of undisguised boredom.

Sir William Wakeham-Tutt, known to his old Army friends as Wacko, piloted his way through the groups of mourners to where I stood. He smelt strongly of whisky and I guessed that he'd had several secret sips from his hip-flask during the service.

'Damn shame about Jack. Amusing fellow... silly thing to do. Pity for a young chap like that to go instead of a stupid old codger like me.' This could not be disagreed with. Wacko was nothing but a nuisance. His face was mottled by the cold of the churchyard and the whisky. He bent closer to me, almost suffocating me with spirituous fumes, and winked one wrinkled mauve lid. 'The women'll miss him most, eh?'

Patience, his daughter and my closest friend, materialised with the helpful swiftness of a tutelary sprite and led him away to a corner where stood Major Bell-Thompson and Sir Brigham Greene, our local MP, thus forming an epicentre of disagreeable old men. I thought I'd better go and help with the modest lunch I'd planned for the sixty or so who had come back to the house after the service. They were drinking deeply. No doubt there was a chill of the mind as well as the body to be shaken off. Mourners are bound to reflect on the unpleasing certainty that, in time to come, they themselves will be boxed and insensate beneath a hoop of flowers. I hoped the post-office amontillado would hold out. Jack would have been furious with me if I had lavished the choice and expensive contents of his cellar on the relations he so despised. It did not occur to me then that he would not know. I could not convince myself that Jack was really dead.

A man, whose name I had forgotten but who had worked with Jack in the City, barred my way. 'Rum talk the padre gave us. Couldn't understand what he was on about!' He beamed with self-satisfaction.

'I thought it was very interesting,' I said, seeing that Mr Molebank, the vicar, was within earshot.

I was lying. Mr Molebank was not a good speaker, though a truly kind and tolerant man, quite exceptionally so for a clergyman. He always started well but then got sidetracked by ideas that suddenly occurred to him. He had begun quite promisingly by comparing Jack with

Orlando Furioso, Charlemagne's bravest, boldest paladin, slain in his prime. But he had got carried away into a discourse about Ariosto's skills as a poet and lost his audience. After nearly twenty minutes of rambling among the complexities of sixteenth-century Italian epic verse, the congregation was so restless that I feared a mutiny.

'Went on a bit, though,' persisted the banker, disregarding my efforts to wink an eye in Mr Molebank's direction. 'What was the poet chappie's name? Harry Austin? Knew a Harry Austin once. In the Guards with me. Don't suppose it could be the same one.'

'I always find the words of the burial service very inspiring.' Mr Molebank came to join us.

'We're Methodists ourselves,' said one of Jack's aunts, with triumphant *éclat* as though announcing that they were worshippers of Amen-Ra.

'I think it was Emerson who said that the merit claimed for the Anglican Church is that if you let it alone it will let you alone.'

Mr Molebank was the only one who smiled at my little offering of wit. The City man and Jack's aunt wore identically blank expressions.

'I think I'd better see to lunch.' I made my escape.

I was just crossing the hall when the front door opened and in came my sister, Beatrice.

'Miranda, darling!' She flung her arms round my neck. 'I've had the most terrible journey. The van broke down outside Maidenhead and it took ages to get it going again. Now I've missed Jack's funeral and you'll never forgive me!'

'Nonsense!' I embraced her warmly. 'It's wonderful to have you here. Such a comfort, you can't imagine! How are you?'

'Oh, fine. But how are you, you poor, poor darling?'

I kissed her again, thinking how lucky I was to have a sister like Beatrice, and how pleased I was to have her there, before my eyes. As she lived in Devon and I lived in Kent, this did not happen nearly as often as I would have liked. I always worried about her. Maeve, a dear – well, fairly dear – friend, said that it was as patronising to worry about other people as it was to feel sorry for them but I don't know how one can help oneself. Whenever I thought of Beatrice I felt an anxiety that was as involuntary as love. Now I could see that at least she was healthy but, oh dear, fatter than ever. She and her husband, Roger, were very poor and he was a strict vegetarian from principle. From what Beatrice said, they lived largely on potatoes and home-made bread with the addition of a few lentils, nuts and root vegetables for variety. While I applauded the ethics wholeheartedly, I deplored the effect it had on their figures. Beatrice was wearing a red hand-knitted jersey and brown stretch trousers, and the effect was of a large robin who had had a particularly good day for worms.

'I'm all right, I think,' I replied. 'At least, I hardly know. I've had so much to do since it happened and so many people to speak to that I'm in some sort of emotional pea-souper. Feelings loom up suddenly in the fog and then disappear without my being able to put a name to them.'

As I stood in the hall, with Beatrice's arm comfortingly around me, my mind slipped into the loop-tape it had played endlessly since Jack's death. I began to live the whole dreadful business through again as I had, several times a day, since it happened.

I had been standing in the pigeon tower when Jack shot himself. It's the most perfect little octagonal building, two storeys high and fifteenth-century, like our house. I don't suppose I'll ever feel quite the same about it, now. It was a bright October day, with a strong suspicion of chill in the breeze and high, thin clouds. I had been leaning against the ladder, looking up through the slanting shafts of light from the pigeon-holes and listening to the resonating coos of the birds. I was only twenty yards or so from the back door, which was open, and the detonation of the cartridge seemed very loud. The pigeons fluttered with fright, and a few small white feathers floated down towards my upturned face.

Ivor had been working nearby and must have heard it, too, for we met at the back door and exchanged wild glances before running into the house. I pushed open the door of the gun room. I heard Ivor draw in his breath and for a moment, perhaps as long as ten seconds, we stood and stared.

Jack lay with his head slightly propped up against the gun cupboard. His eyes and his mouth were half open. I remember noticing how good-looking he was, something I hadn't thought about for a long time. It's odd how trivial one's thoughts are at important moments in one's life. The gun-room window was open and I reminded myself to close it before I went to bed in case of rain. There was a ringing in my ears, like the first silence after a loud, prolonged noise, a sort of interior singing. I felt extraordinarily calm. Then I saw that there was something different about Jack's face. In the last few years he'd been drinking quite heavily and it had reddened his face a little. Now it was an unfamiliar yellowish-white. On his chest the green wool of his gardening jersey was overlaid by a horrifying ugly rust-red stickiness.

'Oh, my God!' said Ivor, at last. 'We'd better . . . Should I . . . ? I don't know . . . I can't think.' His teeth began to chatter with shock.

Though I'm very fond of Ivor, he is the last person to have about one in a crisis. For one second, a feeling of absolute terror made my stomach contract painfully, as though it had been punched hard. Ivor put a hand on my arm and at once, with a sharpness that seemed likely to snap my spine, I felt myself become rigid and my scalp pricked. Something pushed at my leg. I glanced down. Jasper, our black spaniel, was looking up at me, whining and wagging his tail. Automatically I bent to stroke his head and the action restored me to a fragile composure.

'You stay here, Ivor.' I pulled him outside and closed the door. 'I'll go and telephone Dr Kenton.'

I don't know what I imagined Dr Kenton was going to do, exactly. Even in the extraordinary suspension of anything like coherent thought, which had begun from the moment I looked into the gun room, I had realised that Jack was dead. But Dr Kenton had delivered all my children at the cottage hospital and had seen them through their childish illnesses and accidents. Despite being almost seventy, he still worked as hard as a twenty-year-old, up to the elbows in birth, suffering and death, and he understood the puzzles and perplexities of the human heart.

I went to the hall and picked up the telephone. My head was still buzzing with effervescent whistles and the dial seemed stiff and obstructive. The surgery number rang for ages before an unfamiliar voice answered it. 'I'm afraid Dr Kenton can't answer the phone at present.' The voice was cold and unnaturally refined.

'I'm sorry to ring out of hours but this is an emergency. Would you please tell Dr Kenton that Mrs Stowe needs to speak to him very urgently.'

'There's an evening surgery, you kne-ow, if you're not well. What sort of emergency is it?'

The voice had responded to my sharpness with an extra shade of refinement.

'I don't think it's really any of your business but my husband has shot himself.'

I heard her gasp.

'Weel you wait one me-owment, please.' I waited. I must do something about the draughts in the hall. I was feeling shivery. The receiver crackled and then the same voice said, 'Is that Mrs Ste-owe of Westray Me-anor?'

'Yes.'

'Someone is coming e-out to you at once.'

I put the telephone down just as Mrs Goss came downstairs.

'We'll need more furniture polish, Mrs Stowe. That wax doesn't seem to go anywhere. Those old chairs soak it up.'

Mrs Goss hated anything old. She was always telling me about the improvements she and Mr Goss had made to their bungalow. Mr Goss had just finished building a 'vanity unit' for Mrs Goss. Looking at her unwashed hair and sour, lard-coloured face, I wondered that he had thought it worth his while.

'I'm afraid there's been an accident, Mrs Goss.'

My legs were behaving oddly, trembling with shooting pins and needles. Mrs Goss folded her arms and jerked back her head as she always did when I began to tell her something she didn't like . . . usually that a navy sock had found its way into the whites wash again or that the china cupboard door had been left open and the cat had got in.

'Mr Stowe has . . . has . . .'

The room turned swiftly and the floor rose to slap me hard on the face. When I came round, Ivor was bending over me. He held a glass of something. Cognac. I coughed as it caught my throat, but my senses began to return. I felt dreadfully sick. I was lying on the sofa in the library. I suppose Ivor had carried me there. My skirt was screwed up about my waist. I struggled feebly to pull it down. My neck felt cold and wet. Ivor's hand was shaking so much that he was splashing Cognac all over my shirt.

'Poor darling. My poor sweet girl,' he was saying. 'There, there, my buttercup.'

I suppose anyone who didn't know Ivor or me might have thought that there was something compromising in this. But they would have been wrong. Ivor has been our gardener for the last fifteen years, having failed, fairly spectacularly, to live successfully out in the world. There was a short spell in prison, followed by a longer sojourn in a mental hospital. This was a black period for him, his suffering compounded by the fact that he was head and shoulders in intelligence and education above those meant to be treating him. He is inexpressibly tender-hearted and mourns every worm he accidentally chops with his spade. Once I found him in tears over a baby rabbit our cat had killed. Part of our wood was like a miniature war cemetery with row upon row of tiny mounds marked by white plastic plant labels, on which was written 'hedgehog found squashed' or 'striped fish from moat' or 'shrew killed by Dinkie'. This sort of sensitivity is rare and precious in a man. But when Jack was lying on the floor of the gun room, blasted into eternity, it was of no assistance whatsoever.

Ivor had been at school with Jack. They hadn't been friends, particularly, for even then there had been something odd about Ivor. I forgot to mention that he is a poet. As everyone knows, there is little money to be made from poetry and he was too disorganised to garner what scraps there are going. He and I shared horticultural tastes and he worked very hard. In return we provided him with a reasonable salary, a cottage in the woods – which is really a Gothic folly and magically pretty – and he always came up to the house for lunch. He said he was happier than he had ever been in his life. It made me sad to think what his life must have been before.

He and I got on well. He was secretive about his writing, but occasionally he left a poem addressed to me pinned on a tree-trunk and garlanded with moss, or folded into the empty shell of a hen's egg. You might imagine from this that his poetry was not very good but, luckily, it was free from whimsicality and, though I'm not particularly a judge of these things, I thought it was interesting. I stored the poems safely away with the intention of sending them off to a publisher when I had enough for a 'slim volume'.

He always said he loved me but I knew it was a poet's love... someone to write about and dream of and sigh over. Often he would kiss my hand and give me a wren's nest full of wild violets or some specially nice shells he had found on the beach. I was quite certain that this chaste contact was all he ever wanted. Jack always spoke about Ivor's sexlessness with disparagement but I thought it was something of a relief. Not that I'm sexless myself, certainly not, but it – male sexuality anyway – does seem to intrude itself tiresomely on everything that's happening, as I had good cause to know.

Anyway, if one didn't happen to be conversant with the history of Ivor's and my relationship, it might have seemed odd to overhear him call me his buttercup. It was unlucky that Mrs Goss had thrown open the library door at just that moment.

'It's the doctor, Mrs Stowe,' she said, with one of the very liquid sniffs that were her speciality.

A youngish man, tall with dark curly hair, stood in the doorway. He looked tired and rather cross.

'Oh, but I thought... Where's Dr Kenton?' I struggled to sit up. I was very conscious of my skirt being up round my waist.

'Dr Kenton isn't well. I'm the new locum. Rory McCleod.'

He came over and offered me his hand. I realised that I must smell very strongly of brandy.

'How do you do? I'm afraid the shock of finding my husband... I must have fainted... I'm Miranda Stowe.' I stood up and tried to smooth down my skirt.

Ivor sank down into my place on the sofa, tears running down his face. 'You were – unconscious – like Madeline in azure-lidded sleep.' His speech was broken by sobs. 'Poor Jack! What could have possessed him? He had everything a man could desire! How often I've thought of doing away with it all... but never had the courage. Coward!' He struck himself savagely on the breast.

Poets are nothing if not egocentric. I expect they have to be in order to dredge about in the soul. I gave him the brandy, which he sipped as he mopped his streaming eyes.

'This is Ivor Bastable. A family friend,' I said to Dr McCleod.

'I'm the gardener. Don't try to spare my feelings, Miranda. How do you do?'

Dr McCleod shook Ivor's large, earthy hand and then got out his handkerchief. He wiped his own hand vigorously, and his expression was now bemused as well as cross. 'I was told there'd been an accident. Your husband, Mrs Stowe?'

'Oh, God!' I put my hand to my head. 'No, it's all right, Ivor. I've got to be sensible. I'll show you where he is. Ivor, you must go and tell Rose what's happened. Try to break it gently.'

I left Dr McCleod at the door of the gun room. I didn't want to see Jack again. I went through the hall to the kitchen.

Rose had been my nurse once. Next to my three children and Beatrice, I loved her better than anyone in the world. Now Rose was old, eighty-six to be exact, and arthritis was twisting her gaunt frame into something resembling a blasted oak, but she was still my greatest strength and comfort. I saw at once from Rose's expression that Ivor's idea of breaking things gently had resulted in hopeless confusion.

'I can't understand what this addle-brain is talking about. Some poppycock about bodkins and fardels. What is the matter, Miranda darling?'

Rose hated men and she always spoke to them and about them with manifest contempt. She only condescended to endearments with us when things were really bad, so I guessed I must look pretty distraught.

'An accident, Rose ... Something dreadful's happened. Jack has ... Oh, how can I tell the children?'

I felt things begin to swim again but, quicker than a cat's pounce, Rose had me sitting down with my head between my legs.

'That's better,' she said, lifting my head and pressing something cold and damp against my temples. I noticed later that it was one of Jack's socks, which Rose had been darning, dipped in tea. Jack said that wearing a sock after Rose had darned it was like making a pilgrimage with peas in your shoes. The darns were hopelessly cobbled and knobbly, because of the arthritis, but Rose insisted on going through the laundry, looking for mending because, as she said, she wanted to be of some use. 'Do you, Ivor, put that kettle to boil and make her a good strong cup of tea instead of standing there like the Box Tunnel, with your mouth open. Now, Miranda, you tell Rose all about it.'

She held my hand in her own knotted palm and looked at me with eyes like slivers of wet rock from her native Stornoway, almost hidden by enveloping, crinkled lids.

'Oh, Rose!' I hoped I was about to cry and that the tears would bring a proper realisation of what had happened and an end to the ringing noise in my head. I wanted to feel real anguish and loss, instead of this sinister choke-damp of inconsequential half-thoughts. But it wasn't going to be that easy. 'I think I'm going to be sick.'

I was, horribly. Ivor held the bowl for me, which was kind, and made little crooning noises of distress, which was irritating. Rose sat calmly in her characteristic pose with legs well apart and her hands on her knees, waiting till I'd finished.

'That's better. Now you must have something to settle your stomach. Take the bowl away, Ivor, for goodness sake, and stop that mewing!'

Ivor meekly did as he was told, and made me some tea and toast. I tried to eat a little to please them both but I felt weak and faint. The tea was better.

'Jack has shot himself, Rose.' I'd forgotten about breaking things gently.

'Lord have mercy!' Rose pressed her hands to her cheeks in dismay. 'Man is born unto trouble as the sparks fly upward! And that man was more trouble than most!'

She said this almost with admiration. I suppose she felt she could afford to be generous now that Jack was dead. From their first meeting, it had been war to the knife. Most men, when they felt the lash of Rose's severest censure, treated her with emollient politeness, and kept out of her way as much as possible. But Jack only laughed at her, as he did at anyone who tried to impress the force of their personality on him. It wasn't from insensitivity, for he was fully aware of the boundaries that other people marked out for themselves. He simply stepped over those boundaries and behaved exactly as he wanted. While I disapproved of this selfish disregard of other people, there was a part of me that admired it and was almost envious of it. I'm often intimidated by people, even those whom I neither like nor respect. I catch myself out, sometimes, being ingratiating, and then I'm disgusted with myself.

Rose's hand shook as she tidied her darning wools and moved my cup and plate about on the table – the rearrangement of objects was a habit when she was thinking – but she looked calm enough. She had a spirit of endurance that would have satisfied Zeno. She had been alone in the world from the age of seventeen and the only man she had ever loved had died of tuberculosis just before she came to look after me. She was a tough old bird.

'There's Elizabeth to think of. She'll be home in an hour. You'll need your strength. Eat that up,' was all she said.

The desire to propitiate came over me as soon as Dr McCleod came into the kitchen and found me holding an enormous piece of toast. Ivor is incapable of doing anything moderately so I was grasping something the size of a brick, which probably looked callous, if not positively breezy, in the face of my husband's recent death. Ivor was still cradling the bowl of vomit as though it were a libation to the gods. I imagined that my face was almond green.

Dr McCleod looked anything but inured to humanity at its lowest ebb and I longed for dear Dr Kenton. I understood instinctively that, as far as Dr McCleod was concerned, impressions were all against us. Our house, Westray Manor, though not palatial, is large enough to give an impression of money and privilege. I suppose that I, with my eccentric retinue, seemed insulated and protected and therefore beyond the need of kindness from strangers. 'I've sent for an ambulance and informed the police,' he said, looking at me with, I thought, quite unnecessary severity. 'There will have to be a post-mortem, of course.' He rolled his Rs slightly. Naturally, with a name like Rory McCleod, he would be a Scot.

'Must there be, really?' I said, idiotically, as if hoping to persuade him to relent.

'Certainly. Your husband had not been receiving medical attention recently?'

'Oh... let me think. He went to see Dr Kenton about a sprained shoulder just after Christmas.'

Dr McCleod sighed. He seemed very fed up. 'I meant more recently than that. And sprained shoulders are not generally fatal.' His tone was dry.

'That's all you know, young man,' put in Rose, rebuffingly. 'The first intimations of a bad heart are often felt as pains in the arms and shoulders. It's plain to see you've not had much experience.'

'And you are...?' Dr McCleod looked coldly at Rose.

'Oh, I'm so sorry.' I was being propitiatory, again. 'This is Miss Ingrams. She lives with us.'

'I see.'

'Though what business it is of yours...' began Rose. I suppose she was provoked to rudeness by his unsympathetic manner.

'I shall be required to give evidence at the inquest. You'll probably all be asked if you know of any reason why the deceased might have taken his own life.'

He looked at Ivor, probably because Ivor suddenly hiccuped. I expect it was the brandy. He'd got through a second glassful while making the tea for me.

'I resent your insinuations,' said Ivor, in his grandest manner. He has a face like one of the early Plantagenets, rather thin and brooding, with a nose of tremendous length. He became, despite the thorn twigs in his hair and the mud on his breeches, every inch the youngest representative of a noble line... which he was. 'If you think that I've ever given Mr Stowe reason to think that my devotion to Mrs Stowe has trespassed upon the sacred vows of marriage, you stand condemned by your own base imaginings. "Oh, love that never found its earthly close. Streaming eyes and breaking hearts..."'

'Ivor,' I said, desperately, 'shut up.'

The idea that Jack might deliberately have killed himself was so frightening and horrible that I felt my skin suddenly cold with sweat. I rushed over to the sink and was sick again. I felt a hand on my arm.

'You've had a bad shock.' Dr McCleod's voice was

kinder. 'I'll give you something to help you sleep.'

'It *must* have been an accident. It must have been! Jack was so – so confident!'

It didn't sound an adequate reason for my certainty that Jack was incapable of killing himself. I couldn't find the right words to describe Jack's character... his audacity... the fact that he didn't care enough about anything to think of killing himself. He was never depressed – or, at least, I'd never noticed it in the nineteen years of our marriage. Nor was he ever afraid of anything that I knew of. But supposing there were aspects of his character of which I had been unaware? Images of Jack came into my mind. I remembered him when we met at Oxford during my second year, when he was finishing his D.Phil. We were in the same production of *The Tempest*. I had played my namesake and he had been Prospero. His performance had been mesmeric.

I remembered the exultation on his face when he got his first job at the bank, a few months before we were married. And I saw him clearly in my mind here at Westray, rowing up and down the moat, trying to fish out the duckweed. It must have been about thirteen years ago. He was looking up at me, laughing, as I leaned out of the library window. I had shouted a warning that the boat would capsize if he stood up. He had fallen in the moment after, swum to the bank and climbed out, still laughing. I loved him so much then. He had stripped off all his clothes and left them lying on the bank. Rose had met him as he strode naked up the stairs. She had swept past, head in the air, full of wrath.

'Not what you'd call a pretty sight, eh, Rose?' he called down after her.

I had taken his wet clothes to the laundry room and put them in the sink to soak as they stank of brackish water. Then I had gone upstairs to tell him off for offending Rose's sensibilities. He had walked out of the shower, taken me in his arms and pulled me down on to the bed. We made love. We were so happy. It was the day after this that I discovered that for the past year he had been having an affair with Felicity Partridge, one of my closest friends. I was never completely happy again.

CHAPTER 2

'So, you see, I really don't know whether it was an accident or whether Jack meant to kill himself.' Beatrice and I were still standing in the hall. The noise from the drawing room increased as the comfort of warmth and alcohol penetrated the clothing and nervous systems of the mourners. 'It's glorious to talk to you but the draught in this hall is like a cleaver. Let's go into the kitchen. Anyway, I'm feeling guilty. I've left one of my guests to do all the work.'

In my recital of the facts of Jack's death, I stuck to the events of that afternoon. I said nothing about his affair with Lissie. I had never told Beatrice of Jack's unfaithfulness, partly out of pride and partly because I didn't want her to worry about me.

The kitchen was deliciously warm. Rose was sitting in the chair by the fire, with one arm in a sling. James and Elizabeth were leaning on the Aga rail, arguing. They stopped when they saw us and came over to kiss Beatrice. Beatrice and Rose exchanged tender greetings, and Rose explained that she had fallen over that morning but was perfectly all right, just a bruised wrist and no harm done.

'Shouldn't you children be talking to people and taking round drinks and things?' I said.

'Henry wanted to do it on his own. You know how he craves attention,' said Elizabeth, with contempt. 'James and I were bored. I hate talking to grown-ups, anyway. Sorry, not anyone here, of course.'

'But it's so good for you to learn how,' I persisted, unwisely.

'I notice *you* aren't,' said Elizabeth, scowling.

James gave her a light cuff on the head. 'Don't be

cheeky, brat.' He spoke from the superior position of one just eighteen.

'I have been, though. I just came in to relieve Diana.'

'Oh, Mum, you are a fibber!' Henry had come into the kitchen. 'I saw you talking to Aunt Beatrice in the hall for at least ten minutes. It's gruesome in the drawing room. I didn't know Dad had so many really grisly relations.'

'They're your relations, too,' Elizabeth pointed out.

'Well, I'm disowning them on the spot. Can I disown them officially, like changing your name by deep hole?'

'I think you mean deed poll, darling.' James and Elizabeth were in fits of unkind laughter. 'That won't be necessary. We just won't ask them to the house again.'

'I shouldn't think they'll want to come,' said James. 'Fabia was sitting with her eyes tight shut and her head flung back against the cushions, with an expression on her face as though her thumbs were being screwed when Granny was talking to her.'

Though Fabia was also their grandmother, of course, she thought 'granny' and 'grandma' were common and the children had called her Fabia since they were old enough to talk.

'Oh dear, I wonder if I ought . . .?'

'I'll go,' said Beatrice. 'You've got enough to worry about.'

'Thank you. That would be a help. Oh, this is Diana Milne. My sister, Beatrice,' I added, as a tall, strikingly lovely girl came into the kitchen from the dining room. Her face was charmingly sequinned with twinkling fish-scales. 'You look like a beautiful nereid.' I led her to the mirror and gave her a paper handkerchief. 'I'm afraid you must be quite exhausted. It is *so* good of you.'

'Oh, no, I've enjoyed it. It isn't often that I have the chance, these days, to do something uninterrupted. Honestly, it's been a pleasure. There's just the salad dressing to make and then everything's ready, I think. Shall I do it?'

'No, no. You must take off your apron and go and have a drink.'

I fetched olive oil and vinegar from the larder. The children were arguing again over something silly. The anxiety that had been making itself insidiously manifest since Jack's death sent out a warning signal. Of course, the children had always argued. But could this bickering be a sign of serious depression in one or all of them?

When I had seen Elizabeth's face as she sauntered into the kitchen after school on the day of Jack's death, I had thought my courage was going to fail completely and I wouldn't be able to tell her. She was wearing her customary insouciant expression behind a long sweep of fair, wavy hair (she has my colouring... only the boys inherited Jack's red hair) and she smelt of cigarettes, so I knew she had stopped to smoke in the bus shelter with Marlene Cooper. Her eyelashes were spiky with navy mascara and her lips were a sultry shade of tangerine, a look very much at odds with the pale-blue shirt and dark-green pleated skirt that was her school uniform. The brim of her school hat was turned up all the way round in a gesture of defiance that warmed my heart.

'What's for tea, Mum?' she had asked, and without waiting for my answer, unlaced her shoes and left them just where everyone would fall over them. She had spent hours breaking them in so that they wouldn't look new. Now they had all the distinction of Gertrude Jekyll's boots, though no one had yet thought to immortalise them in oils.

I found some fruit cake in the tin and cut her a slice.

'Sit down, darling,' I said. 'There's something I must tell you. You must try to be very, very brave.'

I took hold of her hand but she withdrew hers as soon as I began to speak. I told her as calmly I could what had happened. The piece of cake was poised near her mouth. She drew in her breath sharply and her eyes widened. She put down the cake. 'Why?' she said, at last. She had to clear her throat to get the words out.

'I suppose he made a mistake. Cleaning the gun. I don't know.'

'Dad wouldn't make that sort of mistake.'

Her face was screwed up, as though the light was too bright. I remembered the struggle she had had to break the habit of calling us Mummy and Daddy when she had gone to the local school. When she was eleven we had sent her to my old school in Wiltshire, against all my better instincts. She had been dreadfully homesick. After three terms, I couldn't bear the tearful telephone calls any longer and, to Jack's great disgust, I had taken her away and sent her to our local day school, Bosworth High. I still thought I had done the right thing.

Now she put her head into her hands and made a sound that was half a sigh and half a sob. I put my arm around her shoulders, but I could feel the tension that rejects comfort. She was only fourteen. Too young to have to endure this kind of suffering. I felt a flash of anger. Even if Jack had shot himself by accident, how dare he, father of three children, be so careless? I knew rage was an inappropriate emotion but it was a feeling that grew uncontrollably with every day that passed after the discovery of Jack's body.

Rose came over with a cup of tea. 'Drink this, my chick. You need sugar for shock.'

Elizabeth stayed hunched within the circle of her own arms. Then she muttered a sort of thank-you, took the cup and went out of the room, her head down, avoiding all our eyes.

'Oh dear.' I looked at Rose.

'You didn't think it would be easy,' was all she said. 'Let her be. She'll let you know when she wants you.'

I took Rose's advice. I had no ideas of my own. I was still chasing wisps of thought and forgetting what they were the moment I caught them. A few minutes later we heard strains of the Rolling Stones from upstairs. 'I can't get no-o- . . . satisfaction' went the plangent throb.

'I'm surprised no one corrected their grammar,' said Rose.

The telephone rang. I went to answer it. From the receiver came sounds of distress.

'Hello, Lissie,' I said, at a venture.

'Miranda! Tell me it isn't true!' Another sobbing breath. 'I can't bear it! Oh, please! Please say it isn't true!'

I sighed and drew up the hall chair. 'I'm sorry, Lissie. I'm afraid it *is* true. How did you hear?'

I gathered, eventually, from Lissie's disjointed utterances that she had been to pick up George's heart pills from the surgery. 'The receptionist was gossiping about it on the telephone... She said something about Westray Manor... That's what made me listen... I can't believe it!'

'It's true. Jack has... shot himself.'

I could not believe it either.

'Oh – oh – oh! How can you be so calm? Oh, I'm sorry, darling, it must be the most frightful thing for you. Of course you're distraught! I'll come round at once. Don't do a thing till I get there.'

'No, Lissie, don't –'

But it was too late. She'd put down the telephone.

I had forgiven Lissie – Felicity Partridge – years ago, for her affair with my husband. Thirteen years ago, in fact. Lissie was small and slender and pretty, with captivating dimples and golden curly hair, like those shavings of butter that used to be *de rigueur* in ambitious restaurants during my childhood. She had fallen in love with Jack with all the uncritical devotion of her sentimental nature. When she arrived on our doorstep in such distress one evening, all those years ago, to say that she couldn't bear to lie to me any longer and that she and Jack were dreadfully in love, I had been so astonished that at first I thought she was joking.

I suppose it was naïve of me but I had been without the slightest suspicion. I had noticed that over the preceding few months she had come to see me less often, and that she had seemed rather more than usually tearful and nervous. I had attributed it to the fact that her two-year-old daughter was a terribly bad sleeper and screamed every night for hours. When she had told me that she and Jack were having an affair, I had simply stared at her and said, 'What on earth do you mean?'

She had looked at me with dark blue, frightened eyes and said, 'I love him. I'm so dreadfully sorry, Miranda... I've done the most terrible thing to you and I hate myself.'

A cold feeling had crept into the pit of my stomach, like a snake winding its way into the shadows beneath a stone.

I suppose everyone feels much the same when they discover that the marriage they had thought so happy and successful has been sustained by lies. I need not describe in depth the pain and the humiliation.

'We can't talk here. Come into the library.'

I expect she was alarmed by my face and voice. I certainly meant her to be. As soon as we were sitting facing each other either side of the fire-less grate, I said, 'I want to know everything.'

'It began at your birthday party. At least, I suppose it began long before then, really. The moment I met Jack I think I fell in love with him... I'm so ashamed.'

Out came the story of Lissie's passion. She spared me times and places, though a foolish masochism made me press her for details. As she talked she cried without stopping, her makeup smudging like bruises, the corners of her mouth stretched wide like a child's. The more penitent she grew, the angrier I became. I knew, even as I sat listening and hating her, that she was someone to whom deceit was inimical and that she had detested having to lie to her husband and to me. But I didn't want anything to mitigate my fury. It was my only consolation. It had been going on for eleven months. Heavens, what a fool they had made of me!

When Jack got home an hour later, he found two exhausted, tearful women staring at him with reproachful, reddened eyes. He looked at us each in turn, then sighed and threw down his briefcase. 'I'm going to get us all a drink. I suppose there's going to be hell to pay now.'

It was a remark that grated very much on my ear. I doubted if it would be Jack doing the paying.

'Perhaps you wouldn't mind telling me just how things stand,' I said, with tremulous irony. 'I seemed to have overestimated the value of our relationship by rather a lot.'

'Don't talk in that stagey way, Miranda.' Jack was very cool. 'You know I love you. You're the only woman I've ever loved, as it happens. You won't believe me, I suppose, just at the moment, but I can assure you it's true. I've never loved anyone else. This thing with Lissie, well . . . It was a diversion. Pleasant, amusing, flattering . . . but unimportant.'

Instead of boxing his ears for such a testament of selfishness, I felt an absurd gratitude for this reassurance of affection. Poor Lissie looked at Jack with amazement. Then, holding her arms, she doubled over in her chair and began to make puppyish whimpering sounds. Jack lit a cigarette and poured himself another glass of wine. Mine was still untouched.

'You're not drinking, Lissie?' When she didn't answer, his eyes became harder, with an excited glitter. 'I suppose you came here today to make a row. I hope you're satisfied. You're a sweet girl, Lissie, but you shouldn't play games if you can't stand to lose. I've behaved very badly, I know. I'm ashamed of myself. Now, let's forget the whole thing. It's over.'

Lissie drooped her curly head and hid her face. I felt glad, at the time, to see her thus reduced, but I was astonished that Jack appeared to be quite unmoved by her grief.

'Enough of this torrid scene.' Jack smiled with cruel cynicism. 'Can you drive, Lissie, or would you like me to take you home?'

Lissie got up and ran, bent almost double, out of the room.

Three days later, during which time I had wept and Jack had pleaded with me until at last, out of exhaustion, I had agreed to forgive him – or, at least, to say I had, which was not at all the same thing – I had gone round to see Lissie. I don't know quite what I expected from another painful encounter. She looked so sad and so ill that the bitter things I had imagined myself saying seemed pointlessly vindictive. We ended that interview with tearful promises on her part and softened words on mine.

After a hiatus of a few months, which allowed me to get used to the unpleasant and intrusive image of Lissie and Jack in bed together, I gradually resumed my old affection for her. She was evidently so very unhappy, so repentant and still so much in love with Jack, despite his unkindness, that my anger was slowly extinguished.

Lissie had a generous spirit, she was tender-hearted and guileless. She was also a great deal of fun to be with, and she had exquisite taste. These attributes are not so common that I felt I could dispense with her friendship. In an odd way the affair brought us closer. I tried very hard to make her see what a bastard Jack had been. I failed to convince her. She was, if anything, more besotted. Unluckily, it was I who was persuaded by my own argument and my love for Jack began to falter.

Thirteen years later, Lissie still loved him. She hadn't admitted it but she didn't need to. I could see it on her face whenever she spoke to him or about him. She was, heart and soul, a romantic, and Jack was a romantic icon. His self-confidence, which amounted to arrogance, his intelligence, his energy and, I suppose, his brutality, made him a thrilling blend of prepotent Victorian patriarch and unpredictable gypsy.

On the evening of the day when Jack shot himself, Lissie appeared at the front door, saw me standing in the hall and launched herself, weeping, into my arms. I had been on my way upstairs to take a look at Elizabeth. I could hear the engine of Lissie's car still running on the other side of the gatehouse door, which she had left open. I pointed out that she was filling the garden with fumes and would eventually run out of petrol.

'How can you be so calm? Oh, what does anything matter now?'

She cried so noisily that Jasper set up a loud barking. He was dripping water and trailing weeds all over the floor, so I knew he had been swimming in the moat again. I held Lissie in my arms. My own eyes felt gritty, hot and tearless. Every part of me was stiff with a sickening ache but my mind was disturbingly calm.

I shut Jasper in the kitchen with Rose and Ivor. Ivor had offered to cook supper. He is an imaginative cook but doesn't get much practice so this is usually a disaster. Like most children, I suppose, mine are unadventurous eaters with a list of about ten things – different, of course – that they will willingly eat. None of these lists included eggs pickled in raspberry vinegar or bread flavoured with lavender. But it was kind of him.

I opened a bottle of white wine and poured a glass for Lissie, whom I had left sitting on a chair in the hall, clutching a box of paper handkerchiefs. 'Take this into the drawing room. I shan't be long.'

I ran upstairs and along the landing to Elizabeth's room. I knocked, not expecting to be heard above the blast of 'Hey, you, get off of my cloud', another petty revolt against the rules of grammar. I opened the door. Elizabeth was sitting on the floor, lolling back against the side of her bed. She was wearing sunglasses. Shades, I mentally corrected myself, having earned a great deal of scorn from my children on this point of nomenclature. It was impossible to tell whether her eyes were open or shut. I stood looking down at her for some time. Then I bent and touched her hand. At once it was withdrawn so I knew she wasn't asleep.

'I just wondered . . .'

'Go away . . . please, Mum.'

I went. Lissie was just pouring herself another glass of wine. I put a match to the paper and kindling in the grate and the flames leaped quickly to fill the great cavern of the fireplace. I didn't put on the lights. The glow of firelight would be kinder to our ravaged faces. The warmth, the smell, the sparkle and the crackle of the burning logs was comforting and agreeable. I felt guilty as I thought this. How could I allow myself to enjoy anything when Jack lay dead in a refrigerated box beyond all pleasure? I didn't even know where they had taken him. But perhaps even now his soul was bathing in a brilliance unimaginable.

'Darling, he isn't... here?' Lissie looked up fearfully.

'No. An ambulance came to take him away. I didn't see him go. I was in the kitchen.'

'You poor sweet! What you've been through! Does it hurt to talk about it?'

'No. It's the oddest thing. There was a sudden rush of violent feeling for a few seconds, like opening a door into a hot, noisy, crowded room, and then I seemed to swim away into a dream.'

'Shock, darling, and who can wonder at it? Oh dear, the poor children! Do they know?'

'I've told Elizabeth. I don't know how she's taking it. She's gone dangerously quiet. I'll drive over to tell the boys tomorrow. And I'll bring them home, of course. But I thought I'd better have a night's sleep before trusting myself behind the wheel.'

'Let George go. He'd do anything to help, honestly he would. He'd have come with me this evening but I told him he'd just be in the way. He's very good with children.'

George was good with everyone. He was a kind-hearted, dependable man with a fringe of sandy hair, just where a wreath of laurels ought to lie, and a figure like Humpty Dumpty. I had always liked him. He wasn't fashioned in the image of Heathcliff, and though Lissie was very fond of him, she was often impatient with his practical and stately progress through life.

'Thank you. But I feel I must do this myself. If I chose anyone it would be George. He's a dear.'

'Yes. But...' There was another flood of weeping, punctuated by breathless attempts to tell me how sorry she was for me, and how Jack was the last man to whom it should have happened. She began to list his virtues, a recital that rapidly became a confession of love. 'Of course, there hasn't been anything between us for years. You've got to believe me! He's devoted to you. From the day I told you all about it – you remember, all those years ago – he's never laid a finger on me. He's been completely faithful to you. Say you believe me!'

'I believe you.'

'But I'll be absolutely truthful. If he'd wanted to go on – with me, I mean – I'm not sure that I would have been able to resist him. I hope I would but I can't honestly be sure. It's disgraceful, I know, and I'm thoroughly ashamed of myself. But I want to get it out into the open. I'll love Jack until the day I die!'

I got up and sat on the arm of my chair with my arm round her.

'Dear Lissie. It's all right. I know you loved him. Really loved him. Perhaps... Well, anyway, it's good of you to be so honest about it and I'm sorry that you're so unhappy. Have another handkerchief.'

'This is dreadful. I'm supposed to be comforting *you*. Promise you won't hate me for what I've just told you.'

'I promise. Now, I think I ought to go and see how Elizabeth is. Do you want to stay for supper?'

'Thanks, but if you really don't need me I ought to go and feed George. Since his heart-attack he's terribly fussy about what he eats and when. Dinner has to be on the stroke of seven. Boiled white fish and potatoes without butter. So boring. He loves it, the fuss and the self-importance. But it's mean of me to grumble. When I think of everything you're going through. Oh, Jack!' She burst out crying again. 'Would it help Elizabeth if Alice came over tomorrow?' she asked, when she could speak.

Alice is Lissie's daughter and only child. She is a thorn in Elizabeth's flesh, and this has often caused me tremendous difficulties. Alice is the sort of child whom most adults adore and all her contemporaries despise. She is very small and pretty with the same curly golden hair as Lissie which she wears fastened back from her face with a black velvet padded band. She is a co-operative child and still wears the sort of stripy dresses with sailor collars that Elizabeth had rebelled against from the age of six.

I must admit that there are things about Alice that irritate me, in particular the way she talks with her head held winsomely on one side and her habit of referring to herself in the third person. Also, she always stands with her knees and toes turned inwards and pressed together like a Mabel Lucie Atwell child. Henry says she must have permanently wet knickers and is afraid they might fall down. I try to be nice to Alice. I can't say that Elizabeth does.

Alice isn't very bright and I'm sorry to say that Elizabeth has had her revenge for being forced to spend time with her by exploiting this. She once lured Alice down into the priest-hole, by telling her that she could hear a poor little lost kitten mewing. As soon as Alice lowered herself into the dark, cobwebby space beneath the staircase, Elizabeth had put the tread and riser back in place and pushed home the wooden pegs that secured them.

I had been gardening all afternoon so it was not until Jack came home and heard Alice screaming that she was released. Alice was in a frightening state of distress. Not only was she very thirsty and dirty but she was almost incoherent with terror. I was puzzled when I heard her gibbering about monks and cakes. Elizabeth was sent for. When she saw the state of Alice, she turned rather red and looked a little sorry. 'It was a game. I'm sorry, Alice.'

'But what is all this about a monk coming to tea?' I asked.

Elizabeth went redder. 'Oh, you know the old story about the ghost who lives in the priest-hole. Of course everyone knows he doesn't really exist. I thought Alice knew that.'

'You told Alice she'd have to stay down in the dark with the nasty old ghost! You told Alice!' screamed Alice. 'Alice was shut in the dark with the monk who was going to pull out her hair to make himself a beard!'

I tried to soothe the poor child, but she insisted on being driven home at once. It was some time before she would consent to come to our house again. I spoke very sternly to Elizabeth, but it was hard to induce a sense of guilt when Jack laughed every time the tale was told and James and Henry were openly admiring of her ingenuity.

Then there was the recent occasion, not so painful for

Alice but much more embarrassing, when I asked the church fête committee to stay for drinks after the meeting. Lissie and George were stalwarts on these occasions and had brought Alice with them. The children were, I hoped, playing Monopoly in the kitchen as instructed. I'd forbidden any mention of ghosts on pain of early bedtimes for a whole week. Suddenly Alice appeared in the drawing room.

'What is it, young lady?' The vicar had kindly bent down to Alice's angelic countenance; the better to talk to her as she tugged winningly at his sleeve.

'Please, Mr Molebank, Alice wants to know something. Is it true that you're a pansy? Elizabeth said her daddy said so and I said that it sounded a very nice thing to be. Pansies are Alice's favourite flowers because they have such dear little whiskery faces. Elizabeth said I must come and ask you.'

There was a burst of treacherous laughter from outside the door. Everyone went home quite soon after that, and Elizabeth was severely told off. It will be apparent from this that Alice was not the ideal person to console Elizabeth for the loss of her father.

'Thank you, Lissie, but I just don't know how Elizabeth will be feeling.'

Lissie put her arms round me and kissed me. Her cheek was hot and wet. 'I'll come round whenever you want me, day or night. Promise you'll telephone me if there's anything I can do.'

After Lissie had driven away, I went upstairs. I hovered outside Elizabeth's door. The music had stopped. There was no answer to my knock. I opened the door. She lay on her bed, her eyes closed. From the regularity of her breathing I was sure she was asleep. I thought of all the times I had looked on that sleeping face from the day she was born. I longed to kiss her but it would be cruel to wake her. She had always taken refuge in sleep. I carefully picked up the sunglasses, which were hanging crookedly from one ear, and put them on her bedside table. I closed her window quietly. The breeze that ruffled her curtains was cool now, and smelt of the woodsmoke of Ivor's bonfire.

I was just struggling with the last of Ivor's fish-pie, in which the mashed potato was an off-putting shade of green, angelica having mysteriously become one of the ingredients of the dish, when the telephone rang again. For a moment, I thought it was probably Jack ringing to say he'd be late home. Then I remembered. I felt a frightening flash of anger.

'No, don't worry, Rose, I'll get it. It won't be any good trying to avoid people.'

It was Patience. Patience and I have been friends since we were both thirteen. It was because of Patience that we lived where we did.

When I had found that I was expecting a baby, a year after marrying Jack, we had decided to move into the country. Patience had telephoned to say that there was a moated manor house for sale in Kent, in the next village to her own. Westray Manor had been built in the fifteenth century and not much altered since 1780. It was in the middle of twenty acres of woodland, had a gatehouse, a walled garden, two cottages and a small river that fed the moat. In addition, it was less than two miles from the sea.

The moment I had seen it, at the end of a winding drive through thick woods of oaks, beech and pine, I had fallen in love with it. Before I had crossed the bridge over the moat, before I had opened the gatehouse door and looked into the little courtyard within, I had determined that it should be mine. The construction is brick and timber and stone, round three sides of a square. The fourth side is where the great hall used to be, which was pulled down in the eighteenth century. Now there is a view over a low wall and across the moat to the hills and woods beyond. It has a roof-line of different heights, with tall chimney stacks, stone crenellations and gabled ends. The windows are a mixture of the earlier Perpendicular and later leaded casements. From the thirteenth century, when the moat was dug, to the reign of George III, successive owners have added and subtracted and rebuilt, but the whole is the most harmonious blend of periods you can imagine. I still think it the most beautiful house I have ever seen, and nothing that has happened during the time we have lived at Westray has made me love it less. Of course, there are never-ending problems with damp, there are leaking roofs, crumbling flues, rotten window-frames, flaking plaster. None of this has deterred me in the least.

Jack was never as completely possessed by the house as I was, but he had appreciated its beauty and history and we had been very happy there until Lissie had let in the serpent.

Patience is the kind of friend that everyone ought to have. She is loyal, honest and unselfish. Jack always said she was stodgy and, I suppose, to most men she gives that impression. Patience is stoutly built. Even at school she was hefty and excelled at sending punishing shots from the left wing into goal. She was captain of games two years running, and this was her moment of glory. She has shining brown hair and a white skin. Her nose is broad and her lips plump above a pointed chin. Her eyes are her best feature, a soft periwinkle blue, charmingly triangular in shape which makes her look amused even when she isn't. If she had been a Victorian, I think she would have been considered a beauty. In the second Elizabethan age she looks matronly, with a firm bust and large hips. She always dresses in a seated tweed skirt and has two jerseys, one brown and one green. She has large feet and wears a small size of men's brogues because they last so well.

Something that Jack never took account of was Patience's intelligence. She did brilliantly well at school and should have gone to university as the rest of us did. But her father held that education, particularly of the higher kind, was 'hooey'. That was one of his favourite words. He liked men who shot and fished and took their fences at the gallop, who drank and smoked and kept a wife in the country and a mistress in town. Women were for ornament and procreation, as he never tired of telling any woman who was unlucky enough to come within his conversational range. This was extensive as he always shouted – not because he was deaf but because he was a bully.

Poor Patience. Instead of being allowed to read mathematics at Cambridge, she was sent off to a finishing school in Switzerland where she learned to speak quite good French and fell in love with the ski instructor who, she told me, never so much as glanced in her direction during the nine months she was there. The other girls were similarly disdainful. They all had trunkfuls of French clothes and Italian shoes. Patience, whose mother had died when she was ten, had done her own packing, simply putting in all the things she had worn at school, minus the crested Panama hat and the blazer with the badge. The whole thing had been a lonely and extremely dispiriting experience, and if, she had once said, she felt like bemoaning her lot at having to live with her father, she reminded herself of the days at Château Vervienne and was thankful.

Now I was pleased to hear her calm voice at the other end of the telephone.

'Miranda! Father's just come back from for his constitutional. They're all saying in the village – that Jack is dead!'

I told Patience as much as I knew and she listened quietly. There was a pause after I'd finished. Then she said, still calm but with something of a tremble in her voice, 'I know you've got Rose and Ivor and Elizabeth, but if it would help I'll willingly come and spend the night.'

'You're a dear, but the doctor who came gave me some sleeping pills. I'll go to bed pretty soon, I think.'

'You sound in control.'

'I am, more or less.'

'Good girl. I'll telephone tomorrow.' Another pause. 'Miranda?'

'Yes.'

'I really am most terribly sorry.'

I knew that she was. Patience was incapable of lying even on such an occasion as this. She had been among the tiny handful of women who didn't like Jack. Because she was such a straightforward person herself, Jack's sophistical charm was wholly ineffective. She had no belief in her own ability to attract so his flattery, and the talent he had for creating a persuasive intimacy, did not convince her in the least.

When Jack first met a woman he swiftly sized up the condition of her ego. If they were self-assured he began to undermine their confidence, with coldness, barbed criticisms, ironical disparagement. His victims, usually good-looking women, were piqued by this treatment from a handsome man like Jack. They expected to be calling the shots. Then, when they were in a state either of anger or dudgeon, he would suddenly turn upon them the incandescent beam of his charm. They would be surprised, relieved and intrigued. Jack knew how to fascinate. He played upon the weaknesses of his quarry with infallible skill. Vain women were reduced to beseeching him for attention. The insecure bathed in his approbation, for which they rapidly developed a craving.

He had been annoyed by his failure with Patience, though I didn't imagine that he ever thought of taking her to bed. But it irked him that she, who because of our close friendship came often within his orbit, seemed impervious to his will.

After I had put down the telephone, I went slowly upstairs. Elizabeth was still asleep. I put an eiderdown over her and went to help Rose. She found it impossible now to manage the buttons and hooks and eyes of her complicated underwear. She gave me a softened glance from her generally sharp eyes, which I knew betokened love. 'I put your pills and a glass of water by your bed. I knew you'd forget.'

'Oh, Rose, thank you. I *had* forgotten. Oh dear, what about Puck?'

Puck was Elizabeth's pony.

'Ivor's seen to him. And Jasper and Dinkie as well.'

'Thank goodness. I *am* tired. I don't think I'll need those pills.'

'You take them, my girl. Otherwise you'll be waking up in the night and seeing ghouls.'

'All right, I will.'

But when I lay down in my bed, I thought of Elizabeth and decided to wait a little before I swallowed the sleeping pills. From the time I was five, when Nanny had hit me and I had lost the hearing in one ear, I had always fallen asleep lying on my good ear. It gave me a wonderful illusion of being shut off from the world. I felt, paradoxically, safe in the silence, alone with the beating of my own heart. As a child I had imagined a long staircase with the pulse of my blood as the rhythmic tread of feet going down, down, down. Tonight, in case Elizabeth should call me, I lay on my deaf side and heard all the rustling sounds of the house settling like a great beast on to its knees after the long labours of the day.

When I had been lying there for ten minutes or so, very restless, with streams of indistinct images running through my mind as inconstant as water, the door opened.

'Mum?'

I sat up. Elizabeth's face collapsed suddenly, like a photograph thrown into a flame. I opened my arms and in a moment she was in them. She wept desolately, her body shaking with grief. 'Oh, Daddy! Oh, Daddy!' she cried, over and over again, as though he might hear her and come back.

It was at that moment that it occurred to me, for the first time, that he never would.

CHAPTER 3

The week between Jack's death and his burial hops in my memory from a dreary protraction to a frightening ellipsis, so pliant was time and so disjointed were my thoughts. I woke on the morning of his funeral with a sense of oppression. Elizabeth was still sharing my bed. I looked fondly at the face on the pillow beside me, half covered by a loop of hair, the mouth a little open, the eyebrows contracted into a slight frown. We had talked endlessly about Jack during that last week, and I felt that she had consoled me as much as I had comforted her. Though she was only fourteen she had been fiercely brave, after the first shock, in facing up to his death.

The great difficulty that threw rocks in our path as we tried to accept that he was dead was that we didn't know if his death had been accidental or intentional. The idea, first advanced by Dr McCleod, that he might have intended to kill himself, was terrifying. Elizabeth had raised the question herself quite independently, and I hadn't been able to give her a satisfactory answer. I had reassured her that Jack had been, as far as I knew, happy with no particular anxieties. But it seemed unlikely that he had been so incompetent or, in fact, so ludicrously clumsy as to shoot himself by mistake.

The boys had reacted quite differently. I had driven to James's school, in the centre of London, on the day following Jack's death and, after an awkward exchange of shock, dismay and regret with the headmaster, he had left me alone in his sitting room while he went to find James. James had known without being told that my sudden appearance must mean bad news. He had come in, looking whiter than usual, his red hair more vivid by contrast. When I told him, he walked away from me and stood looking out at the headmaster's garden through the french windows. We neither of us said anything for a while. The he turned and said, 'This must be terrible for you, Mum,' and came and put his arms stiffly around me. If I could have cried at all, it would have been then.

We drove together down to Henry's school, some thirty miles from Westray. We talked about ordinary things. Often we were silent for ten minutes at a stretch. I saw that James's hands shook as he adjusted the visor to protect his eyes from the low autumn sun. I broke it to

Henry as gently as I could. He screamed like a terrified animal, and it took half an hour to calm him and get him into the car. He cried all the way home. Rose and Elizabeth were waiting for us at the door. We went and sat in the kitchen, all of us together, while Ivor made us tea and cried along with Henry in sympathy. Henry sat on my knee and sucked his thumb, something I had not seen him do for many years. I stroked his head until he fell into a sort of doze. Often I looked at Rose with a frightened question in my glance, and always she gave me a nod of reassurance that, in time, the children would recover from this terrible blow.

I had unbounded faith in Rose's judgement. I had been five years old when my sister Beatrice was born. It was nineteen forty. My father disappeared from our lives at the same time. I understood nothing of the war then and, for a long time, imagined that my sister had been sent as a thoroughly inadequate replacement. She had been a charming baby, pink and dimpled, whereas I was thin and pale. The nurse we had had then loved Beatrice to distraction and discouraged my attempts to join the baby-worshipping circle in case I hurt her. Our mother, though averse to all children, seemed to find Beatrice less dull than most. Certainly more interesting than me.

One day, when Beatrice was about four months old, I gave her one of Nanny's precious humbugs out of her special tin, thinking I'd do well to keep in with the object of everyone's affections. Nanny had found Beatrice beet-root-red and not breathing. The humbug fell out when she was turned upside down and thumped, and my sister was saved. I was soundly smacked and sent to bed. I was so angry at the unfairness of this when I had meant to be nice to the nasty, smelly, sicky little thing that I threw all the doll's house furniture on to the nursery fire. I had begun in a rage but I went on because it was such fun to watch the coloured spurts of flame from the glue and to see everything turn black and treacly as it melted.

It was the beginning of a year of misery. The furore that followed the arson episode terrified me, and I grew nervous and clumsy. Nanny was convinced that everything I did was wilful naughtiness. If I lost a glove in the garden or dropped my bread and butter or upset the paint-water jar, these things were put down to bad behaviour and I was scolded and smacked. The reprisal I feared most was when Nanny, bending down with an expression of gleeful spite, would blow out my night-light. I lay for what seemed like hours, with pounding heart, waiting for the Soot Imp, who lived in the day-nursery chimney, to slide under my door and insinuate his long, skinny hand into my bed.

Whenever Beatrice was left unguarded, I used to creep up to the pram and give her a hard pinch for having all the praise and kisses I longed for. Sometimes I was found out, and my disgrace was broadcast over the entire house. I felt that everyone in my small world – my mother, the cook, the maids and Nanny – despised me. Even Danny, the hall boy, seemed to glare at me with a look that cursed. When I grew older I realised that this stare, which had frightened me so much, was due to a quite impartial squint.

One day Beatrice, now eighteen months old and prettier than ever, was taken down to the drawing room to be shown off to visitors, leaving me alone and shunned in the day nursery.

'No one wants to see a nasty, wicked girl,' Nanny said, kissing Beatrice's rosy cheek. Beatrice held up her fat, creased little arms and patted Nanny's hairy face. 'They'd as soon look at that little gypsy girl that comes begging at the door as you.'

The gypsy girl was an object of great fascination and pity to me. She came three or four times a year with her basket of heather sprigs to sell. She was absolutely filthy and her clothes were literally rags. She was almost toothless and covered in bruises. In her eye was the hard, knowing look of one who had abandoned hope with her baby rattle.

With feelings wounded to desperation, I took all Nanny's intimate belongings from her chest of drawers and threw them out of the nursery window. Her grubby apricot-pink bras and knickers and suspender belts festooned the cars and lay on the gravel drive for the visitors to see when they left. For good measure I hurled after them the fat cotton-wool pads and elasticised belts with hooks that Nanny had for some secret purpose I couldn't fathom.

Nanny had completely lost her temper. She had hit me so hard on the ear that it had bled and the doctor had to be called. A perforated eardrum was diagnosed, and Nanny was dismissed.

My mother had brought Rose into the nursery a week later. She had indicated the cot. 'This is the baby. She is, I'm told, a very good child.' She had smiled down at Beatrice and looked almost soft. Then she had turned to me. 'Here is our problem. Miranda is a very bad girl, I'm afraid. I thought you'd better see for yourself what you'd be taking on.'

Rose was like the Scots pine that dominated our Hampstead garden. She went on and on, up and up, formidable, impossible to defy. I hung my head in submission. She had enormous, bony feet encased in black-strapped kid shoes. Rose's hand took my chin and lifted my face towards hers. I looked into her sharp, grey eyes. 'Why, I can see right inside this little girl,' said Rose, in her quick, fierce voice. Her eyes were the colour of dark storm clouds. 'And I can see that she isn't bad at all. In fact, she's a very good girl all the way through. As good as... why, quite as good as the youngest princess in any story about goodness.'

I believed her. It was impossible to think that Rose could ever be wrong. I laid down the burden of my wickedness with amazed relief. I don't remember Rose ever being angry with me. My lapses were all examined and explained and corrected with unfailing patience. My virtues were praised and counted. Beatrice received the same tender, scrupulous care but I always felt that I was the being closest to Rose's heart.

I had been sent away to school when I was eleven. The

parting from Rose had been hard, but every week a letter came, written in the beautiful hand of which Rose was justly proud. And the holidays were occasions of happy reunion. When Beatrice had joined me at school two years later, Rose was dismissed by our mother. It was now 1948 and the war had been over for three years. My father had been killed at Anzio in 1944.

I don't remember being told this. I seemed to slide gradually into acceptance of the fact that he would never be coming back. My mother wanted to go abroad so she shut up the London house. Rose had to find work with another family. I was thirteen, old enough, most people would think, to do without a nurse. But I felt orphaned. Rose and I wrote long letters to each other. I spent all the time I wasn't at school in Italy with my mother, staying in the houses of her friends. They all owned magnificent villas and palazzos, stuck on terraced hillsides miles from anywhere. There was never anything to do in the winter months but shiver over inadequate fires. In the summer you could lie still on the veranda, too hot even to read, watching the paint blister, or there was the option of travelling to the nearest boiling town to look at antiquities.

At the age of eighteen, having won a place at Oxford to read history, I decided that I was old enough to spend my holidays as I wanted, so I took out most of the money in my post-office account. Rose, Beatrice and I went to the seaside for a whole blissful week. We had a glorious time sunbathing on the dunes, walking for miles along the beaches, eating shrimp teas in our modest little boarding-house. In the evenings we read to each other or walked along the promenade, or, best of all, went to see the variety show at the little theatre at the end of the pier. We bought ice-creams and lipstick-pink sticks of rock, and fed pennies into the slot machines half-way along the pier to see 'The Haunted Bedchamber' (Beatrice's favourite) or 'The Execution of Mary, Queen of Scots' (mine) while Rose, with frowns and fierce looks, discouraged the young men who swam in our wake.

Rose came to my wedding, six weeks after my finals. In the photographs she is looking severe, unsmiling, with a large navy hat pulled down low over her forehead. You can see from her expression that she isn't pleased. She didn't like Jack from the beginning. A year after Jack and I were married, and a week before James was born, Rose came to live with us. Elizabeth was born three and a half years later, and Henry two years after that. Until Jack shot himself we lived, on the surface anyway, pretty much like any ordinary family. Now it seemed that we would never be ordinary again.

On his first night at home after his father's death, Henry slept in Rose's room. In the morning, according to Rose, Henry woke up, said, 'I'm starving,' and came downstairs to eat an enormous bowl of cereal with half a packet of brown sugar and nearly a pint of milk. Then he went out to see Puck. When I came down half an hour later, I saw him struggling to launch the boat on the moat, his fishing tackle in the prow. He and James spent all morning fishing things out of the water, everything but fish, that is, for the carp were too wily to be caught.

'I suppose in the old days people threw things out of the window when they'd finished with them,' I said to Patience, who was sitting with me in the kitchen later that day, watching the boys hauling up miscellaneous bones and bottomless saucepans. 'There weren't any rubbish collections and bonfires had to be miles from the house for fear of fire. The water will smell terrible for days now it's all stirred up.'

'They certainly look all right,' said Patience. I knew she meant James and Henry.

'Yes, at the moment. But I just don't know what to expect. It's ridiculous, but I hardly dare to mention Jack's name to them. It's different with Elizabeth. We've talked about him endlessly and it's been a terrific help. But boys are as puzzling as men... even though they're my own sons. There's this determination to pretend that unpleasant things haven't happened. What on earth goes on inside? Are they working things out quietly on their own or simply shelving the problem until the passage of time makes it irrelevant?'

'I'm the last person to ask. The only man I've ever known at all well is my father, and I refuse to believe he's a paradigm of the male sex.'

It wasn't often that Patience allowed herself to be critical of Sir William. I put it down to the fact that all our nerves were on edge.

Everyone behaved pretty much out of character that day. I put through a call to my mother in Florence to tell her what had happened, more out of courtesy than anything else. She had never approved of my marrying Jack and she wasn't the woman to stoop to hypocrisy to save anyone's feelings.

'What do you mean "dead"? Speak up, Miranda, it's a very bad line. Have you been drinking?'

I pointed out that it was eleven o'clock in the morning and that, as she well knew, my habits were boringly moderate. When I got her to understand what had happened, I held the receiver a little away from my ear and let her get on with it. My mother has a very loud voice. It comes from having been surrounded by imbeciles all her life and being obliged to order everyone around if she wants to get a *thing* done.

I haven't mentioned it before because it's something that I don't like people to know straight away. My maternal grandfather was the First World War poet, Christopher Chough. As soon as people know this they see me differently. It seems to give me an interest that I consider entirely spurious. My mother, on the other hand, has been Christopher Chough's daughter all her life and almost nothing else. It doesn't bother her in the least to know that people are thrilled if she accepts their invitation to dinner because then they can say, 'Have you met Fabia Trebor? Christopher Chough's daughter, you know,' and feel that they've scored socially. I find it embarrassing when it happens to me, and I'm always convinced that thereafter they're asking themselves whatever happened to heredity. Some people are disgracefully sycophantic and would fawn all over you even if you told them their food was inedible, their conversation dull and their children hideous. Others are so keen not to seem to be sucking up that they would rather throw themselves out of the window than find themselves talking to you.

Anyway, I've always hated it being known and I can quite see why the children of great men nearly always make a complete mess of their own lives. How can you believe in your own efforts when they are always compared with your celebrated parent's productions, which have all the lustre of acknowledged greatness? There are quite a few of my grandfather's poems that seem distinctly feeble to me, but nowadays even his Army overcoat seems to be an object of veneration.

My mother has always adored the myth-making, and has contributed quite a few faggots of doubtful provenance to the beacon of learning. Like my grandfather's adoration of his own children, for example. My uncle Conrad, a nice weak man, who underscored very neatly what I've just said by wandering from job to job and finally dying as a silent partner in an unsuccessful publishing house, told me the last time I visited him in hospital that he'd hated his father all his life. According to my uncle, Christopher Chough was a sadistic brute who neglected his wife and swore at his children if they went anywhere near him. Also, he liked to do illicit things to young boys. I don't know if this last was true. My mother said Uncle Conrad was a drunken liar. Well, he did drink, certainly.

All my childhood was spent in the shade of my grandfather's genius. My mother thinks that the only fit work for man is Art. Never mind that there are base helots obliged to labour in the abysm, making and mending and growing things, taking care of the sick, upholding the law and clearing out the nation's plumbing. She sees only the artists... painters, writers, composers. Poets, of course. There are others she is prepared to recognise as being on the periphery of all this greatness, such as architects, musicians, actors (stage only) dancers (ballet) and craftsmen, if they are both original and successful. Beatrice did her best for my mother by marrying a potter. This just about squeezed into the maternal category of people possibly worth knowing.

Roger isn't a very good potter. I hope I can say that without being accused of unkindness. Modern pots are something of an acquired taste and the public have not yet learned to love vases shaped like melting kidney bowls, glazed in all the colours of corruption from mouldy-green and bruise-purple to bile-black. I have a cupboardful, going back many Christmases and birthdays. This isn't meanness on my sister's part, rather that the only money they have, not very surprisingly, is what my mother gives them. She is capricious in everything, but most of all with money.

One of the things that attracted me to Jack, apart from the fact that he was handsome, more fun to be with than anyone I'd ever known, and introduced me to sex quite unforgettably, was that he had not one artistic corpuscle in his entire being. He liked reading and listening to music and all that sort of thing – he wasn't a philistine – but he didn't want to create these things himself. He was not contemplative in any way. I really loved that about him.

I hate artists. I had to spend the first eighteen years of my life with them, when not at school, and I can speak from experience. They are the most egocentric brutes imaginable. If their work is going well they bore everyone to death by telling them about it. As though you weren't going to have to spend hours enthusing over the finished article anyway, yawning through two thousand pages of imitation James Joyce or wandering about a hot gallery burdened with a catalogue the size of the *Dictionary of National Biography* or sitting uncomfortably listening to squawks and whistles or trying to think of something nice to say about a lump of granite the colour of school socks with two little asymmetrical holes in it.

If their work isn't going well and they have got writer's block or have knocked the nose off the bust they have been chiselling at for the last six months, then you have to put up with their rantings or their sullens or their alcoholic binges. They whine constantly about being undervalued and badly paid. They are horribly jealous of anyone in the same field who earns a few shillings or words of praise. They are pretty nearly always broke and as mean as hell. If you are so foolish as to offer them a small drink, before you can say John Keats they've moved in, emptied the contents of your larder and drinks cupboard, alienated your entire family and all your friends, and are snoring their heads off in your best bed.

'I simply *don't* understand,' my mother was saying. 'How could Jack have done such a thing? He simply wasn't the temperamental *sort*.'

'I don't know. It was probably an accident.'

'Nonsense! I may not have approved of your marrying him but I'll say this for him. He wasn't so silly as to shoot himself accidentally. Jack was one of the most competent men I've ever met. He *always* knew what he was doing.'

It was the first time I had heard my mother say anything complimentary about Jack. I think it was because they were always in competition with each other. Both needed to be dominant, which had led to some fairly painful encounters.

'I'll come over,' said my mother, unexpectedly. 'When is the funeral?'

'That's very good of you. But isn't it Waldo's exhibition next week?' Waldo was my mother's current lover.

'Yes. But he can manage for two days without me, I suppose. One can't *always* be at other people's beck and call.'

The last time I'd seen Waldo he had given quite a good impression of wanting to manage without her for a great deal longer than two days.

'Haven't you got the Tallows coming to stay any minute? I thought you told me they were bringing their entire family.'

'Yes, and it will be *hell*! Geoffrey Tallow's sister, Gilda, is singing at Verona. She does her vocal exercises for three hours every morning in the *nude*. She says it's the only way she can really *breathe*. It's very inconvenient as the maids can't do her bedroom until after lunch when they expect to have their siesta. She's got a voice like a tin-opener anyway and I'm sure they'll boo her off the stage and I'll have to pick up the pieces. And Geoffrey always quarrels with Waldo. Last time he told him his paintings were exquisitely shallow.'

'Perhaps you ought not to leave them alone, then.'

'Don't you *want* me to come?'

The end result of this rather unsatisfactory talk was that my mother was arriving this very morning and would be expecting breakfast in precisely – I managed to look at my watch without waking Elizabeth – two hours. Meanwhile, there was a great deal to do. Mrs Goss had telephoned the evening before to give notice, saying that Jack's death had been a nasty shock to her system and it wasn't at all what she was used to.

'I, on the other hand, have lost several husbands in just this way,' I told her. I heard her gasp and then put down the telephone. It was a cheap piece of sarcasm but it made me feel better for a moment. I felt really furious. Domestic help was notoriously difficult to get in our part of the world, and I'd only put up with Mrs Goss because she was better than nothing.

It seemed that everyone I had ever met in the course of my life, and a great many more I didn't know, was nobly sacrificing a day's work to come and pay tribute to my husband's passing. It was very good of them, but as we lived fairly remote from anything that might be called a good restaurant I knew I would be expected to sustain them in their grief. I cursed Mrs Goss as I struggled with the breakfast washing-up and tried to make a list of what had to be done.

The real problem was that ever since Jack's death my mind had been in a state of alarming inaction. I really couldn't follow a single thought to its logical conclusion. In addition, I was so tired that I could hardly drag myself about. My head ached permanently and all I wanted to do was lie like Ophelia in cooling water and drift downstream.

Rose was up already and was counting napkins and knives and forks. Then Ivor appeared and, under my instructions, began to scrub potatoes. He worked very fast and very energetically, spraying water and mud generously about. I carried plates into the dining room. The trouble with a funeral is that it is such an open-ended thing. No one would think of attending a wedding or a christening uninvited but the most unlikely people will drag themselves for miles to put in an appearance at a funeral, and they shouldn't have to go away with tongues sticking to the roofs of their mouths and stomachs roaring with hunger.

I had ordered a ham from the butcher and I had poached a salmon the day before. I had also made an enormous quantity of vegetable soup. The baker was delivering ten loaves this morning. It was predictable stuff but I wasn't in the mood for enterprise. I was just crossing the hall to check that there were clean towels and soap in the cloakroom when I heard a crash from the kitchen.

Rose had slipped in the muddy water that Ivor had splashed over the floor. She had been holding a bowl of raspberries that had been flung to the farthest corners of the room. She was clearly shocked by the fall but insisted she wasn't hurt so we got her up on to a chair. I could see she was in pain. Elizabeth had come running in when she heard the crash so I set her the task of picking up the raspberries and washing them while Ivor went to telephone Dr Kenton.

I made Rose some tea and tried to get her to tell me where it hurt but she was so anxious about not holding things up when there was still so much to do that she was uncooperative, merely saying that I was to press on and not give her a thought and she was sorry she'd been such a fool as to fall over. I mopped the floor and put the potatoes on to cook. I was just beginning to slice tomatoes when Jasper came tearing into the kitchen, in a frenzy of barking, trailing weeds over the newly washed floor, and knocked over the bowl of raspberries that Elizabeth had just picked up.

'Miranda? I suppose it's *too* much to expect any sort of welcome,' came the well-known tones of my mother. 'One *drags* oneself half-way across Europe for the sake of one's children and what thanks does one get? Shakespeare knew it all, of course... How *very* much sharper than a serpent's tooth!' The quasi-Lear was standing in the hall while a rebellious-looking taxi driver was bringing in several expensive suitcases. 'I suppose you expect a tip. An extortionate fare isn't good enough for you people these days. *What* is this country coming to?'

'Hello, Fabia.' I kissed her cheek. She was looking stunning in a black wool suit and a black suede toque. She was tall, with a wand-like figure, although she was somewhere in her sixties, and a face that was all planes and bones. Her hair was silver-blonde and cut to chin-length by a genius. 'How was the journey?'

'Revolting! Full of brick-red English holiday-makers returning to their ghastly little hutches. I think the pilot was drunk. We seemed to do a great deal of unnecessary circling. If you scratch that suitcase I shall report you to your superiors,' she said sharply, as Freddy, our only local driver with whom I had always been on excellent terms until now, put down the case with some emphasis.

'Freddy doesn't have a superior. He's self-employed.'

'That explains it. Thank you, that will do.'

She held out a silver coin in a lordly way while I, behind her back, pulled a face suggestive of sympathy and apology.

'I'll go straight up to my room to lie down for half an hour. Just a little *very* weak Lapsang, you know how I like it. And a piece of thin toast. *Un*salted butter.'

She went upstairs, carrying only her scarf. I asked Ivor to take up her luggage and applied myself to Fabia's breakfast. The telephone began to ring incessantly. Virtually every prospective mourner had some message to pass on or some explanation to make concerning their journey. They would be early, they would be late, they would be coming by the A143 if road-works allowed, they would be bringing Great-aunt Julia, they would be requiring petrol, headache pills, a map of the coast as they were going to explore afterwards, could I recommend a first-class hotel at Ramsgate? They all concluded by saying that they hoped I would let them know if there was anything they could do to help. I felt like shouting, 'Just get off the telephone and let me get on,' but, of course, I reassured each caller that no, there was nothing they could do, and yes, I would be sure to tell them if there was.

By this time the kitchen was filled with the smell of burning toast and I was nearly losing my temper when Dr McCleod and Rollo arrived simultaneously. Mrs Kenton had telephoned me the day after Jack's death to commiserate with me and to explain that Dr Kenton was struck down by some mystery illness but they hoped to be at the funeral. I had forgotten that when I asked Ivor to telephone him. It shows what state my brain was in. I tried to conceal my irritation from Dr McCleod, who was quite indifferent to my counterfeit smile. I showed him into the kitchen where Rose was lying on the sofa, and then ran back into the hall to welcome Rollo properly.

If there was one man about whom I sometimes had secret romantic imaginings he was Rollo. We had been at Oxford together and though I had met Jack at my first party and, from that moment on, had been strictly under his aegis, I had always looked at Rollo with interest. I rather think he had returned the feeling, but as he and Jack were friends and Rollo was a man of honour, besides being excellent in every other way, there had never been the opportunity to find out.

We had kept vaguely in touch over the years and Rollo had been several times to stay at Westray. Every year we went to Oxford for his summer parties. These were always just what a party ought to be – interesting people and good things to eat and drink in the seductive setting of his college garden. Four years ago an invitation had arrived that marked a great change in Rollo's life. It seemed that he had acquired his own house, somewhere in Oxfordshire, called Shinlake Manor.

When we got there and saw Rollo's house, a little dilapidated but full of history and almost as beautiful as Westray, I was so fired with enthusiasm that I embraced Rollo fervently. He seemed very pleased and hugged me tightly before turning to someone standing behind him. 'I want you to meet Diana Fairfax. This is Miranda Stowe, one of my oldest and dearest friends.'

He squeezed my hand affectionately as he said this and looked so happy that I was touched, despite seeing at once, from the way he looked at Diana, that he was in love with her and that any little fantasies I had entertained about him were well and truly dished.

The party was a disappointment, although its ingredients were perfect and Rollo was an attentive host. But every time he saw me he wanted to talk about *her*. I didn't exchange a word with Diana myself as she seemed to know a great many people there. Jack was making very fast progress with a blonde girl who exuded a readiness to comply with anything he might ask. I got stuck with an elderly, dazzlingly bald historian, who got very drunk and dogged my footsteps, trying to get me to come up and look at the bedrooms with him. In the end I had to be absolutely rude and we descended to an undignified row of the 'shall–shan't' variety, which did nothing for my temper. I remember that as we drove home I decided that it was positively the very last time I would attend any party of any kind, and that all frivolous, inessential contact with the human race was at an end.

In fact, six months later we went to Rollo's wedding. Diana looked beautiful, if a little stern. She was all of thirty-six or so and waived full bridal flummery for a brilliantly cut, ivory crêpe suit and a charming hat, with a few stephanotis flowers fastened to the brim. She was rather a haughty-looking girl, I thought. I suppose she might have been nervous. I felt I might dislike her until I saw her being very kind to Rollo's mother, who was quite extraordinary, tiny and bone-thin and wearing a startling magenta dress and rose-pink hair, the very last person one would have imagined as a mother for Rollo. Diana had a mother to match in eccentricity: she arrived drunk at the church and had to be carried out bodily during the speeches. But whenever Rollo and Diana looked at each other there was an expression on both their faces that filled me with delight and envy in equal proportions.

That was the last time we saw them. Rollo didn't give any more parties after that, probably because he and Diana had twin boys a year after they married. Now here he was at Westray and looking wonderful, while I knew that my hair was uncombed and my face probably muddy.

'Hello, darling girl,' said Rollo, taking me into his arms and giving me a long hug. 'This is agony, isn't it?'

'Agony.'

'Diana's parking the car. She wanted me to have a word with you alone.'

'That was kind.'

'You know how much Jack meant to me,' said Rollo.

'Yes,' I said, but actually I didn't. To me friendships between men are cloaked in darkness. As far as I could tell Jack never gave a second's thought to any man the moment he was out of his company until the next time he saw him. They never had long talks on the telephone, sent birthday presents, confessed their weaknesses, cried in each other's arms, laughed over past humiliations, agonised over their own children or praised each other's. Any conversation reported by Jack was of the blandest, most impersonal kind, the sort of thing I might say to Mrs Veal in the post office.

'He was an extraordinary man,' continued Rollo. 'I don't think I've ever known anyone so full of energy. It was immensely attractive. He was very clever but he made light work of everything. I don't remember him ever being pompous or self-important, and yet you couldn't help being aware of him all the time. The world will be very much duller without him.'

Dear Rollo. Of course, he knew that the bereaved long

for words of praise for the dead. It is the only comfort. But he did it beautifully, with perfect sincerity.

'Hello, Miranda.' Diana came in, looking stunning in a pale grey silk dress and coat. 'This is all dreadfully sad. I am *so* sorry.'

I remembered that I had not changed, that the obsequies were due to begin in half an hour and that a great deal remained to be accomplished if people were to have lunch afterwards. An insistent smell of burning drifted into the hall from the kitchen.

'Oh God! My mother's toast! Oh, *bugger*!'

I ran into the kitchen and threw a third slice after the others into the waste bin. Diana and Rollo followed. I could see her eyes roving over the mess on the table and the floor. Rose sat in her chair by the fire with her eyes closed, apparently dozing. Jasper lay wreathed in weeds at her feet.

'My bloody daily's given notice and Rose has hurt her arm. I'm so tired I can't think. About forty thousand people are coming to lunch and I haven't begun to make the salads. I think I'm about to implode... if that means bursting inwards from external pressure.'

'Tell me what to do,' said Diana.

She had taken off her coat and was putting on an apron.

'I can't possibly ask you to –' I began.

'Of course you can. I've exchanged precisely two words with Jack in my entire life. "Hello" and "Goodbye". I'm sorry, terribly sorry, for your sake, that he's dead but my presence in church is really irrelevant. I'm going to stay here and get lunch ready. Now, tell me what to do and you run and change.'

She looked at my mud-splashed clothes and wild hair, and I could see that she was thinking I would need the entire half-hour. I couldn't imagine that this elegant creature would actually be much good on the domestic front but it was unbelievably kind of her and I was grateful. I told her everything that I had planned to do, including my mother's breakfast, then raced upstairs.

Twenty minutes later I came down to find several people standing in the hall, dripping blood from their fingers. It looked at first as though some secret society ritual of blood-letting had been taking place, but a word of explanation from a man who worked in Jack's bank put me wise. The children had named our cat Dinkie, after the friendly, intelligent and helpful little cat in Rupert Bear stories. Like the last-mentioned our cat is a glossy, all-over black, but there the resemblance ends. It is one of Dinkie's favourite pastimes to curl up, pretending sleep, on the parapet of the bridge that crosses the moat. People who don't know us well are moved by this picture of feline pulchritude and inevitably the good-natured put out their hands to give the inviting fur a kindly stroke. Dinkie moves like a cobra and takes a slice out of them before they've even made contact. Then he curls up with a seraphic expression in wait for the next victim.

'I couldn't find any unsalted butter,' said Diana, coming into the hall with a roll of Elastoplast and scissors. 'I had to give your mother salted, I'm afraid.'

'We haven't got any. I'd forgotten. She probably won't notice. Let me be nurse. James, go and shoo Dinkie away. But be careful. You know what he's like once he's got the taste of blood.'

I bandaged the lacerations as quickly as I could while Henry answered the telephone. 'It's Maeve,' he said, holding out the receiver to me.

'Tell her I'm sorry I can't speak now. We must leave for the church.'

My mother came downstairs bearing her tray. It was untouched. 'Salt is *poison* to me. And the tea was just a little *too* stewed.'

I am quite certain that my mother does it deliberately. I kissed Henry and made him promise to look after Rose. I had decided that he and Elizabeth were too young to attend the funeral. My mother agreed. She was concerned that they might let the side down by crying in a vulgar, ill-bred way. I was worried that they might find it too much to bear.

CHAPTER 4

The parish church was a brisk five minutes' walk away. Thanks to Dinkie, we would be late if we didn't get a move on. A sharp wind played havoc with our sable draperies. We were a parody, it struck me then, of the hooded, black-habited Dominican monks who had lived at Westray four hundred years ago. We straggled in twos and threes down the drive, our hats and scarves striving to whirl away to the sea. A sudden gust of rain drove us into an undignified run.

The hearse was already drawn up outside the church among an enormous number of cars. I felt a fierce, unidentifiable pain when I saw it. Jack had become the property of Authority since he had been taken away. The Bosworth District and General Hospital had assumed rights over his body, to spread it naked on a table and cut it to pieces if necessary. Now Jack had been sent back to us and we were to begin some mysterious ritual that society had deemed a fitting farewell.

I was angry. Angry with doctors, policemen, undertakers, coroners, anyone who had had anything to say in the matter. Most of all, though, I was angry with Jack. Although I suspected that this feeling of rage was a standard reaction to shock, this did not help. If anything, it made me more furious. James held my arm very tightly. I saw a tear run down his cheek, which he rubbed quickly away. Oh, Jack, you bastard!

'Want to go back?' I whispered. 'It would be all right, darling.'

'No. I'm okay.'

Everyone who had walked down with us dashed to join those already in the church. James and I were to be the only chief mourners. Jack's parents had decided that they'd be better off inside, sitting down, in case there was what Dorothy called 'a nasty wind on the day'.

How right she was. The bell ceased to toll as a sudden

blast blew rain into our faces and the pall-bearers struggled to get the coffin on to their shoulders. I had ordered some simple white flowers for the coffin but early that morning a huge cross of fiery red carnations had been delivered, sent by Miss Horne, Jack's secretary. I told the delivery boy to take them to the undertaker's with instructions that they were to go on the coffin with the family flowers. I was very glad I had done this when I saw Miss Horne's face after the service. It was distorted with weeping. Poor Miss Horne was plain and dull and lived alone in Willesden. Jack had been her entire world. He had called her Horny and, in her innocence, she had loved it. No other man had even thought of being playful with her and she took it as a mark of extraordinary affection. He used to joke about the nickname behind her back and laugh at her devotion. It was just another instance of his capacity for cruelty.

Mr Molebank came up the path at a run, his surplice swelling like a topsail. 'Sorry I'm late,' he gasped. 'Trouble with the boiler – huge flames – didn't like to leave it.'

Mr Molebank lived alone in the large vicarage where he went from crisis to crisis, being the most undomesticated of men and unable to afford to pay anyone to do the housework for him. He never uttered a word of complaint about the discomfort of his existence even when last winter his fingers were scarlet and shiny with chilblains and he had trouble holding his hymn book. He was devout himself but did not expect anyone else to be. But Mr Molebank – or Aubrey, as he had recently asked me to call him – was, I suspected, pretty nearly a saint.

Sucking in long, rasping breaths, he took his place before the coffin, and James and I followed behind it. Together we stepped out of the squalling rain into the darkness of the church and the congregation rose to its feet with a subdued roar like our wood in a storm.

I couldn't believe that there was anything of Jack in the coffin so carefully lowered on to the trestles. I had talked about his death with other people. I had tried to comfort the children. But I still couldn't convince myself. All the time I thought he would walk in and say, 'Just a joke, darling. You didn't really think I could be got rid of as easily as that?'

The congregation got down on to their knees and, with a start, for I had been lost in my own thoughts, I pulled forward the hassock Rose had stitched before her fingers got too bad and bowed my head in prayer.

'Lord have mercy upon us.'

'Christ have mercy upon us.'

I joined in the responses but my thoughts were directed anywhere but upwards. I stared at the mosaic panels of the reredos. It was a beautiful church, baroque and gorgeously painted between mouldings of gilded stucco, built as a private chapel for an enormous eighteenth-century house called Wychford Hall. In its time the house had entertained royalty, most frequently Edward VII when Prince of Wales, but the family who owned it had fallen on hard times. There had been a fire and now the house stood open to the sky, in magnificent ruins. Great fountains, their basins filled with rotting leaves, decorated the grassy sweeps that had once been elaborate parterres. The chapel had become the parish church of Westray. Jack had said it was almost worth the tedium of church services to look at it. He had laughed at the ideas of Christianity. Now, I supposed, he must know all the answers.

It was astonishing how noisy a group of eighty or so people can be. Half of them seemed to be consumptive, sniffing and coughing, clearing their throats and trumpeting into handkerchiefs. The other half dropped service sheets, gloves, prayer books and car keys in a continuous precipitation. By the time poor Mr Molebank's address was nearing its end there was a clatter of restless feet and low grumbles of conversation.

Ten minutes later the service was over. The coffin was taken up, and James and I walked out behind it, falling unconsciously in step with the pall-bearers. It felt dramatic and fanciful, as though we were marching about with Hamlet's body on a platform at Elsinore. A bird flew in at the open church door and swooped over the procession. I remembered the Venerable Bede's sparrow. Like a bird flying through the great hall of a house, we come from we know not where and depart we know not whence. In between, there is a brief period of light and warmth and noise, which is life. Some twelve centuries after the scholarly monk penned his metaphor Jack's brief existence was over and he was . . . where?

I was relieved to see the vicarage roof still visible beyond the trees with no sign of smoke or flames. James cried, very quietly, as the coffin was lowered into the ground. Being nearly a man he kept his most intimate thoughts to himself these days and I, who had once been his confidante in everything, now had to guess what he might be feeling. I was thankful that he could cry.

Dorothy, well muffled, her powdery face streaky, was snuffling into her handkerchief. I felt terribly sorry for her. Donald, Jack's father, looked purple with cold, which clashed strangely with his hair, rather thin now but still as red as Jack's had been. Jeremy, standing composedly between his parents, hands folded together, eyes downcast, didn't look at all sorry, which at least was honest.

When we had first met, Jack had described his parents as being 'prototypic later-twentieth-century lower middle-class'. He hadn't despised them or apologised for them. They didn't interest him so he never thought about them.

The last words were spoken and the last crumbs of earth thrown. James and I went to kiss Dorothy and Donald. I always tried to avoid kissing Jeremy if I could for he was very free with his hands and lips in an unpleasantly secretive way, in both senses of the word. I usually had to resort to a handkerchief afterwards. I was glad to find some planks and ropes between us. Dorothy extended her raddled cheek to be kissed. We had spoken on the telephone, of course, since Jack's death, but I felt that a fresh expression of sympathy for her bereavement was called for. If it had been James or Henry or Elizabeth lying in the ground at our feet I knew I would be a mad woman, beyond reach of consoling words. Dorothy was made of different stuff but the effort ought to be made.

'This is a very dreadful day,' I began.

'Pardon, dear?' Dorothy removed a plug of cotton wool from each ear. 'I get very bad ears if I stand in a wind. What was that you said?'

I repeated my remark.

'I always say it's a lazy wind that won't go round you but has to go through you.' I remembered her saying it, very often. 'I'm glad I thought to put on an extra vest this morning. These October winds can be treacherous. Now, don't let's stand about catching our deaths. You must be wanting to see to the lunch, Miranda. I haven't touched a morsel since breakfast and I'm liable to have one of my turns if starved.'

Grasping her by an arm each, Donald and Jeremy frog-marched Dorothy away towards the grey Rover, which was parked, much to the inconvenience of the hearse, right in front of the lychgate. This was the signal for the other members of the congregation to approach me with expressions of tribute, sorrow or comfort as they deemed appropriate. This was hard work at any time and made worse by a further downpour of rain. Maeve, her face distraught, rushed up to kiss me, knocking off my hat in her enthusiasm and causing a stout, elderly man from Jack's bank to break into a run in its pursuit.

'Darling, I'm so sorry we were late!' Maeve wore a long black coat, the hem of which was several inches deep in mud, and a velvet hat of the sou'wester variety, turned up in front and fastened with a large crimson silk rose. Her hair was dyed a very dark mahogany and cut into short spikes. Her lipstick was startlingly aubergine, which made her look as though she had been eating blackberries but didn't at all detract from the rather sexy *nostalgie de la boue* prettiness of her face. 'The boys overslept and the car wouldn't start. We had to get a taxi. What an extraordinary service! Almost every woman there desperately in love with Jack! Wasn't it romantic?'

The elderly man who had retrieved my damp and now dirty hat gave Maeve a look of the strongest disapproval and staggered away, grunting with the unaccustomed effort of his little run, before I could thank him. Several other people who had been queuing up to speak to me stared at Maeve, with expressions of distaste. Maeve was oblivious to them.

'The weirdest thing, though... I think I saw Jack for a moment, sort of shadowy and transparent, standing by the coffin. I could smell that cologne he used to wear. Spicy and sexy. He was laughing at something... probably us getting down on our knees and praying for him. He always used to say religion was bunk, didn't he? Then I felt terribly cold. That's always a sign of something happening astrally.'

'Yes, well, let's go back to the house,' I said, hastily. Maeve always claimed that she was clairvoyant but, unfortunately, this never enabled her to foresee other people's reactions to her rather theatrical style. I saw Sebastian and Florian, Maeve's sons, standing a little way off. Florian bent to pick a flower from one of the graves and put it in the button-hole of his velvet suit. Sebastian lifted a size twelve Army boot and kicked over the vase. They walked away together, laughing.

I led the way like the head goose in a skein of greylags, the other mourners fanning out behind me. A group of onlookers stood outside the churchyard wall. They were village people who hadn't liked to take up places in the church but, none the less, wanted to be part of the most interesting event that had happened in Westray since the publican's wife had run off with the man from the brewery.

I smiled and nodded and they looked suitably glum. Mrs Veal from the post office was there, handkerchief to her hard, curious eyes. There was a girl holding a very young baby standing with Horace Birt, a fat man with an inflamed face, who farmed the land next to Westray. I didn't like him much and he had certainly not liked Jack, who had told him off several times about his sloppy husbandry. I hadn't realised he was married. As I looked at him, intending to say something palliative, he screwed his blunt red features into a sneer, put his arm round the girl's waist and led her away.

Getting home was as welcome to me then as a tent must be to a man who has spent a particularly raw winter's day sledding across the Yukon, inadequately dressed. If only I had had the tent to myself.

When I had sent Diana and Beatrice to talk to the other guests and had made a large jug of dressing, I went to look at the dining room. Diana had achieved the impossible. The salmon was perfectly skinned and decorated with dill, cucumber and borage flowers. The ham stood on its stand by a newly sharpened carving knife. There were dishes of potato, tomato and green salad elegantly arranged and strewn with spring onions, parsley and lovage. The loaves were wrapped in napkins to keep them warm. A truckle of Cheddar, which I had bought three days ago and entirely forgotten about, stood stripped of its muslin wrapper on a charming blue-and-white Worcester plate. There was a large tureen of steaming soup on a side table. A bowl of blush noisette roses drooped their soft, curved heads to reflect peach and ghostly white in the polished surface of the table.

I went into the drawing room to call everyone for lunch. Beatrice and Diana had cheated. They were sitting on the stairs, out of sight of the other guests, in earnest discussion about the future of modern ceramics. From what I overheard, Diana was being tactful and Beatrice immensely loyal. I opened the door wide, exposing them to the general view. As soon as she saw Beatrice my mother got up and walked away from Dorothy, who was still talking.

'I wondered where you were, Beatrice. *What* have you been doing with yourself? Nothing but eat I should imagine. And you're positively round-shouldered!'

'Lunch, everyone,' I called, hoping to distract my

mother's attention. Beatrice looked upset, almost tearful. Fabia always had this effect on her and probably on many others besides.

'For heaven's sake, don't *loll*, Elizabeth! And take off those *ridiculous* dark spectacles. You might as well have a white stick. James, hands out of pockets! I hope there is no salt in anything, Miranda?'

I gave a little murmured grunt, which might have been yes or no, and then was almost thrown back against the door as Dorothy strode past me to get to the dining room first. Ivor carved the ham while I cut up the salmon and Patience ladled out the soup. People ate as though a siege had been lifted and this was the first break from rats and dandelions they had had in months.

Sebastian and Florian had huge plates of everything. Maeve was currently a devotee of the macrobiotic diet, requiring nice calculations on yin and yang principles and resulting in a monotonous quantity of brown rice. Jasper and Dinkie made themselves scarce the minute they saw Sebastian. He was an unlovely boy, with a shaven head shaped like a thimble, flat-topped and with a neck wider than his brow, a disciple of neo-Nazism. Ivor had once spent two days getting a painted swastika off the gate-house wall. I asked James to keep a discreet eye on him, which he agreed to do as long at it could be at a distance. James and Sebastian were the same age but had not been friends since the age of seven when Sebastian had tried to lower James head-first into the moat. Florian was an entirely different sort of boy. I had once been very annoyed to find him at the dressing table experimenting with my makeup.

'You'll have your hands full bringing up those kiddies on your own,' Donald said, looking at Elizabeth who was leaning against the wall, talking to a man whose name I didn't know.

Her hair looked more like Veronica Lake's than ever. Her skirt was very short and her boots very long. I couldn't remember having seen them before. Was I giving her too much pocket-money? As I looked anxiously at her she pulled her dark glasses from her pocket and put them on with tantalising slowness. I hoped the man would realise that he was talking to a fourteen-year-old.

'I suppose Jack wasn't exactly a family man,' Donald continued. I refrained from comment. 'Stands to reason a chap of his kidney wouldn't want to settle to pipe and slippers. But he thought the world of those kiddies. And of you, my dear.' I tried to look pleased at this tribute. 'Elizabeth looks the spit of you. And Henry is just like his dad. Let's hope he's got his dad's brain, too.' This was annoying but I kept a vague smile on my face. 'As for James, I don't mind telling you I can't make head nor tail of him. Bright enough, no doubt, but too quiet for my liking.'

I felt ruffled by this. Donald had once taken James to a football match. James hadn't been old enough to be able to hide his boredom and dislike of the occasion. Since then they had had nothing to do with each other. Donald lit his pipe. 'You don't mind, my dear, if I smoke this?' He sucked at the tar-clogged stem, making sickening sounds, and then blew a cloud into my face. 'Dorothy doesn't like me to smoke indoors at home, says it gets into the curtains. She's a wonderful woman.'

We looked at Dorothy, who was prodding the tomato salad, her nose wrinkled with suspicion. 'I can't eat all this oil, dear. Upsets my insides. I'll have a plain tomato with a little salad cream.'

She very carefully removed a borage flower from her piece of salmon, holding it gingerly between finger and thumb as though it were a wasp with the power to sting and dropped it on to my plate. I went into the kitchen.

Rose was fast asleep on the sofa beneath a blanket. She looked a slightly better colour now and was breathing deeply. I tiptoed over to the fridge. Fortunately a few tomatoes remained in a bag, a little wrinkled but they would have to do. Salad cream there was not, but there *was* a jar of commercially made mayonnaise. As I was bending down to remove these items I heard a step behind me. I turned round quickly. Jeremy, looking rather heated by wine, was standing unpleasantly close.

'I saw you come in here, Miranda. I've been wanting to speak to you.'

Jeremy was a large, fleshy man. His hair was red, like the other male Stowes, but curly. This, combined with his round face and snub nose, gave him a babyish look, which was made sinister by the little winking grey eyes behind unframed hexagonal lenses. He had fat, wet hands with bitten fingernails with which he was keen on touching one at every opportunity. At least, I hoped it was one and not just me. I found him rather frightening.

'How nice.' I spoke in a low tone and gestured towards Rose to remind him to keep his voice down. 'I'll give you a plate and you can take this to your mother.'

'Just a minute.' He chuckled, a dry little noise like a lawn-mower failing to start. 'I've often wanted to say this. I've always admired you, Miranda. In fact, I might go further than that.' He paused, and I made my expression as discouraging as I could. 'My brother thought he was clever but he didn't know a good thing when he saw it. I'm not like him. I could make you very happy, Miranda.' He stretched his stubby fingers towards me.

'Jeremy, this is all very silly. I'll put it down to the fact that you've had too much to drink –'

Before I could go further, Jeremy plunged forward and clamped his mouth resoundingly on mine as though we were docking in space. I felt something soft under my foot as I struggled to free myself. It was Dorothy's tomato.

'I must apologise for distur-r-rbing you,' said a voice behind us. Jeremy let me go. Dr McCleod, his brow as dark as John Knox's when contemplating the Monstrous Regiment, stood in the kitchen doorway. Stew Harker, the errand boy from the village stores, stood behind him, an infuriating grin on his face.

'Oh, no, you aren't disturbing me,' I began, blushing as I searched for my handkerchief. 'It isn't – we weren't – This is my brother-in-law . . .'

I felt my face burning. Jeremy took up the one tomato

that remained whole and made a cowardly bolt for the dining room.

'I came back to take Miss Ingrams to the hospital. She ought to have her wrist X-rayed. I supposed you would be too busy to take her yourself.'

The cold sarcasm of his tone was wounding. I understood that things looked compromising but I was too cross with Jeremy and too exhausted by things generally to explain.

'She's asleep. Must she be woken?'

I bent over her. She looked so old and so fragile that my heart turned over. The idea of life without Rose was insupportable.

'I think so. The X-ray department is very busy and they've fitted her in specially. Miss Ingrams?' He patted her arm gently.

'You can stop mauling me around, Doctor. I'm quite awake, thank you.'

Rose sat up, furious to have been asleep beneath the gaze of so many. Dr McCleod tried to take her arm but she wouldn't allow it. I fetched her stick, her coat and her hat.

'Quite unnecessary, if you ask me, but you men always think you know best.' Rose's tone was biting.

'It's very good of you to take her,' I said to Dr McCleod, as he followed in Rose's wake.

'It's my job to look after my patients.' He cast aside my gratitude with a glance of dislike.

'What do you want, Stewart?' My voice was sharp.

Stew Harker gave me a little smile that was so full of cunning I wanted to box his ears.

'Telegram for you, Mrs Stowe. Mr Bastable said you was in the kitchen.'

I took the yellow envelope and tore it open. It was from Aunt Nancy. 'SORRY KENT BEE WAY VIEW STOP WAY VIEW IAN SPEAR IT STOP LEN DEAN HE THROW TUESDAY STOP NANCY.'

I puzzled over this message for some time. I rather liked being called a Kent bee. But who were these men, Ian

Spear and his chum Len Dean? Then it occurred to me to say it aloud with my best approximation of a Southern accent. Nancy lived in Virginia and it was a reasonable bet that the telephonist who had relayed the message to Mrs Veal was a native. It read, quite rationally, 'Sorry can't be with you. With you in spirit. Landing Heathrow Tuesday.'

This was good news. Next to Beatrice, Aunt Nancy was my favourite relation. We weren't actually related by blood. Nancy had been married to my father's brother, who had gone down with his destroyer in mid-Atlantic. Nancy had then married a tremendously rich and agreeable Virginian and was deliriously happy spending his money. I was delighted to find that I was still capable of looking forward to things.

The lunch dragged on interminably. Perhaps it was the cold weather that made my guests reluctant to tear themselves away. At last I was able to wave Dorothy, Donald and Jeremy off. Jeremy had given my hand a moist squeeze but I rushed away before he could kiss me. I had had to make Dorothy some ham sandwiches in case she felt faint on the journey back to Basildon. As I buttered bread I had comforted myself with the thought that I probably wouldn't see any of them again for a very long time. They had never seemed to care very much about the children, a feeling returned with interest.

'I've taken Father home,' said Patience, whom I found at the sink wearing my apron and rubber gloves. 'He'll sleep for hours. I'll just wash these glasses for you. I don't know how you're going to get rid of some of those people. Sir Brigham has gone into the library with Lissie. Rather her than me.'

I went to find George and asked him to check that the library windows were properly closed.

'That should settle the GOM's hash.' I had brought a bottle of Jack's best Chablis into the kitchen with me. I poured out two glasses. 'It's strange, isn't it, that winning a seat in the House of Commons seems to release ungovernable torrents of testosterone? What was Lissie thinking of?'

'I think she doesn't know how to say no,' Patience replied, and then blushed a little as she remembered that this incapacity had operated very extensively with Jack.

'I can't tell you what a ghastly experience I've just had!' Lissie came in at that moment. 'What possesses nasty old men with drooping bottoms to think that any girl will be theirs for the asking?'

Lissie was looking very attractive in deepest black from Harvey Nichols. She is the only woman I know who doesn't look awful after crying. She had almost howled during the service. I had been worried that George might suspect that this was more than sorrow for a departed friend.

'I think Sir Brigham has reached the age when any particle of judgement he might once have had has shrunk to a peanut.' Patience sounded unusually savage. Wacko had obviously been very trying.

'We mustn't turn into a coven of man-haters.' I took up a cloth and began to polish the glasses Patience had washed.

'I don't see why not.' Lissie found another cloth and together we worked away. 'As long as we don't expect to do any good by it. There was an article about Women's Liberation in *The Times* this morning. The photograph of the author ruined everything. She was at least a size twenty-two and with a chin like a pelican's pouch. Even Sir Brigham would have been put off. It was obviously sour grapes.'

'Lissie! That's playing into men's hands, if you say that!' Patience was indignant. 'A plain woman has a right to think as she does without being insulted and having all her motives derided.'

'Oh, I know. But where has it got us, anyway? We're still valued for our looks more than our brains.'

'But what a long way we've come,' I put in. 'Think of Caroline Norton and the Married Women's Property Act.

Before she made a stand a woman had no rights over her own children or her own money. That was less than two hundred years ago. Think what Elizabeth Blackwell and Florence Nightingale achieved! What about Emma Goldman and all those others? We should go down on our knees this minute and thank them for the difference they've made to our lives. Of course, things aren't perfect yet. But that's partly our own fault. Our cowardice and apathy have been just as detrimental to the rights of women as lecherous, power-mad men.'

'It's good to hear you sounding like your old self.' Patience smiled as she fetched another tray of glasses from the table.

'I expect you're right,' said Lissie, with perfect amiability.

'Miranda, we've got to go.' Diana came into the kitchen, followed by Rollo. 'The babies have a mad hour, like cats, just before bedtime. We promised to be home by seven. I wish we could stay and help you.'

'You've done so much and I haven't thanked you properly. Please come and stay and bring the children with you, won't you? Come when the weather's fine and we can have long days on the beach.'

Diana said she'd love to and we embraced each other warmly. I was genuinely sorry to see her and Rollo drive away.

'Where is Nanny Trebor?' My mother's tone was imperious. She refused to call Rose anything else. It was her way of reminding Rose of her former servant status. She thought me absurd to keep Rose beyond her days of being useful. Whenever she stayed with me she made a point of finding jobs for Rose to do. 'I see that my suitcases have not been unpacked. She can iron my brown silk for me to wear this evening.'

'In the first place Rose is in Bosworth District and General having her wrist X-rayed, and in the second, dinner will be leftovers eaten in the kitchen and what you're wearing will be more than adequate.'

'There is never *any* excuse for allowing standards to go.

Even during air-raids we changed for dinner and had four courses. Where is Goss?'

I suppose it was weak of me not to be firmer with my mother. But she adored argument and days after you had capitulated from exhaustion and boredom she would refer constantly, and at length, to the subject of dispute to demonstrate her pique that you had actually thought of disagreeing with her.

'Mrs Goss gave notice yesterday.'

'How badly you have managed things, Miranda, if I may say so. So you are to run this large, inconvenient house and look after three *very* difficult children – Elizabeth was quite insolent when I told her that she should not allow that dog in the house – with no help but a senile, crippled old woman and a dangerous, congenital idiot. What *can* you be thinking of?'

'You've forgotten that *I* am here to help Miranda,' said Ivor, who had come in just as my mother was speaking. He had failed to recognise himself from the latter unkind description.

My mother gave a snort of exasperation and swept from the room. On her way out she brushed past Patience, who held a tray of plates and knives and forks. A section of salmon backbone became entangled in the fringe of her elegant, snuff-coloured wrap. It hung behind her like the tail of an exceptionally fanciful chimera.

'Do you suppose that if we simply take everything away it will occur to everyone to go home?' I wondered.

People were sitting very comfortably all about the house, talking to anyone prepared to listen to them. There was no sign of the children. I looked anxiously out of the drawing room window as Jack's Methodist aunt came up to tell me all about her garden. 'You should see our clematis. I've got a stripy one with blooms like dinner plates. That's a drab little thing you've got by the front door. The flowers are no size at all.'

The reams of the old panes gave everyone viewed through them crooked legs like bad cases of rickets. To my dismay I saw Beatrice and the children carrying ropes and clambering down the steep sides of the moat. Elizabeth's pony had escaped from his field again and was standing up to his quarters in the reeds at the edge. Last time he had decided to have a swim it had taken us the best part of an afternoon to get him out.

'Oh, Puck!' I said, with some force.

I think the Methodist aunt must have misheard me for she inhaled to an impressive depth, hoisted herself to her full height and walked stiffly away.

At last we had all the dirty plates in the kitchen and all the remaining edible bits of food stowed in the larder. A handful of guests lingered on but I hardened my heart and decided to starve them out. They had already had cups of tea and the remnants of an old Dundee cake I had found in a tin. Lissie, Patience and Maeve continued with the washing-up while Beatrice and I put Rose to bed. The X-ray had shown a Colles' fracture, which would take at least six weeks to heal. The hospital had set the bone and put a cast on her wrist. They had wanted to keep her in overnight but she had insisted on coming home. Dr McCleod and Ivor had made a chair of linked hands to get her up to her room as she was still sleepy from the anaesthetic.

'I know I'm a tiresome old woman,' said Rose, with a hint of unusual weakness in her voice. 'When you get old it's important to be in the place you know best with the people you know best. That's all I want now. To be with Miranda and the children.'

I had kissed her, sorry to see her resilient spirit broken to the point of admitting sentiment. 'You can get those two out of here,' she added, rather ungratefully as she was no lightweight and Ivor and Dr McCleod were puffing like trains. 'I've never had a man in my bedroom before and it's much too late to begin now.' She closed her eyes tightly and turned her head away.

'Someone let Puck out deliberately,' said Elizabeth, as she stood in the kitchen, muddy to the waist.

'Where are Sebastian and Florian?' I said at once, and then blushed as I caught Maeve's eye.

'They said they were going to play cards in the library while I washed up.'

Naturally Maeve was reluctant to acknowledge her sons' imperfections. Any little lapses were explained away as the result of a broken home. Both Maeve's divorces had been messy. This was not her fault except that she had chosen two such spectacularly horrible men in the first place. Sebastian's father had been a Polish Army officer who had deserted from his regiment and escaped to England. He had married Maeve to avoid being deported and had given her a very hard time, demanding total subservience and a violently active sexual relationship, involving abnormal practices, which she had quickly come to detest. Florian's father had been an aesthete with a strong aversion to getting up in the morning. He was now living a nomad's life with a caravan and a lathe somewhere in Sherwood Forest.

I went into the library. Sebastian and Florian were there, a pack of cards spread out on the table. I noticed that they both had extremely muddy shoes and Sebastian had a gratified look on his face. I resolved to send Ivor to check on the hens at once.

'James, have you seen Ivor anywhere?' I poured my washers-up another glass of wine each and then one for myself.

'Not since ten minutes ago. I'm sorry I lost sight of those two hooligans. Fabia asked me to get her a book. They must have gone out then.' James looked and sounded utterly fed-up. 'I think I'll get back to school as soon as poss. I've got A levels in six months and it's a bad time to miss classes.'

'All right, darling. Whatever you want. I'll drive you back tomorrow, if you like.'

'Thanks.'

'Which book did Fabia want?'

'Burton's *Anatomy of Melancholy*. It took me ages to find. She said it would be more amusing than talking to Dad's relations. Here's Ivor.'

Ivor was humming the tune from last act of *Don*

Giovanni, the bit when he drops through the trap-door and is consigned to the flames of hell.

'Have you been to shut up the hens? I'm a little anxious about them.'

'Don't be anxious, my tulip. Not about the hens, anyway. "Fret not thyself, else shalt thou be moved to do evil," as the psalm says.'

I sniffed. His coat reeked of smoke. 'Have you been having another bonfire?'

Ivor looked guilty. Before he came to Westray he had been convicted of arson. After he came out of prison he had been given therapy for pyromania. We had always allowed him one bonfire a week so that he could indulge the impulse without, we hoped, letting it get out of hand. But I knew he had had a large bonfire the day before.

'Just a very small one. The funeral was upsetting, wasn't it?' His eyes filled with tears.

It was all very well for the psalmist to deliver high-handed injunctions not to fret, I thought darkly to myself.

CHAPTER 5

'My shoes are sopping! I'm going to take them off.' Beatrice stooped to untie the laces of her gym shoes. We were standing in the Quincunx Garden very early in the morning of the day after Jack's funeral.

'Your feet will freeze. You should have borrowed Elizabeth's boots.'

The grass was still wet from the rain of the day before and everywhere smelt strongly of leaves and earth. The sun cast the shadows of slender trunks across the beaded blades between the pattern of crab-apple trees. I had planted this bit of the garden ten years ago: it was especially charming in spring and equally so now, when the crab-apples hung thickly in clusters of yellow, pink and rosy red. Underneath there were drifts – well, on their way to becoming drifts – of blue autumn crocus and white colchicum. We were looking for mushrooms. Beatrice spotted a few in one corner and ran over to pick them.

'This is fun!' She came back to put them in the basket I was carrying. 'Horse mushrooms, aren't they? Do you still find blewits in Puck's field? You ought to take your shoes off. I feel like a child of nature, gathering the fruits of the earth with bare feet.' She suddenly looked solemn. 'Sorry. I forgot. I don't suppose anything seems like fun at the moment. You must miss Jack so dreadfully.' She pressed her lips together and frowned. 'I can't imagine what it would feel like if Roger died.'

'How is Roger?'

'Well, rather sulky, actually. I'm afraid we're not getting on so well. There seem to be a lot more rows. Always about money. I thought he ought to consider getting a job. Perhaps in the art department of one of the local schools. He was as indignant as if I'd suggested he might become a witch-finder general or a concentration-camp guard. I do try not to be dissatisfied. Only it is hard never having any money. And if we don't have children soon I'll be too old.' Beatrice sighed. 'How unfair life is! Your marriage was pretty perfect, wasn't it? An inspiration, really. Almost all my friends are divorced or miserable. Apart from you and Aunt Nancy, I can't think of anyone who's married to the right person. And now a stupid accident has gone and wrecked everything for you! It is hard!'

I hadn't realised that Beatrice had taken this idealised view of my relationship with Jack. I suppose I have always been rather protective of her and as we met only once or twice a year it had seemed a pity to spoil things by grumbling. Perhaps, too, there was an element of pride in keeping quiet about Jack's infidelities. All right. A very large element.

'I suppose night-time must be the worst,' Beatrice went on, misconstruing my silence. She took the basket from me and tucked her arm through mine. 'Poor darling! It must be hell waking up to find he isn't there.'

'Jack and I haven't slept in the same bed for four years.' The expression of amazement on Beatrice's face made me laugh. 'I'm sorry to disillusion you, but Nancy will have to be solely responsible for the apotheosis of the institution of marriage.'

Once I'd begun to tell Beatrice the truth about Jack, I felt I couldn't stop until she knew everything. Our footsteps, as we strolled about, made a muddle of emerald slashes on the silvery grass, very beautiful to see. The wind was cool and damp but the sun caught the fair strands in Beatrice's brown hair and marbled it with gold.

Jack had been furious when I had moved out of the bedroom we had shared for fourteen years. When, all those years ago, I had found out about his affair with Lissie, Jack had worked hard to repair the breach. He told me repeatedly how much he loved me and that I'd been the only woman he had ever loved. I actually did believe him.

It had been his idea to have Henry. I had been doubtful as Elizabeth, at fourteen months old, had only just begun to sleep properly and I was looking forward to unbroken nights and having a little time to myself. But Jack was so confident that another baby was just what I needed that I allowed myself to be persuaded. I've always been much too ready to imagine that other people might be right and Jack's influence was greater because he stood in lieu of all the male family relationships I had never had.

The pregnancy was quite unlike the other two. From the sixth month I began to feel dreadfully ill. One day I couldn't get out of bed because I was so dizzy. My entire body seemed to be swelling in sympathy with my abdomen. Dr Kenton diagnosed pre-eclampsia. I had to spend six miserable weeks in the cottage hospital, hardly getting out of bed. Henry was delivered by Caesarean section. Two days after the birth I got pneumonia. I was too ill to breast-feed him. I hardly saw him until he was a month old.

Jack rose marvellously and unexpectedly to the occasion. Rose was fully occupied looking after James and Elizabeth so, while I was recovering in hospital, Jack took three weeks off from the bank and spent nights walking up and down with Henry, feeding him, bathing him and changing him. Henry screamed with fury whenever he was left alone so Jack took him into our bed every night. It was the only time in the nineteen years of our marriage that Rose and Jack were on good terms. Rose came to see me in the hospital and said that she could forgive a great deal when she saw a big man like Jack lying flat on his back, fast asleep, with a tiny baby spreadeagled across his chest.

I was terribly weak for some time after I came home. Jack had to go back to work so a girl from the village came to help with Henry. I never felt that Henry was my child in quite the same way that James and Elizabeth had been. Rose and I had looked after them between us but Rose's innate tact had always allowed me to take charge. It was to me they came first for comfort, to me they confided their worries when they were old enough to have any, to me that they poured out the intense love that small children feel for the provider of their security and comfort.

As they grew older, James and I remained very much in sympathy. He is like Jack to look at with straight red hair, white skin and green eyes. By the time he was sixteen he was as tall as Jack. But there the likeness ended. James was a serious, introverted child. He wore spectacles and hated any kind of games. I've always considered him to be more intelligent than Jack, though Jack had a sort of cleverness that impressed people. James thinks a great deal about everything. He is soft-hearted, sensitive and, when he chooses, very funny. I suppose it must be obvious to anyone that I think he's wonderful.

Jack didn't understand James and teased him, which James hated. I used to feel furious when he made James feel a fool in front of other people. Jack was competitive with all men, even his own sons. One day I heard James say to Jack, quite quietly after some jibe, 'Dad, hasn't it ever occurred to you that some people are bored by your continual ragging? I am, for one.'

Jack made a face of mock alarm and laughed but I saw that he was discomfited. After that things were more evenly matched between them and I noticed that Jack left James alone.

Elizabeth divided her love fairly equally between her parents and Rose. I don't think she loved any of us as much as she loved Puck and Jasper. Henry adored Jack with a kind of hero-worship that worried me. It might have been jealousy on my part, I suppose. I am jealous, I admit that. When I found out that Jack had been unfaithful for a second time, with a girl who worked at the bank, I had felt excruciatingly, mortifyingly jealous.

It happened on a beautiful morning in May. I had felt suddenly better than for months before Henry was born. I decided to go up to town and do a little shopping. Rose was encouraging. She would manage the three children with the help of Eileen, the girl from the village. I must go and buy myself something nice to wear and get my hair done. I had peered hard at myself in the mirror after Rose said that. I was terribly thin with gaunt cheeks and long, unkempt hair. A lot of it had fallen out after having Henry and it was just growing back in strange wisps round my hairline. My eyes, which are brown, stared reproachfully from my whey-coloured face like Lon Chaney's in *The Return of the Mummy*.

I went to the hairdresser and endured a lot of sympathetic talk about how ill I looked and how my hair was 'just like paper. You can tear it. Look, Janice, at Madam's hair. Never seen anythink like it.' Despite this my morale was improved when I emerged an hour later with a shoulder-length bob that made me look miles better. I went to my favourite shop in Beauchamp Place and bought a very becoming dress. I decided to wear it out of the shop and to have lunch with Jack if he was free. I rang Jack's secretary, Miss Horne, who said that Jack was in a meeting but she would let him know the minute he came out that I had come up to town.

It was a day of sparkling loveliness. I took a taxi to the City and sat in the garden of a little eighteenth-century church, looking up at white cherry blossom against a plumbago-blue sky. Then I walked round the corner to the bank.

A pretty dark girl in a bright yellow suit was standing outside the building. I noticed her at once, partly because she looked so attractive and also because she had an air of excited expectation, which was touching. She looked at her watch and then at her hands, smoothing them together as though she were nervous. She took a mirror from her bag and checked her face. Then Jack came running down the steps and her expression became euphoric. He took her in his arms and kissed her on the lips. She said something that made him laugh and he shook his head. He hailed a taxi. I shrank back into a doorway, my heart thumping with terror at the idea of him seeing me. I felt as though I was doing something disgraceful, as though I was spying on them. They drove away.

I had a mad idea of following them but at once gave it up. It would be quite pointless. I should make a scene and embarrass myself horribly. Suppose she was a client and they were having a business lunch? Kissing was the fashion now. At parties I kissed people whose names I didn't know and about whom I cared less than about the carp in the moat. I expected that in a few more years we'd be kissing the man who brought the registered parcels and Benny Sykes, the milkman. I hoped he'd have got over his acne.

But Jack had kissed this girl on the lips. That was rather different. I felt appallingly weak and ill. I went to Charing Cross and caught the train home. I left the suit I had travelled up in on the train by mistake. When I got back to Westray Rose sent me straight to bed. The children came in and jumped over me and made up their faces with the contents of my dressing-table drawers. Their innocent faces, clown-like with swirls of lipstick and blobs of face cream, filled me with such love that I was comforted. At the same time I felt that I had taken a step away from Jack. He had become someone against whom I must defend myself.

When Jack came home that evening he was particularly buoyant. 'Darling, Horny told me you were in town when I got back from lunch. You shouldn't be so secretive. Of course she'd forgotten that I had to go and have lunch with someone to discuss insurance policies. I'd forgotten to put it in my diary. He was very dull. It would have been much more fun to go somewhere nice with you. What have you done with your hair? It looks marvellous.'

'Thank you. Where did you go for lunch?' I thought my voice sounded pretty natural.

'We went to Simpson's. Very good, but Alan Pemberton – that's the man I had lunch with – only talks about work and his children. Are you all right? You're looking rather knocked up.'

'I probably did a little too much today. I'll have supper in bed, I think. Ask Rose if she'll boil me an egg.'

'All right. You get some sleep, darling. I'll go and see if Ivor's started cutting the yew hedge. He's probably still talking to it and explaining that he's got to be cruel to be kind.'

I managed a weak smile. Jack bent down and kissed my forehead. He stank of Miss Yellow Suit's Chanel No. 5. I recognised it because I used to wear it myself when I was up at Oxford. I closed my eyes and sank down on the pillows, waiting for him to go.

I don't know why I didn't have it out with him there and then. I suppose I wanted to wait until I was calmer, to deny him the satisfaction of seeing me wounded. Because this was the second time that he had been unfaithful, some of the immediate, obvious reactions felt too stale and worn out to bother with. I couldn't be indignant and furious all over again. I had exhausted that with Lissie. Also, I noted with a savage satisfaction, I didn't seem to care quite as much. I was falling out of love with Jack.

Now my feelings were the smartings of wounded pride, the humiliation of being deceived, the insecurity of not knowing what was happening, where and when. I longed to go through his pockets and find something that would turn speculation into absolute certainty. Though it would hurt to have proof, it would also be a relief to know. The stupid hope that I'd been mistaken and that he really had lunched with an insurance man *would* assert itself. But my instinct damped this hope with the conviction that everything in his behaviour confirmed the liaison. The difference this time was that my illusions had already been destroyed. I no longer felt that my world had shattered.

It has often been a comfort to me to recognise that although one can be unhappy countless times until, I suppose, one's dying hour, the unhappiness is never quite the same. For some reason this has always given me strength in the face of misery. There are no dreary repetitions. There are always new sensations to be explored and fresh conclusions to be drawn.

Clearly one of two things had to happen. Either I would go mad with unhappiness or I would cease to care. There was really no choice. I gave myself a few days to think it all over and acquire a little self-control before telling Jack that I knew what he was doing.

It wasn't quite as clear-cut as that. I did have several sessions of weeping, usually in the bath, and there were times when I felt so crushed and miserable that I longed to howl on a sympathetic shoulder. And nearly all the time I felt a horrible sick pain of jealousy, like a stone in the gut, which made it difficult to eat and too easy to drink. I nearly drove into a bridge coming back from lunch with Lissie one afternoon. I had been dreadfully tempted to tell her everything. Perhaps, cruelly, I imagined that it would hurt her as much as me. I'm ashamed of that. Anyway the effort to seem light-hearted had made me careless about how much I drank.

As it was I took a bend a little too fast and had to brake, grazing the wing of the car. I got out to check the damage and then leaned over the parapet to look at the dark tumbling water. I mustn't let Jack or my own silly pride spoil things for the children. The situation was so prevalent these days as to be almost trite. I mustn't allow myself to play stupid, damaging games. I must be sensible. A few not very sensible tears joined the rush to the sea.

On the Saturday that followed the day of my discovery I was on my knees in the courtyard, weeding round the silvery, pudding-shaped bushes of cotton lavender I had planted in the pattern of a lover's knot. Patience was coming to lunch and there was a game pie in the oven, with salad, cheese and a bottle of sauvignon blanc to go with it. The sun was warm on my back and the rosemary hedge behind me smelt tantalisingly sharp. I heard someone walk through the door that opened on to the bridge that spanned the moat. I looked up, expecting to see Patience. It was Miss Yellow Suit.

Now she was wearing jeans and a very tight pink T-shirt. She looked young, somewhere in her early twenties, I guessed, and so nervous that the corner of her mouth was twitching.

'Sorry. Is there a bell? I didn't see it. Are you Mrs Stowe? I work in Jack's office. I'm his new assistant. I've brought some papers for him to sign.' She flushed as dark as a wild peony.

'You *are* a hard worker. Do they always expect you to give up your weekends?'

There was something cold and ironical in my tone and the girl looked away, her eyes glistening. I guessed it all. When she wasn't with Jack she sat waiting for him to ring, feeding off the pleasures of the last meeting, invoking his image, yearning for the day when he would rid himself of his matrimonial shackles and be *hers*. It's an ancient, commonplace drama, with always the same pathetic ingredients of gullibility and self-deception and the uglier ones of vanity and selfishness, but the pains are felt with a fresh keenness each time it's played. I could see that this girl was wretched. I stood up.

'I'm Miranda. Won't you stay to lunch? If you don't mind eating in the kitchen. Jack has gone to buy some fencing posts. I don't suppose he'll be long.'

I had no particular plan. I wanted to show this woman, and thereby convince myself, that I was in control. I refused to be afraid of her. I noticed that her skin was very sallow, the kind that goes into large pores later on.

'Thank you.' She gave me her hand. It was hot and damp. Her upper lip was sparkling with sweat. 'I'm Justine St Clair.'

Heavens! It sounded like the name of the heroine from a women's magazine story. I took her indoors, gave her a drink and introduced her to Rose. I could tell at once that Rose didn't like her by the way she stared hard at the nipples that showed very clearly through Justine's tight T-shirt. 'This is the fashion, is it?' was all she said, giving her a look blent of suspicion and disapproval, as she began to put the knives and forks into tidier formation.

Patience arrived, was introduced and, obedient to youthful training, engaged Justine in small-talk, trying topics as diverse as the best time to prune hybrid clematis (Justine knew nothing about gardening) and the new novel by Angelica Thrift (Justine had never heard of her). Justine's hands shook and her eyes turned constantly and fearfully to the door.

Henry was asleep in his pram beneath the Portugal quince in what was called the drying ground, a little yard between the kitchen door and the old laundry. Justine's eyes went out to the pram and then back to me with what I can only describe as a tortured look.

I realised that this girl believed herself to be in love with Jack. She was so desperate to provoke a change, any change, from the wretched cycle of doubts, hopes and fears that she had risked coming here to face possible disaster. But I also knew the triumph of hope over experience. Had I not believed that Jack's affair with Lissie might be an aberration? I could imagine Justine's frustration in being subject to Jack's callous whims. She and I were struggling for the same thing: instead of being feebly reactive we were seeking some kind of mastery over our own lives.

'Let's start,' I said, cutting up the game pie and putting it on plates.

As the lunch began, Justine had the greatest difficulty in eating anything. When Ivor came in she gave such a jump and a gasp, thinking, I suppose, that it was Jack, that I thought she was going to swallow her fork. Rose fixed her sharp eyes on Justine, and I could tell she was rapidly putting two and two together. When Justine put her knife and fork together leaving half the food on her plate untouched Rose gave several loud 'tuts' of disapprobation. In Rose's book it was ill-bred to make a scene.

Ivor was in one of his romantic moods, giving me a look that was eloquent of love and placing a rolled-up piece of paper by my plate. It was tied with tendrils of virgin's bower.

'I've been experimenting with asclepiadic meter.' His long, thin face looked peaked with effort.

'Asclepiadic... That has a caesura in the middle, doesn't it?' asked Patience, making a sensible guess. I looked at her with affection. She was a trump.

'Yes! Spondee, two or three choriambs, and an iambus!' Ivor was delighted.

As Patience and Ivor tussled with the difficulties of the first ode of Horace and I tossed the salad, Justine looked around the kitchen.

It is a lovely room, very large, with a low, beamed ceiling but full of rippling light reflected from the moat, which runs directly beneath the windows of this part of the house. We had removed the Edwardian range when we came and restored the roasting hearth. It is six feet high and ten feet wide, and on the coldest day can warm the whole room. We found a smoke-jack in one of the outhouses and a basket spit in another. A smoke-jack is fixed in the chimney so that the rising hot air pushes its tin vanes round like a windmill. A series of chains and pulleys connects this to the spit, and the hotter the fire the faster the meat is turned and roasted. Occasionally we cooked large pieces of meat on it but the dripping fat made something of a mess. It was there mostly for the romance of the thing. On one side of the hearth was Rose's chair, and on the other a comfortable sofa. Justine's eyes wandered over everything with an expression of increasing misery.

Elizabeth and James came running in, having been taken out for a walk by Eileen. They held their faces up to me to be kissed before looking shyly at Justine. At once Rose called them to her side, as though Justine might have something contagious, and began to roll lumps of Plasticine into balls for them as vigorously as though she were rolling Justine's head.

Suddenly there were footsteps striding across the hall.

'Sorry I'm late, darling. I met old Budger and he wanted to buy me a drink –'

He stopped suddenly. It wasn't often that I saw Jack absolutely nonplussed. Then his eyes grew cold and his mouth tightened. 'Hello, Patience. Hello, Justine. This is a surprise.' He made it quite clear from the tone of his voice that it was anything but a pleasant one.

'Justine has brought some papers for you to sign,' I said, pleased with the calmness of my own voice. Justine's smile was ghastly. She looked at Jack with eyes bespeaking desperation. Rose tutted again.

Jack clearly remembered the maxim that in skating over thin ice safety lies in speed. 'You don't seem to be eating much. Get them and we'll go into my study. I expect you want to be on your way.'

Patience looked at me in astonishment. Jack often didn't bother to be especially polite to people he considered unimportant but the brusqueness of his manner to Justine was startling. I lifted my eyebrows at Patience and she took a deep breath. 'I always think Kent is most beautiful in May,' she began, nobly.

Justine bit her lips and I saw her eyes fill with tears.

'Why is that lady crying?' asked James, coming to stand by Justine's chair and gazing up at her with intense concentration. 'Does *my* nose go red when I cry?'

‘I can’t stand this,’ said Jack, and walked out of the kitchen.

‘I suppose it’s because there are so many orchards,’ Patience continued, gamely. ‘Everything is pink and white. The hawthorn flowers and cow parsley . . .’

Justine got to her feet. She looked around wildly, tears running down her face.

‘Come on,’ I said, getting up myself. ‘Let’s get this business over with. Back in a minute, Patience.’

‘ “And in green underwood and cover, Blossom by blossom the spring begins,” ’ murmured Ivor, seeming quite unaware of the general embarrassment that prevailed.

I led the way into the hall. Much of my jealousy had dissipated now that I had seen that she was more vulnerable than I was. Also, close to, she was not nearly as pretty as I remembered her. A door banged. Jack came into the hall, looking furious.

‘Justine is rather upset,’ I said, with hauteur. ‘I think you’d better speak to her.’

‘I don’t know what I’m expected to say,’ Jack put his hands in his pockets and glared at us both. ‘I didn’t ask her to come.’

He looked very pale and extremely handsome. I thought it strange that he was most attractive when most horrid.

‘Oh, Jack! I’m sorry, so sorry, to have made you angry.’ Another tear ran down Justine’s cheek. ‘I couldn’t bear another weekend –’

‘For God’s sake!’ He looked at me and spread his hands wide in a gesture of exasperation. ‘The girl’s neurotic. I’ll get rid of her. Sorry, darling.’

‘Jack, this won’t do. You owe her a little kindness.’

Justine spun round with a gasp of fury, her chest heaving. ‘I don’t need you to patronise me! I love Jack! And he loves me! Tell her! Tell her about us!’

Jack hesitated, and then his eyes glittered in a way that was unpleasantly familiar. He looked at me, ignoring her. ‘Well, since you insist. The truth is, Miranda, I’ve behaved very badly. Justine made it fairly clear that she wanted to go to bed with me. And you were... Well, you've been ill for so long... I'm sorry, darling, it's all very sordid. But it was simply a question of opportunity and availability. It was hopelessly weak of me. You've every right to be angry. I promise you it's over now. It didn't mean a thing.'

'Jack!' Justine clasped her hands over her chest as though he had lodged a quivering poignard there. 'I know you don't mean it! It because *she*'s here. I've got to talk to you alone.'

I turned to go but Jack moved ahead of me. 'Don't go, Miranda. I've got nothing to say that you can't hear.' He looked at her and then smiled, cruelly. 'Look, Justine. I shouldn't have gone to bed with you. But you know how it is when someone's positively asking. A man can't resist. It's over now. Finished. Understand? You can have two months' salary in lieu of notice. But next time don't confuse a casual fuck with a great passion. You've made a bloody nuisance of yourself. I suppose that's what you wanted. Now, if you're quite satisfied...' He strode to the front door and held it open.

I've never seen anyone look so humiliated as that poor girl did when she heard what was probably the central experience of her life so far reduced to utter paltriness. She grew very red, then very white. She made a sound of protest, something between a sob and a sigh. Then she crept to the door, casting him a last look of acute suffering to which he responded with smiling indifference.

A week later a parcel arrived, which I opened, thinking it was a pair of pillowcases I had ordered. Out fell one of his ties, cut into small pieces. I was annoyed as it was a particularly nice silk one I had given him last Christmas.

Jack was wise enough not to suggest another baby this time. Instead we went to Venice. The weather was cloudy, in keeping with my mood. On the third afternoon, when the sky was gloomy and the rain slashing, we went back to the hotel and made love. I knew that I had to. Jack would have every excuse for being unfaithful if I refused. He was exultant afterwards. He seemed to think that the fabric of our marriage had been invisibly mended by this act. But I knew that my love for him was hanging only by a thread.

It would be tedious to enumerate the amours that followed Justine St Clair. I think even Jack grew a little bored with them. What he seemed to enjoy most was giving his mistresses their dismissal. He liked me to know about it... perhaps to display his powers of seduction, I don't know. There was always the peculiar glittering of the eye. I suppose, for him, it added spice to our reconciliation. For in those days I allowed a reconciliation. Often I told myself that it would be better to cut and run. I had fantasies of taking the children and going to live with my mother in Italy or of renting a small cottage somewhere and getting myself a job of some kind. I told myself that pride demanded that I should make some stand, deliver an ultimatum, refuse to allow myself to be subjected to what was still, despite all my efforts to distance myself, a painful business.

But there were several objections to this scheme. One was the happiness of the children. I had grown up without a father and I knew the sadness of it.

The only existing connection between my father and myself was a book of nursery rhymes. Inside the front cover, in an idiosyncratic hand, were the words '*To my darling daughter, Miranda, on her fourth birthday, with all my love, Daddy*'. I always kept the book on my bedside table. I knew every loop, every tail, every twirl of the inscription by heart. The Ts were like spears and the Ys were like whips. The cloth spine was worn with much handling and I had repaired it several times. I still looked at it occasionally. As a child I had particularly liked the rhyme that goes 'If all the world were apple-pie / And all the sea were ink, / If all the trees were bread and cheese, / What would we have to drink?' That world, depicted in the illustration as a giant yellow crust with pieces of green and red apple poking through, stuck with trees like slices of cottage loaf and surrounded by shiny, boiling blackness, had represented safety. When I was unhappy as a child I withdrew in my imagination to this apple-pie kingdom where I felt my father lived in spirit.

How could I deprive my children of their father? Of course, he would not be dead and gone entirely out of the world. They would still have had weekends, presents, holidays and letters. But even if this were enough, Jack was careless and selfish. I was prepared to bet that even these inadequate tokens of fatherly esteem would diminish quite quickly.

And there was Westray Manor. It was mine, in fact, having been bought with the money left me by Christopher Chough. But Jack's salary paid for its upkeep and all our living expenses. I had not a farthing of my own. If we decided to live apart, Westray would have to be sold. Westray was my strength, my consolation, my inspiration. To me it was animate with all its past history and all its present beauty.

Of course, I considered having a lover myself. In fact, I firmly intended it. My requirements were simple. A man not absolutely hideous, who could talk tolerably well about subjects other than himself and was not addicted to vice. Most important, he must be unattached. This shows how naïve I still was. I might as well have asked for a prince with ass's ears. After a bit I gave up.

I settled for what I already had... the children, my friends, the house and garden, Rose and Ivor, and I found that it was a life very well worth living, full of satisfactions and good things. As time went on, I minded less about Jack's infidelities. But the less they mattered to me, the more I disliked making love with him. At last, after a particularly grim conclusion to one of his affairs, when the woman had tried to kill herself, I could bear it no longer and moved into the Court Room.

It has always been my favourite room. After the religious community was sent packing, in 1538, Westray Priory had been given to Simon le Bec, a local Baron, as a reward for services to the Crown. It became a

Court-baron and a Court-leet, having powers of jurisdiction over its tenants. All minor local offences were tried at Westray. Because of its importance the room had been panelled and the oak was now silvery with age. An oriel window, matching the one in the library below, gave a view over the woods from which rose the conical roof of the pigeon tower, gleaming with red and grey tiles like a striped medieval tent. The Court Room had a fireplace as large as the one in the drawing room and on winter nights I lay in my gilded chamber, listening to the roaring wind outside and the whistling of the burning logs within and was happy... as happy as anyone could be alone.

CHAPTER 6

At eight o'clock on Monday morning Beatrice and I were alone in the kitchen, drying out after another heavily bedewed expedition in search of mushrooms. There was an hour to wait before Freddy came to take my mother to the airport. It would be a tremendous relief to see her go, though I suppose her constant demands had been a distraction. I had remembered to light Fabia's fire at half past six so that the temperature of her bedroom would be suitable for her levée. She was accustomed to this service during the Italian winter and it did not occur to her that she might do without it for the four days she was at Westray.

'These mushrooms are heaven,' said Beatrice, making large inroads on the ample dish I had fried for everyone's breakfast. 'I've never eaten anything so delicious in my life. What did you say these purple ones were called?'

'The common name is Amethyst Deceiver.' My voice was muffled as my head was half in the oven, checking on the set of Fabia's *oeufs cocottes*. She *never* ate fungi of any sort. Italians are wild about them and Fabia disliked to be one of the throng. She had questioned me closely on the subject of my hens' diet before she would consent to eat their eggs. Fabia's expertise lay in being a nuisance and she was now an absolute genius at it.

'I wish I could stay longer.' Beatrice spoke with her mouth full. 'I know you've got friends to help you and I'd probably just be in the way, but still, for my own sake, I'd be happier to be on the spot.'

'You wouldn't be in the way.' I stopped what I was doing to look at her. Fabia had ordered melba toast with her eggs and I was doing the tricky bit of slicing it down the middle. 'You've helped me so much already.'

'Have I? Have I really?'

Beatrice looked so pleased that I couldn't help smiling. Her modesty was beguiling. Perhaps living with Jack had taught me the value of this quality.

'You have. Talking about the past is agony but I feel better when I have. I must try to be positive. I can't imagine what the future will be and I think I'm rather frightened of it.'

'At least you won't have to pretend to yourself any more,' said Beatrice.

'Pretend?'

'That you aren't minding about Jack making love with other women.'

I was rather floored by this. *Was* that what I had been doing?

'Perhaps you ought to think about talking to someone?' Beatrice suggested. 'I believe they cost a bomb but perhaps an analyst might be helpful.'

'Helpful with what?' Fabia had come downstairs while Beatrice was speaking. 'Waldo has an analyst and, as far as I can see, it has done nothing but make him extremely self-centred. He is always talking about his obsessive-compulsive neurosis. I sometimes feel as though I'm living in a *ménage à trois*. It used to be quite the thing to spend an hour on an expensive sofa in Harley Street, prattling about one's idiotic dreams, but now I think it's rather *vieux jeu*. What is that extraordinary garment you're wearing, Beatrice? One thinks of an armchair under a holland cover.'

'It's called a burnoose.' Beatrice looked a little hurt. 'Arabs wear them to keep themselves warm during freezing nights in the desert.'

'It does bring vast expanses to mind, certainly.'

Fabia was wearing a well-cut taupe coat and skirt which, together with her mink scarf, had probably cost as much as Beatrice's yearly income. Elizabeth and Henry came in with Rose. I'd sent them to help her downstairs. She was still very unsteady, though she said her wrist didn't hurt any more.

'Good morning, Nanny Trebor,' said Fabia, in a voice exceeding her customary more than generous volume. She always spoke to Rose as though she were deaf, although her hearing was good. 'Henry, your hair is much too long.'

'I could have run up and down stairs a hundred times in the time it took us to come down.' Henry was more than usually boastful, I had noticed. 'Is that egg still gooey?' He stuck a finger into the delicate milky film on Fabia's egg before I could stop him and the yellow yolk flooded the ramekin. 'Sorry, Mum.'

I looked at him wrathfully and then, remembering Jack, put a smile on my face while fetching another egg from the bowl.

Elizabeth was helping Rose to lower herself on to a chair. She was being as good as Henry was naughty. Both kinds of behaviour were equally worrying. I regretted that I knew so little about psychology. Elizabeth was wearing a long black mohair jersey and a skirt made out of what looked like an Indian bedcover. Her feet were bare and her toenails were varnished a deep purple, as though she had crushed both sets of toes in an exceptionally heavy door.

'Why does Miranda need an analyst?' continued Fabia, with all her usual tenacity. 'I suppose women these days can lose their husbands without going mad. During the war husbands died like flies. When your father died I carried on exactly as usual and *I* had no mother to drop everything and fly to my side, regardless of the sacrifice involved. I'll have some fresh coffee, Miranda. Coffee that's been reheated is very bad for one's digestion.'

I caught Beatrice's eye and gave her a wink, which unfortunately my mother saw.

'If you're going to grimace, Miranda, I shall begin to think that Beatrice is right and you do need a psychiatrist. One good thing about one's husband dying is that it puts a stop to all that tiresome *bed* business.'

Fabia would have been a great exponent of *fin amour*, had she been born a few centuries earlier. She wanted to be adored with humble gallantry without ever having to give an inch. She thought sex was something over which men made fools of themselves and with which women had to put up for the sake of masculine conversation. Quite why she thought it worth the sacrifice was anyone's guess.

'Though I must say that your father was not one of those men who think of nothing else. He was an artist first and a man second. *What* he would have achieved if he had not died so young!'

She sat for a moment with her head flung back in one of her Mary Shelley poses, the grieving widow sitting on the shore at Spezia, contemplating the blighting of extraordinary talent by cruel accident. Shelley and my father had both been artists and met violent ends, and she was fond of drawing parallels, albeit of a simple kind. She had a room in her house in Italy devoted to the display of my father's remaining canvases. They were very abstract – perhaps cubist, I wasn't sure – in various tones of the same colour. I couldn't tell whether they were good or not. I didn't mind at all that my mother was leaving them to a museum.

'Jack always seemed to me to be the sort of man who was a great deal too interested in sex,' continued my mother. Elizabeth and Henry paused in the business of eating their mushrooms.

'I read something interesting the other day that Picasso

said.' I put Fabia's second egg in front of her and began to cut Rose's bacon into small pieces so that she could manage with a fork. 'He said that there are painters who transform the sun into a yellow spot but there are others who, thanks to their art and their intelligence, transform a yellow spot into the sun.'

'That's a stupid thing to say,' said Henry, disappointed at the turn the conversation had taken. 'I could have said that if I'd wanted.'

'I hope you won't do anything silly, Miranda,' my mother went on. 'Have affairs with married men or anything like that. You must learn to be lonely as *I* had to do. What did you say, Nanny Trebor?'

She turned sharply to Rose, who had made a noise something like 'Chah!' 'That poor creature is becoming addled in her wits,' Fabia said to me, in a voice that was lower but still perfectly audible from anywhere in the room. 'I think, Miranda, that you may find things not quite so easy as you have been used to.'

After I had said goodbye to my mother and then, much more reluctantly an hour later, waved to Beatrice's van as it wobbled down the drive, I made a list of things to be done. 'Put advertisement for daily help in Mrs Veal's window' was at the top of the list. 'Ring James's headmaster'. On second thoughts, that ought to be done first. I just wanted to be sure that James was not in too much emotional turmoil, although headmasters are perhaps not the right people to ask about this kind of thing. 'Find something for Patience's lunch'. The telephone rang.

Half an hour later I put the receiver back on its rest. I had always disliked my bank manager for no better reason than that he was tiresomely self-important and really rather a stupid man. Now I felt I actually hated him for the much less good reason that he was the bearer of ill tidings. The conversation was obliquely apocalyptic of disaster. Jack and I had always been extravagant. We had spent everything that he earned on the children, the house and garden, books, paintings, holidays and cars and never thought of saving. Now the bank manager wanted to see me the next time I was in London 'to discuss the way forward'. My solicitor had made a similar request the day before. I wrote 'Make appointment with bank and solicitor' on my list and then, at the top of the list, I wrote 'Make money'.

'Rose doesn't look very well,' said Patience, after Rose had gone upstairs to lie down. Rose always insisted on having an early lunch and taking herself off when my friends came because she said she didn't want to listen to a lot of silly girls' gossip. It was one of those instances of tact that made Rose so easy to live with. 'She's very grey and shaky.'

'The fall shocked her. She's eighty-six, you know, quite an age. I wonder if I ought to ask the doctor to call again?'

'Give it another few days, perhaps. You're looking under the weather yourself. Dark circles. Aren't you sleeping?'

'Oh, I'm all right. Waking a bit early, that's all. Let's have lunch. I suppose you've got to get back on the treadmill by two?'

'Half past. Oh, I met Lissie on my way up. She nearly knocked me off my bike at Mill Corner. She said she was going to drop in here after she'd been to the library.'

I got out another plate and a glass, and five minutes later Lissie arrived, looking immaculate in pale blue wool with a silk shirt. I was glad to see that the signs of woe were a little diminished.

'I'd love some lunch but only if you're sure I'm not butting in. I've brought a bottle of George's Dom Perignon. I thought we'd better make the best of things.'

Lissie's attitude to everything from low comedy to high drama was essentially one of frivolous epicureanism. We were just enjoying our first glass (Patience was only having half of one because she had to go back to work) when the front door banged and Maeve's voice could be heard.

'I thought I'd come and keep you company.' She came into the kitchen. 'Oh! I imagined you'd be sitting miserably on your own, head bowed beneath the weight of widow's weeds, and here you are having a party.' She looked rather hurt.

I got out another plate and glass. 'I'm so glad you've come,' I said. 'I've got to make plans for the future and I particularly need your advice.'

Maeve recovered her *sangfroid* at this and put a bottle of some peculiarly repulsive-looking greyish liquid on the table. 'It's a Chinese herbal elixir. I bought it last time I was in London. I thought it's probably just what we all need. It has miraculous powers of rejuvenation. Honestly, it makes you feel ten years younger! The man who sold it to me said that his mother-in-law was completely bed-ridden and now, after only one bottle, she's driving round Hounslow on a moped. Apparently it increases a man's ability to maintain an erection while making love for up to four hours. Also it cures epilepsy.'

'It sounds as though it might be a bit strong,' said Patience, as we all stared doubtfully at the bottle.

'Four hours, you say?' murmured Lissie, and then blushed as we all looked at her.

'Oh, come on.' Maeve was impatient. 'Try anything once is my motto.'

And a very great mistake it had been, I knew we were all thinking but were too polite to say. I got out four of the smallest glasses we owned, which we had been given as a wedding present and never used because they were singularly horrible, covered with gilt and a picture of a Swiss chalet on each.

'Terrific glasses,' said Maeve. 'Far out.'

'If you're going to talk like a drugged, alcoholic jazz singer all through lunch, I'm definitely having a whole glass of champagne,' said Patience, stretching for the bottle. 'My God, what have you done to your hands?'

Maeve's hands were covered with the most terrible bruising, yellow, purple and black.

'I've been dyeing. Look! It's called batik. You tie the fabric into lots of little knots and dip it into different colours.' She threw off her coat and displayed a shirt and skin of strange variegation. It reminded me of the sort of painting Waldo did . . . a riot of gloomy streaks entitled *Post Débâcle* or *Storm over Liverpool Docks*.

'Aren't you supposed to iron it when it's dry?' asked Lissie.

'Perhaps it might look better. Oh, Miranda, mushroom risotto! How yum!'

I was in the state of mind that always overtakes me after an admonitory call from the bank manager when for at least twenty-four hours I can hardly bear to spend so much as a ha'penny and I'm saving slivers of soap to stick together in a horrid slimy ball and re-using old envelopes. After about two days of this meticulous economy I forget all about it and slide back to my mildly spendthrift ways, buying paperback books, plants and bars of soap without asking myself if I can really afford to. Being still in the former state of raised pecuniary consciousness I was determined to have mushrooms and raspberries, of which we had had an exceptional crop this year, for supper as well.

'Now, I'm sorry to hog the conversation,' I said, as I handed the bowl of lettuce leaves picked from the garden to Patience, 'but I must consult you all about my future. I know my solicitor is going to say that I've got to sell Westray, buy something small and cheap and invest the difference. But, quite honestly, the thought makes me feel physically sick.'

'That's a typically male attitude,' said Maeve. 'As though a woman is incapable of making any money for herself.' Maeve had just read *The Female Eunuch* and her conversation had taken on a new combativeness. 'Germaine Greer says that of nine million women working in this country only two per cent are in administrative positions and five per cent are in professions. The rest are handmaids to the more important work of men. We're throwing away ambition, talent, stimulation and achievement in order to run around after men and do all the dull things they can't be bothered to do. But, what's worse, we cherish the chains of our bondage. We want men to be figures of authority. The ideal hero of romance is, in fact, a bully who overwhelms the weaker, less potent heroine. And why does he want to bother? Because she is young and pretty and he wants to screw her. We know he isn't going to make the effort to conquer all for the sake of her intelligence, wit and sensibility.'

We were silent for a while, thinking about this. I had to admit to myself that this described some aspects of my relationship with Jack pretty accurately.

'What can we do about it?' asked Patience. 'I don't want to make curtains for the rest of my life. But how can I afford the training to do something more interesting? I have to keep myself and my father. I don't see how I'm ever to be more than a hewer of wood and a drawer of water.'

'I'm afraid I don't want a job,' said Lissie. 'At least, nothing like running Shell or being an orthopaedic surgeon. When George tells me about his day in the office I feel really sorry for him. I have a much nicer time than he does. Perhaps a dress shop would be quite fun.'

Maeve gave a sigh of exasperation and put her head in her hands.

'The fact remains,' I said hastily, 'that I am singularly ill-equipped to earn an honest penny except, perhaps, as a lady gardener at fifty pence an hour, which will hardly pay the telephone bill, let alone food, petrol, clothes, running repairs and so on.'

'What about the children's school fees?' asked Patience.

'Luckily Jack put money into an educational trust fund and so I haven't got to worry about that.'

'You're the only one of us with a degree,' said Maeve. 'That ought to count for something.' Maeve had begun a degree in sociology at Kent but had abandoned the course in her second year to marry the Polish Army officer.

'Yes. History. Couldn't be more useless. I'm not qualified to teach even kindergarten.'

'You can sew beautifully,' said Patience. 'I'm sure I could get Grace to give you a job.'

Lady Grace Cockaigne was Patience's boss. They had met at finishing school, the one useful thing to come out of the experience. Grace was abnormally energetic and capable and should really have been prime minister. As it was, she ran a tremendously smart interior-decoration business, based in London but with provincial – and therefore cheaper – out-workers, of whom Patience was one. I knew Grace slightly – that was all anyone could know her for she never wasted time on inessential conversation. Patience slogged away all day long in an inadequately heated barn with three other women, hemming and herringboning until her head ached and her fingers were sore. At lunch-time and supper-time she cooked wholesome soups and stews for her father, made from the cheapest cuts of meat and whatever vegetables were reduced at the greengrocer's. She rarely complained and I admired her beyond expression. I had to admit to myself, with a sense of deep shame, that one month of Patience's mode of living would send me madder than the combined madness of all the members of the putative Mad Parliament that gave poor Henry III so much trouble.

'I could teach you how to make jewellery,' Maeve suggested. This was particularly kind of her as I knew quite well that the market for silver art jewellery in our area was already swamped by Maeve's own productions and she had a difficult job to sell enough to make ends meet.

'Of course, with your looks, Miranda, you'll soon get married again,' said Lissie.

'You're missing the point.' Maeve was impatient. 'Miranda doesn't *want* to be dependent on a bloke. She needs to find a way of exploring the lineaments of her mind. She wants to be autonomous, free to paddle a kayak up the Irrawaddy or cross the Empty Quarter with a tribe of Bedouin without having to get anyone else's permission.'

'Really?' Lissie looked at me with astonishment.

'Well ...' I couldn't keep the doubt from my voice. 'It's

something that we should all be aiming for ... greater self-reliance and responsibility, anyway.'

'I think you should just aim to keep chugging along for a while without any more great shocks,' said Patience, with what seemed to me admirable good sense. 'You've got to get over Jack's death and that's going to take some time.'

'It's a good thing you won't have to wear black crape and weepers for two years,' said Lissie. 'Think of the expense of equipping the entire family! In the old days, if you had a large family with lots of cousins and aunts and things you'd have to spend half your life wearing black. I don't think black suits me.'

'I expect poorer families simply dyed what clothes they had,' I said. 'In ancient Rome and Sparta the women wore white. That would be even more impractical. In Persia, you know, the colour of mourning is pale brown, a sort of dead-leaf colour. I believe in Syria they wear blue.'

'You've got so much general knowledge,' said Patience. 'I wonder how that could be useful?'

'You could win a lot of money on a quiz show,' said Maeve.

'That seems rather a long way from the lofty ideals you were expressing a minute ago,' I said. 'Anyway, unfortunately my mind isn't very well organised and I tend not to be able remember things when I need to.'

Ideas for my future occupation flowed as I fetched raspberries from the refrigerator and made coffee. It was evident that everyone was suggesting the things that they themselves would like to do. Lissie thought I ought to become a dress designer or an interior decorator. Patience thought I ought to read for the Bar. Maeve had ideas about singing in nightclubs or doing tarot readings or renting a flat in London for high-class prostitution.

'I'm sorry,' I said, as I hunted for an ashtray for Maeve. 'Either the training would be too long, as in the case of reading for the Bar or becoming a dress designer, or I should have absolutely no aptitude, as in the case of prostitution. I've got to do something that's going to bring in money at once.'

At that moment a beam of sunshine broke from behind the clouds and cast a golden path across the floor to where Dinkie lay slumbering by the Aga, flexing his paws and unsheathing his claws in some delicious dream of feline bloodlust.

'I know,' said Maeve. 'Your greatest asset is Westray. People would adore to come and stay here. Seaside holidays in romantic moated manor looked after by elegant and beautiful granddaughter of a poet genius. Glorious gardens, exquisite home-cooked food, a four-poster bed in which Elizabeth the first once spent the night –'

'You never told me that,' interrupted Lissie.

'Maeve!' I was stunned by this unexpected display of common sense. 'You clever girl! You've got it! I'll take in paying guests!'

'I think that *is* the answer.' Patience nodded as she considered the suggestion. 'What a very good idea!'

'I wish I'd thought of it,' said Lissie. 'Oh, what fun! Think of all the interesting people you'll meet! Can I come and be a waitress?'

'We could help with the cooking,' said Maeve. 'I bet they'd love to go home with their yin and yang properly balanced.'

'Could be.' I tried to keep the doubt from my voice.

'Let's drink a toast,' said Maeve, uncorking the elixir and filling the chalet glasses to the brim with the slug-coloured Chinese essence. 'To the Westray Manor Hotel.'

'That sounds like one of those dreadful boarding-houses near King's Cross,' objected Patience. 'Let's drink to the future.'

'To the future,' we echoed dutifully, and sipped.

The taste at first brought to mind those little red squeezy cans of bicycle oil. It was infinitely lubricious, like melted lard. After a second or two our tastebuds were stunned by a bitterness like crushed sloes mixed with raw cocoa, which immediately dried our saliva as though we had been forced to lie for hours in baking sun with our mouths wide open.

'Oh dear! It's absolutely horrible.' Lissie shook her head violently and sneezed several times. I saw Patience put down her glass. Being a sensible girl, she had merely raised it to her lips.

'Hm. Interesting,' said Maeve, who had taken a large swig and virtually emptied the glass. 'It's certainly very potent. I'm feeling more lively already. Quite exhilarated.' She looked pale. 'Perhaps you'd better have it, Lissie, as you're the only one of us with a man.' She giggled. I thought her eyes looked rather bloodshot. Perhaps it was my imagination. Her head drooped until her dangling silver earrings were almost mingling with the swirls of pink and cream at the bottom of her empty pudding plate. She was unusually quiet as the rest of us discussed bedrooms, bathrooms, possible menus, where to advertise and, most interesting of all, how much I could reasonably charge.

After they had all gone, Patience to work, Lissie to go shopping in Marshgate, and Maeve, I suspected, to lie down, I decided to walk down to the post office to put my advertisement for a daily help, now even more urgently needed, in the window. Ivor had kindly taken Elizabeth and Henry to the cinema so I had the luxury of the best part of an hour to myself.

I threw on a mackintosh, found a dog lead and called Jasper. The walk down to the village was beautiful at any time of year, comprising narrow leafy lanes with virtually no traffic. Now there were blackberries in the hedges in every shade of green, pink, red and black. I would make bramble jelly for my prospective guests. Perhaps apple and blackberry pie. Or would they expect something more sophisticated? I must find someone to help me who could do some of the cooking. Two tortoiseshell butterflies fluttered companionably around my head for several yards and then darted off to the last remaining flowers of a wild honeysuckle. Clusters of elderberries and reddening rose-hips glistened among the hazels like some

Fabergé extravagance. The sun was warm and, for a brief moment, I felt almost happy. Then the cloven pine came in sight round a corner and I remembered Jack.

The pine tree had been split by a bolt of lightning many years ago and the two halves had, over the years, curled outwards into a pronounced V. The first time we had driven up to Westray Jack had pointed it out and said, 'That's our cloven pine. It's a good omen. But where is the incredibly useful Ariel?' Because we had met during a production of *The Tempest* and because my name was Miranda, we had made a silly game of relating the play to our lives.

When we took Ivor into our ménage Jack had claimed that we had found our Ariel. And there was something of the relationship between Prospero and his reluctant servant between the two men. Ivor acknowledged Jack's superior strengths and both admired him and chafed under his bondage. When I had pointed out to Jack that he ought by rights to be Ferdinand, instead of Prospero, he had said that he didn't care for lovelorn boys. He was interested in the benign exercise of power.

Had Jack been benign? As I walked along between the high banks with Jasper running just ahead I felt a needling stab of the guilt that was gradually supplanting the anger of those first days after his death. I tried to remember once more what had taken place on the morning of the day he died. It was disturbing that I could recall absolutely nothing of those preceding hours. Had we quarrelled? But, anyway, the idea of Jack being affected by anyone else to the point of killing himself was absurd. Might he have been upset enough to be careless? I remembered those times in our life together when he had displayed surprising tenderness. There was, of course, the period following Henry's birth, which I mentioned before.

And there was the time we had found a tramp lying in the road outside the Magpie and Stump. The man had been drunk, covered with vomit and, I must say, an object of disgust. He was also bloody from a cut head. When Jack had attempted to move him to the side of the road out of the path of cars, he had told Jack to bugger off and go to hell. Jack had put him into the car and taken him to the Salvation Army hostel. Furthermore Jack gave the man a job at Westray, sweeping up leaves and cutting logs on the condition that he never came drunk to work. This worked quite well for a long time, with Stocky, as the tramp was called, turning up with reasonable regularity and claiming his five bob for a morning's work. He preferred to sleep 'out', as he called it, but he managed with a regular wage to look reasonably clean. We were all sorry when he fell off the cliff path one night after an evening of over-indulgence and met his end on the rocks below. He had always been very kind to the children. Henry, in particular, had been devoted to Stocky and was inconsolable for a while.

I could recall several other instances of such acts of charity, and it would have been unjust to say that they were all motivated by benevolent tyranny. There was the time when I developed an agonisingly painful abscess beneath a tooth and Jack had stayed up all night talking, playing cards and reading to me before driving me to London at daybreak the next morning to visit the dentist.

As I remembered all these things I found the guilt much worse to bear than my previous rage. Had I been wrong to separate myself, emotionally and sexually, from him because of his unfaithfulness? Had his affairs been, as he had said, really unimportant? Or were these feelings of culpability just part of the natural process of grief? I was relieved to see the high brick wall of the first village house. My own company these days was almost intolerable.

Having put Jasper on his lead and tied him up outside, I walked into the post office to find two women standing at the grille of the counter in conversation with Mrs Veal. The silence that fell the moment they turned and saw me brought a sudden hot feeling to my face. Had they been discussing me or was I developing a persecution mania along with all the other confusions in my brain? One of the women, whom I knew slightly and to whom I usually said hello, left the shop without a word, not even glancing in my direction. The other moved away and became engrossed with the difficulty of deciding between Rich Tea or Marie biscuits.

I gave my card requesting a daily help, five days a week, four hours a day, to Mrs Veal and made a banal remark about it looking like rain later on. Mrs Veal took the card by one corner, her little finger crooked and expressive of refined distaste. 'I'll see it goes in the window, Mrs Stowe. Thank you, will that be all?'

She glanced at me for the first time, her eyes insolent, and then looked away to busy herself with a pile of pension books. I had been absolutely snubbed. I walked out of the shop in a state of bemusement. Mrs Veal had always been rather unpleasantly sycophantic until today, ignoring the queue to serve me first. I had often heard it said that the bereaved are shunned because people feel awkward and don't know what to say but this was more than embarrassment.

Mrs Kenton was just crossing the road as I left the post office. 'Hello, Miranda. Hello, Jasper. How are you, dear?' She looked at me solicitously.

'Oh, well, all right, really. Everyone's very kind.' Then I remembered Mrs Veal. 'Though some people seem to think that I've disgraced myself by losing my husband.' I laughed, meaning the remark to be taken light-heartedly.

Mrs Kenton put her hand on my arm. 'You mustn't mind, dear, what these small-minded women say. They haven't any of them a grain of understanding about what feelings people have when they experience a terrible shock. Silly tittle-tattlers, the lot of them!'

'Yes, well, I can't imagine what there is to be said.' I was slightly put out by a hint of conspiracy in Mrs Kenton's manner. 'How's Dr Kenton?'

'Kind of you to ask, dear. Not too good, I'm afraid. It's Alzheimer's. What he was frightened of.'

'What's that?'

'Like senile dementia, really. Deterioration of the intellect. There's no treatment. He's suicidally depressed. Oh, sorry, dear. Tactless of me. You'd think that all these years of dealing with illness would have given him some sort of philosophical approach but he won't go out anywhere, won't see anyone. Sits grieving in his study.'

'I'm so sorry. Please let me know when he wants visitors. I'll happily come and talk to him, if it will help. He's done so much for us.'

'Thank you, dear. I'll let you know. But you've got your own problems. Just go steady and don't do anything rash.'

On the whole it was a depressing conversation all round. I was pleased to see the car, with Elizabeth and Henry hanging out of the window, draw up alongside me.

'Lovely film, Mum,' called Elizabeth. 'Anne Boleyn got her head cut off, which was very mean of Henry the Eighth, I thought. She was much prettier than Jane Seymour who had teeth like a snow-plough.'

'You saw all the blood sliding down the axe,' said Henry. 'And all the white tuby bits in her neck. That was the best bit.'

'No, you didn't!' said Elizabeth. 'You're making it up. Mum, he's inventing that bit. There was just a little bit of blood, that's all.'

'You weren't looking! I saw all the windpipes sticking out.'

'Stupid! Of course, there's only one windpipe anyway. You're a complete idiot!'

I refused a lift as I felt Jasper needed more exercise and the car drew away. The children's voices, arguing passionately, were gradually lost as they turned the bend. I walked home as fast as the incline would allow me and reached the front door breathless and hot. Dr McCleod's ancient Hillman stood on the drive by the bridge. I ran in, thinking something had happened to Rose.

'I just wanted to check Miss Ingrams's blood pressure,' said Dr McCleod, bending over Rose as he rolled up her sleeve.

'That was good of you.' I was panting and I felt sure my face was unattractively red.

'Good of me? I hardly think so. I'm not dispensing charity on some lordly whim. It's my job and there are proper procedures, which I'm obliged to follow.'

'Sorry,' I said feebly.

'Great deal of fuss about nothing,' grumbled Rose, extending a scrawny forearm. 'Of course, if you've nothing better to do.'

I hung up my mackintosh and got out a mixing bowl. On the walk home I had decided to relent over the mushrooms, at least as far as tea was concerned, and make a chocolate cake. I ignored Dr McCleod and began to work the butter and sugar together. The kitchen was warm and quiet. I stopped what I was doing to let out a trapped butterfly, which was flapping against the glass. Through the window I could see the children playing with Jasper in the garden on the far side of the moat. Westray was a sanctuary and I always felt better just for being there.

'All right, Miss Ingrams. Pressure's a bit low but nothing to worry about.'

'*I* wasn't worrying. I've got better things to think about,' Rose snapped. She certainly did look tired. 'I'll thank you to leave that alone, young man,' she added, as Dr McCleod attempted to pull down her sleeve. 'You're as bungling and unhandy as an untrained pup.'

Dr McCleod smiled at her as though he positively relished her roughness.

I walked with him to the front door. 'How is she *really*? I'm worried that she still looks such a bad colour.'

'She's a fighter. I expect she'll pull round all right. I'll keep a close eye on her.'

I almost thanked him and then remembered that he was resentful of *politesse*. I didn't think I could bring myself to be quite as rude as Rose was so I said instead, 'I met Mrs Kenton outside the post office. I was very sorry to hear about Dr Kenton.'

'Yes. He knows exactly what course the illness will take. Sometimes it's better to be ignorant. And I'm sorry from a selfish point of view, too. It means I shall have to stay here much longer than I intended until we can find someone to take over the practice.'

'Don't you like it here?' I couldn't keep the surprise out of my voice.

'Oh, it's all very charming to look at, of course.' He spoke with something like a sneer. His skin was very smooth except between his eyebrows where it was creased into deep frown-lines. His eyes were grey, with dark lashes, almost girlishly long. 'I didn't spend all those years training to pander to the over-indulged livers of the rich.'

'Well, rich or poor, I suppose everyone's entitled to medical attention. And the rich ones pay for the poor ones through taxation.'

'That makes you feel pretty smug, does it? The point is that there shouldn't be this great division between rich and poor in the first place. I've spent half my surgery time this morning booking women in for private operations they don't need and trying to cure their husbands of ailments brought about by never taking a step further from their cars than to the door of the office.' He had raised his voice with indignation.

'So you want to work in a deprived area, is that it? We've got to be desperate cases before we merit your attention. I think that's rather arrogant.'

'Arrogant!' He was rolling his Rs with annoyance. 'You're telling me to my face that I'm arrogant?'

'Well, if you can accuse me of being smug I don't see why I shouldn't make some attempt to fight back.'

'You don't begin to understand. How can you?' He gave a bark of a laugh, which made me feel quite furious, particularly since I was aware that he was taking a moral position that could more easily be justified than my own. I couldn't begin to understand how it was that I had Westray Manor and Stocky had had a tree-trunk. I mentally defaced the doctor's image with a worker's cap and a foxy Leninist beard jutting from his chin and tried to keep any hint of apology off my face.

Dr McCleod bared his teeth at me. 'You've probably

spent all your life cushioned from cold and hunger and ugliness. It's quite natural to you that you should enjoy every kind of luxury while other people live at your gate in poverty. I expect you think they aren't trying hard enough.'

'If they're at my gate I'm sorry for them because you don't consider they're in sufficient straits to be worthy of your care. Next time I go by with soup and shawls I'll be sure to tell them to move to an inner-city slum if they want Dr McCleod's attention.'

By this time we had crossed the courtyard to the gatehouse and it was unlucky that Ivor drove past us at this moment in order to put the car away into the coach-house. Jack had always liked cars and this was a pretty silver Aston Martin Volante. Beside it Dr McCleod's Hillman looked ridiculously small and shabby. As Ivor made a sweeping turn to negotiate the corner into the drive down to the coach-house there was the sound of scrunching metal and the Hillman rocked gently. Ivor stopped the car and got out at once.

'I say, I'm most terribly sorry.' He pushed his wiry hair back from his face with one hand while holding up a piece of wing. 'Just caught this with my bumper. Must have been rather rusty, I think. Oh dear, yes, look! The whole thing's only held together by the process of oxidation.' He grinned nervously.

'Please take it down to Bob's garage and get him to put the repair on our bill.' I spoke coldly.

'You think that money is the answer to everything,' Dr McCleod said, snappishly. 'It doesn't occur to you that I need the car every day for my rounds.'

'No. I'm afraid it hadn't.'

He threw off something between a laugh and a snarl and strode across the bridge to his car. He had to kick the door several times to persuade it to open. As he roared away, too fast, down the drive I felt, not for the first time, sympathy for some of those powdered heads that had dropped into Madame la Guillotine's basket. Appearances could be very powerfully against one.

*

'Mum,' said Henry that evening, looking angelic in pyjamas and dressing gown with his hair damp and sticking up from his bath. 'Are you too busy to talk to me?'

We were alone in my bedroom. I had crept upstairs to lie down for a few minutes before starting the washing-up. My head ached violently and I felt horribly depressed. I was worried about Dr Kenton and I was worried about myself. Though I had often hated Jack while he was alive, now that he was gone I missed the security of being in a partnership. Jack had offered protection simply because he was fearless. I had been his wife for so long that I hardly knew who I was without him. But if I felt insecure, how much worse it must be for the children.

'Of course I'm not too busy, darling.' I propped my head up on my hand and patted the bed with the other. 'Come and sit here and let's have a good talk.'

'There was something I thought of today that I particularly wanted to ask you. But I've forgotten what it was.'

Henry traced the pattern on my carpet with his slippered foot. I was apprehensive. It had been a long day, crammed with feelings of every possible orientation. But I knew I had to answer the children truthfully and not prevaricate if they were to come to terms with their father's death.

'Yes, my darling?' I put on what I hoped was an encouraging look and steeled myself for painful discussion.

'I remember.' Henry's delivery was slow and thoughtful. 'What would you do if a flying saucer landed in Puck's field?'

CHAPTER 7

'Miranda, darling, you're looking beautiful but just a little thin,' said my aunt, as we hugged each other by the arrivals gate. Nancy wore canary-yellow Givenchy and drew the eye of every man in the airport despite being sixty-five. We drove back to Westray at high speed. I had driven to meet her in the Volante to enjoy a good run in it for the last time. A man was coming that afternoon to buy it. The interview with my bank manager the day before had been quite as depressing as I had expected. As the weather was unusually mild I had put down the hood, and we felt dashing and adventurous as we overtook everything else on the road.

'It's a brilliant idea!' Nancy was enthusiastic about our plan to open Westray to paying guests. We were sitting down for lunch in the kitchen, about to eat mushroom soup followed by omelettes and a *pis-en-lit* salad gathered by Ivor in the best traditions of peasant economy. 'Sounds like hard work but that never did anyone any harm.'

Nancy had probably never earned so much as sixpence herself but she was rarely idle, despite always having had servants. The children were always very interested in their great-aunt's plutocratic existence.

'Are all the people who work for you quite black, Aunt Nancy?' asked Henry, toying with his omelette to which he had objected on the grounds that it was rather 'eggy'.

'Yes, all of them. Black as your hat.'

'Don't you think you ought to free them?' Elizabeth had just started the American Civil War at school. 'I'm on the side of the Yankees, though of course carpet-bagging was wrong. I'm sure if you read *Uncle Tom's Cabin* you'd want to free them, but I must say it's a terrifically boring book. Miss Betts made us read passages in class. Just imagine being sold away from your family and being beaten and made to work even if you were sick.'

'Bless you, my darling, the people who work for us are perfectly free. They could up sticks at any time and go wherever they want. But Blue Ridge is their home. It would break their hearts to go away. And it isn't only the house and the land they love but all Uncle Robin's family. It isn't the same as servants in England. When Robin was a little boy, Lisa Pearl, Robin's mammy – that means a nursemaid – used to collect fireflies and put them in a jar by his bed as a night-light. Then she'd sing him the old slave songs until he fell asleep.'

'"The fire-fly wakens; waken thou with me,"' said Ivor solemnly.

Nancy knew Ivor well enough not to regard this as an impertinent invitation.

'Yesterday Lisa Pearl came up to the house to wish me a good journey. We sat on the porch and drank whiskey together and we talked of the old days until it was dark. Robin says he owes his enjoyment of life to being brought up by coloured servants... a feeling that everything needn't be taken so seriously.'

'Mum says we're not to call people coloured.' Henry was self-righteous. 'We're to say black.'

'Ah, well, things move slowly in the South. It's hot. You can't imagine how different it is.'

She went on to tell the children about the riding, tennis and swimming parties and clambakes, juleps and cherry bounce. They were most interested in her description of the old johnny house – Virginian slang for lavatory – which was eighteenth-century and panelled and had eight holes.

'You'd have to have a very big family for eight people all to want to go to the lav at the same time,' said Henry thoughtfully. 'Unless they always had dandelion salad for lunch.'

When Henry had exhausted the, to him, extraordinarily interesting subject of lavatories, we made our plans for the afternoon. Nancy suggested that we go at once into Marshgate, where the nearest interior-decorating shop was, and bring back some pattern books. Two of the three bedrooms earmarked for the paying guests needed some refurbishment. 'I'll give you all tea at the Excelsior... my treat,' insisted Nancy, 'and we can be back in time for the car man. Did you say he was coming at six? Now, Rose, won't you come with us? We can drop you off at the Excelsior while we go and look at fabrics. A change will do you good.'

Rose couldn't be persuaded. Nancy had brought her as a present the most beautiful pink cashmere shawl, which Rose said made her think of dawn clouds, and I guessed that she was longing to wrap herself in it and go to sleep for the afternoon. My present had been a crêpe-de-Chine nightdress, very nearly fine enough to be drawn through a wedding ring as in the old stories, of the most glorious shade of duck-egg blue with broad bands of cream lace. Nancy was not only very rich, she was also extremely generous. It's surprising how rarely the two things go together.

We had a lovely afternoon. The children had rides on everything in the rusty little fun-fair, something they hadn't done for years, and then ate enormous knickerbocker glories in the dining room of the Excelsior. Anyone might have thought, looking at them, that they had nothing to trouble them. Henry was very pleased that the Ferris wheel had got stuck when they were at the top. I could see that he would make capital of this when he got back to school.

'Actually the wheel's so small that we could almost have jumped down without hurting ourselves.' Elizabeth was scornful. She had won a bottle of scent on the hoopla stall. I could see the other guests in the hotel sniffing and looking about them to identify the source of the rather unpleasant smell, a mixture of patchouli and cabbages. The woman at the table next to us kept accusing her miniature dachshund of having 'rolled in something'.

When we got home a sleek Jaguar had already drawn up outside the gatehouse and a man, very sleek to match, was just getting out of it. We had gone to Marshgate in my car so that Ivor could polish up the Aston Martin. I left the others to carry in the fabric and wallpaper swatches and took the man, whose name was Derek French, to look at it. Mr French was extremely smart in a chalk-stripe suit and lustrous shoes. His dark hair shone similarly above plump jowls dark with six o'clock shadow.

'Very sorry to hear about your husband, Mrs Stowe.

Mr Stowe came into the showroom just a few weeks ago to talk about a new hood for the Volante. Who'd have thought? Dear, dear.' He shook his head and looked sorrowful.

I murmured my thanks for these expressions of regret. The coach-house is a mere two hundred yards from the house in the shelter of the woods but I could see that Mr French was put out by the dust on his shoes. There was a very strong smell of bonfire smoke in the air but no sign of Ivor.

The coach-house is a pretty, unpretentious building, built in the late eighteenth century and consisting of three bays for carriages and six loose boxes. On the roof is a clock tower. The clock has four faces, deep blue in colour, and it chimes every three hours with a resonant, slightly out-of-tune carillon. Wherever I am in the garden I pause when I hear it chime for a moment's reflection on mortality. Cut in the stone beneath the winding handle are these words: 'Even such is time, which takes in trust, / Our youth, our joys and all we have, / And pays us but with age and dust.' I looked them up once and found that they had been written by Walter Raleigh on the day before his execution. One can only admire his presence of mind.

'A beauty!' said Mr French, cheering up immensely when he saw the car.

'I'll leave you to look at it.' I gave him the keys.

Nancy, Rose and the children were playing Racing Demon in the library, and I could hear screams of excitement. I went into the kitchen and began to prepare supper. Elizabeth and Henry had pleaded with me not to give them mushrooms again so I'd relented and bought a leg of lamb. I had stuffed it with garlic and rosemary, put it in the oven and peeled the potatoes by the time Mr French came back.

'Everything tickety-boo, Mrs Stowe, apart from the hood.' I saw him look longingly at my glass of wine. 'I'll make you an offer.'

I had asked Bob at the village garage to look up the

going price and I was quite determined to accept not a penny less. By the time we had finished arguing, I had prepared the vegetables and was making a raspberry soufflé.

'You drive a hard bargain, Mrs Stowe.' Mr French wiped his face with his handkerchief. It was warm in the kitchen and I saw him look again at my glass of wine.

'Of course, if you don't think it's worth it I'll find another buyer.'

'Oh, very well.' He looked cross. I suppose he had imagined that a woman, particularly a newly widowed one, could easily be swindled out of a hundred pounds or so. I relented and gave him a glass of wine while he wrote out the cheque.

After drinking it he became more genial. 'Lovely house you have here, Mrs Stowe. Your husband seems to have had everything a man could want.' His eyes travelled over my aproned hips and then back up to my face. He smoothed back his hair with both hands and drew in his stomach sharply. 'You must be very lonely without him.' I began to beat egg whites briskly. 'Got some kiddies, have you?'

'Three.' I longed for him to go, but I could see that he had not actually signed the cheque.

'Three! That'll be a job of work, bringing them up on your own.'

I felt that Mr French was becoming too personal but I couldn't think of a way to stop him so I continued to beat away and to smile, but with less conviction.

'You know something, Mrs Stowe? I don't think a woman is fitted to live alone. I don't like to think of you struggling out here, in the wilds of the countryside. I think you need a masculine shoulder to lay your head on. Why don't you and I pop out somewhere for a bite to eat?'

I knew quite well what it was he really wanted to bite. 'As you can see, Mr French, I'm very busy.'

'Derek. Call me Derek. Come on. Let's go and see what the local hostelry has to offer.' He got up and came over to stand next to me.

'I really couldn't think of it.' I felt myself becoming flustered. He was close enough for me to feel him breathing hard on my neck. 'Please, do sign the cheque and we'll consider the business over. Thank you very much for coming all the way to see it. Now I really must –'

With a smack of his lips like the sound Jasper makes when you give him a biscuit – charming from a dog but not pleasant from a man – he put his arm around my waist.

'Oh, excuse me!' Dr McCleod stood in the doorway.

'Dr McCleod! I'd forgotten you were going to call. I'll take you to Miss Ingrams at once. Goodbye, Mr French. Would you mind seeing yourself out?'

As soon as we were in the hall I said, 'Thank goodness you arrived when you did. That man was becoming a nuisance.'

Dr McCleod gave me a look of disbelief, and I felt painfully rebuffed. I really hate people who have chips on their shoulders. It is a kind of dishonesty. Whatever you do or say, they interpret it in a way that is pejorative because they would rather make themselves feel better by thinking ill of you than know the truth of the matter.

The library looks its best by evening light and I could see that the scene before us spoke eloquently of comfort and privilege. The room, originally the servants' hall, had been made into a library in the nineteenth century. Before then the owners of Westray, in common with most of the landed gentry, were not much interested in culture or literacy. It has very well-made pedimented mahogany shelves with brass grilles and a magnificent mahogany desk, which we had bought with the house. There is a handsome chimneypiece with the coat-of-arms of the Victorian owners. Comfortable chairs and sofas with chintz slip covers, table lamps, racks of magazines, my needlepoint frame and all the appurtenances of leisure give the room a friendly atmosphere. It is less formal than the drawing room and we always used it in the winter as there is only the oriel window, which matches the one above in my bedroom, and the door fits quite well.

'Oh, no!' said Rose. 'Can't a body be left to recover in peace? Have you nothing better to do than fash your patients, man?'

'So you're a Scot, Miss Ingrams,' said Dr McCleod, with perfect good humour. Rose was a tremendous snob about accents and rarely used dialect, which she considered low. She must have been really cross to let it slip out.

I ushered everyone back to the kitchen to give Dr McCleod a chance to examine Rose. I was very glad to see that Mr French had gone and that he had signed the cheque before leaving.

'Wow!' said Henry. 'We're rich beyond our wildest dreams! Can we *please* have a colour television? I'm the only boy in our form who hasn't got one.'

'I'm sorry, darling. You'd be surprised at how quickly this money will be used up. I've got to pay the rates out of it besides have new hangings made for the bed in the blue room and make the closet of the red room into a little bathroom. If I manage to make any money out of my guests you shall have one next year. Nancy, you'll never guess what that ghastly man did.'

Everyone was inclined to find Mr French's attempt at dalliance extremely funny. In fact, for the rest of the evening Henry would suddenly burst into giggles whenever he thought of it. It was, he explained kindly, the idea of quite old people kissing each other.

'You'll have to put up with a lot of that,' said Nancy. 'Men find widows irresistible. They imagine you're desperate to be made love to by absolutely anyone. After your uncle died even the husbands of my best friends made a pass. You mustn't let yourself become disillusioned.'

I often thought of these words of advice as, during the next few months, virtually every man able to stand on two legs, with the strength to pucker his lips, made an attempt to seduce me. Except for Dr McCleod and Aubrey Molebank.

On Friday I walked with Jasper down to the vicarage to keep an engagement for tea made earlier in the week. I surmised that Mr Molebank was keen to give me some pastoral care and I was anxious for anything that might lift my mood. I had taken Nancy to the airport early that morning and was feeling tremendously flat after seeing her plane take off. She had the gift of imparting a sense of fun to every small event and we had all been happier than I would have thought possible during the last four days. Now the children were restless and inclined to mope, particularly Elizabeth. She had gone down to the beach to gallop Puck on the sands and I hoped that this would have its usual good effect on her spirits. Henry was at home, building the model aeroplane that Nancy had brought him, with instructions to look after Rose.

My mood was not only gloomy, it was also angry. I scarcely noticed the loveliness of the light as the sun burst from behind black clouds, bathing everything in a sulphurous fluorescence. Maeve had telephoned me at lunch-time and I was able to tell her that the builders were starting work on Monday. They expected to take ten days to put in a small bath, basin and lavatory. The task was made easier because the panelling could be removed to fit in all the plumbing and then put back to conceal all the pipework without need for any further decoration.

'The only thing that's bothering me,' I had said to Maeve, 'is the fact that no one has answered my advertisement for a daily help. I did offer quite a bit over the going rate to try to get somebody good.'

'I expect it's the local gossip that's put people off,' Maeve replied, with a tranquillity that infuriated me.

'Gossip? What do you mean?'

'Oh, it's all over the village that Jack shot himself because you were having an affair.'

'What?'

'Mrs Veal asked me only yesterday if it was true. Apparently Stew Harker found you making love with a man on the kitchen table on the day of Jack's funeral.'

With a rush of real anger, I remembered Jeremy. 'And you said?'

'I said it sounded most unlikely.'

'Thank you very much.'

'Well, I must say I was surprised. It didn't sound like you at all. And why the kitchen table when you've got several perfectly good bedrooms upstairs?'

One good thing had come out of this unpleasant disclosure. After ending the conversation with Maeve on a slightly frosty note, I rang Mead's Provisions in Bosworth and gave them my week's order. In the past I had felt under an obligation to patronise the post office for groceries, although Mead's were superior in quality, range of goods and speed of delivery. I wondered whether it was just cowardice that made me feel that I could never again enter Mrs Veal's emporium. Should I speak firmly to her and set her right as to what had actually happened? Or was that pandering to malicious slanderers? Would she believe me, anyway? I tried to imagine what Nancy's advice would be. She would probably think it funny and tell me to ignore the whole thing. Perhaps I was becoming absurdly sensitive.

The vicarage front door was stiff to open. I found piles of unopened post on the mat the other side. I picked up the letters and put them on the hall-stand. I could have written my name in the dust and made a fairy's dress out of the cobwebs on the stairs.

'Hello? Is somebody there?' called Mr Molebank, coming out of his study. His mild, intelligent eyes displayed ingenuous pleasure. 'Mrs Stowe, this is a delightful surprise!'

'Have you forgotten that you asked me to come to tea?'

'Oh, yes... no! Oh dear! This must be Friday. I'm a fool. Come in, come in.' Mr Molebank was pink with chagrin. 'What must you think of me? To tell you the truth I'm distracted by these accounts. I've no head for figures and the total seems to be fantastic. Now, sit down.' He swept away some papers from the sagging armchair upholstered in brown corduroy. It had smooth greasy patches on the arms and where one's head might rest if one were so trusting. Jasper lay down in the corner, with a grunt of displeasure at being forced to come indoors. 'I'll go and make some tea.'

While he was doing this I found some old newspapers and kindling in the log basket and relaid the fire, which had sunk down to a tantalising pinpoint of vermilion. The vicarage was appallingly damp and even in high summer seemed cold. I had to hunt for the matches before I found them being used as a book-mark in a volume entitled *The Canon in Residence* by Victor L. Whitechurch. I thought this must be something dull and ecclesiastical, but as the fire began to blaze I looked idly at the first pages and was soon convulsed with laughter.

'How nice to hear you laughing, Mrs Stowe,' said Mr Molebank, when he returned at last with the tea. 'I'm sorry I was so long. I couldn't remember what I'd done with the milk jug. Then I remembered that I'd used it to pour disinfectant down the drain. Isn't it a marvellous novel? Would you like to borrow it?'

'Oh, but you're reading it yourself.'

'I've read it scores of times. I should be so pleased if you would take it. I'd like to know that I was able to do at least one person a real service.'

'Thank you, I will. But I do wish you'd call me Miranda.'

'With pleasure. It's quite hard to make the change, isn't it, after so long? Milk in your tea?'

'No, thank you.' I took a ginger biscuit from the plate he held out to me. It was so stale that I almost broke a tooth. I put the rest in my pocket for Jasper when Aubrey wasn't looking. I couldn't afford expensive bridgework just at the moment. 'I suppose we're all very old-fashioned, but it's one of the things I like about living in the country.' I noticed that Aubrey seemed very ill-at-ease and kept shooting perplexed glances at the papers that lay on a table by his side. I decided to risk being interfering. 'What accounts are they? Can I help you?'

'Oh, it would be so good of you. I confess, I have no

head for figures. I just can't make these add up. There seems to be a deficit of eight hundred pounds and I've got to show them to the Parish Council next Friday. Last year we were short of a hundred pounds and no one could find the error. I hope you won't think me over-dramatic but I really fear that that they might suspect me of some kind of skulduggery... at best carelessness, at worst misappropriation. It's such a very large sum. Mrs Scranton-Jones, who is one of the churchwardens, is so severe and always lectures me about spots of soup on the minutes as it is.'

I bent my head over the papers. I was conscious of his eyes fixed expectantly on my face as I attempted to make sense of the seemingly endless columns. Poor Aubrey couldn't have been more than forty-five but already his hair was thinning and he looked careworn. The vicarage had nine or ten bedrooms and it would have been a full-time occupation for one person just to keep it clean. All the downstairs rooms were large, with high ceilings and hardly any furniture. It was a depressing place.

'I think you've gone wrong somewhere here.' I held up one of the sheets, which was covered with squiggles and crossings-out. 'I'm afraid I can't quite put my finger on it, though.' Aubrey, who had been tense with hope, sank back defeated into his chair. 'Why don't you come to supper on Monday and I'll ask Patience Wakeham-Tutt to come as well? Do you know her? She lives at Withington in the next parish. We were at school together. She's brilliant at arithmetic and I'm sure she'll be able to sort you out.'

'How kind of you! I should like that, very much indeed. I don't think I've met Miss Wakeham-Tutt. But I've come across Sir William from time to time. British Legion and that sort of thing. A man of great... firmness of mind. And I'm sure, a splendid old soldier.' He seemed so very pleased that I suspected that he welcomed any chance to escape the discomfort of his lodgings. I ought to have asked him to Westray more often but Jack and Aubrey were utterly different types of men and had had very little to talk about.

Now that he felt that help was at hand, Aubrey relaxed. He was very keen to show me the latest production of the printing press he kept in the dining room. It was an edition of George Herbert's poems, very fine on beautiful laid paper with some charming woodcuts done by a friend of Aubrey's. The printing press was Aubrey's passion and he spent what little spare money he had on papers and inks.

'How are you getting on with your history of Westray Manor? I'm very much looking forward to reading it. I mustn't bully you when it's so kind of you to do it, but don't forget that it will take me some time to set up the type. I'll need two or three months.'

I had agreed ages ago to write ten thousand words on all my researches into the house's past so that Aubrey could print it and sell it in aid of the Wychford Chapel Roof Fund. The Church Restoration Committee, of which Jack and I were members, was planning a pageant to represent the high points of the history of Kent. It was to take place in the grounds of Wychford Hall on Midsummer's Eve. My little essay would be sold at the 'Country Fayre', as Mrs Scranton-Jones insisted on spelling it, on the same day. I couldn't imagine many local people wanting to buy it but Aubrey was so enthusiastic that I felt bound to do it.

'What do you think of the execution of the Holy Maid of Kent? Should we include it in the pageant, do you think? Or might it frighten the young ones?' Aubrey was wholly ignorant of the nature of children.

'If we can make it graphic and horrible, I can guarantee that it will be the most popular item on the programme.'

'Really?' He shook his head in bafflement. 'And I think we must include Sir Thomas Wyatt's rebellion in fifteen fifty-four. We can't manage the whole three thousand "gentlemen of Kent", of course, but we could suggest a crowd with twenty or so.'

'It does give you the opportunity for another execution. Two more if we include Lady Jane Grey. Though the Holy Maid was hanged, in fact. People will enjoy a variety of deaths. I wonder how we can create the impression of a trap-door dropping?'

'Sounds rather dangerous.' Aubrey sucked his biro as he thought about it. I wondered if I knew him well enough to point out that rather a lot of ink was being transferred from the end of the tube to his lips but decided not. 'The terrace of the old house will make an excellent stage. We'll begin with our Anglo-Saxon friends, Hengist and Horsa, I suppose.'

'They'll be cheap from the point of costumes. Coarse woollen cloaks and cross-garters. Perhaps I can make some *papier-mâché* Saxon shields.'

There were so many girls and women in the village who hankered to act and so few female speaking roles that I had offered to do the costumes. Aubrey and I discussed the pageant very happily for an hour, until a groan from Jasper in the corner reminded me that I must be going home.

'Oh dear, and I haven't once asked you how you are all getting on.' Aubrey was sorrowful. He had gone on sucking the biro as we talked and now had a blue goatee beard. 'I was so enjoying our conversation. How selfish of me.' He sighed. 'I really seem unfitted to be a parish priest. When I asked old Tom, the tinker, why he hadn't been here for breakfast recently he said he was tired of tomato soup.'

'That does seem unusual for breakfast.'

'It's what I live on. I'm afraid it's the only thing I know how to cook. I said I could get him some oxtail if he preferred it, but he said not to bother. I don't seem to have the knack of helping people.'

'On the contrary.' I spoke sincerely. 'I've been thoroughly restored by our talk. I was feeling quite murderously depressed. Now I feel much better. Honestly.'

'You're very kind. Let me see you out. Oh dear, what a lot of post! I'd forgotten all about it. There must be a week's worth here at least. A letter from the Bishop!' Aubrey suddenly caught sight of himself in the hall mirror and jumped back with a start. 'Dear me!

Goodbye, Mrs... Miranda. I look forward to Monday immensely.'

It began to rain as Jasper and I set out for home. I enjoyed the sensation of tepid drops on my face. Jasper was pulling like mad on the lead after being for so long on his best behaviour that I decided to risk it and let him off. Sometimes Jasper behaves like a Crufts Obedience Class Champion, almost making a dent in your leg with his nose as he walks smartly to heel. At other times he is indifferent to the loudest yells and whistles. It is all a question of mood. This afternoon he bolted down the road, turned sharp left into a seemingly impenetrable hedge and in three seconds was out of sight.

I forgot to worry about him as I walked back through the village. I saw Mrs Buller looking through her window as I went past. Normally she would have waved. Now she just whisked herself away as I was lifting my hand in salute. It was stupid of me to mind. I knew that in a few weeks some other poor devil would be the focus of gossip and my notoriety would be stale.

I heard Jasper barking somewhere ahead. I turned a bend to see him standing on the verge directing a crescendo of noise towards the bus shelter. From within came the sound of a baby crying.

'Quiet, Jasper!' I shouted. 'Naughty boy! Sit, Jasper!'

Jasper, hearing from my tone that I meant business, rolled over, panting, on to his back.

'I'm so sorry,' I said, as I reached the shelter. 'He doesn't like babies, for some reason. I hope he didn't wake her?'

The baby looked exactly like Charles Laughton but as she was dressed entirely in salmon pink I was on safe ground with regard to gender. The poor little thing was purple in the face from crying and as bald as a plum. I recognised the girl who was sitting on the bench inside, holding the infant in her arms and trying, vainly, to soothe it. It took me a few moments to remember where I had seen her before. 'Aren't you Mrs Birt? I think you were standing with your husband outside the church.'

'Yes, I was there. I remember seeing you.' She tried to smile and I noticed for the first time that her own face was wet with tears. She had a soft, pretty voice, with a northern accent. She was otherwise very plain, very spotty and very young, little more than a child.

'You look rather tired. Shall I hold her for a little?'

I don't know what made me so forward in offering my services. Perhaps it was the extreme youth of the girl as well as the evident exhaustion on her face. It felt strange and, well, I must admit it, wonderful to hold a little warm soft baby again.

'She's been crying on and off all day. I don't know what's wrong with her. And she cried in the night, too, which she don't usually. I'm that worried.'

I held the baby upright against me. At once she stopped crying and began to suck my cheek noisily. 'She's hungry. That's what's the matter with her.'

The girl broke out in fresh tears. 'I don't know what to do! I've been working so hard and me milk's drying up, that's what. Now she'll maybe starve to death!'

'No, no.' I said, very sorry to see her so distressed. 'You must give her a supplementary bottle, that's all. And if you rest and drink more, your milk will come back.'

'I can't rest.' She was weeping so hard that I could hardly understand what she was saying. 'He makes me work all day long and at night –' She stopped and sobbed so sadly that I felt tears come into my own eyes.

'Is your husband unkind to you?' I gave the poor, frantic baby my finger to suck.

'He isn't me husband. I answered an advertisement. I were that desperate. Father Declan said it were the best thing to do.'

'An advertisement?'

'In the *Weekly Furrow*. It asked for a housekeeper, live-in, no outside work. I rang up and he said it wouldn't matter about there being a baby if I kept her quiet, like. I didn't have nowhere to go. The mother-and-baby home needed my room.'

'Haven't you any family? What about the baby's father?'

'There's only me mum. She didn't want anything more to do with me when she found out I were expecting. She's very religious. I was brought up a good Catholic. I know it were a sin but I couldn't help myself. I know it were wrong.'

'Oh dear! Please... try not to cry. You're so young. How could it be a sin? A mistake, perhaps. But you must feed your baby. Have you got a feeding bottle at home?'

'No. I haven't got anything for her, only two sets of clothes the home gave me. They said as I were doing so well with the feeding I didn't need a bottle. And I was, the milk came in a treat, only he has me working all hours of the day. And then at night,' her voice sank to a whisper, 'he comes in and makes me, you know... I didn't... I never thought he meant that... but I didn't have nowhere to go so I have to let him. I haven't got any money and he won't pay me until the end of the month.'

'You mean he forces you to... have sex with him?'

The girl drooped her head and nodded. 'I suppose you think I'm very bad,' she said miserably.

'I think *he*'s very bad!' I felt quite furious. 'You need help. The first thing we'll do is feed this child. Come on.'

'I haven't any money,' repeated the girl, as we both stood up.

'Never mind. I'll lend it to you.'

'That's ever so good of you.' The girl was crying afresh as she followed me the hundred or so yards to the post office.

I was quite beyond caring what Mrs Veal thought as I asked her for two feeding bottles, spare teats, some sterilising fluid and a packet of formula. Her eyes bulged with curiosity as she looked at the crying infant and the baby's mother, now sniffing noisily, and back at me. 'Poor little mite!' she said, half-way to declaring a truce.

But the iron had entered my soul and I wasn't in a forgiving mood. I left the shop and started up the hill to

Westray at a brisk walk, carrying the baby, with the girl and Jasper running to keep up. I'd forgotten how heavy babies are and I soon slowed my pace.

'Where are we going?' asked the girl.

'My house,' I panted. 'It's not far. What's your name?'

The girl's name was Jenny and the baby was called Bridie.

'It's Bridget, really, after the saint but I call her Bridie. It seems more homely. Father Declan said I should call her after a saint. Let me take her now. You look done in.'

'What have we got here?' said Rose, as we walked into the kitchen.

'This is Jenny. I met her in the bus shelter. Her baby's hungry. Henry, put the kettle on. Sit down, Jenny.'

'Let me hold the baby,' Rose took Bridie on her knee, and the baby's urgent cries paused as she looked up into Rose's wise old face. Rose held her tightly and sang to her while I made up the bottle of formula and stood it in a jug of cold water to cool. It had been so long since I had done such a thing that I had to read the instructions on the packet.

'Do you want to feed her?' I asked Jenny.

She shook her head, looking exhausted, her face rubbed into streaks of dirt and tears. I placed a cushion over the wrist that was in a cast and gave the bottle to Rose. Bridie's mouth clamped over the teat and her face became red and then white with emotion as she sucked. Her arms were flung wide and her fists clenched and unclenched with concentration while her eyes rolled.

'She isn't very pretty, is she?' said Henry, watching with great interest. 'She needs hair, I think.'

'How old is she?' I asked Jenny, having signalled secretly to Henry with my eyebrows to keep quiet.

'Nine weeks tomorrow. Is she small for her age, do you think? I don't know anything about babies except what they told me at the home.'

'She's a lovely baby.' Rose spoke firmly for she didn't believe in fussing. 'There's no such thing as the right weight or the right time for a baby to do things. She's alert and that's all that matters. Babies are as different as grown-up people.'

I gave Jenny a cup of tea and some biscuits from the box of groceries that Mead's had just delivered. Then I made up the other bottle of formula and unpacked the rest of the box. Jenny ate as though she were starving. 'Didn't that man allow you to eat properly?' I asked.

'I didn't always have time. Today dinner-time I had to go and muck out the cows. When I come back in he'd ate the lot.'

'I thought the description of the job said no outside work.'

'So it did, but he must've reckoned that I had no place else to go. I had to do whatever he asked.'

I explained Jenny's predicament to Rose.

'She can't go back there,' was Rose's only comment, as she drew the empty bottle from Bridie's mouth and gave her to me to wind.

'I'll have to go back, though, won't I?' Jenny looked wretched. 'He told me to take the baby out because she was crying and getting on his nerves, like. But he'll be expecting me back. I got to do tea at six.'

'Certainly you're not going back there, now or ever. You can stay with us until we can find you a decent place to go.'

'Oh, Miss, you're ever so good!' Jenny began to cry again. 'I'll be so grateful! I'll work ever so hard for you, if you'll let me stay a little! They said I was a really good little worker in the home. The best they'd had. We all had to take our turn with the chores. I really like housework so I often did it for the other girls. Some of them only wanted to read magazines and smoke.'

'Everything'll be fine. Don't cry any more. Shouldn't Bridie be changed before she goes to sleep? She's looking rather drowsy. Henry, run up to the linen cupboard. Somewhere on the top shelf there's a pile of nappies.' I took off Bridie's woollen suit and undid her nappy.

'She's got a very bad rash,' said Rose.

'I know.' Jenny sniffed. 'But I'd nowhere to air them. I

had to hang the nappies on a chair in me room and it were that cold they wouldn't dry. I done me best to look after her but things have been so hard, you wouldn't believe.'

Henry had to leave the room as soon as he had brought the nappy as his sensibilities were too delicate to withstand the washing and changing of Bridie. We decided that Jenny would sleep in the ironing room, which was next to the kitchen. There was already a bed in it, left over from when James broke his leg and couldn't get up and down stairs. Bridie's cot, which Henry and I brought down from the attic, was a pretty French rocking crib all my children had slept in as babies. We put it in its old place in a warm corner of the kitchen. Jenny would be able to hear Bridie at once if she woke. She grew excited when she saw the bed we had made for her baby. 'She'll look so grand in it! Ah, me ducky!' She lowered the sleeping child into the cot and stood looking down at her, lost in admiration at the embroidered and appliquéd linen my mother had sent from Florence when James was born.

'Now we must deal with Mr Birt. You'll need your things for tonight.' Jenny looked frightened. 'You needn't come with me. I'll take Ivor for moral support. You stay here and make your bed.'

I telephoned Mr Birt before setting off. He was simply furious when I told him that Jenny was coming to stay with me and accused me of stealing his workers.

'You haven't paid her anything and you've had a good deal of free labour out of her, as well as other things that no decent man would have asked for. You should be ashamed of yourself. I'm not sure that in a court of law it wouldn't count as rape. You could be in very serious trouble.'

He ranted more than ever when I said this but I knew that he was alarmed.

'If you don't want me to ring up my solicitor to find out, you can put all her things on the doorstep and I'll come in ten minutes to collect them.'

I cut him off in the middle of a sentence of invective. When Ivor and I drove over to Mill Farm there was a pathetic little bundle of things in a carrier bag outside the front door and no sign of Mr Birt.

Elizabeth came in from untacking Puck just as we got back. 'A baby!' she exclaimed, as I explained. 'I hate babies. Don't let it come near me, will you?'

'Don't be silly, darling. She's only a few weeks old. She stays right where you put her. You needn't have anything to do with her but don't say anything unkind in front of Jenny.'

'I'm not a complete idiot, Mum,' replied Elizabeth witheringly.

Conversation at supper was a little awkward. Jenny was shy, and worried, I think, about table manners, though we were eating spaghetti and steamed jam sponge in the kitchen and both my children slouched, sprawled, spoke with their mouths full and generally behaved as badly as usual. She observed carefully what everyone was doing before she ventured to eat. Now that her tears had dried and her face was clean she looked much less plain. She had a high bony forehead, thick with spots and curly dark hair, very greasy and scraped back into a pony-tail. Her eyes were dark, too, with a timid expression that was appealing. I had asked Ivor to stay for supper in gratitude for his being ready to knock Mr Birt down, had he proved intractable. Jenny seemed nervous of Ivor, though he smiled kindly at her.

Bridie woke half-way through supper and cried to be fed. Ivor was very moved by the sight of Jenny holding the baby. ' "The World has no such flowers in any land," ' he quoted from his favourite Swinburne and dropped a lump of mashed potato into Elizabeth's lap as he waved his fork in the air. ' "And no such pearl in any gulf the sea, / As any babe on any mother's knee." '

I think Jenny considered Ivor a lunatic from that moment.

CHAPTER 8

'Are you sure it's wise? Two extra mouths to feed, just when you need money so badly?'

Patience and I were enjoying a glass of wine in the library on Monday evening, waiting for Aubrey Molebank to arrive. Patience was wearing her green jersey, which I always thought suited her better than the brown one. I had told her about Jenny's rescue from the libidinous Harold Birt.

'I don't see that I could have done anything else. The poor child's only seventeen, penniless and completely friendless. I asked her yesterday if there was anyone she should telephone to tell them she was safe – her mother, perhaps – and she told me that she'd sent a card to her mother from the mother-and-baby home when Bridie was born but had never heard a word. The unkindness of it! Apparently Jenny's priest asked her to keep in touch but she hadn't any writing things so she couldn't. After she'd spoken to him on the telephone yesterday, she was so excited and tearful that I've begun to have my doubts about Father Declan. She constantly refers to him in conversation as though he's Almighty God. She hasn't said anything about the baby's father. Of course, I'm just putting two and two together. I could be quite wrong.'

'Poor little thing! I believe it happens more often than one would imagine. It does sound very sad. And how dreadful for her to have this farmer forcing himself on her! I see you couldn't really do anything else.'

'And, as it happens, she's the most tremendous help. When I got up yesterday she'd washed up all the supper things, swept the floor, scrubbed every surface in sight and fed Jasper. She watches me very carefully and then copies what I do meticulously. She did all the ironing yesterday and I couldn't have done it better myself. In fact, I had to tell her several times during the day to sit down and rest. I don't like the fact that she obviously labours under such a weight of obligation that she feels she has to slave all day. It makes me very uncomfortable, particularly when my own children are such a lazy lot. I tried to explain to her that she must rest in order to breastfeed the baby.'

'What did she say to that?'

'She said that she preferred bottle-feeding anyway. She thinks it's more hygienic. I gather, reading between the lines, that she feels breastfeeding is immodest and would rather not have to do it. Rose and I both gave her homilies on the "breast is best" theme but on this, at least, she's intransigent. On every other subject, she seems to regard my least suggestion as a papal bull.'

'Where is she now? I'd be very interested to meet her.'

'She's upstairs at the moment, washing her hair. She's clean to the point of fastidiousness and I was surprised her hair was so greasy and unkempt. Then it occurred to me that she probably didn't have any shampoo. We're having supper in the dining room. Like all infants, the baby's something of a benevolent despot and the kitchen has become her empire. I thought it might be a bit terrifying for a shy bachelor. Rose is in her element. She looks so much better. What little babies want above all is companionship. Rose holds her, kisses her, talks to her, devotes herself for hours to an intense exchange of blinks and grunts. The child will grow up to be a genius, probably, with so much stimulation.'

'I don't know anything about babies. They frighten me, rather.'

'Elizabeth isn't keen either, probably for the same reason. Oddly enough, the boys seem to have taken to her much better. James has always had a strong inclination to be protective. And Henry sees in her the potential to increase the size of his audience.'

'How was James this weekend?'

'All right, I think. Working hard at school, his housemaster says. Yesterday James asked me very kindly if I thought I was beginning to come to terms with Jack's death. He's immensely conscientious and fatherly towards us all, which is very comforting, but I wonder all the time if he isn't repressing his own feelings to a dangerous extent.'

'Perhaps he is – repressing feelings, I mean. But need it be dangerous? I'm not sure I go along entirely with the current trend of minutely dissecting one's psyche. Is it helpful to discover that you've always wanted to murder your mother and go to bed with your father?'

'One thing that's noticeable about any kind of psychotherapy is that people never come away from it cringing with horror at their own selfishness and greed. What they do discover is that from birth they've been the victim of an egocentric, manipulative mother and a sadistic, misogynist father. They've been cruelly spurned by jealous siblings and generally done down by a world full of malevolent nannies, teachers, employers, lovers, spouses and friends. This is possibly true but it takes no account of the fact that they themselves are far from perfect. Of course everyone needs their self-esteem repaired but it isn't any good getting only half the picture. Perhaps I'm reluctant to peer into my own darkest recesses because I'm afraid. But I'd prefer to stumble about by the feeble light of my own little match in the hope that time will do the donkey work.'

Aubrey's psyche was in the last stage of disjunction when he arrived half an hour late. He explained that the shirt he had been wearing was extremely inky and would have disgraced the occasion but the search for a clean one had delayed him. I'm sure that Patience noticed, as I did, that the shirt he wore was damp to the point of being sodden and that he steamed gently all evening as though about to spontaneously combust.

He had brought his accounts with him, as I had suggested. While I did some last-minute cooking, he and Patience looked at them together. When I came back to announce that supper was ready, it was evident that all was well.

'Miss Wakeham-Tutt is a mental giant!' cried Aubrey.

'In fact, we are not eight hundred pounds short, as I feared, but fifty pence to the good! I can't thank you both enough. I've been so worried! I really felt I couldn't face Mrs Scranton-Jones after her remarks last time. Oh, what it is to have a mathematical brain!'

After that it seemed that we were set for a particularly happy evening. Aubrey appeared almost dizzy with relief. Rose, who came to join us when Henry rang the gong, had always liked Patience, considering her a woman of sound sense. She tolerated Aubrey on the grounds that he was an honorary woman, neither violent, autocratic nor licentious. Henry was in a good humour as Bridie had suddenly been inspired by some process of infantile cognition to give an enormous toothless grin. 'It was me she was smiling at,' asserted Henry, as he drew out his chair. 'Hello, Patience, hello, Mr Molebank. I definitely made her smile.'

'That's ridiculous,' said Elizabeth, coming in after him. 'With the squint that baby's got she might as well have been smiling at the kettle or the beams on the ceiling. Or both at once. Probably she'd scream the place down if she could actually see Henry's freckled phiz.'

'I haven't got freckles!' Henry was indignant.

'You're a handsome lad and no mistake,' said Jenny, as she came in, bringing the potatoes. She had divined Henry's character with exactitude.

'Grace will last, beauty will blast,' said Rose. Beatrice and I had been told this constantly during our adolescence when we had been respectively tubby and gangling, both spotty and extremely unlikely to put undue faith in our powers of attraction. It occurs to me now that she may have meant it as a consolation.

I gave Jenny a second look as I took the vegetable tureen, and was very much surprised. Her newly washed hair fell in soft dark waves down to her shoulders. Her complexion had improved already, after two days of washing, rest and proper food. She reminded me of Elizabeth Siddal, Dante Gabriel Rossetti's wife. The oddly angular face, when surrounded by hair and animated by happiness, was not pretty but it had a strong and unusual beauty.

Only Elizabeth seemed a possible source of friction. She answered any remark addressed to her in a slow drawl, which was new and extraordinarily irritating. She was wearing a tiny black skirt, which scarcely covered her knickers, and a crimson jersey, which drooped down over one bare shoulder. Her hair was tied up on the top of her head and she had drawn several spiky eyelashes below her eyes with eyebrow pencil so that her face looked like a painted doll's.

'How are you getting on, Jenny?' said Patience kindly. 'I hear you have a lovely baby.'

'Oh, thank you very much, Miss. It's lovely being here and everyone's ever so kind. Sometimes I pinch meself to see if I'm dreaming. This grand house and all, and a room of me own. And Miss Rose is so good with Bridie. I haven't ever been so happy. This is better than school, even.'

'You liked school?' Elizabeth was drawn out of her sulk by incredulity.

'Yes. The teachers were ever so kind and I liked being with the other girls. I was really sorry when me mum said I had to leave.'

Elizabeth expression was scornful. 'I'd leave tomorrow if I could.'

'Aye, but you've a lovely home to come back to,' said Jenny, mildly. 'Our house were cold and lonely with me mum out working all hours. And I hated the rats in the scullery. I were scared to death of them.'

Elizabeth had the grace to look a little ashamed. Aubrey was interested and began with commendable sensitivity to encourage Jenny to talk more about herself. When he heard the story of Mr Birt – a Bowdlerised version for the sake of the children – he looked at me with such warm approval in his owlish eyes that I felt embarrassed. The telephone interrupted us.

'Is Lizzie there?'

It was a masculine voice, young and with just the same

slow, superior indolence in its tone that had irritated me in Elizabeth. After ten minutes she returned to the table in a much better temper. 'Jasper won't bite, you know. He never does,' she said to Jenny, in a tone that was almost kind.

Perhaps because of the rats Jenny was terrified of all animals, which had exasperated Elizabeth in the way that other people's fears, which we don't happen to share, always do. Jasper sensed that Jenny didn't like him and was inclined to fix his eyes reproachfully on her and growl in a quiet and sinister manner. Poor Jenny had been terrified when, on her first night, Dinkie had leaped upon her bed in a masterly imitation of a friendly domestic pet. Luckily she had hidden beneath the bed covers until Dinkie, balked of his prey, went away.

'All the same, darling, do you think we should have Jasper in the dining room? He does smell rather strongly of stagnant water.'

'You know he'll only bark if I shut him in the kitchen.'

'How remarkable the natural world is.' Aubrey was beginning his second plate of *porc Dijonnaise* with mashed potatoes and French beans. 'Did you know that if a man could jump as high as a flea – in proportion to his weight – he'd be able to jump over St Paul's Cathedral?'

'Everyone knows that,' said Elizabeth rudely.

'I didn't,' said Henry, at once.

'Oh yes you did. You're just trying to suck up. I remember Dad telling us that years ago.'

I experienced an all-too-familiar vacillation of purpose. I was tempted to tell Elizabeth off roundly for her rudeness. On the other hand, I was reluctant to make too much of it so that everyone would feel uncomfortable. Also, I was desperately anxious not to endanger the good terms Elizabeth and I were currently on. The pain of her father's death called for extreme tolerance from the rest of us and would continue to do so for some time. Yet she oughtn't to be allowed to get away with bad behaviour. The result of all this was that, weakly, I did nothing.

Fortunately, Aubrey was the perfect guest and carried on as though he had noticed nothing.

'A caterpillar, you know, can put on ten thousand times its own weight in one day. How much do you weigh, Henry?'

'About eight stone, I think.'

'So if you put on ten thousand times your own weight by bedtime you'd end up weighing ... let me see ... eight hundred tons. No, that can't be right.'

'Five hundred tons,' said Patience.

'Thank you, Miss Wakeham-Tutt.'

'Please call me Patience.'

'Thank you.' Aubrey's conversation was like his sermons, dislocated and circuitous. 'There is a species of bird called the hornbill, which makes a very curious nest. The female is immured in a round shell of twigs and leaves, held together by a sort of plaster secreted by the male bird, with only her beak showing. She stays within this prison until her young are ready to fly. The male bird feeds her with bits of fruit and lizard rolled into pellets. If he meets with an accident – shot by hunters or something – other male birds will come and take over the task of feeding her.'

'That's very nice of them,' said Jenny.

'It isn't kindness, really, but because they are genetically programmed to ensure the survival of the species. Their instinct drives them to reproduce at all costs.'

Could this be the excuse for so much tiresome human behaviour, I wondered, thinking of Jeremy and Mr French and the man who brought the fish on Fridays. Last week, he had run his hand over my bottom when I was leaning over the tray of ice in his van, choosing some smoked haddock.

'What an interesting man!' said Patience, as she was getting into her car to go home. Aubrey had already thanked me profusely and rumbled away in his Morris Oxford. 'He knows so much about so many things. But he's modest and self-effacing at the same time. I don't think I've ever seen such extraordinary eyes. Almost yellowish-gold in the middle with a rim of bright green.'

I had never noticed Aubrey's eyes in that sort of detail. When I met him quite by chance the next afternoon in the Bosworth ironmonger's shop, he thanked me again for what he described as an evening of unmixed delights. 'I owe an immense debt also to your friend. I slept well for the first time for a week. A striking combination of brains and beauty! Those lovely soft blue eyes, the colour, one imagines, of the Madonna's robe. Oh dear, that sounds rather High. I hope none of my parishioners are within earshot.'

He giggled a little at his own daring and went on talking about the excellence of the supper, but I didn't hear a word he said. I was struck by such a pleasing notion that I began at once to lay plans to bring it to fruition. I thought about it all the way home in the car and was still thinking about it as I inspected the progress of the new bathroom and gave the taps I had bought in Bosworth to the builders. I rang Patience, ostensibly to tell her that the fabric I had ordered for the four-poster in the blue room had arrived. She had kindly offered to make the bed hangings in her workroom and to sandwich them in between other commissions so that they would be ready quickly.

'I've got another great favour to ask you,' I said. 'Poor Aubrey will never acquire book-keeping skills. Do you think you might consider looking over the accounts regularly, perhaps even weekly? Then they would be quick to do if they were kept in order. Of course, I know it's asking a lot.'

'Yes, willingly. It would only take ten or fifteen minutes. If he wouldn't think it interfering?'

'I'm quite sure he wouldn't. He spoke very warmly in your praise this afternoon.'

'Oh.' A pause. 'Will he bring them to me at home, do you think, or what?'

I thought of the effect of Wacko on a man of Aubrey's sensibilities. 'I suggest you go to the vicarage, if it wouldn't be too much trouble. He'll have all the receipts there. Don't be too shocked by the state of the place, though.'

'I won't be.' Patience sounded composed.

Then I telephoned Aubrey. 'I hope this doesn't sound too bossy, Aubrey?'

'Not at all. Not at all! You're kindness itself! What a relief it will be! Perhaps Patience will let me give her tea. Does she like ginger-nuts, do you think?'

I was very satisfied when I rang off. If I felt beleaguered by my own problems, I might at least be able to do something about someone else's. I found Henry in his habitual crouch three inches away from the television screen, watching two idiotically grinning men performing with sets of spoons for *Opportunity Knocks*.

'Darling, if they're going to storm the London Palladium they'll manage without your support,' I said, as Henry protested about being hauled off. 'Meanwhile Puck will poison himself if we don't get that ragwort dug out.' I had seen the tell-tale yellow flowers in Puck's field that morning from the kitchen window. Puck never touches it while it's fresh but the minute it starts to die off it's the only growing thing to hold any interest for him. I had asked Elizabeth to do something about it when she came home for school, but she announced that she was staying late for hockey practice.

'Hockey practice?' I queried, foolishly. 'I thought you said last term you hated it.'

Elizabeth gave me a scowl. 'We did the Spanish Inquisition in history last year.' She picked up her school bag and slouched off to catch the bus.

'It's a difficult age,' said Rose, as I looked at her in dismay.

'I know. But it's *always* a difficult age, that's the trouble.'

'Poor child! It's very hard for her. A little grumpiness is natural enough.'

'What bothers me most is that I'm so frightened of upsetting her that I can't react naturally to anything she says or does. Immediately after Jack died we were closer than ever. Now I feel this great divide opening up and I'm too cowardly to do anything about it.'

'Of course there'll be hard times to come. But better say too little than too much as a general rule.'

I went over and kissed her. 'You're such a comfort to me, Rose. I'm so lucky to have you.'

'Tush! Foolishness! You'll wake the baby.'

Rose looked down with a severe frown at the sleeping infant on her knee, but I knew she was pleased.

'Why does ragwort grow where horses can eat it?' asked Henry, as we struggled to get our spades into the chalky, compacted soil. 'It doesn't seem much like the intelligence of nature Mr Molebank was going on about last night.'

'I think it was one of those plants brought over here by the Romans. It grows on the hills outside Rome and they brought it to England as seeds, caught in the studs on the soles of their sandals when they came here in . . .' I sensed by the way that Henry was striding purposefully away to another part of the field that I had lost my audience.

It took us nearly an hour to root up every bit and wheelbarrow the remains away to Ivor's latest bonfire. Henry was slowed down very much by Puck's determination to lick his neck whenever he bent over. 'He really loves me, doesn't he?' said Henry happily. I couldn't bring myself to spoil his delight by explaining that the saltiness of his skin, due to infrequent washing, was the great attraction.

'Don't you think this bonfire's a little near the coach-house?' I asked Ivor. 'A spark could blow over. The wind's getting up.'

Ivor assured me he would put out the fire before going to bed. He looked rather excited, even agitated. I hoped it was just because he had had an unusually stimulating day. He had been up to London to a very smart shop in Piccadilly to sell Jack's guns. They were a macabre reminder of his death. I wanted them out of the house. Neither James nor Henry wanted to shoot. There had been frequent, painful quarrels with Jack about the ethics of killing things for pleasure. It is hardly a subject on which disagreements can be anything other than acrimonious.

I was planning to turn the gun room into a television room for the children. Until now the television had been banished to a very small cold room over the porch. This was not because Jack and I were snobbish about it but rather that too often we had found ourselves sitting in a cataleptic trance in front of *Take Your Pick* and *Double Your Money*, without the will-power to do something either useful or actually enjoyable. So the television had been put somewhere where it required an effort to view it.

I walked into the house by the back door, still very hot from my exertions with the ragwort, to find Dr McCleod in the hall, the telephone ringing and an enormous box being carried in through the front door.

'Mum!' screamed Henry. 'There's a huge green delivery van from London outside!'

'Please go into the kitchen, Dr McCleod. I'll come in a minute.'

I picked up the telephone.

'Hello, Miranda? It's Maeve. Listen, I've got a guest for you! Saturday the tenth. Not this weekend but the next. Aren't I clever?'

'Yes, very. But I don't know if we're ready – the builders may not have finished –'

'Now, don't make difficulties. Janòs won't care tuppence about builders. He'll only want a bed.'

'Ya-nosh?'

'That's right. Janòs. He's Hungarian. A dream. One of the most attractive men I've ever met. And quite, quite brilliant. I ran into him yesterday at the Chelsea Arts Club. I don't mind telling you I've got my eye on him, so no hanky-panky!'

'If he's all you say and he only wants a bed, why don't *you* have him to stay?'

'Because, darling, far more important to him than a bed is a decent piano. I've only got a little cottage piano and all the keys have lost their bits of ivory. Sebastian prised them all off one afternoon when he was younger to make teeth for the snow army he built in the garden. I thought it was so creative that I couldn't be cross.'

'I remember it.' It had been impressive. Sebastian and Florian had worked for a week to make ten life-size figures with sticks for rifles and feather cockades. But I had worried very much about the blood that had appeared, as the finishing touch, on various parts of the soldiers' glacial anatomy. Maeve had said it was red ink but it hadn't looked like ink to me. 'Why does he want a piano?'

'Oh, didn't I say? He's a concert pianist and he's coming to Kent to play at the Titchmarsh Festival.'

The Titchmarsh Festival was held four times a year at Titchmarsh Hall. It was an enormous, rambling house twenty-five miles south of Westray. I had met its owner, Lady Alice Vavasour, once or twice in the early days of living in Kent when I went to charity lunches. Jack had decided I ought to get to know people in the area and encouraged me to do some committee work. But I didn't like the rows that inevitably ensued. There was always one committee member who thought they knew best, and someone else who stormed off in tears, and then there would be endless telephone calls as factions were formed. Also, I didn't enjoy the end result.

I've always thought that a charity ball is a form of entertainment that one must be a masochist to enjoy. To sit in an ugly, cold marquee on a rickety chair as comfortable as the Iron Maiden of Nuremberg, the toes of one's evening shoes curling up like oriental slippers with damp, while one struggles with flabby thighs of poultry and nasty wine is an odd sort of amusement. What a very long evening it is, too. If the object is to see a circle of friends then one might as well set up their photographs on the dining table at home for conversation is impossible. The silliest music you ever heard, from the cheapest band the committee can get, is relayed by amplifiers at such a volume that bells ring in one's head for weeks afterwards. After the second such evening even Jack admitted that the game wasn't worth the candle.

'You've got a Steinway, haven't you?' Maeve went on. 'I thought so. Janòs wants to be able to do a few hours' warming up on Saturday afternoon. He says the piano he's practising on at the moment is hopeless and he's slowly going mad. In my opinion, he's a bit mad already.'

'Oh?' I was suddenly alert. I wanted to run a guest-house not a lunatic asylum.

'Not in that way. What I mean is . . . he's so dedicated to his art that he isn't quite like the rest of us. I don't mean he's actually nuts. You'll like him. Just don't like him too much, that's all.' I assured her that there was absolutely no danger of that. 'I'll take him over to Titchmarsh myself,' continued Maeve. 'He doesn't drive.'

'Well, all right, then. You'd better tell him how much I'm charging for bed and breakfast. Obviously he won't want dinner.'

I named the sum that Patience and I had worked out as fair to the guests but providing a reasonable profit for me.

'That'll be okay. The Festival will pay. I'll bring him over myself from the station on Saturday some time after lunch.'

I went thoughtfully into the kitchen. I had forgotten about Dr McCleod being there. I suddenly caught sight of myself in the mirror. I had a streak of mud from the field down one cheek and a strand of ragwort in my hair. As I tidied myself, he finished taking Rose's blood pressure.

'I can see you're very much better, Miss Ingrams. Is it Thursday they're putting a lighter cast on for you?'

'Mum! It's a television!' shouted Henry, running into the kitchen. 'The biggest you ever saw!'

'There, now!' admonished Rose. 'You've woken the baby.'

'Did you order a television, Mum? It's got my name on the label. Come and see!'

I went with him into the hall and saw that it was indeed addressed to Henry, as well as Elizabeth and James. Inside was a card which said, 'Thank you for a glorious time, love, Nancy.'

'Will you be able to take Miss Ingrams to the hospital on Thursday?' Dr McCleod was standing beside us as Henry tore at the wrapping to expose an enormous screen. I was sure that he must consider me ridiculously frivolous and extravagant to have bought such a thing for the children. I was too proud to explain that it was a present. 'Certainly.'

He nodded and left without even saying goodbye. What made me furious was that I really minded that he always seemed to find me in some way compromised, either in the clutches of a man or drowning in vulgar possessions. I knew the projection was false so why should it matter to me what a virtual stranger (and a disagreeable one at that) thought? I sent Henry to get Ivor's help to move the new television to the gun room and then went up to my room to change, very cross.

CHAPTER 9

The weather changed quite dramatically on the Saturday that was to see the triumphal beginning of my guest-house adventure. I woke early to see clouds as dark as a cinder-path filling the unshuttered window. The unseasonably mild weather had fled, and my room felt cold. Downstairs, the kitchen was warm and quiet. It was rare that I managed to be up before Jenny. She had been with us two weeks now, and whatever bread I had impulsively cast upon the waters by taking her in had been returned to me twenty-fold. She was so willing, so hard-working, so eager to learn exactly how I wanted things done that I felt that I was constantly in danger of exploiting her.

Another worry was that the task of looking after Bridie had been virtually taken out of Jenny's hands. Four days after her arrival we had taken Bridie out in the children's old pram and met Lissie outside the post office. 'A baby!' she had shrieked, and dived beneath the hood. Lissie was mad about babies and a great sadness, on a par with her unrequited love for Jack, was that she had been unable to have a second child. I had several times thought, in fact, that she continued to love Jack so hopelessly as a preferable pain to grieving for the babies that had miscarried.

'What a love! What a honey! The most beautiful baby in the world!'

Bridie, though still, in my secret opinion, bearing a strong resemblance to Henry VIII, was much improved by the jettisoning of the salmon-pink wool in favour of Elizabeth's embroidered baby gowns. Little white bonnets with pale pink ribbons hid the pearly baldness of Bridie's large dome. She gave Lissie the full benefit of her new accomplishment by smiling from ear to ear and Lissie became her slave from that moment. At first Lissie found excuses to come up and see us every day. Books she had borrowed years ago were suddenly returned, and Alice's old baby clothes were brought in profusion. After a bit she dropped the pretence that she had any other reason for coming but to feed, change, bath and kiss Bridie.

It gave Rose a chance to rest, which I was glad of, but between them Bridie's needs were so well taken care of that Jenny hardly laid a finger on her own baby all day. It was obvious that she much preferred housework. 'She'll come round to it,' Rose assured me. 'She's had a cruel start. No proper support. She's bound to have found it hard. And seventeen's too young to be unselfish. It's against nature. Give her time.'

I thought I saw guilt flash from the corner of Rose's dark grey eyes, and I noticed that after this conversation she often called Jenny over to take the bottle from her and feed Bridie herself. Who has not found that children, in their scatheless innocence and promise of continuity, are the greatest comfort in adversity? I knew that without my own children I should never have been able to continue my own life after Jack's death with anything like composure, so I couldn't blame Rose or Lissie.

After I had prepared lunch for five people – James had elected to stay at school this weekend to go to a party in London – I went up to change. The chairman of Jack's bank was coming to take me out. At the time of Jack's funeral he had been in New York and was, so he told me via his secretary, deeply grieved that the claims of international monetary affairs had required him to absent himself from the occasion. I was glad that I had put on an elegant *café noir*-coloured wool suit when he turned up to collect me in a Rolls-Royce. He was a solemn man, much taken with his own importance, and we were driven in great state along the sea-front at Marshgate by a smartly uniformed driver, who turned the wheel between his hands as delicately as though stroking a kitten.

The inhabitants of Marshgate, unaccustomed to such otiose grandeur, gawped from the pavement as we purred beneath the *porte-cochère* of the Excelsior. The driver helped me to disembark with an iron grip on my elbow, as though I were an elderly dowager pickled in gin. My companion, though short and immensely fat, had a deportment to rival Mr Turveydrop's. As we arrived at the entrance to the dining room he drew himself up to his full five feet and three inches. The head waiter flew down from the far end of the room and rushed us to the best table overlooking the sea. Two more waiters flapped napkins in our faces and presented enormous menus.

As a pre-war baby, I was pretty well inured to eating nasty things. Rationing and boarding-school food had combined to make a lean and unappetising diet during my adolescent years. Now, in the early seventies, thanks to a new spirit of indulgence begun in the sixties, it was possible for the determined and well-heeled epicure to dine out in London without despair. Unfortunately, triumphs from the capital lost something in translation to the provinces. Everything sounded promising, if you like *coquilles Saint Jacques* and that kind of thing, but it all came in boxes and had been in the deep freeze for months. I warned my host *sotto voce* that this would be the case. My discretion was scattered to the winds. Mr Defresnier, for such was my companion's name, called the head waiter in a peremptory voice and demanded to know what was fresh as Mrs Stowe – he indicated me with a nod – seemed to think that much of what was on the menu was frozen.

The head waiter, whom I had known for many years and who was called Luis, turned his eyes on me with a look of rebuke similar to the *coup d'oeil* Julius Caesar probably gave Brutus. We ordered, or rather Mr Defresnier ordered for me, *bortsch à la Tsarina*, followed by *fricandeau à l'oseille*, with Excelsior potatoes and buttered spinach. My host, who had not addressed a word to me since we had taken our places at the table, studied the wine list in silence, his plump lips pursed and a frown quilting his brow. The suspense, as the wine waiter hovered at his side, pencil tip poised on pad, grew almost unendurable. A silver revolving trolley rolled by, bearing little porcelain trays of wholly meretricious *hors d'oeuvres*. At first sight it looked various and colourful but a second glance identified baked beans, tinned sardines and quite the nastiest food ever invented, something called Russian salad, a *macedoine* of carrots and turnips with citrine-coloured peas bathed in salad cream.

Finally Mr Defresnier rapped out his order for wine in excruciating French and told the waiter to remove the ashtray. As it happens, I don't smoke but I was tempted to order a large cigar. Mr Defresnier put his hands together before him on the table, fixed his small topaz eyes on me and began to speak. He told me how certain it was that Jack would have been made a director within the next year if he had lived, how devastated they had all been to hear of his death and how irreplaceable his special talents were. Without pausing to allow me to acknowledge these compliments, he went on to talk about the difficulties of recruiting people who were not merely clever (these, it seemed, were ten a penny) but who were able to take instructions from superiors, who were flexible, courteous to their fellow workers and eager to promote the bank's business twenty-four hours a day. I was just thinking that absolutely none of these desirable qualities applied to Jack, who had been arrogant, lazy when it suited him and off-handedly rude to anyone he disliked, when the soup arrived.

It tasted like a tin of beef consommé, gingered up with sherry, in which a few strands of raw beetroot lay in a disheartened way on the bottom of the plate. Mr Defresnier drank half of his, then pushed it away and continued to talk to me about the bank. The beetroot shreds were rather unmanageable, especially with his sharp eyes fixed unwinkingly on my face so I put down my spoon. Luis clicked his fingers. He stood within four feet of us throughout lunch, his entire body inclined in an attitude of service, which would have inhibited anyone but Mr Defresnier. I could hardly bring myself to catch his reproachful eye. A battery of stainless-steel dishes came winking through the swing doors like Philip of Macedon's silver-laden ass. The *fricandeau* turned out to be lumps of some mysterious meat – I thought it was probably veal and was thankful Elizabeth couldn't see me eating it as we had all promised her faithfully that we never would – with carrots and onions, served with greasy fried potatoes and very wet spinach boiled to an emetic slush. It was quite what I had expected but Mr Defresnier was clearly disappointed. He pushed it about on his plate, chewed silently for a minute and then gave up and began talking again. He spoke in stately periods, as though reading from a script.

I continued to eat, for I was hungry, and responded with nods and smiles, stretching my eyes wide in astonishment as he made particularly emphatic points. Occasionally Mr Defresnier addressed a question to me, but the moment I opened my mouth to reply he immediately turned to Luis and asked for a window to be closed, a glass to be changed, water to be brought or the wine to be plunged in ice. I soon understood that I was not expected to bear any part but that of listener.

I hardly had time to put my knife and fork together on the plate before Luis commanded an underling to whisk away my plate. He brought us the menu for puddings himself which was a great piece of condescension. Mr Defresnier ordered two *crème de riz à l'Excelsior*, but I knew from experience that this was just rice pudding with a tinned apricot floating on the top so I called the waiter back and asked for cheese. Mr Defresnier seemed startled by this display of independence. He began to look at me with an expression I didn't quite like. Then he reached inside his coat and pulled out an envelope.

'As you are no doubt aware, your husband made wholly inadequate provision for a pension.' I did know this. Interviews with my bank manager and solicitor had made this point painfully intelligible. 'A man his age has no thoughts of dying,' continued Mr Defresnier. 'Inside this envelope is a cheque. It is an acknowledgement of his service to the bank and an expression of our sympathy for your great loss.'

I was surprised and rather touched. It had not occurred to me that the bank would willingly part with sixpence, if not actually threatened with a writ. I longed to tear open the envelope and see how much it was for, but he continued to hold it firmly between his fat, manicured fingers. He stared at me a little longer with the same speculative expression, then he called for the humidor. 'Normally I do not smoke during the day but for once I shall indulge.'

There was a great deal of irritating fuss while he rolled and rattled and sniffed and squeezed the cigars and then more ritual as one was cut and lit. I was longing to go home, but nothing could hurry this man, certainly not consideration for anyone else. He leaned forward and blew a curl of smoke into my face. 'You must be lonely, Mrs Stowe, without your husband.'

I thought of Westray, and of the five people at this very moment sitting round the kitchen table eating the onion and mushroom tart I had left for them. Perhaps six, if Lissie had stayed. 'Not really. I –'

'You're clearly a very intelligent woman.'

If so, he must share with Maeve extraordinary powers of extrasensory perception to have discerned this as I had said perhaps a total of twenty words amounting to nothing more brilliant than 'yes' and 'no' and 'no more potatoes, thank you'.

'Money is not everything, as I know only too well.' Mr Defresnier leaned forward as he said this, and laid his dry, cold hand on mine.

I knew he was lying. I withdrew my hand. 'You're very kind. I really must be going home, I'm afraid. I have guests arriving this afternoon.' Only one guest actually but the plural added a degree of exigency, I thought.

'Yes. A remarkable woman.' Mr Defresnier smiled for the first time, disclosing teeth the colour of teak. No wonder he was generally so grave. 'I would like to help you in a way that is a little more . . . personal.'

I noticed that several more waiters were drifting towards our table, as though drawn by irresistible forces. One so far forgot himself as to let slip the contents of his tray. I was reminded of the Magnetic Mountain of medieval stories, which drew the nails out of all the ships that approached it. It ought to be easy to tell people to push off but I've always found it difficult. I stood up and began to walk through the long, by now virtually empty, dining room. I could hear footsteps padding along behind me on the thick, red carpet. In the foyer Mr Defresnier managed, though his legs were shorter than mine, to get between me and the door. 'Well, Mrs Stowe?' He placed one hand on my arm. The smoke from his cigar separated into two thin streams, one for each of my nostrils.

'Miranda! What a stroke of luck!' I saw Aubrey's *bête noire*, Hilary Scranton-Jones, pushing through the revolving door. 'I was just coming to find a telephone. Too annoying! I've had to leave the car at the garage. Oil leaking all over the road! I was going to tell Guy to come and fetch me.' Her eye ran over Mr Defresnier, who removed his hand from my arm. 'Oh, but perhaps you won't be able to give me a lift. Are you madly busy?'

'No. But I haven't my own car here.' I introduced Hilary. Mr Defresnier bowed his head and then stared past her to a revolving stand of coloured slides by the reception desk. 'Do you think we could give Mrs Scranton-Jones a lift? It's on our way.'

He bowed his head again and walked over to the door without looking at either of us again.

'Oh, I say, a Rolls!' Hilary's tone was one of girlish excitement. 'You are a dark horse, Miranda!'

I explained that I had been having lunch with Jack's former boss and that there was no mystery in it. But I knew that she had seen his hand on my arm. Hilary Scranton-Jones was a scandalmonger of the worst kind. She was gushing to one's face and behind one's back wholly malevolent. All the way back to Westray her eyes turned from me to my companion, filled with wild surmise. Mr Defresnier, taking up more than half of the back seat, spoke not a word but gazed straight ahead, puffing smoke into the interior of the car until our eyes watered. Hilary kept up a flow of small-talk, which I did my best to answer.

I was very sorry that the driver took a wrong turn, which meant that we reached Westray before Hilary's Bella Vista at the other end of the village. As I was getting out of the car, Mr Defresnier took the envelope from his pocket and handed it to me without a word. Hilary's eyes nearly popped from her head with enthralled conjecture. I thanked Mr Defresnier for lunch and he twitched his chin upwards, which I assumed was a gesture of farewell. They purred away, he staring straight ahead and she waving at me through the window, her eyes sparkling with malice.

'Mum! Four thousand pounds! We're rolling in it!' Henry was leaning against me, reading over my shoulder.

'Can I have a new saddle, then?' asked Elizabeth.

'Well, darling. We'll have to see. This is the rates demand I've been expecting.' I picked up the top envelope from the pile of letters waiting for me. 'And here's the bill from the garage. I'm afraid we really ought to keep the money for necessary expenses. But if you could find a good second-hand one . . .'

Elizabeth gave me a despiteful look from kohl-rimmed eyes and allowed the door to bang behind her as she went out.

'How was your lunch?' asked Lissie kindly, as she ironed a minute woollen sock.

'Frightful. Almost not worth four thousand pounds.'

'That bad!' I told Lissie all about it and she was sympathetic. 'What time's this pianist chap coming?'

'In about half an hour, if his train's on time.'

'Maeve's rather keen on him.'

'I wish I could like as many men as she does. I'm beginning to feel unattractively crabby and priggish, constantly spurning aspirants for my body.'

'It's going to be difficult to find someone after a man like Jack.' Lissie's expression grew dreamy. There arose a smell of scorching wool. 'Damn! He was such fun . . . so irresistible.' Then she blushed at her own lack of tact.

I wondered whether to tell her that I had managed to resist him for four years, but thought better of it. It would hurt her terribly to know that she was just the first of countless affairs. It was probably better to have romantic feelings for a man who was dead. Jack could no longer be a threat to her marriage with George.

'Snow's forecast for Kent, did you hear?'

'No. But I thought the sky looked ominous as we drove back from Marshgate. Maeve had better take a shovel when she goes over to Titchmarsh. I wonder if I should lend her my car. Hers is so unreliable.'

'I shouldn't,' said Lissie, with an expressive look. 'You know how things fall to bits in Maeve's hands.'

'Only, I think, because she lets the boys have them.'

'Exactly.'

'That must be Maeve now,' I said, as I heard footsteps in the hall. 'Let's go and meet Mr Wunderbar. What could be Hungarian for wonderful?'

'Who's wonderful?' said Maeve, evidently overhearing

my remark as she stood shivering by the front door. She was wearing a very muddy, hairy blanket, smelling strongly of dog, and holding a handkerchief to her nose, which was bright red.

'Maeve. You don't look very well!' I exclaimed. This was an understatement for, nose apart, all the rest of her, of which there was a great deal exposed, was lavender-coloured with cold.

'I'm not. I woke up this morning with the beginnings of a chill and then, once he'd heard me sneeze, Janòs insisted on having the car windows down all the way back from the station. He says he can't risk getting a cold as he's got another recital next week.'

'That is the truth of it,' said the man standing beside her. I saw at once why Maeve was keen to lay claim to him. He looked like an advertisement for fresh air. His skin was brown and clear, his hair shining and black, his eyes large and dark beneath straight, thick brows. I have always found the description of eyes as 'liquid' faintly disgusting. His eyes were very bright and shining, if not actually fluidal. He looked more like a corsair or a safe-cracker than a pianist. He was of medium height and very well made. His broad shoulders were encased in a leather coat, and a red wool scarf was tucked cosily about his neck. Maeve, no doubt with seductive intent, wore something flimsy and low-cut in white cheesecloth.

I took away the foul-smelling blanket and exchanged it for one of my jerseys. Then I sent Maeve into the kitchen to warm up. Lissie said she would make her some tea.

'Where is the piano?' Janòs seemed unrepentant, despite the reproach implicit in our fussing over Maeve. I took him into the drawing room. 'It is not bad.' He ran his hands over the keys.

'Not bad! I thought it was rather good.' I felt a little annoyed. 'It was only tuned a few weeks ago.'

'Yes, it is in tune.' His English was quite good and his accent, I had to admit, very attractive. 'But the touch is uneven. See!' He played a scale. It sounded all right to me.

'You hear the middle notes there? They are heavy. Slow. I look inside.'

He opened the lid, put his head inside and began fiddling with the dampers. I looked at his well-shaped bottom and legs, encased in jeans and ending in expensive brown boots. I recognised the Artist. Politeness was a fribble, either bourgeois if the artist was left-wing or lower-middle-class if viewed from the right. Nothing must get in the way of the pursuit of Art. I left him to it and went to join Maeve and Lissie in the kitchen.

'You ought to be in bed.' I looked at Maeve, who was shaking with cold.

'I think I'll go there right now. So as to be better for this evening.'

The glance she gave me was unfavourable, if not actually baleful.

'What's the matter?'

'I'm worried about you and Janòs. I thought he definitely warmed to you in the hall.'

'Really? What can it be like when he takes a dislike to someone? What can be the adverse of ignoring someone completely and never once glancing in their direction?'

Maeve gave a chortle of laughter. 'I love you, Miranda. You look so sweet and innocent and you're so sharp, really. Put my bad temper down to pneumonia. I must be better by tonight. I've got the most marvellous dress.'

'Warm, I hope. You know it's supposed to snow?'

'No, is it? Damn! Well, it's crushed velvet, quite warm, I think, except it's cut away at the back almost down to my bottom.'

'You must have a wrap or something.'

'Certainly not. My bottom's my best feature.'

As it happened, the Polite World was denied the opportunity to judge this. Maeve rang me at six o'clock to say that she had a raging fever and was incapable of standing upright.

'Shall I come and look after you, you poor girl?' I asked, feeling sympathetic for she did sound terribly ill.

'No. Florian's here. And all I want to do is sleep,

thanks. You've got to take Janòs to Titchmarsh. He's supposed to be there by eight. How are you getting on with him?'

'Superbly well. I haven't seen him since you left. Jenny took him some tea at four. He told her he didn't want anything to eat. If he's drunk the tea, it was with one hand for the scales haven't stopped. I wonder if the audience is in for a surprise. I haven't heard anything like a tune yet.'

'He told me that he doesn't like practising what he's going to perform on the day. He just wants to get his muscles and brain pepped up. Apparently he had quite a row with the Titchmarsh people over it. He wanted to rehearse yesterday. They wanted to rehearse this afternoon. In the end he said he'd play without a rehearsal and they'd just have to take the tempo from him. There's some ill feeling, I gather.'

'From the two-and-a-half-second glimpse I've had of him I don't imagine he'll care. I'll get him a taxi. I hate driving in snow.'

But Freddy was booked for the evening. I thought he sounded a little cool. The effect of my mother had not yet worn off. I resigned myself to the role of artist's accessory and went upstairs to change. After some thought I selected a long black strapless dress, the severity relieved by a triple-strand pearl necklace and pearl-drop earrings. In the unlikely event that Titchmarsh Hall was heated, I would look *soignée*. Otherwise the short, dark-red velvet coat, which I chose to go over the top, would have to stay on, in which case I would be warm.

When I came downstairs at seven o'clock all was quiet. I went into the drawing room. Janòs lay asleep on the sofa. He had removed his boots. I warmed to him just a little, seeing this unexpected gesture of consideration. 'I'm sorry to wake you,' I said, touching his arm. His eyes sprang open and he looked wide awake at once. 'You should go and change now. We must leave in a quarter of an hour.' He continued to stare at me. His eyes looked quite black in the half-light. 'Maeve is ill so I'm going to drive you there.'

'Good. That is good.' He got up. 'Where are my things?'

'I've put them in your room. I'll show you.'

'Okay. Come on.'

He bounded up the stairs in front of me two at a time. It seemed that he had vaulted out of sleep with the energy of a ten-year-old. He looked around his room and nodded. 'This is good. A bathroom. Very good. I take ten minutes to change.'

He looked much older and more impressive in white tie and tails, and a new seriousness seemed to have come over him. He was frowning and abstracted, and I almost asked him if he had got his music but remembered in time that he was not one of the children and could manage these things for himself. Ivor had nobly offered to cook supper. He was furiously beating egg whites with a balloon whisk in a copper bowl when I went in to say goodbye. Not for him the quick and easy way with the electric beater. A pile of rose-hips on the kitchen table looked very poetic and emblematic of the rural idyll. I hoped the children would be co-operative.

'Goodbye, sweet Eglantine.' Ivor gave me an approving smile. ' "O thou art fairer than the evening air . . ." Don't worry about a thing. I've brought the car round for you and put a rug in the back in case. No snow yet. You'll be all right.'

We drove to Titchmarsh Hall more or less in silence. I suppose Janòs was thinking about the recital. I was concentrating on finding the way. The quickest route on the map was across country on small B roads. It was unusually dark, which made the sign-posts difficult to read. I didn't dare to ask Janòs to look at the map in case I disturbed an important train of thought and ruined the performance.

We reached Titchmarsh Hall at the time specified. The fabric of the building was invisible in the darkness but I remembered it as being a cross between an enormous Italian villa and a prison. It was built of yellow brick with four large towers at each corner like lookout posts. Titchmarsh Hall belonged to John Vavasour, Lady Alice's husband. It was rumoured that her family thought that she had thrown herself away by marrying a man without a title and no income to support his estate. It was public knowledge that they lived by selling off parcels of land and that both their children had turned out extremely wild. I was surprised to see that the car park was already full and deserted by mankind. Maeve is always unreliable with times and dates. I knocked gently on the front door. When there was no answer, I redoubled my knocking. The door opened.

'Shh! The concert's begun,' said a man in evening dress with an expression of the strongest vexation. He had a nose larger and more hooked than the Iron Duke's and a pointed bald head, which emerged like a mountain peak from a fringe of grey, cloud-like curls. A label on his lapel proclaimed him to be Major Bernard Kitterbell. 'Do you have tickets? We're dreadfully oversubscribed this evening. Everyone's braved the cold to hear this new Hungarian pianist, who's supposed to be so amazing, and the bloody little swine hasn't turned up. It's positively the last time I have anything to with this wretched festival. I'm going to have to announce in a minute that he isn't here and –'

'Hold on, hold on,' I interrupted. 'Here is the bloody little swine.'

I introduced them. Major Kitterbell made some attempt to repair things with Janòs while I looked about. The hall was very large and very cold, though there was a powerful and unpleasant smell of burning dust, intimating that the central heating had been turned on specially for the occasion. A giant Victorian refectory table with bulbous imitation-Tudor legs bore a hideous bowl of Benares brass filled with faded dried flowers, and there were two huge terracotta jars filled with bent pampas grass. A stuffed bear, its eyes and teeth long ago fallen out, did service as a hat-stand.

'Oh, God! It is terrible! This is not music!' Janòs put his

hands to his ears to defend them against the strains that reached us from the ballroom.

'It may not be quite up to your standards, Mr Decksie, but I can assure you for an amateur string quartet they have a very high local reputation –'

'Décsi. My name is Janòs Décsi. You pronounce it "Ya-nosh Day-chee".'

'Oh, I see. Daychee. All right. Well, as I was saying, we at Titchmarsh are very proud . . .'

But he was wasting his breath. Janòs had walked away. To the right of the hall was the conservatory, full of giant palms and ferns. Janòs paused to light a cigarette and then strolled out of sight among the pteridophyta.

'Well, I must say –!'

Major Kitterbell evidently thought better of giving way to temper, merely shooting me an angry glance before hurrying back into the ballroom. I tiptoed in after him and found an empty chair on the back row. The musicians were getting to the end of a spirited version of Borodin's second string quartet, which the audience seemed to be enjoying, swaying, tapping and humming along with the tune and no doubt wishing they were in a warm cinema with comfortable seats, watching *Kismet*. It was not a brilliant performance, in fact there were bars that were unrecognisable, but they kept going and ended together on the same beat with a flourish. Major Kitterbell walked up to the platform, while they were bowing their thanks for tumultuous applause.

'There will be a short interval, ladies and gentlemen, before the next item in our concert when Mr Jaynoss Dexy will play Rachmaninoff's third piano concerto.'

The audience made polite expectant noises and then rushed from their seats to the bar, which was set up on long tables in the drawing room. I joined the queue for wine cup, very much not my favourite drink but I felt I needed something to cheer me. The air was filled with flying whiskers shed from ancient fur stoles and tippets.

It struck me, not for the first time since Jack's death, that I had not fully appreciated the general usefulness of husbands. Besides all the obvious things, like fetching drinks and calling taxi-cabs in the rain, they establish one's reputation. I seemed to be the only unaccompanied woman in the audience, as far as I could tell, and I became aware that people, particularly the men, were staring at me. I felt the beginnings of self-consciousness. In a moment of optimism I had slipped off my coat. Now I had the sensation of being very naked about the shoulders and bosom. I caught the eye of a man with long ginger sideburns and a moustache. I looked away quickly but not before seeing that he had begun to push through the crowd towards me, twirling the end of his whiskers in a predatory way. In front of me in the queue I recognised the second violinist from the quartet that had just finished playing. He looked old and safe. I congratulated him on his performance.

'Actually I got a bit lost half-way through but, thank God, we recapitulated. I'm so glad you enjoyed it. Every year I think it'll be the last time I play – getting too old, you know – but they always persuade me.'

He certainly did look ancient. His dinner jacket was going green with age and he looked sadly indigent. I asked my new-found friend how long he had been playing the violin, and he told me about his boyhood longings to be a professional. His father had considered this a worthless ambition and instead he had become a farmer. 'Not a good one, though, my dear. Too vague. Heart not in it. Always wanted to do something creative, don't you know?'

I certainly did. I explained that much of my youth had been blighted by being spent with those of a creative leaning. The old man was delighted by this and laughed so much at everything I said that I felt really encouraged. I was just thinking how charming and perceptive he was when Lady Alice Vavasour came in, parting the crowd as though her heavily freckled pigeon chest were the prow of a majestic ship. Her pale, protuberant eyes stared through her guests. Her tones were patrician. 'Too potent! We shall all be on the floor before the evening is over!' She poured a large bottle of lemonade into the bowl containing the wine cup and left, without a glance at anyone, steaming her way through the small craft that bobbed against her bows.

'I don't think I'll bother to have any more,' I said gloomily. 'It tasted like Corona the first time round. A gnat couldn't get tight on it. I notice we weren't favoured by gracious smiles or words of greeting.'

'It was a bit offhand, wasn't it?' said the old man, a twinkle of cordiality in his eye. 'I think it's bred in people, that kind of careless sovereignty. She's good at heart. If you were in need of help or had some ghastly illness, you'd see the best side of her.'

'That seems too high a price, even for so great a privilege.' The old man seemed to enjoy this feeble little joke enormously. 'Anyway,' I became bolder, encouraged by his admiration, 'isn't that more a case of patronage rather than good-heartedness? I don't see why perfectly hale people like me who aren't specially in need of kindness shouldn't be favoured with some ordinary token of acknowledgement.'

'You're right, my dear. But I doubt if it's quite the case of arrogance that you think. Rather more a question of manners of the old school. It probably would not occur to her that her guests might be offended. She sees herself, no doubt, as an institution, a member of the *ancien régime*, entitled to certain privileges in return for undoubted responsibilities.'

'Perhaps it's as well that someone who has the looks and charm of a floating battery is insensitive to the opinions of other people,' I exclaimed, unable to hide my indignation. My companion threw back his head with such roars of laughter that everyone around looked at us inquiringly, hoping to share the joke. I felt a little repentant. It does not do to be catty, except with one's intimates. 'That was unkind of me. I expect she has all sorts of difficulties we know nothing about. And it can't be much fun to have to live in a house that's much too big with dwindling servants and expanding bills. The house smells like a cheese and the carpets have the texture of fudge.'

My companion was about to say something when we were interrupted.

'Miranda, darling! How dreadfully I've missed you! You've been hiding yourself away. Confess!' A woman I hardly knew flung her arms around me, enveloping me in a cloud of Arpège. Her eyes were bright with curiosity. I knew she wanted to hear about Jack. I wasn't at all sorry to see Major Kitterbell flapping his arms in the doorway.

'Take your seats, ladies and gentlemen, please! The second half is about to begin.'

We applauded as the East Kent Philharmonic took their places. The leader came in and they tuned up. There was a long pause. Some of the audience started to fidget and whisper to each other. I felt nervous. Where was Janòs? I turned my head anxiously and saw him stalking along the gangway between the rows of seats. A trickle of polite applause began, which grew louder as the conductor took his stand on the rostrum.

Janòs spent at least a minute adjusting the stool and half a minute more flexing his fingers, flicking out his tails, pulling at his collar and checking his cuffs. He glared at the audience and then stared thoughtfully at the keys. I began to have a terrible fear that he had forgotten the notes of the first bar. This was quite as bad as watching my children play in the school concert. Finally, when the tension in the audience had become almost intolerable, he nodded to the conductor, threw back his head in a gesture that I already recognised as characteristic and began to play.

CHAPTER 10

From the very first notes the audience was in a state bordering on infatuation. The least musical person in the room must have been enslaved by the passion and probity of the performance. Virtuosi are conspicuously romantic. Janòs looked so handsome, so severe and so unreachable that I was convinced that every woman in the room was enjoying some delicious figment of fancy about him, more or less erotic according to nature. What the men were thinking, I couldn't imagine. Those who were not longing for the music to end so that they could get home to dog, pipe, and whisky *may* have been intellectually and emotionally engaged with the music.

Shakespeare said there was no one so 'stockish, hard and full of rage but music for the time does change his nature'. The cathartic properties of music are celebrated but none the less I was taken by surprise. Despite the chill in the ballroom my skin began to burn.

Jack had always derided Rachmaninoff's music on the grounds that it was noisy and theatrical. Janòs gave the piece an eloquence that lifted it far above sensationalism. The cadenza of the first movement was moving to the point of being spiritually agonising. The lovely Russian melody of the *adagio* made me shiver with unidentifiable longing. The restlessness of the third movement was so impassioned that it seemed impossible that he could remain so coolly concentrated. From time to time he threw back his head to indicate the re-entry of the orchestra. He made no movement that was not essential to the performance. The intense beauty of the brilliant and sonorous coda broke down my thoughts until every part of my mind was given to the music. I sat absolutely still, as though in moving I might break the spell.

At the end there was a moment of silence. Then the audience sprang to their feet and began to applaud. Some of the less inhibited shouted, 'Bravo.' The orchestra rose spontaneously and joined in the frenzy of clapping. Janòs stood, bowed to left and right, and permitted a small smile to appear momentarily on his face, which had remained withdrawn and stern. Then he shook hands with the conductor and the leader of the orchestra and strolled from the platform. I experienced a complete discontinuity of time before the concert and after it.

'Ladies and gentlemen,' Major Kitterbell was standing up before us, waving his programme for silence, 'after that superb rendition of Rachmaninoff I know we all want to thank Mr Janice Deckers for being here tonight and making this undoubtedly the best concert of the season.' There were some 'hear, hear's and another storm of clapping. 'We will now have the customary closing speech from our host, to whom we are, as usual, enormously grateful, and then you are advised to make your way home as quickly as possible as it has begun to snow. Ladies and gentlemen, our chairman, Mr John Vavasour.'

There was a burst of good-natured applause as, to my horror, the old man with whom I had exchanged such pleasurable animadversions on Lady Alice in the interval stepped up on to the stage.

'My dear fellow members of the Titchmarsh Music Society and honoured guests, I must be very brief as I'm sure you are all anxious about getting home. I'd just like to thank the orchestra for their spirited playing,' (more 'hear, hear's) 'and, of course, Mr Janòs Décsi who, for some forty minutes or so, transformed the world for me. I'm an old man, and I've heard a great deal of music in my time, but I can say with truth that I've never heard anything to top it.' (More vigorous clapping.) 'Also I must thank my wife for the very large part she has played in the organisation of the event.'

Lady Alice bowed her head in a queenly manner and people clapped again, though with less enthusiasm. I shuddered at the awfulness of my blunder. My self-esteem must be shockingly low to descend to spiteful remarks about some harmless woman I hardly knew. I felt thoroughly ashamed.

As I shuffled with the other guests towards the back of the ballroom a dark, good-looking man said, 'Good evening, Mrs Stowe.' He was lost in the crowd before I could identify him.

Janòs stood, with his hands in his pockets, by the front door. Major Kitterbell was talking to him, but as soon as

Janòs saw me, he abandoned the Major in mid-sentence, walked towards me and gripped my arm. 'Let's go. I'm hungry. Have you something I can eat in your house?'

'Lots of things. If we can get there. I'm worried about the weather. Goodnight.'

Major Kitterbell's last words of effusive oblation were lost as Janòs hurried me down the steps. The snow fell fast in sweeping circles as the wind sidled through the bushes, which stood in sullen masses around the house. Already the ground beneath our feet was padded with slippery flakes.

'Come. Let's run.' Janòs took my hand.

The leather soles of my shoes could find no purchase, and I seemed to be half skating, half flying. As I struggled to find the keys, snow gathered in the upturned collar of my coat and slid down my neck. I was shivering so much that I could barely turn the key in the ignition. The roar of the engine and the beam of the headlights was reassuring.

'Good. This is very good.' Janòs sighed with satisfaction, undid his scarf and coat and hurled them on to the back seat.

'Good, that the car's started, yes. But look at the weather!'

The windscreen wipers screeched in protest as ledges of snow continually built up on the blades. We followed other cars in procession down the drive and turned left with half of them at the junction with the main road.

'Don't worry,' said Janòs, with tremendous and, as far as I could see, quite unfounded confidence, leaning forward to wipe the inside of the windscreen with his hand. 'There is no hurry. We have all of the night in front of us.'

'And I shall be very disappointed if I don't spend nearly all of it in deep sleep in my own bed.'

'You are an anxious person, no? Full of trepidations?'

I was too busy staring ahead, trying to focus my eyes on whatever external road markers might be discernible, to take issue with this disparaging suggestion. The snow was driving horizontally into the windscreen, and every few seconds I found my mind drifting to watch the pattern of white flecks on the blackness. I began to see configurations in the dots, like paintings by Seurat or Signac. Some orange lights at a roundabout, usually a vexatious sight, were a welcome relief, showing me the whitening verges and the snow-laden branches of the woods on either side. Then we turned off into a B road and I was left with the visual acuity of a mole. The mesmerising effect of the blowing flakes grew much worse.

'This is cosy,' said Janòs, with every appearance of delight.

'I'm glad you're enjoying it.' I decided to drop the sarcasm for a moment. 'You played wonderfully. I shall never, ever forget it!'

'Always after a performance I am intoxicate. The thing is done and it has been done well. Sometimes it is better than others. That is of course. Tonight was not the best but it was good. You are hot, with this thing on?' He had his hand on the switch of the heater.

'No. There is every possibility that my blood is becoming gelid in my veins. Getting home is dependent on my heart being able to carry on pumping, so if you'll leave the heater on and the windows shut we may have a chance.'

'You think badly of me because I make Maeve drive with fresh air?'

'You may have given her double pneumonia.'

'I hope not. But let me explain. I do not want, my dear Mrs Stowe, that you and I shall start out bad friends. You see, there are many, many good pianists. And few possibilities for playings. I am good, yes. I lie if I do not say that. But there are ten, maybe twenty, even thirty good pianists in the world, all wanting the same little platform. How can I rise above them? By putting everything that I have into my work. But they also, these twenty, thirty others, are saying the same thing. So I have to put more, I have to go further than I imagine I can go. You see? Nothing must stand in the path. I stop for one second and someone else has taken my seat. If I do not play I am nothing. Worse than nothing. I am a failure. If I play with Maeve's cold, my playing is maybe a small bit less good, I am finished.'

'Goodness! Can it be worth so much effort?'

'For me, yes. For those who fall away, who becomes teachers, it is evidently not worth. When I was a boy, in Hungary, I told myself that if I survive I will fight to be good... to be great... to be the best. I make my pact – you say pact? – with God or the devil. Perhaps with both.'

'I suppose things were very bad, then?' I asked, feeling reluctantly sympathetic despite all my old reservations on the subject of artistic monomania. 'I'm afraid I don't know much modern history. The Hungarian uprising was... um... nineteen fifty-six, wasn't it?'

'Things was bad, yes. Very bad. In nineteen fifty-six I was fifteen.' I did a rapid mental calculation. That meant he was thirty-three, six years younger than me. 'I was already a musician. But I had to take a gun in my hands and kill. My brother was ten years old and he, too, went on to the streets to fight. Two hundred thousand Hungarians escaped over the border into Austria and I with them. I was wounded in the shoulder. Friends took care of me. I never saw my family again. My father was shot in January nineteen fifty-seven after the Soviet suppression of the so-called counter-revolution. My mother die a year after that.'

'Oh dear, how very sad. I'm so sorry.' I had heard a little catch of breath as he mentioned his brother so I didn't dare to ask his fate.

'Sad, yes. Now it is sad. At the time it was... *rémisztö*... terrifying, you might say. We had nothing to eat. We drank from filthy puddles. We ate grass, mud, rats, cats. My shoulder was poisoned. I was mad with fever for a while. I give up hope.'

I was silent for a while, trying to imagine it. He had been younger than James then.

'I don't suppose one can ever get over anything like that,' I said at last, 'but I hope you can sometimes find... peace of mind.'

As I said this a car loomed suddenly up in the pointillist windscreen. I jerked the wheel over to the left and we sketched an elegant parabola on the road. I pulled the wheel again and we were going forwards once more. After a short pause brought about by fright we both started to laugh.

'Yes, I have peace of mind but not when you drive like that!'

'I'm so sorry. My nerves are hopelessly on edge.'

'Oh, you need not apologise. You are so good to drive me.' He paused for a moment and then put a hand on my arm. 'And you, too, Mrs Stowe, you have your sorrows. I ask Maeve about you and she tells me that your husband is dead, very, very recent. I am sorry for that. Very sorry.'

'Yes. Thank you. Do call me Miranda.'

I didn't say any more. He left his hand resting on my arm and I felt the warmth of it gradually penetrate the sleeve of my coat. It was comforting. I was very tired. The concentration required was exhausting. I found myself yawning until my eyes watered. We were cut off from the world in our warm, dark cave . . . I pulled my thoughts together. I had very nearly fallen asleep.

'Not much further now, thank heaven,' I said at last. 'Only two miles from here and then we'll be able to have something to eat and get to bed. I can't wait to –'

Whatever I had been going to say was lost in an intake of breath that became a scream as we left the road and plunged, bonnet down, into a drift.

'Are you all right?' I said, as soon as my heart stopped bursting in my throat and I could speak.

'Yes. Okay. You?'

'Just a little shocked. I've banged my knee.'

'A little adventure, eh? Well, Mrs Stowe, what is to do now?'

I put the car into reverse and pressed the accelerator. There were sinister noises from the spinning wheels, the car groaned and then lurched another foot deeper into the ditch.

'I don't suppose anyone will come along now.' I

switched on the interior light and looked at my watch 'Twenty minutes to twelve. This is a quiet road at the best of times. As far as I remember there's no telephone box anywhere nearby. There's no help for it, I'm afraid.'

'You mean we must go out and walk? Ah, well. Two miles, you say? That will not take long.'

I turned off the engine, removed the keys from the ignition and took the torch from the glove compartment. Thank goodness Ivor had put in the rug.

'I hope you'll be all right with just your coat.'

'Certainly. I shall be warm as pie.'

'Toast, I expect you mean.'

'No. Pie. Pies are warm.'

'Well, let's not argue.'

I opened the door and put out an experimental foot. My leg disappeared up to the knee in snow.

'We'd better get going. This isn't going to be pleasant.'

We stumbled out of the ditch and into the road. It was, mercifully, only two or three inches deep in snow. I mentally kissed goodbye to my black grosgrain evening shoes, of which I was very fond. The beam of the torch was a pallid yellow against penumbrous hues of grey. The wind soughed in the trees, which were invisible except as an opaque black presence, and the snow fell lightly and unceasingly. At first I was warm with the rug about my head and shoulders. Janòs set a brisk pace and soon took the torch from me so that I could tuck my hands inside my sleeves. Neither of us had gloves and our hands were the first to suffer.

'You know Captain Scott? Of Antarctica?' I asked.

'No.'

'He wanted to walk to the South Pole. In about nineteen ten.'

'What for?'

'To be the first there. There was a Norwegian going, too, a man called Amundsen, and it came to be something of a race.'

'A race, huh? You English are great colonisers.'

'It was wanting to be first, I think.'

'Ah, well. We are all mad in degrees.'

'There's an account of their journey called *The Worst Journey in the World*, written by one of the men who went on the expedition. Of course, winter in the Antarctic is perpetual night and a hundred degrees of frost is quite usual. Their sweat froze so that their clothes were as stiff as boards and they were stuck in bending positions, pulling the sledges. Their fingers were covered in blisters and the liquid in them froze, too, so that their hands were like bunches of marbles. It took an hour to work their way into their sleeping bags. Their teeth froze and split to pieces. Their toenails came off.'

'And you think all this will happen to us tonight?' Janòs seemed to think this very funny.

'Actually, my feet are already cold enough for frostbite. I can't feel them any more. Did you have stilts as a child? I did and it feels like walking on them.'

'I have been in Russia. There you must constantly rub your nose with snow to stop frostbite. Here is nothing. A little cool, perhaps. Did they get there first?'

'Who? Oh, Scott. No, Amundsēn got there first because he used dogs to pull the sledges. Scott thought it would be unfair on dogs so he had some special motorised sledges made. But they weren't any good, they broke down all the time.'

'Oh, my! You English are . . . crazy!'

'I don't think so. I think it was right.' I forgot the transcendent playing and became indignant as he continued to laugh. There was nothing of the maestro about him now. 'They knew that the conditions would be appalling. It's one thing to decide to inflict them on yourself. Quite another to impose them on other creatures.'

'Yes. All right. Don't be angry.'

'Actually, they did take some ponies,' I admitted. 'I can't quite see what the difference was. And they shot them at the foot of a glacier when the ponies couldn't go any further. I always hated that bit as a child. It seems the *ne plus ultra* of ingratitude.'

'So these men endure all this to find they have been – what is the expression? – popped at the post?'

'Pipped. Worse than that. They all five died.'

Janòs threw his hands into the air and let out a great sigh, either from regret at this sad end or from astonishment at human folly. He continued to walk steadily, his head up and his shoulders back as though strolling on a mild summer day. I wanted to pause and catch my breath but I knew the intense cold would be worse the minute I stood still so I kicked off my beautiful and now ruined shoes and kept going, trying not to think about my feet. I pulled the rug over my mouth, as my throat hurt with breathing in the snow, and for a while we walked in silence. I stopped thinking about Scott and the Antarctic and imagined being a soldier in Napoleon's army, retreating from Moscow across thousands of miles of birch-forested, sub-zero steppe.

'Ah! It has stopped snowing,' said Janòs, taking his hand from his pocket to put his arm about my shoulder. 'See, how beautiful. There is the moon.' He was right. It was astonishingly beautiful. For a moment as the moonlight poured down through a gap in the clouds, the trees and the road became an intaglio of bone-white, slate and silver. No owls hooted, no foxes barked, even the wind had lowered its sighs to a soft breathing. 'Ravishing. I am ravished.' He was looking down at me as he said it. Embarrassed, I turned my head away to escape the keen glance of his dark eyes. 'It is much further? You are very cold, poor Mrs Stowe?'

I shook my head. To speak would have meant removing the rug from my nose and chin. We would soon be at the bottom of the drive. Now I was hardly conscious of walking. I heard the grinding of snow beneath our feet, felt the weight of my clothing and the moist scratchiness of the rug over my face. As we turned into the drive I closed my eyes and winced as they smarted and stung. I kept them closed, guided by Janòs's arm as we walked up to the house, stumbling, sliding, thoughts dream-like.

'Ha! The ordeal is finished. Here is the house,' said Janòs.

The light from the hall windows cast a gleam over the soft white mounds of the parterre. Janòs pushed open the front door. Jasper ran up to me, whining with pleasure, his claws scraping on the flags. Otherwise the house was quiet. On the table in the hall was a bottle of whisky, a Thermos flask, mugs, glasses and a plate covered with a napkin.

'Sandwiches! Oh, wonderful! I must eat. And you must eat too. Sit here.'

Janòs pushed me down on to the stairs and the next thing I knew he was holding a mug of scalding coffee to my mouth. As I sipped it, I could feel it burning my throat and chest.

'Good. Now eat.'

It was an effort to chew. My face hurt as I moved the muscles in my cheeks. Janòs had eaten four sandwiches before I had finished my first. I think they were egg and watercress. I gave the rest of my sandwich to Jasper and then rested my hand on his smooth, warm head. The hall light burned amber and wavering through the whisky in Janòs's glass. My eyelids drooped.

'Come. You must go to bed.'

Getting upstairs was the most exhausting thing I ever remembered doing in my life. I was too weak to straighten my legs properly.

'Which room is yours?'

'That one.'

Janòs opened the door, switched on the light and lifted me on to the bed. I lay with my eyes closed, vaguely aware of the sound of a match striking and, very soon after, the spitting of twigs and kindling. I was seized by a painful fit of shivering.

'Come on. Drink more coffee.'

It had the oddest taste. Perhaps my taste-buds had frostbite.

'There. I turn off the lamp. We have only firelight now. Soon you will feel the warmth. I am going to take off your clothes but you must help me. No, don't be silly, this is not a time for modest. You might become ill if you do not get warm.'

I did try to help but my fingers were useless. There was a tearing sound as he pulled off my dress but I didn't much care. Then I was pushed beneath blankets and the eiderdown. I opened my eyes again and saw Janòs sitting at the foot of the bed chafing my feet. It was perfect agony as they began to regain some feeling. Then his hands were rubbing my back. Suddenly I was aware that he was taking off his clothes.

'What are you doing? This really isn't a good idea.'

'I will warm you with the heat of my body and finish the sandwiches at the same time. I hope you will not object to a few crumbs. I am careful but, you know, it cannot be avoided.'

He got into bed. His body gave out a delicious warmth and I lacked the resolution to move away.

'Ah, that is better!'

He put one arm beneath my shoulders and I rested my head on his chest while he continued to eat. I glanced up and he smiled down at me, his eyes black and full of amusement as he munched the last of the sandwiches with an expression of satisfaction.

'I think I just finish the whisky.'

'Should you?' I murmured. 'There was at least half a bottle.'

'You English... always so proper even when dying of cold. You drank a third yourself. I put it in your coffee.'

That explained the odd taste and the smouldering sensation I had now in my stomach. I never drank whisky as a rule, hating the taste.

'Better now?'

'Much better. Still a little shivery but all right. Very comfortable.'

'I have the coffee if you don't want more.'

I shook my head and closed my eyes. I was not so drunk or so tired that I didn't know that I was lying naked in bed with a man, also naked, whom I had met for the first time that afternoon. But no doubt alcohol and exhaustion had something to do with finding myself in such a situation. I drifted into a delicious dream.

I was dancing, almost floating, to delightful music. There was some restraint on my neck and it was impossible to turn up my face to see who my partner was. I could see only his dress shirt and the beautiful black pearl studs he wore. Then I noticed that instead of a dinner jacket he was wearing a grey military coat, coarse and mud-stained. With a dreamer's prescience I was unsurprised to find myself at the battle of Borodino. To the left I recognised the Shevardino Redoubt. Powder-smoke hung in the air like a bitter cloud. I fought for breath as my partner held me tighter. There was tremendous noise and turmoil, cannon boomed continually. The grip round my waist was killing me now. I could scarcely breathe. A fusillade of muskets crackled in my ears. A rust-red dot appeared on my opponent's chest and spread rapidly as I stared at it with fascination. The pressure relaxed on my chest. I looked up and saw Jack's white, dead face.

'What's the time?' I muttered, opening my eyes. My neck, which had been resting on Janòs's arm, was stiff. It must have been his heartbeats that had made me dream of battles. My own heart was pounding.

'Two o'clock. I heard a chiming just now.'

'That's the coach-house clock.'

'Does it have coaches in it?'

'No. Cars. I'd look a little silly driving about in a landau, don't you think? Besides, it would take so long to get anywhere.'

'You at least should say "motor car", you know. I am a student of England's great culture. When I was a boy I read everything in English I could find. My professor had many books by a writer called Gertrude Rince. You have heard of her?' I shook my head. 'All her people, dukes and countesses, live very happily in big houses and play billiards every night with brandy and soda. They have servants and much money and great possessions. They are unlucky in their loves but they forget it all in a splendid game of tennis or a dinner of ten courses. The dukes are wicked but there is usually an interesting secretary, an amusing bishop and an adorable butler.' I began to entertain the deepest respect for Miss Rince's powers of imagination. 'I love these books. What is my disappointment you can imagine when I land at the Heathrow Airport as a boy of nineteen and see instead of beautiful lawns and lakes and peacocks a terrible *hiba* of dullness, horrible houses and streets and traffic.'

'It must have been a shock.' I smiled. The nightmare was beginning to recede. 'But you didn't expect us all to live like that?'

'Yes. In these books even the beautiful but unworthy girl who falls in love with the handsome and devastating – devastating is the word? – young master of the great house, she live in a charming village bungalow –'

'Cottage, I think you mean.'

'Yes, that is right, cottage, with kittens and those flowers, hillyhocks. You laugh. That is good. You are especially beautiful when you laugh.'

'Hollyhocks. The flowers are called hollyhocks.'

'And that is not such a funny word? It seems to me quite as ridiculous.'

'I'm sorry you're disappointed with England.'

'Ah, well, that was fourteen years ago. Since then I have been five times to England and I have met lords and ladies and been to their great houses. But they look like other people, often ugly and not well dressed, and they are ignorant like dogs. A romance with them is not possible. In my books they all know poetry and music and all are handsome. Oh, that Lady Alice, so cold and depressing! She say to me afterwards, "Very nice, Mr Desky." Nice! The woman is a fool besides looking like the leg of a chair. You English women are too thin. You yourself, Mrs Stowe, are a little bit thin. You have been too sad to eat after the death of your husband?' He ran his hand down my body and let it rest on my hip.

'Shouldn't you be going to your own room now? I'm sure you must need some sleep.'

'How can I think of sleeping when I lie naked with a wonderful girl?'

'Na-ked. It has two syllables.'

'Besides, I never sleep after a concert. I am too – how you say? Charged up? Now, if you permit, I am going to make love to you. I thought you should have a little sleep and get warm first. I wait in patience but now you feel delightful.'

'Just a minute!' I sat up in bed and looked round for my nightdress. 'I think you're taking too much for granted.'

'You don't find me attractive?'

'Yes. No. It isn't that. I don't know you.'

'But what do you want? We have talked very much. Also, I feel that we have much, much more to say. That is perhaps more important. You have slept so charmingly in my arms. You want that I court you for many months as in the stories? Well, if I must I will, but it is a shame.'

'I don't want to be made love to as a matter of convenience. Just because you have a romantic dream about English women and you can't get to sleep after a concert. It has to be more . . . particular.'

'Ah, I see. You are very wrong. I do not want to make love to you from convenience. If I lie in Lady Alice's bed at this moment I would wish her goodnight politely and hope very much that she will not steal all the blankets.'

I laughed despite myself. 'But just the fact that you don't find me repellent isn't enough.'

'For a clever girl you are being really very stupid. The first moment I saw you I say to myself, this girl is beautiful. I desire her. I want more than anything to make love to her.'

'You said all that in the quarter of a second you allotted me before getting to grips with the piano? You must be a fast thinker.'

'I say more than that, you sarcastic woman, but it would not be proper to tell you all that I thought. Now that I know you I feel more than this. It is not only physical desire. Though that is strong. Terribly strong, as the devastating hero says. It is something else. Though our lives, our experience, are so different yet I am in sympathy with you. You feel that?' He looked at me gravely.

I did like him. And, of course, the truth was that, besides being still in the grips of an almost embarrassing *schwärm* about his playing, I thought he was probably the most attractive man I had ever met. 'It's just not that simple...' I began. 'There are the children, and there's Maeve.'

'The children are asleep. Forgive me, I do not see what they have to do with it. You generally ask them before you make love with a man?'

'No, of course not.'

'And what has Maeve to do with this?'

'Well...' This was certainly awkward. It would be a betrayal of friendship to explain that she had planned to have Janòs for herself. 'I think she might feel that you are *her* friend and...'

Janòs continued to look at me, his eyebrows raised in inquiry. 'It is because you miss your husband? You are afraid to be sad that it is not he? That I can understand, poor girl.'

I thought it was exemplary to take this attitude. Most men, I imagine, would be piqued at the idea. 'No. It honestly isn't that. I can't explain –'

'I can. You think too much about everything. Because you have been hurt you are afraid. You do not want to love again and be vulnerable.'

As Janòs said this I felt a pain so violent that my eyes started with tears. He had, more than he could possibly know, gone straight to the heart of the thing. He bent his head and kissed my eyelids.

'Don't cry, my dear Mrs Stowe, there is no need. You will see.'

He kissed me again, this time on the mouth. Tears began to fall in earnest. I was furious with myself. Now was not the time. Of course it was that damn music that had unlocked dangerous emotions.

'Yes, cry. You need to cry. My poor, beautiful girl.'

He kissed me again. I responded. I couldn't help myself, I found I had absolutely no power of resistance. Jack had been my first and only lover. I had assumed that he was good at making love because I had enjoyed it and because so many other women had risked so much to take him to their beds. But making love with Janòs was as different as shouting and singing. When making love, Jack remained, on some level, remote, playing the game his way and calling the shots. Sometimes I had the impression that I was an engine being expertly stripped down.

I was astonished by the tenderness and generosity of Janòs. The intensity of his playing was recognisable in his love-making. He talked to me, first in English and then, as we became increasingly sick with desire, in Hungarian. I forgot the pain in my feet, that we were strangers, that I might have to pay for this rapture. Best of all, I forgot Jack.

Some time afterwards he sighed and rested his head on my outstretched arm. 'Magnificent! Thank you, my dear, my darling Miranda. I tell you the truth now. I never make love so well with a woman before.'

'It was . . . oh, heaven!'

'Yes? I knew that you enjoy a little. That, one can always tell. So it was, in the end, Mr *Csodálatos*? Mr Wonderful? Ah, it is good to hear you laugh!'

CHAPTER 11

Day filled my bedroom with dazzling light. As consciousness returned I felt my spirits soar. It must be wrong to feel this happy. I put out my hand to touch Janòs.

'Mum?' said Elizabeth's voice from the doorway.

I sat up and looked around wildly. I was alone in my bed.

'What's the matter?' Elizabeth gave me a hard stare from a mandarin-white face. 'You look frightened.'

'Nothing, darling. I was half asleep. Goodness, how brilliant the light is! All that lovely snow. What have you got on your face?'

'It's called Porcelain Lily. Aunt Nancy left it behind in the bathroom. It's a very posh jar.'

'I hope it isn't bad for your skin.'

'You always think things are bad for me,' said Elizabeth impatiently. 'It's very undermining of my self-confidence. If I go out, you think I'm going to be run over by a bus, thrown off by Puck or slip down between the train and the platform. If I stay in, I'm going to choke on a pen top or fall on the fire or accidentally drink a bottle of bleach. It's a wonder I'm still here and not covered with scar tissue.'

'Sorry, darling. I expect I *am* over-protective. It's because I love you.'

Elizabeth screwed up her face into an expression of disgust. 'I'd rather you loved me a bit less, frankly, and let me have a bit more freedom. Marlene's mother says Marlene's got more sense than her and Marlene's dad put together. She lets Marlene do whatever she wants.'

'Than *she* and Marlene's dad, darling. Well, from what little I know of Marlene's parents I should think that's quite possible.' I repressed a grimace as I thought of Mr and Mrs Cooper who, if village gossip was to be believed, had set the house on fire several times by smoking in bed and who had been seen hitting each other on many Saturday nights outside the Magpie and Stump. 'I don't see why we should run our lives according to the dictates of the Coopers.'

'You're the most terrible snob, Mum. I suppose I'll be the only girl in the class who isn't allowed to go to the inter-schools hockey match.'

'Well, if you really want to go... When is it?' It sounded harmless, though painfully dull, I thought. Probably I *was* rather too strict with the children. Jack had often accused me of excessive anxiety on their behalf.

And now was not the time to quarrel with Elizabeth. It was terribly important that the children should feel able to confide in me.

'Friday, seven o'clock until ten.'

'That's a very strange time to have it. Won't it be too dark to see the ball?'

Elizabeth sighed again. 'The pitches are flood-lit, ac-tu-ally.' She drawled the last word in a way that made me long to box her ears, though I had never believed in smacking the children and hadn't allowed Jack to, either. 'Good. I'll put my name down, then.' She disappeared and then pushed open the door again. 'By the way, the pianist is downstairs having breakfast. He's really dishy, isn't he? I noticed that Jenny's put on that dress you gave her and is virtually doing pirouettes round the kitchen.'

As the door slammed I realised that the entire conversation had been a manoeuvre to get permission for the hockey match. Ought I to ring Miss Weston-Waite to check? Goodness, how suspicious I was! Perhaps Elizabeth was right and I *was* undermining her confidence. I heard the coach-house clock strike nine times. I pulled on a dressing gown, ran downstairs and telephoned the local garage. They said they would go at once to tow my car out of the ditch. Then I hurried to Rose's room. She was sitting waiting patiently for me. I was glad to see that Jenny had remembered to bring her some tea.

'So sorry, darling. Fearfully late night. The car ran into a ditch and we had to walk the last bit.'

I picked up her woollen spencer and petticoat.

'The exercise seems to have done you a lot of good.' Rose's eyes scanned my face. 'I haven't seen you look like that for a very long time.'

'It was a marvellous concert.'

'Must have been.'

There was a silence as I struggled with Rose's lisle stockings.

'I hope you'll not do anything rash, my girl.'

I laughed. 'I don't know what you're thinking, Rose, but you needn't worry.'

'I wondered yesterday when I met him. I thought he was too handsome for anyone's good.'

As Rose and I entered the kitchen Janòs, who was sitting at the table next to Henry, stood up politely. Rose gave him a cool nod. I bent to stroke Jasper. I wanted a few seconds to school my face into an expression of indifference. When at last I lifted up my head he was looking at me and immediately my treacherous knees felt like broken flower-stalks. I permitted myself a decorous smile. Rose made a sound between a sigh and a groan.

Jenny put a plate of sausages, bacon and eggs in front of Janòs with a strange swooping movement that was almost a curtsy. He thanked her with a smile and she dropped the cloth she was holding.

'Let me pour you some toast,' I said, picking up the coffee pot.

'Mum!' Henry was giggling. 'You're in a funny mood this morning. And you don't usually wear a skirt on Sundays unless someone's coming to lunch. Why've you put lipstick on?'

The difficulties of conducting any kind of liaison – I hesitated to call it a love affair, just in case I was taking too much for granted – in a large household were brought decidedly home to me. Elizabeth came in and sat down opposite Janòs. He stood up and gave her a little bow. I could see she was rather stirred by this. Her eyes returned constantly to his face as she leaned back in her chair, chewing toast and marmalade. I hoped this fierce scrutiny from beneath heavily mascaraed lashes would not put him off his breakfast.

'Have I really got to go back to school tonight, Mum?' asked Henry plaintively. He seemed the only one of us impervious to the fascination of Janòs.

'Well, sweetheart, you've missed so much already. Don't you think you might?'

'Of course he can,' said Elizabeth. 'James and I have been back weeks. Why's Henry got to be different?'

'You're just at a silly old day school. And James is almost grown-up,' said Henry, before I could speak.

'Anyway, I've got a specially imperial nature. My house-master said so. It takes me longer to get over things.'

'Perhaps he meant impressionable?' I suggested, as Elizabeth snorted tea over the table. 'Did he really say that? More than the other boys? I wonder why.' I think that if schoolmasters realised how anxiously their words are weighed – and generally very much taken exception to – they might well refrain from making off-the-cuff comments about their pupils. 'Elizabeth, darling, would you mind using a handkerchief? I really think, Henry, that it's time to get back into things. We've all got to make tremendous efforts and be very brave –'

'Oh God, not a sermon!' Elizabeth interrupted. 'We get all that crap in school at assembly time.'

'Elizabeth!' Rose was shocked. 'That language is unsuitable for the breakfast table!'

'Well, if absolutely *everyone*'s got the right to boss me about I think I'll push off to the stables. I don't know why you want to stay here anyway, Henry. It's the most hopelessly uncool scene.' She buttered a large slice of toast with deliberation, smeared it with two huge spoons of marmalade, gave Janòs the full benefit of a smouldering pout and left the room.

'Oh dear,' I said, watching her go. 'I'm so sorry, Rose. You know how much she loves you.'

'I do. And I can remember her mother aged fourteen. I'm not going to be hurt by a little adolescent rudeness. She's wanting to hurt as she's been hurt.'

'I hope you'll say that when I go through adolescence,' said Henry. 'In my experience, by the time anything's my turn everyone's sick of being tolerant and understanding and I just get a thick ear.'

The pathos of this was spoiled by our laughter.

'You'll get away with anything, young man,' said Jenny admiringly. 'Handsome and clever as y'are. There's Bridie crying. Shall I fetch her to you, Miss Ingrams? I better get on with the dishes.'

'Henry and I'll wash up,' I said quickly. 'Rose is looking tired.'

'I knew it!' Henry was indignant. 'Just because I don't go slamming out of the room I get all the lousy jobs. I'll just see if Elizabeth needs any help with Puck.'

Janòs appeared quite undisturbed by this inordinate domesticity. He ate his breakfast and drank his coffee with an air of relaxed abstraction, but the minute Rose had got up to walk over to her usual chair by the fire he leaned across the table, took my hand and raised it to his lips. I experienced a seismic shock from the top of my head to my toes. 'I need not go away this morning,' he said, very quietly. 'I can stay until tomorrow.'

'There's no need for whispering, Mr Dexie.' Rose's tone was severe. 'I can easily leave the room if you have something particular to say.'

'Janòs is staying until tomorrow, Rose.' I tried to speak casually, though I could have screamed with delight. 'It's a wonderful opportunity for him to rest and see a little more of Kent.'

'Ah, we shall not bamboozle Miss Ingrams. Bamboozle is a Gertrude Rince word. I say it right? It is Mrs Stowe who is the attraction, as the wise Miss Ingrams has already understood. Now, if you permit me the use of your piano, it is necessary that I practise for this morning.'

'Certainly. Shall I bring you some coffee in an hour or so?'

'I say yes so that I see your face for one moment to spur me onwards. Oh, the distraction of a lovely woman! What men has to put up with!'

He went away with a particular smile on his lips that told me he had intended to tease Rose.

'Miranda, my girl, you'd best look out for yourself. That man is dangerous.' Rose was bristling.

'Dangerous? What do you mean?' I went over to the sink to begin washing up and to hide the expression on my face, which I suspected was what Henry would have called soppy.

'He's too young, too good-looking and too – too unassailable. A man must be a little weak to make a good husband. The wife, if she's lucky, can be his weakness. Men don't aspire to a state of grace. They can only tumble into it.'

'Goodness, Rose! Aren't you rather jumping to conclusions? I met Janòs for the first time yesterday afternoon.'

'And a lot can happen in less than a day. You don't need to tell me. I can see for myself. I know how unhappy that man made you.' I understood her to be speaking of Jack now. 'But that makes you more likely to make a mistake. I'm old and I'm ready to go. You be careful and let me go peacefully.' I looked at her sharply when she said that and, on an impulse, went over and kissed her. 'Now you're getting me soapy. I think I'll close my eyes for a few minutes.'

I finished tidying the kitchen and went into the hall to get my coat. A cannonade of octaves thundered from the drawing room. I let myself out through the front door, in a dream of happiness and guilty expectation. The car stood on the drive, slightly scratched on one side but otherwise unharmed. I drove through the snowy village to Maeve's pretty cottage, which stood by itself next to a little mill-stream. Even the knowledge that I would have to make an unpleasant confession couldn't quell my excitement.

Maeve opened the door. She wore a white nightdress, trimmed with torn lace, and a grubby pink wrapper edged with ostrich feathers. She was terribly pale with dark rings beneath her eyes. She peered at my carefully composed, solemn expression. 'Oh, Lord! You don't have to tell me. And it was wonderful. Oh, well, come in. I knew it would happen anyway. Life is a bugger!'

'Oh, Maeve! I'm so sorry!'

'Rubbish! I never saw anyone look less sorry about anything in my entire life. Sit there.' She pointed to a sofa that was draped with Indian shawls on which lay two sleeping cats. I removed part of a fish skeleton before squeezing myself between them. An inglenook fireplace took up nearly all of one wall. It was piled with burning logs and the room was stiflingly hot. A sitar jangled a shimmering *raga* from the gramophone and the air was sickly with incense.

'How are you feeling? I brought you some eggs.' I held out a box of blue eggs from my Araucana hen that I knew Maeve liked.

'It'll take more than half a dozen eggs to make up for an act of deepest treachery.'

'I really am sorry –'

'Oh, don't be silly! It's all right, really. I couldn't have gone to bed with anyone last night. I felt too damned ill. And it isn't as if I've got any claim to him. I knew I'd lost him the minute I had to give up the idea of going to the concert.'

I felt a little piqued at Maeve's assumption that I was a sexual pushover. But then, I thought, that was just what I had been.

'I didn't intend it to happen. It's just that the car got stuck in a ditch and we had to walk. By the time we got home I was deep-frozen and Janòs very kindly thawed me out.'

Maeve winced. 'I can imagine. Let's not get too graphic. I'm quite jealous enough as it is.'

'I do feel guilty. And you look so ill.'

'Actually, I'm feeling a little better today. And in a few days, I'll be fighting fit. Then perhaps it'll be my turn to deliver Janòs to an engagement. I know he can't get to sleep after a performance without making love.'

She took a French cigarette from a packet and lit it, smiling at me wickedly as she did so. I repressed a bossy urge to tell her not to smoke when she was ill.

'Did Janòs say that? I didn't realise that you were on such intimate terms.'

Maeve gave a shout of laughter, then coughed and clutched her chest.

'This tastes filthy.' She ground out her cigarette in an empty baked bean tin, which stood on a table beside her. Not quite empty judging from the angry hiss. 'That really got you, didn't it? No, my poppet. In fact, Janòs and I have never discussed anything my old granny couldn't hear. I just said that because I know musicians. It happens to be true of a lot of them, that's all. They get so high on the terror and glory of it all that they have to come down in the nicest way possible. It was a guess. And if it's true of anyone it's bound to be true of Janòs. He's an absolute duck, isn't he? Bee-oo-tiful.'

'Mm.'

'You needn't pretend you're not dippy about him. It's written on your face, my dear.'

How inconvenient it was to be apparently so scrutable.

'I expect it must seem to you that the funeral baked meats are scarcely cold –'

'Oh. don't bother about that!' Maeve waved away all my pretensions to decorum. 'I know perfectly well that things had been lousy between you and Jack for years.'

'Well! I don't know how –'

'Come off it, Miranda. Jack ran after women like a stag in rut, didn't he?'

To my intense humiliation I found that my eyes had filled with tears. It was that wretched music. It had unlocked my feelings and left me frighteningly vulnerable and volatile.

Maeve was at my side in a moment, breathing cigarettes and cough medicine all over me. 'I'm so sorry. That was stupid of me. Now I've really hurt your feelings and I didn't mean to. Jack was the biggest fool I've ever met. He had you and it should have been enough for a man twenty times as good as he was. That was the trouble, Miranda, darling, he just wasn't good enough for you. You're a lovely, intelligent girl, and I don't blame Janòs for one minute for falling for you. In an open contest I wouldn't have stood a chance, I know that.'

It wasn't possible to withstand Maeve's generosity. She was cranky and infuriating, but she was immensely kind and also not a fool. I was only sorry that there was now every chance that I had caught her cold. I kissed her cheek and said it was quite all right.

'There, now. Everything's all right between us, isn't it?

I'm not cross that you've had a gorgeous time with Janòs and you aren't annoyed with me for being a brute.'

I assured her that everything was very much all right and asked her if she would like to come up to Westray for lunch.

'I don't think so, thanks all the same. Not while I look like an old sick rat, cornered in a cellar. I wouldn't want to blow my chances with Janòs completely. No reason why we shouldn't share him, is there?'

I shook my head cravenly, though privately I thought that if my wishes came into it at all there was every reason. I emerged with relief from the soupy atmosphere of Maeve's cottage into fresh air and drove home. As I let myself in through the front door I saw Elizabeth leaning, with closed eyes, against the door of the drawing room. Janòs was playing the Schubert prelude in C minor. Her pale face was screwed into an expression that touched me deeply. I could see that she was moved by the romance and excitement of the music. I tried to tiptoe past her to the cloakroom but she opened her eyes. As soon as she saw me she moved away, assuming an air of nonchalance.

'Oh, doesn't he play lovely?' said Jenny. She was sitting at the kitchen table with a sleeping Bridie in her arms, listening to the faint strains from the drawing room.

'Lovely,' I agreed, putting on the kettle for the prodigy's coffee.

Ivor wasn't with us for lunch as he was making his monthly visit to his brother, who lived in a very grand way in Essex. I was thankful for his absence. Since it seemed to be the work of a moment to divine something particular in my relationship with Janòs, it was hardly likely that Ivor would miss it. There never had been and never would be anything more than a romantic *tendre* on his part between Ivor and me but I was anxious not to hurt his feelings. We had excellent tender, rare roast beef for lunch, followed by apple charlotte.

'I suppose we should be thankful not to have had mushrooms,' said Elizabeth. 'But I do feel that if I see another apple ever again in my life I shall have a nervous breakdown.'

'Tush!' said Rose, who had noticed the way Elizabeth could hardly tear her eyes away from Janòs.

Even Bridie had now fallen victim to Janòs's charms for he had taken her from Jenny's arms, held her on his knee and made ridiculous faces at her, to the baby's huge delight. Elizabeth's dreamy gaze didn't falter even when Janòs stuck out his tongue and wrinkled his nose hideously.

'Who's going to come with me for a walk on the beach this afternoon?' I asked. 'The sun's trying to come out and it will do us good.'

Everyone, except Rose, wanted to come. We got out the push-chair as the pram was too heavy to push over sand, and wrapped Bridie and ourselves in scarves and hats and gloves as well as our thickest coats.

The sea was in its greyest mood, huge breakers running violently against the groins and dissipating in froth and foam. Gulls and oyster-catchers ran up and down the shining sand, while putty-coloured clouds whizzed at high speed over our heads. The hunt for trophies began – who could find the biggest, prettiest shells, the freshest, longest seaweed, the brightest, smoothest pebbles? The brine stung our lips and tasted delicious. We were deafened by the tumbling breakers and the shrieking of the birds.

Janòs was entranced by everything. I watched him running about with the children, wading the shallow channels, vaulting the groins. I was happy to walk along with Bridie and let Jenny run with the others. Bridie's little face was turned up to the scudding clouds as she stared fixedly in a waking dream.

At last Henry leaped a groin and fell into a pool of water on the other side. He was immediately freezing cold and inclined to sulk. It was time to go home. We each gave him something dry to wear. This was Janòs's idea. He started by giving Henry his coat and said he was much too hot anyway, Jenny gave up her gloves and I parted with my hat. Elizabeth said he could have her jeans as her coat was quite long enough to make it look as though she was wearing a skirt. Henry's good humour was restored.

Elizabeth took off her coat in the hall with an air of deliberation. She was wearing a long jersey and tights, which were perfectly decent but there was something flaunting in the way she walked very slowly upstairs, with a languorous swaying of her hips. Janòs looked at me and smiled. I hung up everyone's coats, put away all the boots, which had been flung down, and went to make tea. While Jenny cut bread for toast, I built up the drawing room fire. I had lit it before going out and the room was already warm. The tapestry of Diana and Actæon glowed blue and green and gold. The sofas on either side of the great fireplace upholstered in yellow damask, and the crimson and blue Turkey carpet were a magnificent foil to the soft, sombre panelled walls. As I poured the tea, my mood was one of guilty exhilaration.

'What shall we do with all the things we found on the beach?' asked Elizabeth, cursing as she dropped a second piece of bread from the toasting fork on to the fire. 'Why can't we have a proper toaster like the Coopers? It has two slots for the bread and it chucks the toast out when it's done.'

'I am familiar with the modern toaster,' I retaliated. 'I haven't just flown in from Mars. I just don't happen to want more gadgets than are necessary. The Aga makes perfectly good toast for breakfast and I happen to think that nothing beats bread toasted over an open fire. You've just got to stick it more firmly on the fork. I agree that we ought to do something with all the things we picked up this afternoon. It seems wanton just to throw them away.'

'"Wanton" is a good Gertrude Rince word,' said Janòs, who was sitting with his head thrown back and his legs stretched out before him. He looked quite wonderful. Dinkie strolled in and, sensitive to the magnetism that Janòs seemed to be effusing, made a bee-line for his knee. Despite our warnings Janòs stroked his head and Dinky purred, wearing his most hypocritical melting expression.

'This is English eccentric. You keep an animal who tears you to pieces. This I enjoy. But if you,' he spoke now to Dinkie, 'draw the blood I have no hesitation in wringing the neck.'

Dinkie continued to look seraphic.

'When I was a girl,' Rose began, with something sharp in her voice that reminded me to stop looking at Janòs, 'it was the fashion to make centrepieces for the dining table. They got very elaborate. Shells were very popular, I remember.'

'What a good idea! A marine tableau,' I said, with all the hearty enthusiasm of a parent hoping to see a little creativity. 'You can use the table in the north window as it has a marble top.'

Henry and Elizabeth brought in our afternoon's spoils and began to arrange them. The bladderwrack and sea oak were very effective, once the Sellotape had been persuaded to hold them in festoons along the edge, but the shells didn't make much impact.

'I know,' said Elizabeth, forgetting to drawl, 'let's use the shell box from your bedroom in the middle to make it look more important. Can we?'

'Yes, of course. And what about the mermaid fan? You could stand it up behind the shell box.'

The box had been brought back from Italy by Fabia and usually stood on my dressing table. It was *papier mâché*, decorated with the most exquisite tiny pink and grey-and-violet striped shells and in the centre was a galleon in full sail made of mother-of-pearl. The mermaid fan, as we always called it, was of mysterious provenance. I had had it in my possession as long as I could remember, and because Beatrice and I had so often played with it as children, it was slightly torn and some of the paint had cracked away from the silk. There was a painting of a naked girl on it, her nether parts gracefully hidden by rocks and seaweed and beneath it was written the invocation from *Comus*.

Sabrina fair
Listen where thou art sitting
Under the glassy, cool, translucent wave,
In twisted braids of lilies knitting
The loose trains of thy amber-dropping hair.

At moments of trial, such as giving birth, having a tooth filled or after backing the car into the stable door, I always say these beautiful, soothing words to myself and they never fail to provide comfort. They have for me the power of a phylactery, reminding me that all is not vile.

The children were delighted when their handiwork was admired, and Elizabeth didn't object when I put my arm about her waist and tweaked away a little piece of bladderwrack that had caught in her hair. I sent Henry off to pack the things for school that I had put out on his bed before lunch.

'Will you play something?' I asked Janòs. 'I shall have to leave in an hour to take him back to Nethercoat's.'

Janòs played some Chopin nocturnes and mazurkas, tender and sparkling by turns. I stared at the fire and it would be a thumping lie to say that I thought only of the music and not a great deal about the night to come.

'Can Janòs come with us to take me back?' Henry asked, when he came down with his suitcase. 'I can introduce him to Mr Bellamy. He's always going on about the importance of cultivating our minds. He has really stinking gramophone sessions of classical music.'

Elizabeth wanted to come too, but as usual she had left an entire weekend's homework to be done on Sunday night. It took less than an hour to reach Henry's prep school. We endured a tedious twenty minutes with Mr Bellamy, who lionised Janòs quite shamelessly.

'Don't forget to write, Mum,' were Henry's last words, as he trailed his newly cleaned blazer across the quadrangle on his way to the dormitory.

'Of course I won't forget. See you on Friday.'

'At last! I wait all day to be alone with you,' said Janòs, as we got back into the car. 'I have not realised that to be the lover of a respectable woman is a very crowded affair. I do not dare to lay a finger on you in case the children see me assaulting their mama. They would object, you think, on behalf of their papa?'

'I think it would hurt them dreadfully.'

'Well, I suppose there is something to be said for the wait. It becomes – what is the word? – more tension, which is not unpleasant.'

He placed his hand on my knee as I drove. He was quite right. The heightened expectation made it quite hard to concentrate on what I was doing. We talked idly of this and that, both, I suspect, thinking of something else, and his hand on my knee seemed to burn.

As it happened, anticipation was to be intensified to almost unbearable levels. Everyone was tired because of the walk and the sea air, and by half past nine, the animals were fed and the doors locked. I tested Elizabeth on her French verbs, undressed Rose and then went to my room and lit the fire.

For a time I lay on my bed, allowing my mind to float without direction. Then I felt suddenly self-conscious, undressed quickly, put on my crêpe-de-Chine nightdress and got into bed. After half an hour I was rather cold so I changed my beautiful nightdress for a warm winter one and got back under the eiderdown. After another twenty minutes I came to the conclusion that the fresh air had tired Janòs so much that he had fallen asleep. Could I bring myself to go and wake him? It was, after all, 1974 and women were no longer expected to be passive and subservient in matters of sex or anything else. Sorrowfully I concluded that, foolish and absurd as such bashfulness was, I couldn't make myself do it.

Just as I was beginning to drift into sleep I felt a warm hand on my shoulder.

'Are you awake, Miranda? May I come into your bed?' He was beneath the bedclothes before I could do more than open my eyes. 'Oh, my! I begin to despair of finding myself here. Every time I creep out of my room the door of Elizabeth flies open and she is standing in the corridor.

I say I go downstairs to fetch a book. When I come up she is waiting for me and we talk for ten minutes about what I think about girls and horses. Are they a substitution for boys? I explain that I know nothing of this but we have a friendly talk, I say goodnight. I wait five minutes and slide out again of my room. Bing! She is there! I say I want a glass of water. She kindly fetch it for me. We say goodnight once more. The third time I think she become suspicious. I am slow to think what I can be doing this time. I say I have the headache. She fetch me pills. I wait ages in my room. Success! There is no little girl waiting. But I think by now my beautiful woman is asleep and has altogether lost interest in making love with me.'

'Poor Elizabeth. I hope she doesn't suspect anything.'

'The truth is that she has got a little passion for me. It is nothing and will go away. It is something to do with the music. It is romantic for women.'

'Really?' I smiled to myself.

'Oh, yes, really. You think I am very conceited? Always it is so. It is not me myself that they loves.'

'Oh, shut up! You know perfectly well everyone in this house, with the exception of Rose who hates all men, is nursing the most appalling crush on you.'

'Crush? What is that? It sound painful.'

'Agony.'

'*Elbüvölö*! I have this crush also. All day I am in a torture of wanting to do this. And this. And... this. Together we put ourselves out of the misery, eh, my very dear Mrs Stowe?'

CHAPTER 12

'What do you think? Was it a success?'

It was lunch-time on Monday and my interlocutor was Lissie. I realised that she was referring to my first experiment as inn-keeper.

'Yes. I should say so.'

'He paid up without a squeak?'

'Well, yes. In fact, he stayed two nights and insisted on paying for both.'

'So I should jolly well hope. Why not?' Lissie looked at me, rather puzzled.

'Oh, I don't know. He'd originally booked for one. You know...' My voice trailed away. Talking about Janòs made me feel a frisson, at the same time guilty, delicious and worrying. Since driving him to the station at break of day I had thought of him very frequently, and always with a sharp little stab of desire at once overlaid with anxiety. He would be half-way to Berlin by now and I had no idea when or even if I would see him again. Janòs had said nothing about further meetings and I was too proud to raise the subject myself.

'Well, I must say you look more cheerful than I've seen you for ages. Obviously rising to the challenge has done you good. Did Maeve have her wicked way with him, do you know?'

'No, poor thing.' I was in one way perfectly sincere: I was sorry for her. 'She had dreadful flu and couldn't go to the concert, after all. I took him instead.'

'Oh, what a shame! And she was so keen to go. Did you enjoy the concert?'

'Yes, very much. What was your weekend like?'

'Perfect hell. We got to Marjorie's just as the snow started. She was having a dinner party and the bad weather meant that none of the local guests came. Marjorie got into a fearful grump about it. We were stuck for the evening with a ghastly couple who were staying the night. Colonel and Mrs Dewitt. She was diamond hard, smoked like an exhaust and wore lipstick so thick you could have carved your name in it. She was full of bright, condescending chat, part of her duty as the Colonel's lady, I suppose. Lady!'

Marjorie was Lissie's mother-in-law, and there was ill-blood between them. I had met Marjorie once or twice and agreed with Lissie that she was a horror.

'They bitched all evening about some poor woman at their poxy golf club who was, according to Marjorie, "just a trifle MIF".'

'MIF? Madly Incestuous with Father?'

'Nothing so interesting. It means "Milk In First". If you put the milk into the cup before the tea it's instant and permanent social death.'

'It sounds like an exceptionally dreary dinner party, I must say.'

'Obviously not as much fun as your evening. So who's next for bed and board?'

'A couple called Paget. Next Friday. It's their honeymoon. They're staying two nights. My aunt Nancy met them by chance in a restaurant and persuaded them to come to Westray. I must try and get things just right for them. And a man called Tremlow. I suppose he saw the advertisement in *The Gentlewoman*. He's here for a whole week. Apparently his nerves are bad and he's seeking absolute peace. I did warn him about the children. Do stay to lunch, won't you? Mushrooms are off because of the snow.'

'Well, it all seems to be humming along nicely. Thanks, I will.'

On Tuesday afternoon, when I was walking down with Jasper to the post office with my weekly letter for Henry, I met Patience. She was walking along with her head in the air and an unusual swing in her stride.

'Hello, Miranda! Where are you off to?'

I held up my letter. 'Henry is very particular about hearing from me on Wednesday even though he comes home every weekend. Cold, isn't it?'

'Lovely, really. Refreshing. I adore winter. That robin has hopped all the way up the road with me. It's strange that robins like humans. Did you know there's a tradition that robins cover any human corpses they find with leaves?'

'There's a bit in Shakespeare about it. *Cymbeline*, I think. I'd like to believe it.'

'Do look at those spindle berries. They look marvellous

against the snow. I love the country. I could never live in a town, could you?'

'I don't think so.' Patience's buoyancy of mood was striking. Her eyes looked particularly blue and bright and she emanated well-being. 'Have you been to help Aubrey with the accounts yet?'

'I went yesterday afternoon. What a hopeless muddle! Like the house. It could be a wonderful place to live. That lovely old garden going down to the river. And the rooms aren't at all bad. It's just so dirty and untidy. Aubrey made me tea and he'd bought some of those marshmallow tea-cake things from Mrs Veal. It was so sweet of him that I had to eat one. I loathe desiccated coconut. After we'd done the accounts he showed me his printing press. It was fascinating.'

'Fascinating,' I agreed. Patience had been badly bitten, there was no doubt of it. Her eyes had that look of blissful reminiscence that, no doubt, mine had when I could slip Janòs's name into the conversation. The moment came at once as Patience asked me how the house guest had behaved and whether I thought it was going to be all right. I was discreet, as anyone might have been hiding behind a hedge, but I thought Patience was looking at me rather attentively by the end of my recital.

'I wonder what made him decide to stay a second night? Is he really as attractive as Maeve said?'

'I should say so, yes.'

'M-hm. I see. And you walked back two miles through the snow? You must have been frozen. Romantic, though.' She looked at me inquiringly. I suppose the expression on my face must have been revealing for, before I could say anything, she began to laugh. 'Good! Wonderful! I'm so pleased. Can I come and have tea with you? I must hear all about it.'

'You're not shocked? After all, we'd only just been introduced, virtually. And there's Jack . . .'

'No! Good heavens, what a prude I must seem!' I didn't think that but I suspected that Patience was probably a virgin and I wouldn't have blamed her if she had thought it was all rather tasteless with Jack so recently dead. 'I think it's marvellous, honestly! As for Jack *de mortuis nil nisi bonum* and all that, but the way he behaved ... Well, you don't need telling. Oh, what a white-pebble day!'

This was an old joke between us, referring to the Ancient Roman custom of dropping a white pebble or a black one into an urn, according to whether the day had been good or bad. At the end of the month the contents of the urn would be examined and thus the felicity of the month was simply but effectively reviewed. I posted Henry's letter and then Patience linked her arm with mine and we walked back together up the hill.

'Is it love?' asked Patience, in a low voice as we came within view of the cloven pine. 'Or just sex?'

I bent to let Jasper off the lead as he was doing his prancing-horse-choking-to-death imitation. 'I haven't the faintest idea. Wasn't it Carlyle who said that love has many points in common with delirium? It certainly feels like the latter.'

'But that would suggest that love is only an illusion which you're bound to recover from. That's too cynical. Perhaps it's the need to escape from oneself. The desire to join with someone else ... to shed the burden of solitude.'

'Or perhaps the longing to see yourself differently through the eyes of someone who loves you. But that's rather cynical, too. It suggests pretence again. It *ought* to have something to do with the happiness of making others happy.'

'As I've never been in love I can only theorise. I've always been invisible to men. I've had passing infatuations for individuals from time to time, of course, but the least contact with the object of the passion has killed it off immediately. I've always wanted men to be like stronger, more honourable women. But they've always turned out to be embarrassingly weak and selfish.'

'Well, my experience, as you know, isn't much. I think when I discovered that Jack was being serially unfaithful my self-confidence was dealt such a blow that I protected myself by simply not finding other men attractive.'

'So this pianist does mean something.'

'I suppose he must. Yes.'

By Friday all the preparations for the paying guests had been made. After endless discussions and changes of mind, the menus had been decided. There were bottles of Malvern water and boxes of biscuits on bedside tables, vases of hellebores on dressing tables, extra blankets at the foot of beds, pen, paper and envelopes on writing desks and selections of light prose in bookshelves.

'What do you think honeymoon couples need especially?' I asked Lissie and Maeve, who were helping me prepare vegetables in the kitchen shortly before the guests were due to arrive. Jenny was laying the table in the dining room. Patience had torn herself reluctantly away to go and cook faggots and boiled potatoes for Wacko. The girl was a saint.

'Not a sex manual, these days,' said Lissie. 'People don't go to the altar without having been to bed together first, do they? Even George and I, all those moons ago, had one or two goes first to make sure that we could. Not that it was altogether successful. George always came at once. It was years until anything happened to me.' She suddenly looked at me and blushed, and I guessed that her initiation into the pleasures of love-making had been in the arms of my husband. Poor George. Poor Lissie.

'Our generation was unlucky.' I cut into a red cabbage and admired the intricate convolutions of white and magenta, like contour lines on a map. 'Just too old to benefit from the sexual revolution of the sixties, yet young enough to be aware of sexual opportunity spread around like a smörgåsbord.'

'It's a miracle our generation ever managed to enjoy it at all,' said Maeve. 'Because Pa was an archdeacon, Ma felt it incumbent upon her to convey to us girls that sex was felt as a regrettable necessity by my father and a cruel infliction by her. She wanted us to think, if think we must, that they nobly got together to do their duty, like having the Bishop to lunch. Something onerous and time-consuming, which bores you to sobs but you know you ought to do it.' Maeve had thrown off this early teaching with a gusto I admired wholeheartedly. 'But there's nothing to stop you now, Miranda.'

I could hardly blame her for the craftiness of the smile that accompanied this remark.

'Of course, they'll have brought cases of contraceptives,' continued Lissie.

'You're becoming something of a *voyeuse*, you know,' said Maeve, with characteristic frankness. 'Always imagining other people in bed together. Better watch yourself. Unless there's a possibility of persuading George into an open marriage.'

'There's as much likelihood of that as George volunteering for the space programme,' replied Lissie, gloomily. 'I can't imagine how another woman would put up with him, honestly, if they hadn't got fond of him over the years. Every night, after cleaning his teeth for two minutes and gargling for one, he gets into bed and reads the business section of *The Times*. If he feels like making love he pats me on the bottom and says, "How about it, old thing?" in just the same voice he uses when he asks Buster if he wants to go for a walk. You may be amused,' Maeve and I were rather heartlessly laughing, 'but it's all so unsexy! And why must he always do his pyjama jacket up to the very top button?'

'I seem to remember that on Cary Grant it looks rather fetching.' I started to peel some chestnuts, always tricky and tough on fingernails. 'And there's a great deal to be said for dependability. George is a darling. Kind and loyal and funny. You must admit he's got a sense of humour.'

'Oh, yes. But who wants someone to be kind to them in bed? Unless you've got flu or something. Sometimes I want uncontrollable lust, perhaps even brutality.'

'Aha! *The Female Eunuch* again,' said Maeve, with triumph. 'You're conditioned to remain infantile and passive. Our greatest desire is to hand over responsibility for ourselves to another parent figure. What you're actually looking for is the father-phallus.'

'No, really?' Lissie paused in the act of chopping onions. 'But my father was bald and freckled and only interested in cricket.'

'That has nothing to do with it,' said Maeve, impatiently. 'I don't mean you want to go to bed with your own father, you chump, but you want to be treated as a sex object without volition, in order to reassure yourself that you conform to society's ideal woman, all curves and hair and doll-like features.'

'No, I don't,' said Lissie, with decision. 'I just don't want to be bored. If you're saying that I ought to hanker to go to bed with a man who wants to discuss Shakespeare and who talks to me in the same way he talks to his colleagues on the nine-fifteen, well, that sounds deadly dull if you ask me. Contrast that with a marquis, with a cruel mouth and an impetuous, overbearing temper, and I bet any woman would choose the latter.'

Lissie's sexual fantasies were interrupted by the clang of the door-bell as it bounced on its spring. I went to answer it. Mr and Mrs Reginald Paget stood on the doorstep with their suitcases. I told Jasper to stop barking, asked them to come in and called Elizabeth and Henry to take the cases upstairs.

Mrs Paget was thirty-something, tall, angular and pale, and very demurely dressed in mackintosh and brown tweeds. My mother would have summed her up in two seconds as 'dowdy'. Her hair, something between fair and mouse, was arranged round her face in pin-curls of the sort we used to manufacture for each other at school with two crossed kirby-grips. She was very shy and smiled all the time, in a vague way, while darting uncertain looks at me and round at the hall, and at Henry as he came leaping down the stairs.

'How do you do?' said Henry, offering his hand to Mrs Paget in his most juvenile-lead manner, all precocious charm.

She took it as nervously as if Henry had been a prince of the Blood Royal. I made a mental note to tell Henry that it was not good manners for the man to hold out his hand first. No sooner had I thought this than Mr Paget thrust a giant hand almost into my face. 'How d'jer do, Mrs Stowe? Call me Reggie, won't you?'

It was apparent at first glance that Mrs Paget had 'married to disoblige her family', as the saying goes. Mr Paget, or Reggie as I must call him, was stocky without being fat, with dark curly hair, prematurely balding from a pronounced widow's peak. I judged him to be several years younger than his wife. He wore a camel coat with a velvet collar and a shiny suit like a gigolo's. In contrast to his wife's faltering gaze, he looked me in the eye with intimidating self-assurance. He was my idea of a shady character, the sort of man known to the police but clever enough not to get caught. He looked me up and down with an insolent smile. His skin was a curious shade of orange. I suspected a fake tan. He smelt like the cosmetics department of Harrods.

'Nice boy, you got there, Mrs Stowe,' he said, to Henry's retreating back. His accent was an uneasy American, which slipped from time to time into Australian. 'And this is the young lady of the house, I guess?' Elizabeth came slowly down the stairs with a sinuous movement from hip to hip, like a mannequin on a catwalk. She wore a dress with a plunging neck-line, which exposed a childishly bony chest. Her face was as white as Harlequin's, her lips were blood-red and she had drawn a teardrop under one eye with eyebrow pencil. 'What a little heart-breaker!' Reggie said, almost under his breath. 'Takes after her mother.' He gave me an impudent wink.

'Will Miss Weston-Waite approve, darling? That's a very elegant dress but do you think it's quite suitable?'

'I'm glad you like it. It's yours. Do you mind if I borrow it?'

'So it is. No, I don't mind. I haven't worn it for ages, anyway. But is it quite the thing for an inter-schools hockey match?'

'Oh, Wettie-Waite won't notice. She won't be able to unglue her eyes from Gillian Walsh. She's the games captain, and Wettie-Waite's so madly in love with her she can hardly blow her whistle when Gillian scores a goal.'

'Yes. Well. This is Mrs Paget. My daughter, Elizabeth.'

Mrs Paget looked quite frightened, and I didn't blame her. Reggie shook Elizabeth's hand for longer than I thought necessary.

'I can't have the little lady carrying my heavy suitcase,' he said, staring at Elizabeth in the manner of a predator examining its lunch. He looked up at Rose, who was slowly making her way down the stairs towards us. 'And this must be Gran. Charming family you have, Mrs Stowe.'

'This is Miss Ingrams.'

'Oh, pardon me, my mistake.'

Rose murmured a frigid 'good evening' to Mrs Paget and touched for half a second the hefty paw held out by Reggie, before continuing her stately progress to the kitchen.

I showed them to their room. Reggie threw his case on to the bed. I stifled a protest. He felt the mattress. 'Very nice. Very nice indeed. A lovely old-world touch this four-poster. It'll be very cosy, won't it, Priscilla? It's our honeymoon, you know,' he went on, regardless of his wife's evident embarrassment. 'Spliced at three o'clock today, weren't we, Priscilla? And come down here to comply with the terms of the Marriage Act, ha, ha!'

I left them to unpack and went back to the kitchen.

'Pretty ghastly,' I said, in answer to Lissie and Maeve's eager inquiries. 'Well, perhaps that isn't fair. She's all right, rather schoolmistressy and quiet, but he's quite a horror. What on earth could have made her marry him? Or he her, come to that?'

'Perhaps she has money,' suggested Maeve.

'And he's good in bed,' said Lissie.

'There you go again,' said Maeve.

We had decided earlier, after much discussion, that I should eat in the dining room with the paying guests to ease the burden of conversation, and Ivor had been deputed to act as host. I had given Jenny plenty of instruction in the art of waiting at table, and I thought she had pretty much got the hang of it. I had tried to persuade Rose and Henry to join us but they were adamant that they would rather eat in the kitchen. Elizabeth was to be picked up by the mother of a schoolfriend and taken to the hockey match. I was thankful that she would be out of Reggie's way. Maeve and Lissie said goodbye, with obvious reluctance. I gave everyone the strictest instructions not to let Dinkie out of the kitchen and went to give the Pagets a drink in the drawing room and await the arrival of Mr Tremlow.

I usually enjoyed having people to stay. But it is a different matter if one is charging for it. Mistakes will not be glossed over as with friends. Shortcomings will, no doubt, be resented, and there is an unpleasant consciousness of value for money. I felt apprehensive as I checked that the flowers were not wilting, that the glasses were polished, the fire drawing well and the day's newspapers and *Country Life* tidily arranged on the table.

'Wow, terrific room!' Reggie entered the drawing room with a bouncing stride on the tips of his toes, arms held out from his sides and dangling as though he had not been a biped very long. He came to stand close to me in front of the fire. The temptation to move away was almost overwhelming. 'Like the house. Very tasteful. These genuine?' He indicated the furniture. 'Must be worth a bob or two.' He had changed into a suit, possibly even shinier, and beneath it he wore a pale mauve shirt with a frilled front. His fingers were bright with gold, a signet ring on the little finger of his right hand and a wedding ring on his left. He whipped out a comb, ran it briefly through his hair, returned it to his inside pocket and gave a little sigh of self-satisfaction.

'Priscilla's just putting on a dress. She'll be down in a minute. She's had an upsetting day. Fool of a brother turned up at the register office and tried to get in a fight with me. Doesn't approve of me. Ha, ha! Priscilla's dad was a solicitor and had a bit of property besides. Left her quite comfortably off. Brother thinks I'm after her money.' He assumed an expression of sorrow and affront, but his eyes continued to gleam with guile. 'My best man had to get a little rough with him. Priscilla's not used to that sort of thing.' He moved closer. His eyes, protruding and moist, like sucked toffees, held my gaze.

'Will you have a glass of wine?' I asked.

'I fancy something a bit stronger. Gin and It, half and half? A man on his honeymoon's got to keep his pecker up, eh?'

He laughed very heartily at his own joke and nudged me with his elbow. I smiled to show that I wasn't a prig and went to the kitchen. I found a bottle of gin in the larder. A further search produced a very old bottle of sweet vermouth with two inches of dull red liquid in the bottom. I speared a maraschino cherry with a stick and, rather inexpertly, made him a cocktail which was, perforce, much more gin than It.

'All the trimmings, I see, Mrs S,' he said, appreciatively. He drank it down very fast and sucked at his cherry with a sozzling sound, which I would certainly have ticked Henry off for making. 'Shy little thing. Priscilla, I mean. Not my usual sort. But I like a bit of class in a ch— girl. She had everything as a kid. Convent ejercation, detached home, pet retriever, the works! My old man had a barrer in the Old Kent Road. I left school at fourteen and set up on me own, selling spare parts. Motor accessories, they're called now. Of course, some'll think I married Pris for her money but that's not at all the case.'

'I'm sure it isn't.'

'When a man's thinking of settling down, he looks for something a bit different. A proper mother for his kids.' He tried to look righteous at this point, but his eyes were cunning. 'Someone who won't play the field with your mates. Priscilla's inexperienced but she ain't cold. She wouldn't let me – you know – before we were spliced but I could tell she's got a bit of passion about her. A bloke can sense these things.'

I was half glad and half sorry that the door-bell put an

end to these confidences. It could not be said that Reggie's conversation was dull.

'Mrs Stowe? I am Maurice Tremlow.'

Mr Tremlow took off his hat, a dashing black fedora, disclosing a magnificent head of white hair and a broad forehead. He was very brown and had a quantity of wrinkles that would have made any woman, except, we must suppose, the genuinely liberated, chuck themselves under the very next train. He was about seventy, I guessed, of medium height and tending to fat. His rotund form was encased in a stylish Bohemian cape with crimson frogging. He had not lied in his letter about the attenuated state of his nerves. His hand trembled as it held mine and his eyes filled with tears that remained unshed. 'So good of you to have me at such short notice. What a beautiful house! Fifteenth century?'

'Yes. Let me take your coat . . . cape. Are you interested in architecture?'

'Oh, yes. My word, yes! It's hard to imagine not being interested in something so very central to our lives. The printing press of all ages, according to . . . someone. I've forgotten who. G. K. Chesterton said that there are no uninteresting things, only uninterested people. Do you agree with that?'

'Well. I suppose I do. It takes a little thinking about. Henry! Come and take Mr Tremlow's case, darling.'

'So this is Henry. Well, well.' Mr Tremlow shook Henry's hand and stared keenly at him. 'A good, strong, intelligent face, if I may say so.'

As far as Henry was concerned all gross flattery was permitted.

I took Mr Tremlow up to his room. 'Charming! Delightful! Most welcoming!' He sank on to the bed and tapped his chest. 'Out of condition. Too much good living. You're near the sea, aren't you? I shall walk there every day. Nothing like ozone for the lungs. That, and a lean, healthy diet. I can tell I shall be able to sleep here. Liable to insomnia, you know, but here I shall go out like a snuffed candle.' He laughed, but at the same time his eyes filled again with tears. He dashed them away with the back of his hand.

I asked him if he would like a drink before dinner but he said not. 'Expect I've kept you waiting. I had to wait for a taxi at the station. I'll just have a wash and then be downstairs directly.'

Mrs Paget was in the drawing room when I returned. She had put on a brown jersey shirtwaister, fastened uncompromisingly at the neck with a diamanté brooch, fashioned like a beetle. Her enormous shoes were the last word in good sense, flat and plain with plenty of room in the toe. She wore her hair fastened to one side with a tortoiseshell clip, and no makeup. I wondered if Reggie hadn't made something of a miscalculation as to the promise of passion, but reminded myself that still waters run deep. She wanted sweet sherry. I had to go back to the kitchen for the bottle of Bristol Cream that I used for trifles.

Ivor came in, looking as though he was swimming in a suit several sizes too big for him. Usually he wore knee breeches and a Norfolk jacket. I thought it was very nice of him to make such an effort. He bowed over my hand and kissed it, looking very much the gentleman, if somewhat eccentric. He went to stand by Mrs Paget and asked her how she liked Kent.

'It's rather cold, isn't it?' was all she had to say, in a flat, precise little voice.

'Ah! "Thou art a summer bird, which ever in the haunch of winter sings the lifting up of day".'

'Pardon?'

I thought she looked rather offended to be called a bird. Mr Tremlow came in, very elegant in a midnight-blue smoking-jacket and patent evening pumps. Despite his size he was light on his feet, and his hands were white and beautifully shaped. He moved them expressively whenever he spoke. I introduced him to the Pagets and we went into the dining room.

Jenny brought in the soup. Lissie and I had decided on *potage solferino* as it was both good and economical, made of tomatoes, potatoes and leeks, and no one could object to it, however simple or sophisticated their tastes. The cookery writer whose recipe it was had been urgent in her recommendation of the addition of cayenne pepper so I had put in the merest trace, as I knew Henry and Jenny wouldn't like it. Mrs Paget took one sip and put down her spoon. 'I'm afraid I can't eat spicy food.'

'Oh dear!' I was mortified. 'Is it too hot for everyone?'

'Not a bit of it!' said Mr Tremlow.

'This soup has class,' said Reggie, with gusto, cramming the entire spoon into his mouth and swallowing it down with audible gobbles.

'Perfectly delicious, Miranda,' said Ivor.

All the men asked for more, which was reassuring. Mrs Paget was discouragingly taciturn, occasionally pressing her napkin to her lips. It's strange how if silence falls when there should be conversation, one's normally busy, possibly even fertile, brain becomes an arid, featureless landscape where ideas of the most limited kind, let alone something *à propos*, whisk instantly out of sight.

'Do you live in London, Mr Tremlow?' I asked, feeling instinctively that he was my best ally.

'I do, temporarily. But I've spent most of my life in Italy. My darling wife was Italian. I only arrived in England a few weeks ago after thirty years abroad.'

'Very nice, those Italian ch— girls, ain't they?' contributed Reggie. 'Big black eyes and . . . you know.' He made circular gestures with his hands before his frilled shirt-front. Mrs Paget closed her eyes and resorted once more to her napkin.

'Do you know Italy, Mrs Paget?' Mr Tremlow asked. The skin round his eyes folded like paper fans as he smiled kindly at her.

'I've never been abroad.' She gave him one of her quick, doubting smiles. 'Mother and Father always took a house at Burton-on-Sands for three weeks in the summer. Father didn't like foreigners.'

'Are you fond of the sea?' I asked, eager that she should

find something to enjoy. 'It's very near. You could go for a walk tomorrow on the beach.'

'Thank you, but I have a delicate chest and I think the cold would be too much for me. I prefer to read.'

'What sort of things do you like to read?' asked Ivor, suddenly looking interested.

'I like biographies about the Royal Family.'

'Ah. History! Miranda is a fine historian, you know.' I made an embarrassed disclaimer but Mrs Paget looked at me as though I were large and insectivorous with a stinging tail. Ivor had worked up a full head of steam, conversationally, and noticed nothing. 'Seneca made an interesting comment about temporal power. "However many people a tyrant slaughters, he cannot kill his successor." Obvious when you think of it, but a good point, wouldn't you say?'

He looked expectantly at Mrs Paget. Ivor is a considerate man and it would never be his intention to make people feel uncomfortable by talking over their heads. I knew perfectly well that Mrs Paget's reading was confined to the sort of books that go into great detail about whether the little Princess Margaret Rose liked shrimp paste or jam for tea, what comedy turns the Queen Mother enjoyed at the Royal Variety Show and what sort of soap 'Crawfie' used for the infant bath. I think Mr Tremlow understood it too, for I saw a ripple of amusement run through the hachure lines on his face as he took up Ivor's question.

'I have always valued the remark that Fortune rarely accompanies anyone to the door. It has the same kind of cynical wisdom. But however much men affect to recoil from power and its corrupting influences, who has not grasped it with both hands when it is offered them? Take Cromwell, for example. Heroic intellect, philistine of genius or barbarous regicide?'

While Ivor and Mr Tremlow had an argument about the Interregnum, which they both seemed to relish, I relaxed a little. The fire cast a generous and friendly glow, the candlelight sparkled on the well-polished silver, the dark red chrysanthemums gave out a delicious musky scent. Reggie appeared to be enjoying himself. He drained his glass, then turned his brazen stare to me.

'That's good stuff. I picked up several cases of best Bolly the other day.' Picking up, I imagined, was a euphemism. 'Intellectuals, eh?' indicating Ivor and Mr Tremlow with a nod of his head. 'That's all very well but women don't go for it, do they? He married?' He looked at Ivor, who was expounding his theory of popular unrest.

'No.'

'Thought not.' He lowered his voice fractionally. 'You don't mind having a nancy-boy about the place? I can't understand why women like them. I suppose he's safe.' Reggie laughed abrasively and unconsciously fingered the waistband of his trousers. I averted my eyes. 'He a relation or what?'

'He was at school with my husband. He helps me run the house and garden.'

'Hubby pushed off, has he? That's bad. He must be a *very* fussy guy.'

I was relieved to see Jenny with the next course. Reggie seemed to have very little idea of the parameters of polite conversation. The casserole of pheasant, with chestnuts, roast potatoes and red cabbage, looked tempting and smelt good, I thought.

Priscilla's father had clearly been an autocrat and, as far as his daughter was concerned, his slightest pronouncements were canon law. He had never eaten game because, being wild creatures, they were necessarily scavengers and their diet was likely to be unhealthy. Nor would he have approved, apparently, of the cold beef, which was all I had to offer instead of the pheasant, on the grounds that meat once cool was indigestible. She ate the vegetables with an air of silent martyrdom.

'Come on, Pris!' Reggie's voice was sharp. 'You'll need to eat something. I don't want a fainting woman on my hands. Don't mind her, Mrs S. She doesn't know what's good for her. She soon will.' He laughed loudly, with his mouth full of food.

'It's absolutely delicious,' said Mr Tremlow, tucking in with complete disregard of the lean, healthy diet he had mentioned earlier.

'First class, Miranda!' Ivor gave me a glowing look across the table. 'You're looking very beautiful tonight,' he added, in what was meant to be a whisper. Reggie's eyes narrowed as he looked thoughtfully from Ivor to me.

Mr Tremlow was the perfect guest, and asked me to tell him something of the history of the house. I told him all I knew about its first existence as a priory and about the early years in private ownership, in particular that of Margaret le Bec whose arms were above the fireplace in the dining room. He was particularly interested in the letters that had been found behind the panelling upstairs when the Victorian owner of Westray had put in the first bathroom. 'Are they still in the house? I should so much like to see them.'

'The originals are in the local museum but we have copies. I'll show them to you after dinner, if you like.'

I tried to shift Jasper away from my leg. After chasing cats, with the exception of Dinkie, swimming in the moat, and bones, he liked best to press himself against any stationary member of his family, usually Elizabeth. As she was out he had made do with me. He leaned more heavily as I moved away.

'My goodness, this dog is an affectionate creature,' said Mr Tremlow, bending to look under the table. 'He's been lying on my feet throughout dinner. It's rather flattering.'

Mr Tremlow and I were sitting at opposite sides of the table, at least five feet apart. I put my hand down and felt, instead of Jasper's silky head, a trousered, muscular knee. Reggie winked.

'These letters, now. Tell me about them,' said Mr Tremlow, helping himself to more pheasant from the dish Jenny offered him.

'Some time after becoming a widow, Margaret le Bec converted to Roman Catholicism. There were several recusant households in this area, probably sharing the responsibility for hiding Catholic clergy. It's clear from the letters that Margaret and the priest, who was her spiritual mentor, became lovers. The letters are very sad, really, all about the imperilling of their immortal souls. She must have been a brave woman. It was no joke being a Catholic in those days.'

'What say ye in answer to the "Bloody Question"?' quoted Ivor.

'Pardon?' Priscilla looked quite fierce.

'Priscilla doesn't like language,' said Reg. 'She's always ticking me off. Of course, when you're courting you have to let the little woman have her own way.' He looked round at us all with a sly smile, which boded ill for Priscilla, I thought.

'I was speaking of the interrogation all suspected Catholics had to undergo in the reign of Elizabeth,' explained Ivor kindly. ' "Would you defend England against the Pope if he himself invaded?" It's known as the "Bloody Question".'

Priscilla's pale eyes looked beseechingly at her husband as she tried to get her mind around the concepts involved. 'I don't know,' she said, at last. 'Father didn't like Catholics. He was a Baptist, Strict and Particular.'

'Drink up, my girl.' Reg spoke in tones of authority. 'You haven't touched that wine. You want to relax. You're all of a jitter. You'll feel better in a while.'

I began to understand why Priscilla had married Reg. Her father had been an ignorant despot and Reggie offered the same security. You would have thought she must have been spoiled for choice. Jenny brought in the *crème brûlée*. She really was doing her job beautifully.

'Now, that does look a bit of all right. You'll eat that, Sugarlips, if you know what's good for you.' Reggie's advice was bordering on a barked command. He had drunk twice as much as anyone else and his face was red. I felt more than ever that I should not like to tangle with him. Priscilla tapped nervously at the crystalline disc sitting on the custard.

'Give it a whack, doll. I know you've got it in you – as the bishop said to the actress, if you'll pardon me.' Reggie made a face that was a grotesque parody of an apology.

Mr Tremlow made a sound something like a choking cough. Priscilla, scarlet with embarrassment, hit the *brûlée* hard and a sharp, triangular piece flew out and struck Ivor smartly on the cheek.

After dinner Mr Tremlow sat next to me on one side of the fire in the drawing room, looking at the Margaret le Bec letters, while Reggie and Priscilla occupied the other sofa. Reggie's large hand was on Priscilla's knee as he sipped at a generous brandy and soda.

'Very stylish,' he said, looking round. 'Take note, Pris. I shall want something like this to come home to.' He stood up suddenly. 'Goodnight, all. Time we were turning in.' He winked at me. '"Go forth and multiply," the good Lord said, and I like to do my bit.'

Priscilla, blushing until her eyes watered, crept after him, pausing awkwardly at the door to whisper goodnight.

'Oh dear. What a dreadful man!' I said, when I was certain they were out of earshot. 'It wasn't quite the evening of seamless congeniality I'd planned.'

'I've had a perfectly lovely time,' said Mr Tremlow. 'But I worry about that poor girl. He seems something of a rogue to me. While you were making coffee he was telling me about his wife's money.'

'She does seem frightened of him. I would be myself – Hello, darling,' I broke off as Elizabeth put her head round the door. 'Come and meet Mr Tremlow.'

'Hello. I'm on my way to bed. Come on, Jasper. Goodnight. See you in the morning.'

Jasper rose reluctantly from Mr Tremlow's evening pumps and followed her out of the room.

'That was rather abrupt. Difficult age. I'm sorry.'

'Don't be. She looks a dear girl. Lots of character.'

'Do you have any children?'

'Sadly I . . . My God, what's that?'

A scream rang through the house, quickly followed by

another. I flew up the stairs, my mind filled with horrid images. Mr Tremlow followed as fast as his weight permitted. The cries came from the Pagets' room. Had Reggie unveiled himself and the shock of masculine anatomy been too much for a delicately nurtured woman? Henry and Elizabeth stood on the landing convulsed with laughter as the sounds from within the bedroom calmed to low sobbing. I heard Reggie's voice very loud and annoyed as he told Priscilla to pull herself together.

'What have you done, you horrible pair?' I asked in a low voice.

'It was to pay her out for what she said about you,' explained Henry. 'I just happened to be listening at the door when they were dressing before dinner. She said that you were too smartly dressed to be respectable.'

'Did she, indeed?' I was not altogether displeased. Then, remembering, 'You know you shouldn't eavesdrop. It's very bad behaviour.'

'And he said that you were a juicy piece but she was much more his type. Honestly, she's the dullest, wettest-looking woman I've ever seen. You're miles prettier!'

'I couldn't agree more. Miles,' panted Mr Tremlow, who had caught up with us.

'Thank you, both of you. So what form did your revenge take?'

'That green plastic scorpion I got in my stocking last Christmas – you remember. Well, I put it into one of her slippers. I just meant to give her a little fright. I didn't think she'd scream the house down.'

'Thank God!' said Mr Tremlow. 'I feared I was going to be obliged to force my way into their bedroom and command him to unhand her. He's bigger than I am.'

'Well, you'd better apologise in the morning. I don't suppose she's used to children. It was very unkind of you.'

'She did scream, though, didn't she?' Elizabeth giggled. Her makeup was smudged all over her face. I wondered again about the hockey match.

'I thought all the windows were going to crack.' I started to laugh. 'That girl has lungs.'

Elizabeth came and put her arms round my waist. 'I do love you,' she said, before going off to her own bed.

Suddenly I felt the evening hadn't been quite such a disaster, after all.

CHAPTER 13

Reggie was first down to breakfast. He looked like an advertisement for a brand of men's wear, in yellow cashmere jersey, Paisley cravat and cavalry twill trousers. Everything was obviously new. No doubt Priscilla's money was already coming in useful. I abandoned Mr Tremlow to an undiluted dose of Paget wit, and got on with cooking porridge and bacon and eggs. After breakfast, for which Priscilla failed to appear, Mr Tremlow asked me to show him the house.

'That man is a crook,' he said, trotting after me into the library. 'He was boasting about his dealings with the Inland Revenue and it became quite obvious that he ought to be in prison for fraud. That poor girl he's married should be rescued.'

'I don't think she'd thank you for it. However miserable he makes her – and I think it will be very miserable indeed – she'll do what he tells her. Men can be absolute super-rats and women go on loving them for it. Think of Wagner and Augustus John, to name only two.'

'You're probably right. Oh, I like this room! The best kind of Victorian domestic architecture. Well made, comfortable, graceful. And, my goodness, what an interesting collection of books! The Paduan School, Fauvism, baroque formalism, nuagism . . . Oh, my!'

'Do use the library whenever you wish,' I said, quite forgetting my intention to confine paying guests to the drawing room. I liked Mr Tremlow and it was hard to remember that the basis of our relationship was financial. 'All the art books in this corner belonged to my mother, who lives in Italy, and my father, who died during the war. I hardly ever look at them myself. I'm much more interested in fiction and history.'

Mr Tremlow, hands shaking with excitement, had taken down a volume and was already immersed. I left him there and went off to make the beds. When I returned three-quarters of an hour later, he was sitting behind the desk with a pile of books in front of him. He looked up as I came in. 'Tell me, Mrs Stowe, while you've been gone I've been thinking. How do you account for the masochistic tendencies of the fair sex?'

'Well, it so happens that it's a question to which I've given some thought.'

I went over to sit on the window-seat, looking down over the moat, and Mr Tremlow turned round in his chair to face me. He was wearing a coat and trousers of navy drill and a yellow silk bow-tie, very unEnglish. A faint dribble of sunlight gave his white hair a silver aureole. A branch of *Viburnum bodnantense* had fallen from the vase on the desk beside him. Mr Tremlow picked it up and turned the pink blossom constantly in his hand as we talked, inhaling the sugary scent. He looked like a man who enjoyed life, despite the abrasion of his nervous system.

'I think it's the direct result of women being brought up to please. This is all Freud, of course. I can't claim any original thinking here. Looking back, I can see that unconsciously I've allowed the boys much more scope for rebellion. I expect it also has something to do with knowing so little about men, being brought up in an entirely female household. With Elizabeth I felt more confident that I knew how things should be... how she should be.'

'She appears, from what little I've seen, to have thrown off the maternal yoke pretty effectively.'

He smiled as he said this. I found myself, almost before I knew what I was doing, telling Mr Tremlow all the things that worried me as far as the children were concerned. It was only when I had finished giving him an account of Elizabeth's reaction to her father's death that I suddenly remembered that Mr Tremlow was a guest in my house, seeking rest and recuperation. 'I'm so sorry. You can't possibly want to hear all this. You're a very good listener and I got carried away. To answer your original question, I think the hideous and unreasonable demands that super-rats make on women give them a feeling of self-fulfilment. To put up with being insulted, beaten and betrayed, and then to come back for more with an expression of love is an affirmation of all their training.'

'You're a feminist?'

'Well, naturally I'm in favour of anything that makes women happier and freer. Who wouldn't be? But I've never done anything to advance the cause, like marching with banners or writing polemics, which could justify me in calling myself a feminist. I'm ashamed to say that I've left it up to others to do all the hard work and collect all the brick-bats.'

'Why?'

'Cowardice, I suppose. Laziness, perhaps. I admire intensely women like Mary Wollstonecraft and Harriet Martineau. The trouble is that it's so hard to live properly, isn't it?'

'I wish you could have met my wife. She'd have loved you. Lucia was extraordinarily intelligent, though she could barely read or write. When I first met her she was just eighteen years old.' Mr Tremlow sighed. 'I shall never forget the first sight of her, walking with her goats down the mountainside. Imagine ... the twisted trunks of the silver olive trees, the darting lizards on the rocks, the coil of sunlight trapping the red earth, no sound but birds and goat bells. I was hungry, thirsty ... a little lonely, too. She gave me a piece of the cheese she had made herself that morning. The freshness, the sweetness of it! I thought I must be in Elysium.'

Mr Tremlow was silent for a moment, thinking. I waited for him to go on. 'Lucia was an orphan. Every day she milked the goats herself, made the milk into cheeses and took the goats up to the best pasture. Every evening she milked the beasts again and cooked a supper for her five younger brothers and sisters. They all went to school, girls as well as boys. She was strict with them. Every one of those children finished their schooling and two went to university.' Mr Tremlow stopped for a moment, and I saw that his eyes were wet. He did not attempt to hide his emotion but after a while went on. 'How much she taught me! Until I met her I had no idea how steeped I was in convenient lies.'

'You must miss her terribly.'

'Well, I do, of course. But for me she is somewhere nearby, even here in this English paradise, which would have been so utterly strange to her.'

Mr Tremlow was far from the *beau idéal*. One could not imagine him setting out on the Siege Perilous. But he seemed to have discovered, none the less, an experience of love that was exemplary.

'Could it be, do you think,' he went on, 'that women are genetically predisposed to choose the leader of the herd, regardless of moral considerations? Perhaps men choose pretty, healthy young women to produce pretty, healthy children, and women choose strong, aggressive men who can most effectively protect them and their children. Perhaps it has no psychological significance at all?'

Lissie put her head round the door just as I was wondering whether this postulation might be correct. I introduced Mr Tremlow.

'How do you do? Who's that ghastly man smirking and winking in the drawing room? He can't be one of the newly wedded.'

'I'm afraid he is. We were just talking about horrible men... about the strange attraction they have for apparently sane women.'

'Easy. It's because nice men are so dull.'

I concluded that our various interpretations of the phenomenon said more about our characters than anything else. I showed Mr Tremlow the rest of the house while Lissie went to coo over Bridie and help Jenny peel potatoes for lunch. He was interested in everything, from the priest-hole to the sixteenth-century dog-gate. I was fired by his enthusiasm to begin my project on the history of the house for Aubrey's midsummer pageant. It would be the perfect antidote to frequent, unsettling thoughts about Janòs.

At twelve I drove to the station to meet James, who was coming home for the weekend. The thrill of seeing him step on to the platform had never lessened in all the years he had been at boarding school. He seemed to have grown taller in the two weeks I hadn't seen him, and being a prefect for nearly a term had made him magisterial. It was hard to see myself as the parent. While I was chopping onions to make a *pissaladière* for lunch he questioned me closely about my weekend guests. 'I don't like the idea of just anybody being able to come here. This Paget bloke sounds like a real villain. I don't think Ivor will be much protection. You're surrounded by children and old women, no disrespect to Rose.'

'We have to live in the world as it is, darling. I can't lock myself away.'

'Dad let us all down. I shan't ever forgive him for that.'

'James!' I was astonished and horrified. 'Surely you believe that it was an accident! And if it weren't – if he wanted to kill himself – how desperately sad that would be. Deserving of our pity, surely, not blame.'

'You always want to excuse everyone. You want everything to be tidy and cosy. I believe that people should be responsible for their actions. And I wasn't just talking about him killing himself, though if he intended it, it was an act of disgraceful cowardice and disloyalty to you. I meant the way he behaved before he died. You know, with those other women.'

'Oh, darling. I didn't realise you knew. I *am* sorry.'

'There you go again. What are *you* sorry for? I don't suppose you enjoyed it. You mean you're sorry I should have to face the distasteful fact that my father was a philanderer, to call it by a polite name? Well, I'm not a child and I prefer to see things as they are. Oh, Mum, don't look like that!' He came over and put his arm round my shoulder.

'What am I looking like? Hurt? Humiliated? Yes, I felt all those things but now he's dead surely we ought to forget our quarrels.'

'What good's experience if we don't learn from it? The past's got to affect the present. You can't pretend it wasn't important because it's over.'

'Who says anything's any good? Perhaps the existentialists are right.'

James launched himself into a diatribe against existentialism, and I listened as I fried potatoes with garlic and sage, delighted not only to be released from the necessity of justifying myself but to hear him so fluent and full of ideas. Jack's presence had always acted as a damper to James's enthusiasm. Jenny came in with Bridie and blushed with delight when she saw James. He seemed quite pleased to see the baby. He elected to join the dining-room party for lunch, presumably because he felt it his duty to check over the guests.

I was relieved when Priscilla appeared in answer to the gong. Though I had tried very hard to banish prurient imaginings on the subject of her defloration, from time to time as the morning progressed they would creep in. I couldn't feel Reggie was the ideal man for the job. However, she looked substantially the same when she came downstairs. When she shied at the *pissaladière*, on the grounds that onions gave her indigestion, Reggie told her to eat it up and shut up, and instead of throwing it at his head, that is just what she did. The courtship was clearly over. Predictably, James took an immediate dislike to Reggie and contradicted all his flagrantly boastful assertions. I was grateful to Mr Tremlow, who turned the conversation constantly to tranquil topics like the egg production of the hawksbill turtle and ancient methods of bartering in Papua New Guinea.

After lunch I proposed a walk on the beach. Reggie said he would take Priscilla for a tour of Marshgate. I arranged for Freddy to collect them. We were very glad to see them go. A frail sun had made short work of the remains of the snow, and skirted among wisps of white cloud like a poached egg. A stiff wind ruffled the feathers of the seagulls and blew Jasper's ears inside out. The sand was hunched into dun-coloured spars. Jenny and I took it in turns to push Bridie. After a while the push-chair got stuck in the wet sand and we carried her. I was enchanted to find that she held up her white-bonneted head and clung on to me with her small pink hands. I ran with her a little way, and she opened her mouth wide in surprise at the buffets of wind in her face. When she saw Mr Tremlow's black cape blowing up like the wings of a fabulous creature she screamed with pleasure.

'I'm delighted to be the cause of her first real laugh. I feel like a good fairy bestowing wishes. She shall have a laugh like silver bells.' Mr Tremlow capered ridiculously among the sand dunes, skipping and waving his hands until his fedora was snatched from his head and bowled along the border of pebbles and seaweed that marked the last high tide. Henry was the one to restore it to its owner. He received Mr Tremlow's expression of gratitude as hungrily as the dunlins tugged at the worms, hiding vainly beneath the sluggish sand.

I could not help thinking of the last time I had walked by the sea, six days ago, with Janòs. It was all very well for me to decry Elizabeth's desire to please the male sex. I looked at her. She had a handful of shells and was wandering a little apart from the others, with her eyes intent on the ground. Her white face was wet with sea spray and touches of pink showed through on her cheeks. I remembered holding her in my arms years ago as I held Bridie now, walking on this very beach.

I noticed coming towards us a dark-haired man. For a second I thought, I hoped, that it might be Janòs. Then, a moment after, I realised the absurdity of the idea. This man, anyway, was taller, with longer hair. He was pale and had none of Janòs's characteristic energy. He slouched along with both hands in his pockets, eyes on the ground in a manner that was almost depressed. When he came nearer I recognised Dr McCleod.

'Good afternoon,' I called, as we passed each other.

He nodded and walked on, without smiling. I felt rebuffed. It took some minutes for the prompting of memory to remind me that I had, in fact, seen him at the Titchmarsh Festival. He had looked so different in evening clothes that he had disappeared into the crowd before I had recognised him. He was either offended or discouraged by my failure to acknowledge him then.

'He's a dear old gentleman, isn't he, Miss?' said Jenny, indicating Mr Tremlow, who had swooped down with a shout of triumph and carefully dislodged from the sand a tiny shell, coral-pink with four rounded whorls.

With a bow he presented it to Elizabeth. 'I think you'll find that it is called *Chauvetia brunnea*, my dear. Very rare. A pearl for your collection.'

Elizabeth dropped him a curtsy and thanked him.

'A dear,' I agreed. 'He certainly makes up for the others. The thought of dinner tonight is almost more than I can bear.'

'What ails thee, Mistress Stowe?' Mr Tremlow executed a rather wobbly arabesque. 'Know ye not that I have magic powers and can dispel all troubles?'

'I don't think even your mighty potency can do anything to alter the repellent nature of Reginald Paget.'

Later that evening after dinner, as I was undressing her, Rose and I had a proper talk. She was more communicative than she had been for ages. Since breaking her wrist she had distinct good and bad days. On a bad day she was morose, breaking her long silences only with sombre scriptural utterances. She had no opinion of organised religion, as it was exclusively in the custody of men, but the Bible was, for her, the source of all wisdom. She relished its precepts and the sonorous beauty of its prose. Tonight, however, she was prepared to chat in the vernacular.

'How do you think it's going?' I asked, as I brushed her

thin, faded hair, once so brown and springing. 'Do you think the children mind very much? Having to share the house with strangers, I mean.'

'It'll be hardest on James,' Rose said, to my surprise.

'Really? I should have thought it would matter to him least. He's so grown-up now and often chooses to go to parties rather than come home.'

'But when he does it's you he wants to see. You'll naturally have less time to give him. He's not a man yet, for all his clever talk and masculine ways. And he's never liked change.'

'That's true.' I paused, while Rose sipped her hot milk and whisky, a nightly indulgence she considered heinous but worth going to hell for. 'I hadn't thought of that.'

'Now, don't go worrying. Life isn't quite what we want, ever, for any of us and the learning comes from making do. He'll mind, but that's not to say it won't be good for him. As for Henry, the more the merrier. I saw him making up to Mr Tremlow before dinner. He'll blossom with new relationships. Help him get over his father.'

'Mr Tremlow is an ideal grandfather figure, I should have thought.'

'Not a bad man.' This from Rose was clarion-voiced praise. 'As for Elizabeth, I don't really know, to say the truth. She's got secrets, and that's natural at her age but she thinks a great deal too much of the men. She's unsettled, but she's bound to be that, paying guests or no. My chief worry, when I can gather my failing wits together enough to worry, is you, my girl.'

'Me? Oh, Rose, that's kind, but you really needn't concern yourself with me.'

'That's where you're wrong. Everything depends on you. If you go down, we all go down and that's a weight of responsibility. It was a very bad mistake to marry that man and it'll be a while yet before you're safely out of the woods. He died not a moment too soon, in my opinion.'

'Rose!'

Rose rearranged the powder bowl and brush and comb on her dressing table before continuing. 'If the choice was to leave Westray or go back to that man's bed, it's best that he died when he did. You'll admit that sooner or later.'

'Oh, but that wasn't it . . . You're very hard on Jack . . .' As violently as though I had been catapulted from the dark into the light, I suddenly remembered Jack saying to me, 'Either you let me back in your bed or I'll divorce you for mental cruelty and you'll have to sell the house.'

How could I have forgotten this? The preceding hours before discovering Jack's body had until this moment been blank. But now with a most unwelcome clarity I remembered the sound of his voice, his attempt to sound careless. 'Don't think I don't mean it. I've already been to see Mould. Ring him up if you don't believe me.'

Leslie Mould was our solicitor. I did believe Jack. Countless times over the last four years he had tried to get me to make love with him. He had bullied and pleaded, even squeezed out a few tears, perhaps genuine, I don't know. Once he had tried force. He had sulked for days, stayed away for weeks at a time. But I had been beyond any pressures that he could have brought to bear. It had gone on too long. I had at last achieved indifference, or something like it. It had taken twelve years, but having got it I was incapable, even if I had wished, of feeling love or desire for Jack.

I knew he had girlfriends in London. I took messages for him over the telephone punctiliously. I cooked him food when he was at home, gave him clean sheets, took his clothes to the dry-cleaners, did everything that a wife might be expected to do. I was polite, knowing from experience that saying bitter things gave me pain and Jack pleasure. Some husbands would have rejoiced in this arrangement. I suppose it was pride that made it unacceptable to Jack.

Now, as I folded Rose's vest, I felt a horrible, pinching fear as I contemplated what else I might have forgotten about that morning.

'Goodnight, my love,' said Rose, unexpectedly, as I helped her into bed.

'Goodnight, darling,' I said, turning out the light and bending to kiss the drawn cheek. I felt a little movement towards me. Rose, customarily shy of demonstrations of affection, looked at me with full eyes before turning away to sleep.

I went to bed in the silent house and lay awake for at least an hour, thinking about Jack. Next door was Mr Tremlow, dreaming of his beautiful goat-girl, perhaps, and further down the landing Elizabeth was, I hoped, in some adolescent fairyland. Henry claimed that he never ever dreamed anything but saw stars and rockets in his head all night long. James's hopes and desires seemed to have narrowed recently to the haunts and purlieus of Oxford. At the head of the stairs were the Pagets... I turned hastily on to my good ear to prevent myself from hearing anything disagreeable and thought about Rose. She was so weak and tired now, not ill but simply worn out. I felt a tear roll across the bridge of my nose and drop on to the pillow.

Some fitful hours of sleep later I awoke to hear tapping on my door. I immediately thought of Reggie, who had tried all evening to advance the flirtation he had begun the day before. I sprang out of bed, full of righteous anger, and threw open the door. Jenny stood there in her nightdress. She shrank back when she saw the expression of wrath on my face. 'I'm ever so sorry to wake you, Miranda. I didn't know what to do!'

'It's all right. I'm not angry with you, Jenny. I thought you were Reggie.'

Jenny looked startled but continued, in a piercing whisper, with her tale. 'I were getting up to see to Bridie. I opened the shutters so as I could see better to make up the bottle. There's ever such a bright glow down the drive where the coach-house is!'

'Oh, God!'

I snatched up my dressing gown, looked for my slippers but couldn't find them, and ran to the window on the landing. Splashes of red and gold shattered the darkness. I flew downstairs to the telephone and dialled 999. When I had given my name and address and described the nature of the emergency to a man who seemed to be afflicted with deafness and who responded so slowly that I imagined him pausing to lick his pencil and scratch his ear before writing anything down, I told Jenny to go back to Bridie, who was yelling loudly.

'We don't want to wake anyone. The children might be frightened, and an arsonist living in the garden isn't exactly a draw to paying guests.'

I let myself out through the front door and ran over the bridge. Supposing the fire had crept round to Puck's stable? I put on a spurt and hardly felt the ground beneath my bare feet.

'Miranda! Thank God!' Ivor's large shape loomed up in the darkness. 'I was coming to wake you. Have you called the fire brigade?'

'Yes! What about Puck?'

'He's all right. It hasn't reached the stables yet but I've taken him down to the old barn to get him away from the smoke. Oh, God, Miranda, I'm sorry!'

'Never mind now. Can we do anything?'

'Nothing. The tap's frozen. We'll have to wait for the firemen.'

It was hard to believe in the impartial and heartless nature of what seemed like terrifying animosity as the flames crept along the walls and closer to the clock tower. Our nostrils were filled with bitter smoke, and we tasted the acrid fumes on our lips. When I shut my stinging eyes I saw on my inner eyelids scarlet and silver images like destroying hands. The noise was tremendous, and ash blew over us like spitting rain.

My efforts to keep the thing quiet were, of course, useless. The children, Reggie, Priscilla and Mr Tremlow appeared soon after the fire engine, which came wailing and flashing up the drive, hauling the village from sleep with its own *son et lumière*. The firemen rushed about with impressive efficiency. I saw that we could do nothing but get wet and in the way.

We stood in the hall, dazed with shock and sleepiness. Henry looked like a singer from *The Black and White Minstrel Show*, having attracted more ash and soot than the rest of us put together.

'I never knew fire was so noisy,' said Elizabeth.

I saw that she was trembling with cold and fright. 'We'll go and get warm in the kitchen. Come on, everyone, there's nothing to worry about. They'll soon put it out,' I said, trying and failing for a note of cheerfulness. 'What about a cup of tea?'

Reggie took a grizzling Priscilla upstairs with unsympathetic firmness. Elizabeth said that tea was the very last thing she wanted. Henry was all for returning to the fire to see how it was going. He was recovering his usual buoyancy and, I could see, had plans for playing some heroic role. I sent him back to bed with instructions to wash his face.

'Talking of washing, Mum, your feet are bleeding on the rug,' was Henry's parting shot. 'If *I* did that you'd say I was making a mess.' He grumbled to Elizabeth about the unfairness of life all the way upstairs.

'I suppose it was Ivor?' asked James, his face very white. 'Honestly, he's getting worse. Of course I like him, we all do, but this isn't supposed to be a rest home for the criminally deranged.'

'Well, people do sometimes get worse, darling. You have to put up with people's vagaries and hope they'll put up with yours.' My feet were hurting now. James gave me a look that accused me of being tolerant to the point of feeble-mindedness.

'I'd like that cup of tea,' said Mr Tremlow. 'Come along, Mrs Stowe. You could do with one too, I'm sure. You will tell me where things are and I'll make it.'

I protested against this idea but he was firm. He made me sit by the Aga with a cup of tea in my hand and my feet in a bowl of warm water. He was surprisingly authoritative and I was glad of it, for the fire had shaken my sense of purpose.

'You know,' said Mr Tremlow, gorgeous in a purple and green Paisley dressing gown, as he drew up a chair next to me, 'I always think a little chaos – a few unforeseen events – are an excellent thing.'

'You do?' I had been trying to work out the cost of the repairs to the coach-house. I felt steeped in gloom.

'Yes. You see, we all struggle for security. Houses, jobs, bank accounts, mortgages, insurance schemes. We marry to have a companion, have children to give us a share of the future. We try to hedge our bets, anticipate, stay ahead of the game. But it's all an illusion. The bigger the kingdom we build for ourselves, the more we have to lose. Houses burn down, we get the sack, banks go bust, spouses divorce us or die, children move to the other side of the world. It's good to be reminded that we can't hold on to anything. We mustn't lose our sense of adventure or our faith in our own ability to survive. How are those poor feet?'

He meant me to be comforted and I *was* comforted. When Ivor came in, he found Mr Tremlow tenderly drying my feet. 'This is wonderfully biblical,' said Mr Tremlow. 'I'm only sorry my hair isn't long enough to make a towel.'

'The fire's out. They're getting ready to leave,' said Ivor, in a suppressed voice. 'Half the roof's gone and one pair of double doors. The walls are black but otherwise all right.' He sank down at the table and buried his head in his hands. 'I'm more sorry than I can say. Oh, what a fool I am!'

'It's not as bad as all that,' I said. 'No one was hurt.'

Ivor burst into tears. Mr Tremlow poured him a cup of tea, put it at his elbow and went tactfully out of the room. I got upstairs at last, having reassured Ivor that our friendship could withstand the burning down of the coach-house. The fire in my bedroom had sunk to a few smouldering gleams. I didn't bother to turn on the light but hobbled across the room and prepared myself for the icy embrace of the sheets, my hot-water bottle having gone cold hours ago. But the bed was warm.

'Aha!' said a sleepy but unmistakable voice. 'I fall asleep several times waiting for the lovely Mrs Stowe. Oh, your hair smell delicious! *Füstölt Kolbász*... smoked sausage! What an appetite for conversation you have in the middle of the night. Almost I think to go downstairs. But no, I tell myself, this will make complications and spoil the surprise. You like surprises, yes?'

CHAPTER 14

If I had been an Ancient Roman I should have found it immensely difficult to select the appropriate pebble for the urn that Sunday. Janòs woke me early in the morning and we made love in a deliciously leisurely fashion, without the desperate hunger of a few hours before. White pebble. He told me he had to leave for London immediately after lunch. Black pebble. And so it continued. I imagine the Romans had just the same trouble and always spent the last hour before bedtime in torments of indecision.

It was unquestionably blissful to rediscover the pleasure of sexual passion with someone who made me feel that we were intimates as well as lovers. Jack had once told me that he preferred to make love to women about whom he knew nothing and cared less. Now I understood that he had always deliberately disengaged himself emotionally and it occurred to me, for the very first time, that Jack did not like women.

The second good thing that followed hard on a dawn that was not so much rosy-fingered as grey-fisted was the result of an early telephone call. I had never had an extension to my bedroom because I felt strongly that at Westray wiring, and the concomitant boring of holes and knocking in of tacks, should be kept to the strictest minimum. None the less, it was maddeningly inconvenient to have to stumble on sore feet down the stairs in response to a faint, insistent ringing from the hall. A man, whose larynx sounded as though it had spent a lifetime being exsiccated by cigarette smoke, asked for Reggie.

Reggie was terse with the disturber of his dreams and grew yet more laconic as the conversation went on.

'I've got to love you and leave you, Mrs S,' he said, finding me in the kitchen. I had decided, reluctantly, that it was too late to go back to bed and that I must get Janòs out of it and start Rose's porridge. 'Business calls. That little fracass turn out all right, last night? Priscilla got hysterical. Terrified of being burned in her bed. I put a stop to all that nonsense. If you've been brought up hard like I was you don't have nerves. They're an upper-class luxury, they are.' He gave a short bad-tempered laugh, and I thought, not for the first time, that he was very like Mr Bounderby. He whipped out his comb, ran it through his oiled locks and returned it to his inside breast pocket in a characteristically swift movement. 'You've looked after us very nice. I like to see a woman in the kitchen. Pity we couldn't have got to know each other a little better, but you gotta take time by the fetlock as the saying is.'

'Forelock.'

I was so accustomed to correct the children that I spoke without thinking. I was sorry at once.

Reggie looked cross.

'Have it your own way. Those of us who got our ejercation thumped into us at the school of hard knocks are strangers to fine words and folderols. Some of us has the cares of the world pressing on us.'

The cares of the world took Reggie and Priscilla away at ten o'clock. Their agent was a man named Prance. He was as nasty a bit of work as I have ever seen. Mean little eyes gleamed in a skull shaped like the Sugar Loaf mountain. I wondered what there was about Reggie to make Prance, who was a foot taller, with an impressive musculature that strained at the seams of his coat, so subservient. He made no protest as Reggie loaded him with all the suitcases and the camel overcoat and balanced Priscilla's handbag on top for good measure. Prance tottered across the bridge and stowed everything into the large maroon Jaguar waiting on the drive.

'Here you are.' Reggie peeled off a lot of notes from a roll he had pulled from his back trousers pocket and handed them to me. 'I've added a little extra as a tip for personal services.' He winked at me.

I understood that this was for the benefit of Prance, who had returned and stood awaiting further orders. I wished that Freddy, the taxi driver, had not arrived at the door at that very moment. Freddy explained, with great haughtiness, that he wanted to check what time the foreign gentleman was requiring his services. He had tried to telephone but the line had been engaged.

I said goodbye to Priscilla, who this morning had black ravines under each eye and a wild look. It is said that every man makes his own hell but I was confident that from now on Reggie would do it for her. I saw them go, with relief, and took Freddy into the hall. Janòs came downstairs while I was looking for the train time-table.

'I grow tired of waiting for you, my darling. Also I am hungry.'

I gave Freddy, who was by now frozen with disapproval, the time-table and left them to sort it out between themselves.

Just before lunch I heard Maeve's voice in the hall. 'Thought I'd come and run my glimmers over the beautiful Abdallah. You don't mind, I hope.'

'Not at all. Who's Abdallah?'

'Literally, you mean? He was the father of Muhammad and so scrumptious that when he married two hundred virgins broke their hearts and died of disappointed love.' Maeve had had a brief flirtation with Islam before becoming a Zen Buddhist and after a phase of Rosicrucianism. 'Metaphorically I mean Janòs, of course. That's him I can hear practising, isn't it?'

'How did you know he was here?'

'Easy. I read it in the tea-leaves.' She lit a Gitane and puffed smoke over the roast potatoes, which I was in the process of basting. 'Oh, how good those smell!'

I noticed that she was looking particularly attractive, in a tight black jersey and a swirling gypsyish skirt. Her short hair was mulberry-coloured and her eyes stared dramatically from black rims, which were exaggerated into Cleopatra-like points at the corners.

'Like to stay to lunch?'

'You generous girl! Not only willing to share your paramour but your potatoes, too. Actually, I heard the news from Mrs Veal. I was just getting in some logs when she loomed up over my garden gate. She couldn't wait to tell me that she'd heard from her brother-in-law, who's a fireman, who'd heard it from Freddy Beach, you know, the taxi man, that he'd brought a young man of foreign extraction from the station to Westray Manor at two o'clock in the morning. It was the lateness of the hour that set the village agog.'

'What else did that intolerable woman say?'

'Not much. She was hoping to get some dirt out of me, but all I could tell her was that he was a pianist and dizzily handsome and that you'd met him for the first time last weekend and were mad about him.'

'You didn't say that! Oh, Maeve, how could you?'

'What's wrong with that? It's true.'

'You could have made up some story about him being a cousin or an interior decorator or something. You didn't have to practically describe us in bed together.'

'I don't see why I should have to perjure my soul for the likes of Mrs Veal.' Maeve was currently Anglo-Catholic. 'Anyway, interior decorators don't generally call on their clients at two in the morning. Why you worry about what other people think of you I don't know. I've never given a damn.'

'If I could stop minding for my own sake, I should still mind for the children's. It's embarrassing for them to have everyone talking about us.'

'They'll have to toughen up, in that case. You're much

too protective. I let my boys see the world as it is. No namby-pambying for them.'

And perhaps that's why one's a neo-Fascist and the other's a transvestite, I thought, but immediately repented of this unkindness. I don't subscribe to the view that mothering, good or bad, forms people's characters. If only it were as simple as that. I just wanted my children to enjoy childhood as much as possible. Thanks to Jack there was now a very important entry in the register of sorrows.

'You know what the Greeks said,' continued Maeve.

'Which particular Greeks?'

'Oh, I don't know exactly. At this distance it hardly matters. What a pedant you are!'

'Sorry.'

'Anyway, Aeschylus or whoever it was said you have to suffer unto truth. Meaning that when you're wretched you learn useful things, and when you're happy you just skim along not taking in anything much.'

'A masterly translation, if I may say so.'

'I love it when you're sarcastic.' Maeve ground out her cigarette in the pile of potato peelings.

'Must you do that? There's a perfectly good ashtray in front of you.'

'It's all organic. What a fuss you make about trivial things. Do you think you might be anally retentive? My analyst says nanny-reared children almost invariably are. But I had a nanny who could have understudied for Mr Hyde without makeup. I bet I was out of nappies before I left the maternity home. My analyst says I'm the least anally retentive woman he's ever met.'

'As a chat-up line it's certainly original.'

'Oh, do you think he's going to make a pass? I *had* wondered. Good. He's quite succulent when he takes his specs off. If only he wouldn't clean out his ears with his car key.'

'Maeve! Surely it's professional misconduct or something.'

'Is it? I should think it happens all the time. Whenever I

talk about my first marriage and the terrible things Titus used to insist on doing when we were making love, poor Mr Postlethwaite, that's my analyst, goes lobster-pink and keeps having to go off to the lavatory. I think I've got him in a permanently inflamed state. That's good. I don't see you laughing often enough. Anyway, I meant to ask you straight away about the fire but I got sidetracked. What started it, do you know?'

'Ivor, I'm afraid. But for God's sake don't spread *that* around the village. He's been in trouble – serious trouble – before because of it. For the last few years he seemed to have it under control. Jack's death started it all up again. He just can't resist making fires. It's a compulsion.'

'No! Gripping! Go on!'

'There isn't any more to tell. It's really rather sad. He was so miserable last night. You wouldn't laugh if you knew.'

'Gosh, sorry.' Maeve was kind-hearted, no one more so. 'Poor bloke! It's just that I've never met a pyromaniac before. I shall view him with new eyes. You must ask me to lunch when he's here.'

I had deliberately avoided doing any such thing in the past because Maeve was one of the few people that the gentle Ivor didn't like. On the occasion of their first meeting they had had a stormy argument about pacifism. Maeve had quickly and accurately taken Ivor's measure and decided to tease him. She had pretended to be tremendously pro-war. Things had got quite ugly as Maeve knows how to be provocative. She believes that quarrelling is an aphrodisiac. Which explains quite a lot about her life, really. Ivor hates rows and it had taken weeks for him to get over it. However, that was all a long time ago.

'I certainly will if you'd like it. But you're not to torment him. He's had a spell in a mental hospital, you know.'

'No! More and more interesting! Ah, the piano has fallen silent. Just a minute.' Maeve took one of my rubber gloves and tossed it on to the table with a theatrical gesture where it fell into the baking tray in which I had just melted fat for the Yorkshire pudding. 'I challenge you, Miranda, to *guerre à mort*! Or perhaps *guerre à lit* would be more accurate.'

I retrieved the glove, washed it and returned it to its partner by the sink. 'I don't accept the challenge. If I ever find myself resorting to stratagems to attract a man I shall know it's time to take a vow of celibacy.'

'Ha, ha, ha!' said Maeve. 'What a weight of self-delusion you bear, my poor child.'

The rose-pink shavings of beef fell from the knife like large petals. The Yorkshire pudding had risen in golden billows. I had braised celery and flavoured carrots with French mustard and rosemary.

'This looks sufficiently ambrosial to make me immortal. Lucullus would be well contented to sup with Lucullus,' said Maurice. After the excitements of the night before, Mr Tremlow and I had progressed to Christian names. He had been appointed to the head of the table by default. I hate cutting up meat and James always cut slices as thick as linoleum. Ivor had not made an appearance, which was worrying but I hadn't had time to make inquiries. I expect Jack's absence from the head of the table must have been in everyone's thoughts, though no one mentioned him. I felt sad that a conspiracy of silence about his death had grown up among us. 'I'm delighted that my old skills haven't quite deserted me,' continued Maurice. 'My goodness, how it takes me back. In Calabria we had whole pigs sometimes, roasted over a fire out of doors but there was no finesse about cutting it up.'

'Who's Lucullus?' asked Henry.

'He was a Roman general and a great gourmet. When a superb feast was prepared for him he was asked who the guests were to be. He replied as I have stated.'

'If I'd said that, everyone would have told me to shut up. If you're a Roman you can say really stupid things and centuries later people are still thinking how jolly clever they are and making you translate them. It's unfair.'

'You English have the reputation for food of the most disagreeable kind,' said Janòs, 'but this I do not find. It is yet another thing that you do like an angel, Mrs Stowe.'

He smiled at me in such a way that my heart-rate doubled, I swallowed much too much horseradish and began to cough.

'What else does Mum do besides cook?' asked Henry.

I gave him an indignant look from watering eyes.

'Of course, you Hungarians know all about food,' said Maeve, getting straight into provocative mode. 'Paprika stew, paprika potatoes, paprika soup, paprika ice-cream . . .'

'Yes, Miss. A good joke but you cannot make me angry. What patriot feelings I have are in things higher than the national diet.' He smiled at Maeve.

I wondered, jealously, what effect this was having on her.

'I don't think food's a bit important,' said Elizabeth. 'What matters are things like great art and music. I listened to your playing this morning. It was dreamy.'

Janòs bowed solemnly to her but made no reply. I was amused. Very recently Elizabeth had expressed such forthright views on sadistic mothers who made their hapless daughters take piano lessons that I had allowed her to give them up. She had pinned her hair back on one side and let the other side fall across her face, from behind which she peeped at Janòs. Her shirt was unbuttoned almost to her belt.

'I see your programme at the Wigmore Hall next month is all Brahms,' continued Maeve. 'Those poor old Romantics are so done to death it can't be possible to say anything new about them.'

'At every single performance it is possible to say something new. But not everyone can hear. It requires the audience to listen, yes?'

'Oh, goodness me, what a cheat!' Maeve was warming to her theme, sensing a slight engagement with the argument on Janòs's part. 'Anyone could go on giving the same tired old interpretation and pretend that it's going over the heads of the audience.'

There was much more in this vein. Maeve and Janòs were sitting opposite each other across the middle of the table, and soon the conversation became too splenetic to allow contributions from the rest of us.

I tried to talk to Rose, who sat on my right. 'I think the sun's going to come out in a little while. Shall we walk down to look at the coach-house after lunch? I want to see the extent of the damage and you haven't had any fresh air for ages.'

Rose stared at me from eyes that held a suggestion of defiance. It was not one of her good days. ' "Though your sins be as scarlet they shall be white as snow." Isaiah, chapter one, verse eighteen.'

I couldn't think of a suitable reply. I went to get the lemon meringue pie. Dinkie was crouched over it on the kitchen table, having eaten a neat semi-circle out of the biscuit-coloured ripples. It was sheer spite on his part as he hates sugary things. He gave me a smug look from his peridot eyes.

When I returned to the dining room it was to hear Maeve say, 'The only reason you play Rachmaninoff is because it's just the most seductive stuff ever written. It's tart's music.'

Janòs, who had been looking very cross, suddenly began to laugh. 'You try to make me angry. I see what you do. Oh, no, Maeve. You want to enslave me but I am bound to the mast and there is wax in the ears. I drink to the sirens.'

He raised his glass to her in mock salutation. Maeve blew him a kiss. I almost banged the lemon meringue pie on the table.

'Must you go now?' I heard Elizabeth saying to Janòs, as they stood in the hall after lunch. I was in the cloakroom putting on my coat and gloves and neither was aware of me.

'My dear Elizabeth, I must. I shall come back soon, if your mother will permit.'

'Oh, she will, I know. I want your advice, Mr Décsi. I'm thinking of taking up the piano again. Do you think my hands are the right shape?'

I came out of the cloakroom to see Janòs bending over her outstretched hand. Elizabeth bent forward until her breasts were absolutely under his nose.

Janòs let her hand drop abruptly. 'You want my advice. I suggest that you clean that rubbish from your pretty little face and go and read some charming fairy-tales. I do not want to be arrested for seducing little girls.'

I made a pretence of looking for my bag so that they should not know I had overheard. When I joined them, Elizabeth was fiery red and her eyes were very bright.

'I won't be long darling,' I said to her, my heart wrung for the wound she had received. 'When I get back from the station we could show Maurice the garden, couldn't we?'

'I think that's the most boring and stupid suggestion I've ever heard.'

She walked slowly upstairs with great dignity, but her head began to droop before she was out of sight.

'Next weekend I play in Venice,' said Janòs, as we drove through the village.

'Lucky you. I've only been there once.' For a moment I saw Jack's face in the bedroom at the Hotel Fedele. Outside the rain had fallen like silver ropes and his smile, after we had made love, had been triumphant.

The picture vanished as Janòs said, 'Why don't you come with me?'

'Oh! It's a wonderful idea but I couldn't. I couldn't leave the children.'

'Why not? It is two nights. Saturday and Sunday. You have visitors?'

'No. Maurice leaves on Friday. I'm sorry you didn't have a chance to talk to him properly. He's very intelligent and knows so much about so many things.'

'What stops you, then? The children can be for two days without their mother.'

It was on my lips to deny it, and then I remembered how young Janòs had been when he had had to do altogether without family or ties of any description. I would never be able to make him understand.

'Well, there's Rose, too. She's so frail.'

'That girl, Jenny, who is in love with your son, James, seems managing.'

'Capable, I think you mean. Yes, I suppose she is. Is she really in love with him, do you think? But she has a baby to look after. It wouldn't be fair to load everything on to her.'

Janòs spread his hands. 'It seem I make a mistake. I think this affair is important. But for you it is just a time-passing.'

'Pastime. No, you're quite wrong. It *is* important to me. Very important. But you must see that I have other obligations.'

Janòs was quiet for a moment. Then he said, 'I see that I am on the bottom of a long, long list.'

We drove up to the station in silence, and Janòs opened the door and got out. I thought he was going to go without another word and I was wretched. I wound down my window. He came round and bent to my level.

'We have a saying in my part of Hungary. You must feather your wishes or they cannot fly. It means that you must take trouble for what you want.' He stuck his head in through the car window, and kissed me lightly and briefly on the lips. Then he strode off into the station without another glance in my direction. I put the car into gear, my state of anguish not helped by the sight of the station master and the porter, grinning like buffoons.

'What did you say this bit of garden is called?' asked Maurice when, an hour later, we braved the chilly wind for a tour of the grounds. We had reached a hedged compartment about thirty feet square. Four fastigiate yews marked the corners of an octagonal pond, in the centre of which stood a rather battered statue of Aphrodite.

'Temenos.'

'Don't tell me. My Greek's a little rusty but still in place, just about.' Maurice stared up into the racing clouds for inspiration. 'I've got it. A sacred piece of ground.'

'Quite right. You see, it's dedicated to Aphrodite. The children, ironically enough, call it my Jealousy Garden.'

'Why?'

'Because I grow only green flowers in it. There are hellebores, *Ribes laurifolium* and stachyurus in late winter, then Solomon's seal and *Daphne laureola* and all the euphorbias in spring. In the summer there is the green rose – *Rosa viridiflora* – and lime-coloured tobacco plants, moluccellas, angelica and *Alchemilla mollis*. Then comes a wonderful green zinnia called 'Envy'. It's a marvellously tranquil place to sit in and contemplate whatever's bothering you. That's why I have that camomile seat over there.'

'Oh, please! Let's go and sit on it.'

'It isn't at its best at this time of year.'

'I don't care. Imagination is the eye of the soul, according to Joubert.' Maurice plumped himself down on the camomile with a flourish of his cloak. 'Ah! What a pretty place this is, even in winter. Its charm is in its restraint. Now, tell me what's ironical about calling this your Jealousy Garden?'

'Oh. Did I really say that?'

Maurice smiled and nodded.

'I can't imagine why.' I felt myself grow warm. 'At least... that isn't true. I *do* know. But it isn't at all interesting.'

'I'm interested.'

'Really, it's a very uninspiring story and one I shouldn't dream of boring anyone with.'

'Forgive me if I've been inquisitive.'

'You haven't been. But it's all about something that's past and needn't be dragged back.'

Maurice flexed his elbows, clasped his hands together on his knees and made himself comfortable. Dinkie, who had followed us companionably around the garden, suddenly changed into a tiger and gave the falling leaves hell. Jasper leaned against Maurice's knees, with the lofty expression of a dog who has a great deal on his mind.

'Lovely, isn't it?' Maurice seemed content to watch the tiny currents and eddies on the dark surface of the pool. 'I could sit here for hours. No doubt the damp camomile promises rheumatism for my bottom but no matter. Perhaps you're right. Sometimes the past is better left alone. It's too painful to sift it.'

I don't know to this day what persuaded me to begin the tale of my life with Jack. One minute we were sitting in a congenial silence, contemplating nature, and the next moment I was deep in a frank confession that tossed discretion to the winds. It seemed as though Maurice had charmed the words out of me as he sat, grave and silent as one of the Seven Sages of Greece, his eyes shining faintly in the shadow of the brim of his fedora. The narration came easily as he refrained from expressions of disapproval or blame or even surprise. I realised for the first time as I spoke about Jack that, despite the unhappiness of our marriage, there was a residue of . . . not love, that was too strong an emotion but something like sore regret for the man he had once been, the *primum mobile* of sexual love, mentor of my youth and father of my children.

'I suppose it was as much my fault as his that things went so badly wrong,' I concluded. 'I shouldn't have minded as much as I did. You see, it didn't matter how often he told me that he loved me, I still felt rejected, humiliated and . . . desolate. Intellectually I knew that this was nonsense. But something much stronger than my intellect had control of how I really felt.'

'The heart has its reasons.' Maurice spoke for the first time for many minutes. 'I do understand.'

'Do you?' I had been staring at the ground while I spoke. Now I turned to look at him. I saw that his eyes were suffused with tears. 'Oh, I'm sorry.'

'Don't be. At my age one has seen so much that – weal or woe – crying comes easily.'

'I've been very selfish, burdening you with these sordid troubles. Ultimately it's all unimportant.'

'Ah, don't say that! Don't be polite. Don't shut yourself away. "Give sorrow words: the grief that does not speak whispers the o'erfraught heart, and bids it break." Shakespeare knew what he was talking about. I'm getting old. I don't want the fripperies of small-talk. I exult in your confidence.' He got up and twirled on the spot. 'You see, no rheumatism. I wax fat like Jeshurun on your trust. Now, take me to see those hens and we'll agree that fidelity is an indispensable component of love.'

'This is Heloïse,' I said, taking a handful of corn from the bin and bending down so that the hen could peck from my hand. 'She's a Lavender Araucana and lays eggs with greenish-blue shells. And this is Abelard.' I pointed to a handsome grey cockerel, who was flapping his wings, warning me to not take liberties with his mate. 'He hasn't suffered the same fate as his namesake but I threaten him with it because he's so noisy. Ivor made the hen-house. Isn't it lovely?' It was of Gothick style with castellated towers at each end and an ogee-shaped pop-hole. Abelard stretched his neck and crowed.

'That's a pretty one.' Maurice pointed to a hen with downy chestnut plumage who was scratching the ground and turning her head on one side to spy the tiny insects which are fowl caviare.

'A Partridge Silkie. That's Ivor's favourite. He calls her Xanthippe because she squawks and scolds all the time. There never was such a scholarly hen-run.'

Walking back towards the house we passed again through Temenos. A piece of paper tied with plaited grass lay on Aphrodite's plinth.

'Thank goodness! If Ivor's writing poetry, he must be holding together, just about.' I picked it up and unrolled it. I had become increasingly concerned at Ivor's non-appearance, fearing that he would be brooding on the accident to the coach-house, and I had already decided that I would go down to his cottage later that afternoon to talk to him if he would allow me. 'I wonder if he overheard our conversation about Jack. But he's the soul of honour and would have gone away the moment he heard our voices. He has an almost supernatural ability to drift unseen about the garden.'

'He's in love with you.'

'Well, only in an Ivor-ish sort of way. Poetically.' I read the two stanzas, which were predictably about guilt, despair and love. 'Do you know? This is really good! I've always thought that he has an original and imaginative voice. This has an argument as well as beauty.'

'May I see?'

I gave the paper to Maurice. He read it as we walked along. I tucked my hand through his arm to guide him beneath the iron hoops of the rose garden, which in summer dripped with white petals but now bore only crumpling leaves, yellow and sere. 'I agree with you,' he said, at last. 'A lot of contemporary verse is pleasingly sensual and not much more. But this has something to say. Suppose I let a friend of mine who works for Flogam and Knoutem see this? Or is it not meant for publication?'

'I'll give you the portfolio I've collected of Ivor's poems. Who is there in the world who doesn't want recognition? We won't say anything to Ivor. I wouldn't want to get his hopes up. As you must have gathered, he's rather . . . sensitive.'

'I like the people you've collected around you. I wish I'd known your husband. He must have had something exceptional about him or you would not have chosen him.'

'Come and see his grave with me.'

I had been once to visit it since the funeral, but I was made so self-conscious by the attention my presence in the churchyard attracted that I had not done so again. Villagers had materialised from nowhere and gathered by the churchyard wall, lingering ostensibly to blow their noses or tie a shoelace but really to detect, I now realised, some sign of consciousness of guilt.

'These flowers are new.' I placed the wreath of red roses, which was rather battered by wind, more securely against the wooden cross that marked the mound. 'Here's a card. "From Horny, with love". Poor Miss Horne. Hothouse roses at this time of year! How she loved him! These must be Lissie's flowers.' I pointed to the bouquet of longiflorum lilies. The greenish-white petals stirred faintly in a sudden gust and a small black beetle scurried from the depths of one and dug its way out of sight into the earth.

'Lissie. Ah, yes. I remember. The first lapse.'

'Yes. But I honestly have forgiven that. She's one of my dearest friends.'

'And this little posy?'

I looked at the small bundle of bramble flowers and traveller's joy with one drooping wild rosebud at its centre, tied with wisps of straw. 'That has Ivor's hallmark. How like him to put flowers on Jack's grave!' I paused for a moment. 'You may have noticed that there aren't any from me. Jack despised sentiment. Of all the women who loved him I can, at least, claim to be the only one to whom he showed himself as he really was.'

'He must have been a man of great fascination. But hardly, one thinks, with the temperament for *felo de se*.'

'I'm beginning to accept that I shall never know the answer to that.'

'Are the natives friendly?' Maurice looked up suddenly.

'What? Oh, bother! They are such ghouls!'

'Take my arm, Miranda. We shall brave it out!'

We marched so swiftly upon the picket that its members scattered in embarrassment. Poor Maurice was out of breath by the time we reached the foot of the drive so we slowed our pace for the long stroll up to the house. As we rounded the last bend Westray came into view.

'Do you know? I can't think of a lovelier house anywhere. I *am* enjoying my visit. Tomorrow, if it isn't raining, I'll go down to the beach and do a little sketching.'

He began to describe his house in Calabria as we made

a detour to look at the pigeon tower. I saw the red hills, the poplar groves, the brilliant light and intense shade, the green shutters, the cream and pink oleanders. Talking of Italy made me think regretfully of Venice. Janòs and I could never be anything more than occasional lovers. Our lives were quite incompatible. I knew that I must take my imagination firmly in hand and crush silly romantic hopes. I smiled to myself at the idea of abandoning my responsibilities to gallivant abroad with a young, tempestuous lover. I was too old, too discreet and much too sensible for such folly.

CHAPTER 15

The *acqua alta* surged beneath the duck-boards on which we teetered across the Piazza San Marco, cigarette packets and *biglietti* floating on the tide like urban bladderwrack. We walked crab-like on the narrow planks to accommodate the German and Japanese tourists and their garlands of photographic equipment. Behind the golden domes of the basilica the sky was white with cold but no rain threatened. Janòs strode ahead. A new side of his character had been shown to me since we had met at Gatwick. He was imperious with members of the cabin crew, and they fussed over him as if he had been royalty. I was surprised to find that we were travelling first class.

'Well, naturally. I do not intend to spend two hours with my knees in my ears, annoyed by screaming babies.'

'It does seem a little extravagant.'

'I cannot understand you English. You will inconvenience yourself whenever possible, mortify your fleshes with cold and eat nasty things – I except you in this, Miranda – and yet you spend much more money on your houses and gardens than most Europeans, who are living in modest apartments.'

'I expect that must be why. Economy must be made somewhere, I suppose.'

'Well, I have no house or garden, so I can spend my money on just what I wish. And that means the little less hell of travelling first class.'

'Really? You haven't got a house anywhere?' I was startled, having thought that everyone, apart from tramps, must have some kind of dwelling they called home.

'No. I have none. Where would I have it? And why? Always I move about to play. In between I go where I want to hotels that I like. Sometimes I stay with girlfriends. A house would be a trouble.'

I reflected that we could hardly be more different. For me, my house was second only to my family in importance.

We had been whisked by motor-boat over the lagoon to our hotel. Overhead the seagulls shrieked or stood silent on the posts that marked the deep-water channels. The sky and the water melted into each other, a study in *grisaille*, until La Serenissima rose slowly from the horizon in dizzying reflections of rose, ochre, pumpkin, smoke and gamboge. The receptionist of our hotel almost sank to his knees with remorse. 'Your room is not yet ready, Signor Décsi. With infinite regret I must ask you to wait twenty minutes here in the foyer where we shall bring you refreshment.'

But Janòs was impatient, furious, unmanageable. I assumed that this was because of the tension that he said built to intolerable proportions before a performance. He took my arm and said that we would go to Florian's instead, for a glass of Prosecco. We left the receptionist almost in tears. On our return our luggage had been carried to our room and I think they would have carried us, too, if it would have done any good. The room had a view from its balcony across the lagoon to Santa Maria della Salute.

'Oh, look! Look!' I called, struggling to open the great windows. 'How beautiful!'

'Yes, how beautiful. I have looked already,' said Janòs, coming up behind me and turning me firmly round. 'I have forty minutes before the beginning of the rehearsal. Those idiots almost spoil everything. Now, let me undo the buttons. Oh, God! You are like a parcel! Layers upon layers of wrappings. Ah! These little buttons are provoking. All week I wait for this moment and now I am ready to cry like a child who is frustrated.'

'It is winter, after all. Is this a good idea? Won't it make you late?'

'Well, if you will permit, it shall be quick. Tonight, it shall be long. All night, if it pleases you.'

I was just thinking that this was a delightful idea when the telephone began to ring.

'Leave it!'

'Oh, but hadn't we better –?'

'Answer it at your perils!'

I had been afraid that Jack might haunt me in Venice, but I had forgotten the irresistible persuasion of Janòs's love-making. He was in a state of extreme tension and this communicated itself in a way that, it would not be an exaggeration to say, shattered all expectations. For a while afterwards I lay with my eyes closed, regretting the ebbing of sensations of physical pleasure, thinking that I *must* be in love with Janòs, whatever that could possibly mean. The telephone rang again.

'Signora Stowe. *Momento, per favore.* You are connected.'

There was a tremendous hissing and then I heard a voice I recognised as Jenny's. 'Miranda?'

'Yes. I can hear you, Jenny. You needn't shout.'

Jenny was yelling, as though mistrustful of the power of telephone lines to cross frontiers. 'It's Elizabeth, Miranda. She's poorly. Doctor said to ring you.'

'What's wrong with her?'

I sat up in bed so abruptly that Janòs rolled away from me. 'Hey! What are you doing?'

'Sh! Tell me what's wrong, Jenny.'

'She complained at lunch of a pain in her stomach. She

couldn't eat anything and she looked ever so pale. Eeh, she did sweat, though! Rose told her to go and lie down. I went up to see how she were getting on an hour later and she were in tears with the pain. Then she got up to try to go to bathroom and she fell down in a faint, like. There were blood everywhere.'

'What?'

'Blood. Like a period but ever so much. Rose said to call Doctor so I did and he came real quick. He's taken her to the infirmary. He said to call you when I told him you was gone abroad.'

'Oh, God!' I clutched my head and tried to think. 'All right, Jenny. I'll catch the first flight home. Ring the hospital and get a message to Elizabeth that I'll be there as fast as I can.'

'You are not going!' Janòs was sitting up now and swinging his legs out of bed.

'I must go. Elizabeth may be very ill. She's in pain and bleeding. She fainted.'

'She is not alone. She has medical help. And Rose and Jenny.'

'I'm her mother. I must go.'

I was already dialling Reception. 'Hello? Yes, Mrs Stowe speaking, room forty-six. Please get me on the next flight to London. It's very important. Yes, first class if necessary. At once. I'll come down to the desk.'

'I don't believe it!' Janòs took hold of my arm in a grip that made me wince with pain. 'You leave me now like this? It is just this kind of thing to make me play badly.'

'Of course I don't want to go! But I have to!'

'I see.' Janòs was pulling on his clothes, as cold now as he had been heated a moment ago. 'Go, then! You are already leaving my mind. Women! They are all the same in the end.'

I understood that he intended to persuade himself of this fact. Any idea of wounding me was already far from his thoughts as I had ceased to be of any importance.

'Goodbye, darling,' I said, as he picked up his coat and

scarf and walked out of the door. 'Please telephone,' I added, to the empty room.

Two hours later I was sitting in a plane as it rolled slowly across the tarmac to its position at the end of the runway. The engines screamed and then we were airborne. Dusk was falling. Venice was dyed in shades of cobalt and lavender and beaded with yellow dots.

I stared out of the window, no longer seeing the darkening expanses of cloud, and thought of Elizabeth. She had seemed perfectly well when I left. I ran back over the past week in my mind for any signs of illness. As she always wore that strange white makeup it was impossible to tell whether she had been unusually pale or flushed. She had eaten well, I was sure. She had been rather droopy and irritable, but that was fairly normal these days. Poor darling! She must be terrified, being rushed to hospital. How could I have left her! I must be the very worst of mothers. I drank two glasses of *spumante* very fast, but waved away the little plastic tray of food.

Why had I allowed myself to be persuaded? Things had seemed to be generally so improved the week before that I had thought I could allow myself this indulgence. Henry had telephoned me from Nethercoat's that Monday evening to say that he had got the part of Henry V in the school play. 'Masses of speeches, Mum. I'm the main part!'

'Yes, darling. I am familiar with the play.'

'We've just been shown the film. Terrific battles. I'm not going to wear my hair like Laurence Olivier does, though. He looks like a stupid girl. I'm going to have a suit of armour. You've got to come and see it!'

'Darling, if I had to crawl every one of the thirty miles on my hands and knees I should be there. Absolutely nothing could keep me away. I'm very proud of you. I know you'll be good.'

It was not entirely maternal infatuation that made me say this. Henry was a good actor and could remember his lines easily. But in addition he had a keen enjoyment at being the centre of attention that, on the stage, was extraordinarily attractive. It must be what is called star quality. Of course, he had inherited this from Jack.

James had telephoned from Westminster later in the week to say that he had been asked to spend the weekend with friends and they were going to Covent Garden to see *Tosca*. He seemed very pleased by the idea. I had noticed his musical tastes changing from the obligatory pop to something more thoughtful. At eighteen he was more or less in charge of his own life. I felt that my role was purely advisory now.

When I had told Patience that Janòs and I had parted on less than good terms at the railway station and explained the reason why, I had been startled by her reaction. 'He asked you to spend two days in Venice with him and you refused? Either you aren't really interested in him or the balance of your mind is disturbed! What an invitation! It's exactly what you need. An opportunity to have some fun for a change!'

Maeve, who had unexpectedly joined us for lunch that particular Tuesday, was even franker. I hadn't been going to say anything about it for fear of upsetting her but Patience had no such scruples.

'Miranda!' Maeve had paused in her consumption of *spaghetti con funghi e piselli*. 'You're crazy! Ring the man at once and say that you're going!'

'That's very generous of you in the circumstances –'

'Oh, rubbish! I'm not interested in exclusive rights, if that's what you mean. You know what I think about monogamy. You can't stop people desiring each other by putting an embargo on touching. It's exactly the way to inflame secret passions. I'm convinced there wouldn't be half so much human sexual activity if everyone could go to bed with whomever whenever they pleased. We'd all be attending classes on macramé and barbola work out of sheer boredom.'

'That seems to suggest that all the enjoyment of sex lies in intrigue,' I objected. 'What about the simple physical pleasure of it?'

'Surely it isn't possible to have such a thing without an emotional overlay of some kind,' suggested Patience, tentatively. 'You've *got* to have some feeling about another person. Suppose you made love with a complete stranger and the room was in total darkness. Wouldn't you be unable to prevent yourself fantasising and supplying a mind and a physical shape to the flesh?'

'I'm surprised at you, Patience,' said Maeve. 'So this is the way your thoughts run. It's the most delicious idea, I grant you.'

'I'm not saying it's what I want to do,' said Patience, her cheeks glowing.

'I should absolutely hate it.' I shuddered at the thought.

'And why?' Maeve's eyes were filled with curiosity.

'I'm not sure. I should be afraid.'

'Go on. This is interesting. What of?'

'I should feel I was giving something of myself away. To someone I wouldn't know I could trust. And . . . they might look horrible.'

'Mm, that's a very revealing remark.' Maeve savoured this for a while. 'What would that matter if the lights never went on and you never saw them?'

'I must be very superficial, I know.'

'Or very romantic,' said Patience. 'I don't see why you should be ashamed of minding about appearances. Most people do, though luckily we don't agree about what's attractive.'

I thought at once of Aubrey Molebank. He was intelligent, compassionate and considerate, and I was very fond of him. But I would have been prepared to hand over large sums of money not to go to bed with him.

'Anyway,' said Maeve impatiently, 'what it comes down to is that if you don't ring up Janòs, undisputed cynosure of all female eyes, and tell him you'll go to Venice with him you need a spell of careful medical supervision. Perhaps that ducky new doctor would provide it. Have you seen him?'

'You don't mean Dr McCleod? He's such a disagreeable man. And he has an appalling chip on his shoulder.

He thinks I'm a spoiled, selfish little madam who drove Jack to his death with my coquettish behaviour.'

'He's got a very pretty girlfriend. Or perhaps she's his wife. I saw them driving off together yesterday. He didn't look at all disagreeable, I can tell you.'

'Well, I don't like him. How can I ring up Janòs when I have absolutely no idea of his telephone number or where he is?'

'Hello, everyone,' said Lissie, coming into the kitchen. Her eyes were bright and her cheeks pink with cold. She looked very charming in a camel coat with a fur collar and matching fur hat. She gave us each a kiss and then looked round the room.

'Bridie's asleep,' I said, knowing at once the object she sought.

'I hope that's fake fur,' said Maeve disapprovingly.

'Oh, yes, I think so,' said Lissie vaguely, her blue eyes quite guileless.

It was obvious from twenty paces that it was mink, but I'm sure that Lissie had never given it, or the ethics of wearing fur, a single thought beyond whether it was becoming or not.

'Look, she's just woken up,' said Lissie, lifting Bridie up. 'Isn't she utterly adorable.'

'Very much like the things Sebastian and Florian used to make at kindergarten. Wobbly clay lumps with blobs for eyes and matchstick holes for nostrils. She's like a cartoon, just a sketch of what she might grow up into.'

'How can you?' Lissie clutched Bridie so close to her that the baby started to whimper in protest at having her breathing impeded by mink. 'Look at her darling little gummy mouth.'

We looked obediently as Bridie dribbled furiously and stared back at us with round eyes. Then she smiled suddenly, an enormous toothless grin, and I noticed that we all, including Maeve, beamed back.

'I give in. She's irresistible. Now, Lissie, do help us bully Miranda into going to Venice with her *amoroso*.'

Lissie paused in the act of wiping Bridie's face, and looked at me with patent astonishment.

'Oh, don't let's talk about it any more.' I got up to make some coffee.

'Haven't you heard, then?' went on Maeve, obliviously. Or perhaps she was not as oblivious as she seemed. 'Don't you know about Miranda's great love affair? Of course you've met Janòs. You were here when I brought him that day I went down with flu. But perhaps you didn't know that they fell straight into each other's arms?'

'No. I didn't know.' I watched Lissie as she bent her head over the baby. She had her back to me as I put the kettle on the Aga. When I sat down again I caught her eye, and she was gazing at me with an expression of absolute amazement.

'Is the kettle on?' cried Maurice, coming in opportunely. 'It would be a kindness to rotate me on the spit to bring me to room temperature. That beach was the site of a wind symposium today. Not only a mistral and a sirocco but a peesash and a harmattan as well, with a simoom to keep them company.'

He began to peel off his gloves and scarf. This was his second day of sketching. The day before Ivor had carried down a canvas windbreak and erected it near a rocky promontory while Maurice had carried his easel and drawing paper and I had brought the brushes and paints. Maurice said he could only paint if he wore his special painting hat, which was a Borsalino, the type of hat Carlyle took to wearing in his old age. Apparently it drew stares even then in a much more hat-accustomed age, being broad of brim and high of crown. Maurice looked at least as extraordinary in his but I saw that it was admirable as a shelter from the elements. The only trouble was that it would not remain on his head. Maurice solved the problem by tying it on with his braces. We left him, an improbable figure crouched behind green and white striped canvas, his easel propped upright with a cairn of rocks, but on such a day only seabirds would look at him and wonder.

The day before he had refused to show me what he had done because he said he never liked people to see his unfinished work. But now, when politely pressed, he opened his portfolio. 'Here we are! Westray Rocks. What do you think?'

We looked in silence. I had been prepared with some delicate little compliments but they seemed inappropriate.

'Good heavens!' Maeve was the first to recover her wits. 'It's stupendously good!'

'Look at the water!' said Patience. 'I've never seen it look like that even in a Turner. Full of light. You feel that wave's going to roll at any moment.'

'It's beautiful!' said Lissie. 'You know, you could sell this. I'd buy it like a shot!'

'Well, actually, I do sell my paintings,' said Maurice, modestly. 'It's how I earn my living.'

'Can I buy this one?' asked Lissie.

'I'd love to sell it to you but it's promised. I'm having an exhibition in January, and the fellow who's putting it on wants half a dozen water-colours to round it off. I'm tremendously flattered that you like it.'

'Fancy you being a painter,' said Maeve. 'Did you know, Miranda?'

'I had no idea. I should rather say, fancy you being a *good* painter. I've spent prolonged periods of my life knee-deep in painters but I've only met a few whose work gave me positive pleasure to look at.'

'What do you think about Miranda going to Venice, Maurice?' asked Maeve. 'Do you think she should?'

'Venice! Can there be any question about it?'

Maurice and I discussed the matter in more detail after the others had gone home. I was turning a leg of lamb into a *daube à l'Avignonnaise* for supper and he was sitting at the table, preparing a piece of paper for the next day's work by applying a dilute coat of paint with a brush and a sponge. He called it 'laying a wash'. Rose was asleep on the sofa, tired out after a morning at the hospital having the cast removed from her wrist. It seemed perfectly natural for Maurice to be in this familial setting, as though we had known one another all our lives. I explained about Venice and Janòs.

'Good, good, good! Just what you need. Distraction. Something for yourself. Naturally when a woman has children she's going to be pretty much tied up with them, but before you know it they'll be off your hands and then you'll be adrift. It's just the time for you to begin to look for new experiences.'

'Oh, don't! If you knew how frightened I get when I try to think of some sort of future occupation.'

'Frightened?'

'At the idea of being judged by my peers and found wanting. I've been a free agent so long, you see. And I'm thirty-nine. It's probably too late to make a go of anything.'

'When I decided to stay in Italy I had the same problem. I was forty-something. My Italian was rough. I took all kinds of jobs, washing up, being a waiter, breaking horses, keeping bees... anything I could get. As my Italian improved I became a teacher in the local school. I was married to Lucia by then. I used every skill I had to earn a wage except the one thing I longed to do. But one day I saw Lucia asleep on our little veranda and the temptation to draw her became too much for me. I took hold of pencil and paper. It was thirteen years since I had drawn so much as a stick man. I sold that sketch the same day for more than I earned in a week schoolmastering.'

'How extraordinary that you waited so long.'

Maurice fidgeted with the points of his scarlet waistcoat, while sucking the end of his brush. 'The time wasn't right. It isn't only a question of technique, after all, but of knowing who you are and what you want to say.'

'You think a fallow period can actually be helpful, then?'

'Yes, I do. Of course, opera singers and athletes can't wait. But lots of things you might do are all the better for simmering. I suppose I'm sounding a little like Dr Pangloss – "All is for the best in the best of all possible worlds." But you will find, I hope, that when the moment is right and you apply yourself to whatever it is that your talents direct, you can do it easily and naturally. It's a little like marriage. The temperaments must be sympathetic but there must be synchronisation of development also.'

'It's a consoling theory. If only I had some idea of what talents I might have.' I adjusted the rug over Rose's legs. She stirred slightly and muttered something I couldn't hear.

'I wish you'd known her earlier,' I said, in a low voice, tucking Rose's hand, white and thin-looking from the weeks in the cast, beneath the cover. 'She was the mainstay of my childhood, you know. I owe everything to her.'

'Really? Parents not up to scratch, then?'

'My father was killed in the war. I can't remember anything about him. My mother is, well... not very interested in small children.'

'Not interested in anyone but herself, I think you mean.' Rose opened one eye and threw off the rug.

'I didn't realise you were awake, darling. Can I make you some tea?'

'That would be vairry nice.' I had noticed that Rose, who had always been such a snob about dialects, was sounding more Scottish by the day. 'So you're going to Venice with that young conquistador. On your own head be it, my girl. He'll make any woman pay for loving him. You think I'm just a silly old spinster but I've eyes to see and I've been a long time in this wurld. I know about men, though I've not let them take liberties with me the way you girls do these days.' She unconsciously drew her grey worsted-clad knees together as she spoke.

'I think you're one of the least silly women I've met, married or not,' said Maurice. 'And I claim, also on the grounds of longevity, to know something about the fair sex. Whether we either of us really know anything at all is quite another matter. Ha!' He held out the paper at arm's length. 'Manganese Blue and Paynes Grey, with a touch of Rose Madder. A bold combination but rather winning, I think.'

'Old fool!' said Rose.

The telephone rang. It was Janòs.

'You can tear yourself away from all the people and all the works there to talk to me for two minutes?'

'I can.'

'Then I want to say that I am sorry for being in the branches when we say goodbye.'

'In the branches?' I thought for a minute. ' "Up in the boughs", I think you mean. At a guess that's another Miss Rince expression and rather dated, though charming. I forgive you, anyway.'

'Oh, it is so good to hear your voice! How I wish that I could take you away with me! It is not much to ask, is it? Two days in the most beautiful city in the world. After Budapest, naturally.'

'No, I agree it isn't much.'

There was a pause. 'You will reconsider?'

'Yes.'

Maurice and I had many little talks in the three days that remained of his visit. By Friday there could hardly have been anything about my life he didn't know. In fact, I made some useful discoveries about it myself as one always does when talking with someone who is perceptive and interested. He was equally forthcoming, happy to talk of Lucia. He spoke of her last illness and early death, aged only fifty, with the most touching tenderness. Everything he knew that was valuable, he said, he had learned from her. I was really sorry when Friday came and he had to leave. A parcel arrived for him on the morning of his departure.

'Aha! I got the secretary of my club to send it,' he said, jumping up. We were in the library awaiting the arrival of the taxi. 'It's a present for you.'

'How kind! And when I've so loved having you as well.'

'Have you really, my dear girl?' I saw that his eyes grew moist. 'It's been wonderful for me. The fellows at the club are all very well and my dealer looks after me, like a virtuous son with a refractory parent, but it isn't at all the same as being in a family. I don't say I'm lonely, exactly, but I do miss the company of women. That makes me sound like an ageing roué. It's nothing to do with that. It's a question of sympathies.'

'I understand perfectly.' I was unwrapping the parcel. Inside the box was a great deal of tissue paper. I experienced the apprehension one always feels when undoing a present in the presence of the donor. Lies may be necessary. Inside the tissue paper was something very strange indeed... not unlike a tortoiseshell cow's horn. I lifted it out. 'It's very... unusual.'

'It's just a little joke between us, my dear. It's Harriet Martineau's ear-trumpet. You know, after all our chats about the great feminists of the past I thought you might like... I've had it about me for many years, always rather treasured it as a symbol –'

I cut him off in mid-speech by throwing my arms about him. 'It's the most perfect present! I'd forgotten – the poor thing was terribly deaf, wasn't she? This has been shouted into by every eminent Victorian. Dickens, Charlotte Brontë, Mrs Gaskell, Browning, Tennyson – What a piece of history!' I kissed him again.

'I'm glad you like it. I want my things to go to a good home. When you get old you want to shed your possessions. I've carried that ear-trumpet around with me for forty years.'

'I'm so proud that you've given it to me. Now you *must* come back and see us, if only to ensure that it's being properly looked after. What are you doing for Christmas? Why not spend it with us?'

'How glorious that would have been. A proper family Christmas! But I've promised to have lunch on Christmas Day with my dealer and his wife. It's very good of them but actually I slightly dread it. They're madly *jeunesse dorée* with a Belgravia flat furnished entirely in white. They always wear white clothes, too. Oh, the terror of spilling! Of course, I could come down afterwards, say by tea-time?'

We had agreed on this plan and parted with assurances on both sides that we would spend the interval steeping our souls in things worth looking at. For Maurice, it was the cubists at the Tate, for me it was Tintoretto, Tiepolo and Titian.

As it turned out the only Venetian masterpieces I saw before landing again at Gatwick were postcard reproductions in the departure lounge at Venice airport. I bought one of Tiepolo's *Annunciation* to send to Maurice, and one of Marcus Curtius leaping into the ravine to save Rome by the School of Titian. The expression on Marcus Curtius's handsome face, of high-minded superiority, reminded me vividly of someone. I couldn't think who it was.

Ivor was waiting for me the other side of Customs.

'How is she? What's happening?' I asked, as soon as I saw him.

'She was in the operating theatre when I called at the hospital. No one would tell me anything.'

Despite a heavy suitcase, I broke into a run on hearing these words. We drove through the darkness at great speed. I cared nothing about Janòs. I would, oh, so willingly, have struck a bargain with God never to see him again if only Elizabeth would be all right.

Bosworth District and General was a nineteenth-century building, converted from the workhouse, with newer bits tacked on. Reception was in darkness and everything was folded up and put away, as though illness were a governable occurrence.

A nurse directed me to Night Sister's office. It was unoccupied. I walked fast down a deserted corridor, glazed to shoulder height with shiny brown tiles like a floodmark of gravy. I passed dimly lit double doors, shrouded trolleys and increasingly exhortatory notices – stern injunctions against the leaving on of lights and the removal of linen without signing for it, and warning of hideous penalties for failing to leave the sluice room tidy (underlined three times). It seemed an ugly and unfriendly world, whose sole purpose was, judging from the number of fat pipes that ran along the walls, the conduction back and forth of vast amounts of hot water. The smell of dust, rubber and germicides was sickening. I passed from the hard, flickering light of neon strips to the comparative patches of obscurity in between feeling more and more frightened. At last I heard footsteps. I turned a corner to see Dr McCleod walking towards me.

'Oh, where is she? Please, I must see her!'

'Apparently she's just come out of theatre. I'm going there myself.' Then, looking at my face in the blaring light from overhead, he added, quite gently, 'She'll be all right.'

'Will she? Really? Will she be all right?'

'Yes, I promise you.'

I let go of his hand, which I had taken hold of without thinking what I was doing. 'What's the matter with her? She seemed perfectly well this morning.'

'It was an ectopic pregnancy.'

'What?' I was certain that I must have misheard him.

'An ectopic pregnancy. The foetus develops in one of the Fallopian tubes and causes severe pain, and bleeding –'

'That's not possible.' My head began to feel very light and dizzy. 'Elizabeth is only fourteen – she's a child!'

'Fourteen's quite old enough, as you must be aware. There's no doubt about it. The operation was to remove the foetus. Though at this stage it is, of course, minute, it's large enough to cause rupturing of the tube. It's a life-threatening complication of pregnancy. We couldn't wait for your consent. Mrs Stowe? Are you all right? Do you want to sit down?'

'No! Let's go to her quickly! Oh, I can't believe it! She's just a child! How could she have . . .' My voice trailed away as I remembered those hockey practices after school.

'It happens all the time to girls even younger than she. I'm afraid class is no barrier to these unfortunate accidents.'

'Oh, for heaven's sake! You must think me a complete fool! But it's no good trying to talk to you! You're just hopelessly prejudiced!'

We walked very quickly side by side in silence the rest

of the way to the recovery room. My fears had inflamed my anger to unprecedented levels. I felt quite murderous. I glanced at him once and recognised Marcus Curtius without the helmet. He looked aloof and superior.

'Is this the mother?' A stout woman with a very tall starched hat pinned over a grizzled perm barred the door. Having looked me up and down once, she turned her gaze to Dr McCleod. She went immediately on to the list of things I dislike intensely, like African marigolds and sautéed kidneys.

'Yes. This is Mrs Stowe.'

'And you are?' My tone was as imperious as I could make it. The woman's face spoke of insolent stupidity. There was vindictiveness in her stony eyes and contumacy in her greasy snub nose and narrow mouth. The arms folded across her chest were brawny but, in my fury, I could easily have knocked her down.

'This is Sister Tugg.'

'I see. Well, Sister, I should like to see my daughter.'

'I'm afraid that won't be possible.' Sister Tugg gave an unpleasant little smile. 'She has not yet come round from the anaesthetic. If you telephone tomorrow morning at nine, we shall be able to tell you how she is.'

'I'm not leaving. My daughter needs me, and I intend to be here when she wakes up.'

'This is a hospital, Mrs Stowe, not a luxury hotel.'

'Really?' I feigned an expression of surprise. My voice was as coldly sarcastic as I could make it. 'I'm prepared to overlook its shortcomings. A comfortable chair will do. I expect you can organise that.'

'I hope you are not going to be difficult, Mrs Stowe.' Sister Tugg's neck was suffused with a red tide of anger.

'It is rather late to telephone Sir Humphrey Bessinger but I shall certainly do so if you continue to be uncooperative.'

Sir Humphrey was chairman of the hospital governors. He was a devotee of the poetry of Christopher Chough and pressed invitations continually upon us. He had several times offered a princely sum for the painting of my grandfather, which hung on the stairs at Westray. Also he was susceptible to widows. From the way he had put his arm round my waist and kissed my cheek lingeringly at Jack's funeral I was prepared to bet that he would have the entire senior nursing staff put on sluice-room duty if I requested it.

Sister Tugg lost some of her buoyancy. 'Well...'

It was enough. I moved towards the door and she was forced to step aside or collide with me. Inside the recovery room two nurses were engaged in yawning conversation as they put instruments from a table into a cabinet. Elizabeth lay on a trolley, her hair fastened up in a green cap, a small trail of saliva depending from the corner of her open mouth. She seemed profoundly asleep. I took off my gloves and took hold of her hand. It was terribly cold.

'Oh, my poor darling!' I whispered.

She stirred slightly and her eyelids twitched.

'Here's a chair,' said Dr McCleod, who had come in behind me. 'Sit down. You look all in.'

'How is she, do you think?'

'She's a good colour.' Elizabeth was a faint pink, her skin as fine as Bridie's. 'It might be a long time before she comes round, though. Are you sure you want to wait?'

I was about to reassure him on this point when Elizabeth suddenly opened her eyes.

'I'm here, darling. How are you?'

I scanned her face anxiously but I don't think she heard me. Her eyes closed again. I was vaguely aware that Dr McCleod had gone. Both nurses came in and out constantly, allowing the door to bang behind them each time in a way that exasperated me but I was too preoccupied to say anything.

Something like half an hour passed, during which I sat in silence, before Elizabeth opened her eyes again and fixed them on my face. 'Mum?'

'Yes, darling?' I took her hand. Elizabeth looked over to the door as it opened to readmit Dr McCleod, then vaguely round the room and then back again at me. An expression of intense pain appeared on her face. I rose from my chair in terror. 'Where does it hurt, sweetheart?'

Dr McCleod bent over her and asked her if she could tell him where the pain was.

Elizabeth shook her head and a flood of tears burst from her. 'I do wish Daddy hadn't died!'

CHAPTER 16

'Mrs Stowe?'

The voice broke rudely into my dream. I sat up and gazed uncomprehendingly at Dr McCleod as my eyes accustomed themselves to bright daylight. Then I turned my head and looked at Elizabeth. She had been terribly sick in the night and had cried on and off for ages. Now she was propped up in bed with a tray in front of her, bearing a bowl of corn flakes, which she was pushing about with a spoon. Though there were dark shadows under her eyes, she seemed calm. She gave me a thin smile. 'Hello, Mum. It's lucky you don't snore. Everyone else has been awake for hours.'

I looked about me. We were in a ward with eight beds. Four were occupied. There was a great deal of noise. Every trolley had a squeaking wheel, every nurse had a loud voice and a heavy hand. Curtains were dragged along rails, to form private cubicles, with a rattling screech that set my teeth on edge. I must have been tired beyond measure to have slept through it.

'How did you sleep?' Dr McCleod sat down on the end of Elizabeth's bed. I waited for her to reply and then realised that the remark was addressed to me. 'How was the chair? Not too bad, I hope?'

I was about to say that, thanks to the chair, I should in future be able to charge money exhibiting myself as the Hunchback of Westray, when I remembered that Dr McCleod had gone to a great deal of trouble to have one brought up that was larger and more padded than anything the ward offered. 'Not at all bad, thank you,' I said politely.

An auxiliary nurse stopped in front of us with a trolley. 'How about a nice cup of tea, Mrs Stowe?' she asked, with a professional smile.

'Yes, please. Very, very weak. No milk or sugar.' She gave me something the colour of oxtail soup. It was hard to drink it without shuddering.

Dr McCleod hastily waved away her offer of 'a nice cup of tea', which seemed to be the token of her vocation. 'Filthy stuff. It's really rusty water. They drain it off the radiators.'

I hadn't realised that he was capable of dissident jokes, even of the mildest kind. He was cradling one knee in his clasped hands and looking very kindly at Elizabeth.

'I don't think I can eat these,' she said, referring to the corn flakes and looking at him guiltily.

'Don't then. I'm not here in an official capacity. You're Mr Morton's patient now. I'm here as a friend. If you take my advice, you'll eat as little as you can while you're in hospital. Look what hospital food has done for Sister Tugg. She's a really hateful woman. I shouldn't mind in the least if she got stung to death by wild bees.'

Elizabeth laughed. I instantly felt better. Perhaps we were not heading inexorably for disaster, after all.

'What about having her combed to death like poor St Alphage?' I suggested.

'Are you a Catholic?' Dr McCleod looked at me in surprise.

'No, but I spent large parts of my childhood in Italy, touring churches. I'm a walking *Book of Saints*. Are you?'

'I was brought up one. My mother is very devout. My father was born a Catholic but he died believing in nothing at all, not even in the power of doing good and the ability of mankind to love each other. I don't think there ever was a man so disillusioned.'

'That must have been very painful for him. And rather sad for you.'

'I've always reacted against his pessimism. He was a doctor, too, working in the slums of Glasgow. He felt himself to be helpless in the teeth of his patients' determined pursuit of self-destruction. He was a romantic idealist, really, and he couldn't forgive laziness, selfishness and stupidity.'

There was something familiar about this. I thought the son was probably more like the father than he had any idea of.

'It's very good of you to come and see Elizabeth. And on Sunday, too.'

'It was on my way. She's looking fine. I know what some of the staff here are like – narrow-minded, intolerant. I hope they won't try to intimidate you. Still, I needn't worry, I suppose. You made short work of Sister Tugg.' He gave a short laugh. 'You'd never think that these women are supposed to minister to the sick. They're more likely to give them a good drubbing.'

'Now, Dr McCleod.' A nurse stood over him with an arch smile, 'You know we don't allow sitting on beds. You'll crease the counterpane. Matron is due on her round in ten minutes.'

'In that case I'm going to run away before I'm folded up and put into a cupboard. I'll call in tomorrow, if I get a chance.' He looked at Elizabeth. 'Remember, if they try to bully you, you must stick out your tongue as far as you can at them and say you're doing throat exercises specially prescribed by Dr McCleod.'

Elizabeth giggled. 'He's got a beautiful voice, hasn't he?' she said, when he had gone. 'I love that accent. It makes me think of *Kidnapped* and Alan Breck and wild, windswept, heathery mountains.'

Which was just where I looked as though I had spent the night, I thought, as I stood before the only mirror I could find in the bathroom. It was about four inches square and hung in the darkest corner of the room, but the sectional scan I did of my face showed a makeup-less, pallid complexion and hair like Uncle Ebenezer's. A large notice told me that I must NOT repeat NOT under any circumstances remove the plug of the wash-basin. I looked, with some surprise, at the slightly perished rubber bung. As an object of desire, I could not imagine it tempting anyone.

The imminent arrival of Matron threw the nurses into a frenzy. The patients lay chastened in their beds, chests constricted by vigorously tucked-in sheets, necks bent to acute angles on beaten pillows. They had put themselves beyond the pale by being ill, they were outcasts, dependants, ciphers.

'We have been a naughty girl, haven't we?' Matron said, in a disapproving voice, as she stood at the foot of Elizabeth's bed. She was a thin woman with upswept spectacles and teeth that sloped inwards like a shark's. Elizabeth looked miserable. I guessed she was too weak to command her usual vocabulary of defiance. I braced myself to defend her.

'Well, well, you're nothing but a child, really.' Matron suddenly turned a smile on me that was conspiratorial. 'You must be very angry, Mrs Stowe. These men want more than locking up. Prison's too good for them. I hope you're being looked after. We do our best but you get a very low type of girl applying to nurse these days. I'm always telling Sir Humphrey that we must pay the nurses more and attract women from better backgrounds.'

None of the nurses standing around her dared to express indignation by so much as an eyebrow twitch, but I thought I detected some swellings of bosoms beneath aprons. I understood that Matron was being lenient with me, almost friendly, because we were in some unholy alliance based on class. Repulsive though this was, I decided, on the basis of tiredness and cowardice, to go along with it.

'You've had a severe lesson, my dear.' Matron wagged a skinny finger playfully at Elizabeth. 'All men have the beast in them and you mustn't let them have what they want.' The very young, weedy-looking male student doctor, who was accompanying Matron on her round, looked abashed. 'Pretty girls must be especially on their guard and listen to what their mother tells them.'

'Hateful cow,' said Elizabeth, after Matron had swept from the ward. 'What did she mean about prison?'

'Oh, well, it's illegal, you know, to make love to girls under the age of sixteen.' There had so far been no opportunity to discuss the identity of the co-author of her predicament. I felt, anyway, that it would be better to wait until she was at home. 'Let's not worry about it now, darling. You must just concentrate on getting better. This afternoon I'll dash into Bosworth and see if I can find you some good books to read, shall I?'

Elizabeth's eyes filled with tears. 'I don't really want to do anything. I'm so tired and my stomach hurts like mad.'

'You're depressed. It's not surprising. You'll feel better in a day or two.'

'Aren't you angry with me?'

'Angry? No. I'm upset... and relieved, of course, that you're all right... and full of self-reproach that I allowed you to get into this mess...'

'I don't see that you had anything to do with it!' snapped Elizabeth. 'Oh, Mum, don't look hurt! You're always looking hurt, these days, and it gets terribly on my nerves, that's all.'

'It must be because I am hurt, then,' I said crossly. 'I don't enjoy seeing my children unhappy. Am I supposed to pretend to be unfeeling? You expect rather a lot, I must say!'

'Oh, I don't know. I'm sorry. Well, I'm an idiot, I know. You don't have to tell me.'

'I didn't think I had.'

'A nice cup of tea, ladies? Ooh, sorry!' said the nurse, slamming a trolley into the end of the bed with a clatter that made my head ring.

Elizabeth dozed all morning and looked a lot better when she woke up. I left her at one o'clock to go and find myself something to eat in the town, as hospital rules precluded visitors from a share of the powdered scrambled egg, tinned tomatoes and ice-cream scoops of lead-coloured mashed potato that were on offer for lunch.

I found a café that served soup and sandwiches. The tomato soup was tinned and the sandwich filling slyly fugitive, but it was a great deal quieter than the hospital as I was the only customer and the waitress acknowledged my order with nothing more than a sullen grunt. I bought *Horse and Hound* and two historical romances for Elizabeth, and a copy of *Vogue* and a novel by A. P. Herbert for myself, feeling that we needed something entertaining and cheerful. As an afterthought, I bought a bag of apples and a box of Elizabeth's favourite chocolates.

When I got back to the ward there was a young man, a boy, really, sitting by Elizabeth's bed. He stood up when I reached them and looked thoroughly uncomfortable. I knew at once, without being told, that this must be the culprit for whom Matron reserved the direst of punishments. He looked no more than fifteen or sixteen years old, tall and gawky but not unpleasing in appearance. His hair was long and stood out in thick, black corkscrew curls around a face that looked vulnerable. He had large, nervous hands, with butterflies tattooed on the backs, with which he twisted the hem of his T-shirt into knots.

'I'm Miranda Stowe, Elizabeth's mother,' I said, seeing that they were both overcome by the awkwardness of the situation. I held out my hand.

'I'm Johnny. How do you do.' He took my hand in his damp palm. 'I'm sorry Elizabeth's ill,' he said, desperately.

'It's good of you to come and see her. How did you know she was here?'

I could see the nurse, who was on the afternoon shift, gliding nearer to hear what we were saying. Even the patient in the next bed, who had seemed so inert as to be possibly already dead, perked up enough to raise herself on one elbow. I smiled at Johnny encouragingly.

'She phoned me. My grandfather brought me. I had to come and see she was all right.' Johnny looked absolutely miserable. 'I live with my grandparents. He wants to see you. He's in Matron's office.'

Matron's office was in the furthest reaches of the hospital in one of the new wings. It was light, peaceful and cheerfully furnished. An elderly man was sitting by the window. He got up as soon as I walked in. For a moment I couldn't think who he was, though his face was familiar.

'This is the most terrible business. I couldn't be more sorry about your daughter,' he said, as he came over to shake my hand. 'John Vavasour. I remember meeting you at the last music festival, when you kindly brought that marvellous chap to play. What a pity this is! I can't tell you how distressed my wife and I are about it. You must be very angry with my grandson.'

'My daughter asked me that – if I was angry with her, I mean. But anger seems to me a wholly inappropriate reaction. I don't for a moment think they intended any great wickedness or thought about the consequences of what they were doing. They're still children. Of course, it was irresponsible. But I feel so very sorry for them both.'

'I'm relieved to hear you say that.' Mr Vavasour's hand was shaking as he gestured to a chair. 'Won't you sit down? I really feel I must. This is the last straw, to tell you the truth. My daughter, Johnny's mother, lives in California. She belongs to some strange religion. I can't understand it at all. The man who is the lynch-pin – guru, I think's the word – seems to be an out-and-out bounder. He's made her give him all her money and abandon her family. I believe he sleeps with all the women in turn.' Mr Vavasour shook his head. 'When I think what a sweet girl she was... Johnny's father is in prison for smuggling drugs. My wife and I have had to look after him and his sister for the last three years and it's almost more than we can manage.'

'I thought he looked a charming boy.'

'Did you? Did you, by Jove! You're a generous woman, Mrs Stowe, and I must say that if the circumstances were other than they are, I should be thoroughly glad to have this opportunity of knowing you.'

'Thank you. Of course, if anything had happened... if

Elizabeth had died as a result . . . I expect I would have had very different feelings. But now, though I'm worried about her, naturally, I don't think we should make more of this than we can help. They've both had a dreadful fright. Perhaps, a little later on, a good talking-to is all that's necessary. It's obvious that they're both looking for affection and reassurance in a world that's let them down rather badly.'

I told him about Jack's death, and he put his hand on mine and pressed it briefly in sympathy. We had a frank talk about our feelings of inadequacy as guardians of the morals of youth. When Matron returned, and insisted that we had tea with her, Mr Vavasour and I were on the best of terms. I noticed that Matron had Lapsang Souchong with slices of lemon as thin as rice paper. There had to be some compensation for daily immersion with 'the worst type of girl' about which she grumbled at length, overjoyed to find herself hobnobbing with the County.

Mr Vavasour took Johnny away, and Elizabeth and I settled down with our novels and chocolates.

'What do you think this is?' said Elizabeth, in a low voice, as supper was brought to her.

I looked at the gelatinous spheres swimming in a viscous sauce and shook my head, at a loss. 'Giant tapioca? But those are carrots. It must be savoury. Could it be tripe?'

'I think it's something left over from the operating table.' Elizabeth giggled and took a mouthful. 'God, I can't possibly eat it. I think I'll finish the chocolates instead.'

'Will you mind if I go home soon, darling? I think I must go and see what's happening to everyone, and you're so much better now.'

'No, that's all right. You ought to get some sleep anyway.' Then she giggled again. 'Sorry about being sick on your shoes.'

'Think nothing of it.'

When I left the ward an hour later she was absorbed in

her novel, eating apples and yawning by turns. All violent feelings seemed to have subsided. I went to Reception to telephone for a taxi.

It was wonderful to be home. Ivor, who had kindly helped out with the cooking during my absence, had left some supper in the bottom oven of the Aga for me in case I came back. Jenny and Rose fussed around me, exclaiming at my exhausted appearance, asking about Elizabeth, begging me to put my feet up and rest. I sat on the sofa next to Rose and ate with relish the carrot and walnut soup Jenny brought me. 'Mm, how absolutely delicious! It's lovely to see you all. Elizabeth will be home the day after tomorrow and have her stitches out on Thursday. Was Henry all right? I did hope to catch sight of him before he left.'

Ivor had set out to drive him back to school a quarter of an hour before I reached home.

'He seemed bonny enough,' said Rose. 'Full of this play he's doing. We had to listen to his speeches all weekend. If he hasn't got them by heart it's not our fault.'

'Such a clever lad,' said Jenny admiringly. 'It wouldn't surprise me if he were a film star when he's grown-up, like. They're such handsome boys.'

She sighed, and I knew she was thinking of James. Her skin was free from spots now, after weeks of proper food and washing, and she was looking very lovely indeed. I ate the leguminous stew, whose main ingredients were Jerusalem artichokes, beans, carrots (again) and cabbage, with less enthusiasm. It seemed a rather gaseous combination. I could not manage any of the carrot cake.

'We shall be seeing carrots in the dark,' was Rose's caustic comment.

It was clear that Ivor had carried out my injunction to be economical, and use our own garden produce as much as possible, to the letter.

The next morning, as I drew up at the hospital, Sir Humphrey was just stepping out of his Daimler.

'Miranda!' He loped across the tarmac towards me like an elderly, arthritic gazelle. 'What a delightful surprise! Nothing wrong, I trust?'

I explained that Elizabeth was recovering from a minor operation. I could tell that he hadn't heard a word I had said, he was so busy straightening his tie, pulling down his cuffs and generally prinking his plumage. He had an asinine grin on his face.

'It's my day for hospital meetings.' He made a face expressive of boredom. Matron, who had come out to greet him, saw the grimace and looked rather hurt. 'Will you improve the day and have lunch with me? They do a reasonable roast beef at the Six Jolly Porters.'

'Thank you.'

'Good! Splendid!' he panted, his tongue almost hanging out with enthusiasm, and stepped back hard on Matron's foot.

I could hear Elizabeth giggling with someone as I entered the ward. A screen prevented me from seeing who her visitor was until I had reached her cubicle.

'What are you two laughing at?'

Dr McCleod, who had been sitting on her bed, stood up and looked uncomfortable. 'Oh, well. Perhaps, now I think about it, it was feeble, really. Better forget it.'

'I thought it was funny,' said Elizabeth. 'Mum won't mind. I'll tell her. How did it begin?

"There was a young girl of Madras
Who had a most beautiful ass
But not as you'd think
Firm, round and pink
But grey with long ears and eats grass."'

Dr McCleod looked relieved when I laughed. 'I was afraid you might think I was corrupting youth.'

'Good heavens, no! It could hardly be more innocent.'

'May I share the joke, Elizabeth? Good morning, Dr McCleod.' Matron and Sir Humphrey appeared, with startling suddenness, round the screen, followed by the shy student doctor and two nurses.

'Dr McCleod was cheering me up,' said Elizabeth. Her expression was demure but I detected a glint in her eye. 'He told me this limerick. Let me see if I can remember – oh, yes.'

She got as far as 'firm, round and pink' when Matron drew in a sharp breath and said, 'Thank you, I don't think we want to hear any more,' and swept augustly away with her entourage. Sir Humphrey fluttered his fingers at me. I thought Elizabeth might burst her stitches with laughter.

'Wicked girl.' Dr McCleod was laughing, too. 'It's going to take me months, perhaps years, to repair my relationship with Matron. And you may laugh, Mrs Stowe, but you'll be tarred with the same licentious brush. Matron saw you giggling.'

'Good. The last thing I want is a relationship with that woman. She's an insufferable snob.'

McCleod looked at me in some surprise. 'Actually, it's my day off. What about having lunch with me?'

The moment the words were out of his mouth he looked as though he would have liked to recall them.

'Oh, what a shame! I would have liked that very much – but I've already said I'll have lunch with Sir Humphrey. Oh, it is a pity!'

'Oh, no. It doesn't matter at all. Goodbye, Elizabeth. I'll come and take your stitches out on Thursday. Goodbye, Mrs Stowe.' He was gone.

'Golly, Mum! You are a clot! I'd a million times rather have lunch with Dr McCleod than with that senile old prune. He dyes his hair.'

'So would I, but I'd already agreed to have it with Sir Humphrey.'

'So what? You could have pretended you had to rush home or something. He'll never ask you again.'

I realised that she meant Dr McCleod. She was probably right.

Lunch with Sir Humphrey was gastronomically an

improvement on the one I had eaten the day before but conversationally I preferred the sulking waitress. Hilary Scranton-Jones, as luck would have it, was also dining at the Six Jolly Porters, and her female lunching companion was obviously being filled in, over her prawn cocktail, on all the gossip, for she frequently glanced round at our table as if to check for herself what was going on.

I realised fairly early on that Sir Humphrey was an idiot, which went some way to explain his success in public life. He talked volubly about Christopher Chough – what a brilliant and courageous man he had been, how powerful and sensitive his poetry was. It brought to mind a conversation I had had with Maurice. When I had confessed that I thought my grandfather's poems were, on the whole, overrated and that his popularity was due to an excess of sentiment and a sneaky sort of self-conceit that passed for heroism that I found rather repulsive, Maurice had been delighted. It was just what he thought himself, he told me, but had been afraid to say for fear of wounding my feelings. We had a glorious time rubbishing the *genius loci* of my childhood. Maurice had said that all war was a filthy excrescence on the backside of humanity and attempts to make any aspect of it glorious were immoral.

Sir Humphrey at last abandoned the topic of my grandfather and moved on to more personal things. He wanted my advice. He was afraid that I would think him ungallant but since his wife had died four years ago he had had no reliable female friend to whom he could turn. How I wished that Hilary Scranton-Jones could have heard this designation. Apparently he had been having a great deal of trouble recently with Matron, who had taken to ringing him up at all hours, ostensibly to discuss hospital business. She would then go on to talk about the isolating consequences of power, how life was like a voyage on unpathed waters and how sensible it was for those in the same boat to share the rowing. 'The poor woman's brain is softening, I think. I couldn't make head or tail of half she said to me last night. I wonder if she was hinting that I ought to take her on a cruise.'

I could see that Sir Humphrey was out of his depth when it came to metaphor. He didn't want to hurt Matron's feeling, but he was running out of excuses to put off the invitations to tea and supper with which she bombarded him. How could he discourage her without making their work together at the hospital difficult and embarrassing?

'Why not tell her you're engaged to be married?'

'Miranda! That's quite inspired!' He wrinkled his nose and whickered like a horse with pleasure. 'Now, why didn't I think of that?'

I refrained from telling him that it was because he had the intelligence of a woodlouse.

'That's what I'll do. Thank you, Miranda.' He grasped my hand firmly before I could snatch it away. 'You see, a man does need female counsel. That woman's been driving me dotty and she must be fifty if she's a day!' He whickered again. 'The thing's preposterous!' I couldn't see why. Sir Humphrey, despite the ginger dye, looked at least sixty. I tried to disengage my hand but he held on to it firmly. 'Now who shall it be? The future Lady Bessinger, I mean.'

'I should invent a name. Someone you've met in London. You can make up reasons why the engagement is to be a long one. She's nursing her sick mother, perhaps. After a year or two Matron will have forgotten all about you.'

'I want you to have dinner with me to celebrate. We'll go to the Savoy. When is your next free evening?'

'Oh. Um... How kind. But I'm afraid I can't accept any invitations until Elizabeth is better.'

'Of course! Do forgive me, I'd forgotten. Naturally you are a dedicated mother.' He waggled my imprisoned hand. 'It's a very moving thing for a man to contemplate... maternal devotion.'

His eyes, rather rheumy, looked mawkish. Afterwards I wondered why I had not told Sir Humphrey that I was engaged to be married myself. Perhaps my own intelligence was nothing to boast about. I spent the afternoon in the ward with Elizabeth, having bought a fresh supply of historical novels, some bananas and several packets of biscuits. I left at half past seven, having arranged to take her home the next morning. I drove back to Westray with a mind more or less blank from tiredness. When I had got back to the ward after lunch Elizabeth had said, 'You've been an age! I've nearly gone potty with boredom.'

I treasured this remark. After all, it seemed that I had been able to do something for her. It was necessary that she and I should have a serious talk later when she was stronger. I couldn't actually forbid her to have a sexual relationship. Or, rather, there was no way of enforcing the ban unless I locked her permanently in her bedroom. As I drove through the village I saw that Maeve was at home. All the lights were on and the cottage looked pretty and welcoming. I decided to stop and have a drink with her. It was only just after eight and I knew that she never had supper until much later.

Loud pop music from within drowned my knockings so I pushed open the front door. Florian lay on the sofa, his eyes closed, listening to Procul Harum. He was wearing one of Maeve's evening dresses and fanning himself with an ostrich plume. 'Hello, Miranda.' He opened his eyes. 'Care for a joint?'

'No, thank you. Is your mother at home?'

'Yes. She went upstairs. Said she couldn't stand the music.' He giggled to himself. 'Let's face the music, tee hee!, and dance.'

He kicked both legs into the air, exposing a pair of long, lace-edged knickers, and giggled convulsively. I climbed the stairs, narrowly avoiding stepping on Maeve's ginger tom, who was sleeping on one of the treads. I stopped to apologise and then I heard Maeve's voice. It had not occurred to me that she might not be alone.

'Come on, darling. Let's have a tiny smoke first.'

'No. I do not want that rubbish. You ask me to come to

bed with you and then you want only to play about. Get off that silly little frock. I lose my patience.'

I stumbled down the stairs, the cat running ahead of me, and went quickly past the still giggling Florian to the front door. The night air seemed freezing on my burning face. I got into the car and drove home. Rose had gone to bed but Jenny was sitting in the kitchen.

'No, I don't want anything to eat, thanks,' I replied, when she asked if she could get me anything. 'I think I'll go straight to bed.'

'You do look all in. There's a note here from Mr Detchy. He came this afternoon and was ever so annoyed that you weren't at home. Mrs FitzGerald came by to see how you'd enjoyed yer holiday and he went home with her.'

I took the piece of paper she held out to me. Jenny had lit the fire in my bedroom. I put Janòs's note into the flames, without reading it, and watched it burn. Then I undressed and washed and got into bed.

There was a dreadful sick feeling in the pit of my stomach and what was most hateful about it was its utter familiarity. It was the old enemy that I thought I had defeated. How well I recognised every painful beat of my swollen, jealous heart. I lay on my back, watching the firelight playing upon the beams of the ceiling, and though my throat was tight I would not let myself cry. Instead, I thought about the bedroom in Maeve's cottage and what they were doing there. With infinite care and thoroughness, I excised Janòs from my affections and thrust him out of my life.

CHAPTER 17

'But what do you expect? You abandon me at the worst time and I am supposed to run after you like a faithful little dog?'

Janòs's sloe-black eyes were reproachful. We were standing in the drawing room. It was eleven o'clock the next morning. I had come downstairs, having fetched Elizabeth from the hospital and put her to bed, and was in the process of thinking about what I might give her for lunch when I found Janòs standing in the hall. Despite my good intentions, I had felt a familiar excitement on seeing him. I read myself a brief lecture. He must have seen at once that something was very wrong for he looked at me hard and long before speaking.

'So. How is the invalid?'

'She's all right, I think. Just a bit tired. She'll be better when the stitches are out. More comfortable.'

'She had an operation? Jenny would tell me nothing.'

'Come into the drawing room, will you? I don't want her to overhear.'

'So what is the mystery?'

'She was expecting a baby but it went wrong.'

Janòs whistled. 'A child like that! Poor little girl! And you,' he looked at me calmly, 'you are hating men and furious with her?'

'No, it's nothing like that. I can understand that she was looking for something... love, comfort, perhaps excitement. I'm not angry at all. Sad, really.'

'You look stern... even fierce. I do not dare to say that I love you.'

'No. Don't say it.' I moved away from him. I must change those wilting flowers, I thought, distractedly. I noticed that the seaweed from Elizabeth's table arrangement was beginning to smell like the jellyfish Henry had once kept as a pet. 'When I got back from the hospital last night I stopped at Maeve's cottage. I wanted to talk to someone about Elizabeth. Florian told me Maeve was upstairs. I don't know whether he intended to be malicious or not. Anyway, it doesn't matter. Luckily I heard you talking before I interrupted you and made a complete fool of myself.'

'I see.' Janòs put his hands into his pockets and leaned back against the piano. It was then that he made the remark about the faithful little dog. I ignored it.

'I'm sorry I had to leave you in Venice. How did the concert go?'

Janòs shrugged his shoulders. 'Not bad, I think. But I was angry, so angry with you. Then a day passes and my anger goes. I want again to see you. I want to talk to you, to hear your voice. I want to make love to you.' He came up close to me and put his hands on my shoulders, then round my neck and kissed me. 'Don't be angry because I make love with Maeve. I like her but I love you.'

I would not allow myself to return his kiss. 'I'm sorry, Janòs. It's no good.'

'What do you mean? It *is* good. Listen, idiot, I can't tie myself sexually to one woman for the rest of my life. I don't want to tell you lies. Of course there will be other women. But that has nothing to say to my feelings for you. Cannot you understand?'

'Yes, perfectly. But it *does* say something about your feelings for me. You would expect me, I suppose, not to make love with other men?'

'I assume that you would not want to.' I smiled but said nothing. 'Oh, come, Miranda. It is different for a man. Be honest.'

'No, it isn't! That's just where you're wrong! I wouldn't make love with other men because I wouldn't want to hurt you . . . because I thought our relationship was worth the self-restraint. But you don't understand women like me. Perhaps it's a cultural difference. That's just one of the things that makes a love affair between us difficult. The other thing is that you will never understand that for me my children are just as important as your career.'

Janòs shrugged. 'Children grow up.'

'Yes. And how they grow up is very much my responsibility. Just as you can't allow yourself to make a single mistake because of the consequences it may have for the rest of your career, I mustn't make mistakes either because my children will suffer the consequences of mistakes I make now for the rest of their lives. Perhaps for sixty or seventy years. It's every bit as important, but you can't see that.'

'Well, perhaps you can teach me. I am willing to learn.'

'If it were only that we might try, I suppose, but there are other impossibilities. You've always lived at some extreme or other. My life is constructed on a more temperate scale and I want it to go on like that.'

'You mean you cannot change to adapt to me? Or you will not?'

'I don't think that I could. Anyway, one thing I'm sure of and that must finally put an end to all doubts... all vacillations. I can never again love a man who is unfaithful. I would rather live alone. I mean that from the very bottom of my heart.'

Janòs held his head in his hands. 'This is about your husband? I begin to see.' He sighed. 'Why do you not tell me this thing?'

'Because I wanted to forget it, I suppose. I'm ashamed of minding so much.' Despite myself I felt tears rising. They must have been tears of self-pity, not very admirable. 'It hurt me. Perhaps other women don't mind when their husbands are unfaithful. All I can say is that I did mind, very much.'

'All right. It is all right.' Janòs stroked my arms and spoke soothingly.

'That's just what it isn't! It hurt me then and it hurts me now to talk about it. It makes me feel as though I'm a neurotic, jealous fool and I won't have any more of it. No. Never again!' I was almost shouting as I said this.

Janòs held out his arms in a gesture of despair. 'What more can I say?'

'Nothing. It isn't any good. You see, we don't want the same things. And that's more important than absolutely anything else. More important than desire, comparable intelligence, compatible tastes. I still find you desirable but that's all. I don't love you any more.'

'Well,' said Janòs, sadly, 'it is something to know that you once did.'

When he had gone I went out by myself to Temenos,

the Jealousy Garden, and sat there on the camomile seat for half an hour. The noseless stone face of Aphrodite regarded my misery impassively. There are as many ways of loving as there are people, probably, but the variations are so slight as to be insignificant. She had seen it all before. If I did not learn from experience, I told myself firmly, I deserved to be wretched for the rest of my life.

I lived through the next ten days in a state of gloomy resignation. I felt like a mariner to whom the voyage has become wearisome but who is, none the less, thankful to have avoided shipwreck. The approach of Christmas prohibited much introspection. It was a time when Jack's absence would be continually in our thoughts. I asked Patience and Wacko to lunch on Christmas Day, feeling that we must at all costs – and the cost of entertaining Wacko was considerable – be busy. Then I decided to ask Lissie, George and Alice for good measure. Then, when Maeve looked rather sad on hearing our plans, I found myself asking her and the boys as well. So we would be sixteen with Maurice. I found myself relying quite a bit on the idea of Maurice coming.

Maeve and I had had a long palliative talk, which had acted as a postscript to the Janòs affair. She had been both defiant and apologetic but I assured her that I knew perfectly well that if it hadn't been her it would have been someone else. I had already known that the relationship had too many counts against it. I was thankful to finish it before the usual depressing compromises had been made to try to salvage a doomed love affair. She was aghast to find that I had imagined myself in love with him.

'If only I'd known it was that important to you!' she had groaned. 'I do feel bad. Anyway, I didn't enjoy it nearly as much as I'd thought. He was pretty offhand. I expect he was thinking of you.'

I thought this extremely generous under the circumstances.

Elizabeth had been very quiet since coming out of hospital. Johnny had telephoned several times and they had had long conversations.

'It's no good, Mum,' she told me, in a rare burst of confidence. 'I'm completely put off sex. We only did it three times and look at the result! I think I shall become a nun. Johnny and I are good friends but I certainly don't want anything else.' She shuddered.

'You'll find it will be much easier when you're older. You'll know how to use contraception properly –'

'Oh, not another lecture on contraception!' she interrupted. 'I had to listen to all that from Matron. And I'd heard it all before from the biology mistress. I'm a world authority on Dutch caps and the Pill. It wasn't that we didn't know, just that we weren't organised, that's all.' She paused a minute, then said, 'Will it really be easy when I'm older? It seems a thoroughly confusing and strange business.'

'Well, to tell you the truth I think a lot of adults find it like that too. That's why everyone is obsessed by it nearly all the time.'

Elizabeth giggled. 'But is it really enjoyable? I can't say I liked it very much, honestly.'

I thought fleetingly of Janòs. 'Yes. It can be absolutely one of the best things in the world.'

Henry had arrived home from school in a mood of huge excitement and wandered all over the house exhorting us to go once more into the breach and close the wall up with our English dead until Rose threatened to commit a violent crime so that she could be taken away to a nice peaceful jail. But by Christmas Eve Henry had grown silent and gloomy, and Rose confided in me that she had actually offered to hear his lines, so alarming was his quietness.

'Mum,' he said, as Patience and I were decorating the staircase with holly, yew, larch and dried cardoon heads sprayed gold, 'must we have the carol singers in tonight?'

I remembered the carol singers coming on Christmas Eve the year before. Jack had arrived home from the bank just as the dozen or so singers were standing in the drawing room, having drunk their sherry and eaten the mince pies we always provided. No doubt, Jack had been wishing a tearful mistress a libidinous farewell before her seasonal excommunication, which accounted for his lateness. As the singers had courteously sung 'O Come All Ye Faithful' in gratitude for the victuals, Jack had stood behind the carollers and joined in. He had exaggerated the solemnity merely by opening his mouth very wide and glancing heavenward with reverential eyes. The children, Rose and I, trying to look jolly and pious at the same time, had been utterly confounded, red in the face and throats aching from suppressed laughter. 'I think we ought, darling. It's a tradition that goes back long before we came to Westray.'

'Actually,' said Patience, 'Aubrey spoke to Mrs Warrington – you know, the woman who organises the singing – on the telephone while I was at the vicarage helping him put the candles and things into the oranges for the Christingle service. He suggested that they should, just for this year, give you a miss. He thought you might prefer to be quiet.'

'Did he? That's so like Aubrey. A kinder man never breathed. What is he doing for Christmas? Apart from taking services, I mean.'

'He told me he'd ordered a pork pie specially from Mead's. He said he didn't trust himself to cook a turkey without giving himself food-poisoning but he felt he ought to celebrate the birth of Christ with something more festive than tomato soup.'

The result of this poignant conversation was that I telephoned Aubrey on the spot and asked him to join us for Christmas Day, and he said he would be absolutely delighted. I noticed that, from then on, Patience smiled to herself when she thought no one was looking and was inclined to hum 'God Rest Ye Merry Gentlemen' as she tripped up and downstairs with branches and florist's wire.

Late on Christmas Eve the decorating was finished. Standing in the hall, looking left to the drawing room and right past the library and stairs into the kitchen, everything was romantically embowered, mossy and verdant.

It looked as though the house had turned itself inside out or the woods outside in. Our hands were scratched, our backs hurt, our knees were bruised but the effect was of a fairy-tale grove. Elizabeth spent a long time scooping up earwigs, spiders and beetles, which had inadvertently come into the house, and putting them into the courtyard garden.

A fresh fall of snow during the night was benevolent for even James went out before breakfast on Christmas Day to have a snowball fight with the others. I was delighted to see him chasing Henry, threatening to stuff a snowball down his neck. James had worked for several hours every day of the holidays so far, and while I was glad that he took his A levels seriously I would have given anything to hear one of his terrible jokes. He behaved like a man of thirty rather than a boy of eighteen, offering to help with the household accounts and to do the annual cellar check that Jack had always done just before Christmas. I accepted all tenders of help, but I would much rather have seen him relax and enjoy himself. Jenny followed him about, when she wasn't doing things in the house or looking after Bridie, and tried to get into conversation with him. The scraps I overheard were not encouraging. He seemed to be lecturing her on the Napoleonic wars.

After breakfast Ivor dropped Rose and me off at the Westray church, then he and Jenny drove on to the very nasty modern Roman Catholic church in Marshgate. He always said that it was his greatest test of faith, having to worship in a neo-brutalist, concrete dog kennel. The children voted with one voice to stay at home and look after Bridie. As I was listening to Aubrey, prattling on about Persia in the seventh century, I looked at the gilded *papier-mâché* ceiling and was obscurely pleased that at least we were not usurping the old religion as the building was eighteenth-century to the foundation stones.

Aubrey drove us home and opened the champagne, while I welcomed the arriving guests. The presents were put under the Christmas tree, which stood in the corner of the drawing room. Elizabeth, Henry and Alice were appointed to hand them out. I gave Elizabeth a coat, which was almost identical to one she had admired in *Vogue* but had cost a great deal less. Henry got the radio-controlled helicopter as requested, and for James I had bought a gramophone, advertised 'as new' in the local newspaper. I think they were pleased.

The children had clubbed together to buy me an electric fruit-juicer. This was an exceptionally thoughtful present as it would save masses of time before breakfast, squeezing oranges for guests. I had agreed beforehand with Patience, Lissie and Maeve that we would exchange nothing of value, but still the books and soap and chocolates mounted into great heaps as there were so many of us. Sebastian said he didn't believe in Christmas and therefore hadn't bought anyone anything. I noticed that he made a careful hoard of all the socks, cologne and records he was given. Florian gave me a book entitled *Sexual Practices of Sapphists*. I had given him a collection of Keats's poems, so I suppose we were even.

At last everything was given out and exclaimed over. Patience, Lissie, Maeve and I went to get lunch ready. I refused to let Jenny help. She was no more than a child herself. It was, she told us, her first proper Christmas, as her mother had always spent Christmas Day working in the hotel where she was a waitress and Jenny had been sent to an aunt, who was very religious and didn't believe in rich food or spoiling children with material trumpery.

Jenny had been thrilled to the point of tearfulness with the watch we had given her. The children had all contributed pocket-money so we had been able to buy her one with a pretty red morocco strap. She confessed that it was the first watch she had ever owned. I was very glad that since Elizabeth's return from hospital she and Jenny seemed much more friendly. I was touched by Elizabeth's dawning interest in Bridie.

Lunch, despite Wacko getting drunk and telling stories that might have been risqué if they had been comprehensible, was cheerful. The dining table seated twelve comfortably and sixteen was a squeeze, but this seemed to contribute to greater conviviality. Elizabeth had back-combed her fringe so that it stood straight up as though in shock. She wore a strange white garment, which I recognised, after a brief scrutiny, as a dress shirt belonging to Jack. Each fingernail was painted a different colour. The effect was stylish but I did feel a burst of disloyal envy when I saw Alice's smart navy blue dress with its white frilly collar. This dissolved the minute Alice put her head on one side and said that Alice always felt sad at Christmas because there were so many children in the world not having such a lovely time as she was. Even Aubrey, who might have been expected to applaud this sentiment, looked rather sickened. James, Henry and Elizabeth viewed Alice with cold contempt. I am sorry to say that when Dinkie, hiding beneath the dining table, savaged Alice's leg and the children were sent for sticking plaster, there was a burst of extremely audible laughter from the hall.

George carved the geese, and Ivor handed the plates round. As there had been, he said, a division of labour, based on gender, in the production of the lunch, so there would be one in its clearing away. The men would do the washing-up. In the event, as could have been foretold, George, Ivor, James and Aubrey did it all while Wacko slept by the fire and Sebastian, Florian and Henry were nowhere to be found. Two plates were broken and almost everything had a smear of grease on it and had to be rewashed the next day, but the thought was kind.

After lunch we played charades. My team's word was 'cornucopia'. I went into the kitchen to find a piece of newspaper that I could make into a Bishop's mitre to go with my old evening cloak for 'cope' and was horrified to see Jenny leaning with her arms on the table, sobbing. Eventually she sniffed out an explanation. 'He thinks I'm stupid! And I am! There's no two ways about it. I don't know the half of what he does and he'll never like me because I'm not clever. We weren't ever taught nothing but sums and reading and how to make soup. I'm not good enough but I do love him so!'

Afterwards, when I had it out with James, he said he thought he'd been very tactful. 'I couldn't encourage her, Mum. That wouldn't be fair. I only said that my tastes were rather bookish and I didn't think hers were. God, she asked me to kiss her! What was I supposed to do?'

'Darling, it was difficult, I know, but I think your idea of tact is, perhaps, not quite all you imagine.'

'Should I have done what Dad would have done? Kissed her and gone to bed with her and *then* chucked her?' James's tone was bitter.

'No, of course not. You did the right thing. Just be kind to her, won't you? Make it clear you don't despise her. I've promised to recommend some books to read. She seems keen to improve her mind. Why don't you help her?'

James looked unconvinced of the wisdom of this but muttered that he would do his best.

By the time I had got Jenny to powder her red nose and join us for tea Maurice had arrived. 'Dears, the most extraordinary lunch! White food to go with the white flat and the white people! Risotto with white truffles to begin and then turbot, *pommes purée* and *endives à la creme*, followed by vanilla soufflé and meringues. It was just like stepping into an underexposed film.'

He was looking very Christmassy, with a band of holly round the crown of his fedora and a large necklace of mistletoe pinned to his cape.

'Did you really go on the train looking like that?' asked Alice, in awe. She was unused to eccentricity, her parents being patterns of English restraint.

'No, I came by van. But you'll spoil my surprise. First I must have sustenance and then I shall give you my presents. How wonderful the house smells!' He sniffed extravagantly. 'Bosky and florescent.'

'Here's some fruit cake,' said Elizabeth, taking it to him as he sat down by the fire and held out his hands to the blaze, Jasper leaning lovingly against his knee. 'Mum'll bring you some tea.'

'Thank you, my dear girl. It's very good to be here.'

I saw him look searchingly at Elizabeth. When he had telephoned earlier in the week to confirm the time of his arrival, I had told him about the abortive trip to Venice. Henry brought Maurice our present, which I had found in a Brighton antique shop: a pair of Berlin woolwork slippers with roses and a dog, something like Jasper, embroidered on the toes, not very much worn. He put them on. They must have been made for a woman, but he had small feet and they fitted him perfectly. 'Thank you, Miranda. Thank you, my darlings. They are perfectly beautiful!' He was very moved and dabbed his eyes with his napkin.

'Ivor is making the Wassail Cup,' said Elizabeth. 'It's his job every Christmas. The Wassail Cup belongs to Westray Manor. Whoever buys the house has to buy the Cup. It's mentioned in some records. Mum can tell you all about it. Ivor puts in ale – ugh, horrible taste – and herbs and things. He also puts in a lot of ginger wine, which I quite like. Now, we'd better watch the last bit of the charade. Henry gets livid if we don't all concentrate like mad when he's acting. There never was such a little show-off.'

Henry took the house by storm as Zeus breaking off the goat's horn and giving it to Amalthea, played very winningly by Lissie, in gratitude for her care of him in his infancy. Baby Zeus was brilliantly and unconsciously played by Bridie. Henry cast thunderbolts to transform the horn into the cornucopia, from which poured corn, fruit and flowers and then went on striking god-like attitudes to tumultuous applause until Sebastian picked up one of the apples, which had tumbled on to the drawing room carpet from the old gramophone horn, and threw it at Henry. It brought up an angry red mark on Alice's cheek and made her cry very much.

The Wassail Cup was a welcome distraction. It was a large bowl, engraved with the arms of Westray's seventeenth-century owners, and we used it only once a year, at Christmas. Otherwise it was kept in the Court cupboard in the dining room. Jack and I had always gone to the bank's New Year's Eve ball in London, which had prevented us from observing the proper tradition of using the Wassail Cup on the last day of the old year. Several weeks ago I had received an invitation to the ball accompanied by a note from Mr Defresnier, saying how much he was looking forward to seeing me again. I had been delighted to send a refusal.

'It's mostly lemonade,' I reassured Lissie, as Alice stopped crying long enough to drink a glass. 'Ivor never makes it very strong so that the children can have it. Try some yourself.'

There was a great deal of aniseed in it, one of those strange flavours that grows on one. Everyone had a second glass.

'I am the Lord of Misrule, self-appointed,' said Maurice, standing up and stepping over the sleeping Jasper, 'so you must obey my every command and I bid you go into the hall to see what I've brought. Follow me, everyone!' He skipped from the room.

While we had been watching the charades someone, presumably Maurice's driver, had brought in an assortment of strangely shaped objects. Every parcel was wrapped in blue paper with white fluffy clouds in gouache and real feathers stuck on them. 'Not Christmas, I know, but holly's damned expensive in Berkeley Square.'

For Rose he had brought a pretty little porcelain cup with roses on it and for Jenny a necklace of amber beads that he said would suit her pre-Raphaelite beauty, which pleased her very much though she didn't know what it was. For Ivor there was a copy of Browning's 'Pippa Passes' bound handsomely in blue hide as he said Ivor was the only person he knew who was clever enough to understand Browning. Ivor was delighted. For Henry there was an enormous and excitingly shaped parcel, which turned out to be a magician's cabinet. It was Chinese lacquer red, big enough to hold a small adult, with "Marcello the Marvellous" in loopy writing on the side.

'It will make things disappear,' explained Maurice. 'It

belonged to a friend of mine who was a magician. He's given up now but I said I knew a boy who'd take care of it.'

Henry was ecstatic. James was given a gold hunter fob watch, very handsome and, I thought, probably very valuable. Maurice said he had owned it all his life but he rarely needed to know the time any more. I was astonished when I unwrapped my own vast and weighty present to find a beehive. 'A swarm will be delivered after the Christmas holidays. I realised when you showed me the garden that this was the one thing it lacked. You needn't make honey, if you don't want to. They will just buzz about pollinating things. I've studied bees all my life, and I can tell you there are few creatures more fascinating.'

'How clever! What a *wonderful* present!' I was genuinely thrilled.

'Good, good, good! Now, as Lord of Misrule, I command you all to brave the cold and come outside at once, before it gets dark, to see what I've brought for Elizabeth.'

'Oh, crikey!' said Elizabeth.

On the other side of the moat stood the most perfect little open carriage. It was green with yellow coach-lines, two wheels and long shafts, which rested on a trestle. 'It's a governess cart,' said Maurice. 'A little jaunting carriage for the poor lonely governess to take her charges out in on fine days. What do you think?'

He looked at Elizabeth. She stood with her back to us. She was the only one of us not exclaiming and admiring. I saw her put up her hand tentatively to touch the rail that ran round the top of the pretty tub-shaped chassis. I was quite sure that Maurice would not misunderstand her silence. At last she turned, and her expression made my throat feel tight. She put her arms round Maurice's neck, hiding her face. 'How did you know it was what I've always wanted?'

'I think you mentioned it when you were showing me Puck. Then I happened to see this advertised and I thought it might be just the thing. The harness is on that wall. I hope it'll fit him all right. Tomorrow you can try it on and we'll go for a drive.'

'I must get in it.'

Maurice turned the handle of the little door at the back and Elizabeth put her foot on the iron step. Inside were two seats facing each other covered in green leather. Elizabeth sat down on one of them, her eyes shining. 'It's so lovely, I don't know how to thank you.'

'My darling, if it makes you happy that's all I want.'

When Elizabeth ran down to the stables with Henry to put the harness in the tack-room I felt that I must say something. 'I know, I know!' Maurice held up his hand. 'You're going to say you can't accept it. Now, listen! This exhibition has already created a lot of interest and I've got commissions falling out of my ears. Some chap who's seen the paintings of Westray Rocks has asked me to do a series of four for a princely sum. What does an old man like me want with money? I'm seventy-two. I've got everything I want. You can't imagine the pleasure it has given me to –'

'I only wanted to say that it's the kindest and best thing you could have done.'

After this we all rushed, shivering, indoors and had several more glasses each of Ivor's Wassail potion.

'Gosh, this stuff is really growing on me,' said Lissie, after her fourth glass. 'It tastes even better after going out in the cold. How marvellous that it's virtually non-alcoholic!' She hiccuped and giggled.

'Now, everyone, lights out! It's time for Murder in the Dark!' Maurice had also been at the Wassail Cup, and the tinsel he had made into a crown was hanging giddily over one ear.

We cut up bits of paper and marked M and D on two for murderer and detective.

'It's such a funny word, isn't it?' said Henry, starting to laugh. 'De-tec-tive. It's the silliest word I ever heard.' He went off into a fit of hysteria and between bursts of laughter muttered the syllables over and over again.

'Darling, do get a grip on yourself,' I said urgently. 'Don't spoil things by behaving like an idiot. You're very over-excited.'

'Gettagrip, gettagrip,' repeated Henry, in a very annoying way.

'I think you'd better go and sit quietly in the kitchen for five minutes,' I said severely. 'Calm down.'

Henry went off, still laughing wildly. I noticed that everyone else was inclined to uncontrollable giggling, particularly Sebastian and Florian.

'I'm the detective,' said George, solemnly, when we'd all chosen our bits of paper.

Something about his pompous manner struck me as being absurdly funny and I began to laugh myself. It was odd that I'd never noticed before what a charming laugh I have, silvery as they say in romantic novels... It was at this moment that I realised that there was something wrong with me. The children always tell me that my laugh sounds like a rook cawing. It isn't quite as bad as that but very definitely not silvery. I realised that I was drunk and, looking around at the glowing faces of the company as they perused their pieces of paper with idiot grins, so was everyone else.

'Let's have some more Wallais – Wallis – Wassail Cup before we go and hide,' cried Maeve.

'I don't think we ought,' I said, to an empty hall as everyone rushed with their glasses back into the drawing room.

'Ivor!' I grabbed him by the sleeve. 'What did you put in that stuff? It's much too strong.'

Ivor beamed down at me, his fair hair sticking up like a saintly nimbus. 'Stop worrying, darling. I only put in two pints of ale and half a bottle of ginger wine to ten pints of lemonade. Bridie could drink it without ill-effect. You're looking remarkably lovely tonight, my angel.' He stooped forward to kiss me, missed and almost toppled over.

'Ivor, you're stewed! You must have put in more than that!'

The ringing of the telephone interrupted my incoherent thinking. 'Hello? Hello? Yes, this is four six two eight. Who? Oh, Janòs! Oh dear!'

'What is the matter, Miranda?' Janòs's voice sounded far away.

'No. Nothing. I'm fine. Too much to drink, I think.' I let rip with another silver scale of notes and then pulled myself sharply together.

'You do sound drunk. I am shocked.'

'No, no, I'm all right now, honestly.'

More hopeless tittering. Despite the laughter, I was not really enjoying myself. This was a very strange kind of intoxication. I seemed to be floating several inches above the ground.

'I miss you, drunk or sobered. I'm lonely without you. I love you.'

'I'm lonely without you, too.'

'Well, then. I am this moment in Boston. I could come tomorrow night?'

'No. No, you mustn't do that.' Suddenly I was far from laughter. Though my thoughts were scattering the moment I tried to gather them, I knew that I must not let him come. 'Don't come. I do love you in a way – at least I desire you – but that's not the same thing. You'll put me through hell and I've spent quite enough of my life there as it is.'

'So it is goodbye, then.'

'Yes. Goodbye, goodbye, goodbye...' I found I was talking to a buzzing sound. Janòs had put the telephone down.

I turned away from the telephone.

Ivor was still standing behind me, his face white and his lips trembling. 'My God! You were in love with that fellow and I never knew! I must be the world's biggest fool!'

I tried to piece my mind together, though it would insist on roaming off like a particularly playful *ignis fatuus*. Ivor had not known about Janòs, never having seen us together and he had assumed, when I said I was going to

Venice with a friend, that I had meant a girlfriend. I had deliberately misled him with the best of intentions.

'To think that all these weeks I've been telling myself to hold back, to let you get over Jack's death before I . . . and all this time you've been making love with that fellow . . .' Ivor opened the front door and went out, letting it slam behind him.

The Wassail Cup was full to the brim, which awoke suspicion even in my distracted brain. I carried it carefully into the kitchen and flung the contents into the sink. A smell of brandy, probably the latest addition, was strong enough to make me cough.

I went upstairs to my own bedroom and lay down on the bed. As the room was in complete darkness it was as good a place to hide as any. The blackness before my eyes shimmered into little sparkling dots which, as I stared at them wondering what they could be, flared into brilliantly coloured flowers. I enjoyed this for some minutes until it occurred to me that the phenomenon was unusual, to say the least. Someone, or some two, had added substances to the Wassail Cup that were making me hallucinate. I knew that Maeve had flirted briefly with mescaline and LSD supplied by Sebastian and Florian.

The door opened and somebody crept forward in the dark. I heard soft footfalls and breathing, quite close to my face. I held my breath. Hands patted up and down the bed. I reminded myself that this was just a game. Or was it an hallucination? To this day, I simply don't know. A hand touched my leg and paused. Then it worked its way up my body until reached my throat. I screamed, 'Jack!' very loudly, and sat up in a state of terror. The hand released me at once. There was a sound like suppressed laughter and then the footsteps tiptoed away.

I rushed downstairs to find the hall in brightness and the game over. There was some confusion, as George was confronted by four victims instead of one and it turned out that Wacko had been the murderer and misunderstood the rules of the game. I wondered if it could have been Wacko in my bedroom but somehow I didn't think so. For one thing he was really tight and could not have tiptoed to save his life.

When George had ponderously worked his way to a conclusion that satisfied him, we discovered that Alice and Rose were missing. A search was instituted, and Rose was found fast asleep in the kitchen with Bridie in her arms. Lissie began to panic and look behind curtains and under rugs and in vases. At last Alice was found, asleep on the floor behind the sofa in the drawing room. This effectively broke up the party, for which I was extremely glad as I felt we would all be better in our beds, sleeping it off.

Patience, who had returned after taking Wacko home, insisted on driving the Partridges back as she said that neither George nor Lissie was in a fit state to drive. I could only be thankful for Patience's presence of mind.

'Why aren't you in a condition of inebriation bordering on lunacy?' I asked her, as we bundled my guests into Wacko's ancient Rover.

'I thought something was different about Ivor's potion after we'd been to look at Maurice's presents. It seemed much more potent so I didn't finish my third glass.'

'Sensible girl! I wish you'd pointed it out to the rest of us, though.'

'I didn't want to seem like a kill-joy. I suspect that I appear awfully dull to many people, especially men.'

I kissed her and said that no one who was silly enough to mistake common sense for dullness was worth worrying about. At least, that is what I meant to say but the Wassail Cup made anything but the most straightforward syntax tricky.

Aubrey said that he would walk home with Maeve, and they would return the next day to fetch their cars. The FitzGerald boys had gone off on their own some time before. Everyone rolled away down the drive with scraps and tatters of thanks and appreciation floating out into the night.

Somehow I scrambled eggs for supper, fed the animals and put Rose to bed. The children, Maurice and Jenny all voted for an early night, which was entirely out of any of their characters and just showed how devastating had been the onslaught of the Cup.

I got into bed with even more pleasure than usual, and drifted at once into the most delicious series of dream adventures. I had just agreed to stand in for Catherine the Great in a plot that was virtually a rerun of *The Prisoner of Zenda* when the clamorous pealing of bells across the length and breadth of the Russian Empire for my coronation became recognisably our own front-door bell. I switched on my bedroom light. It was half past two in the morning. Very cross indeed, I pulled on my dressing gown and went down to answer it.

Two police officers stood on the doorstep. 'Mrs Stowe? Sorry to disturb you at this hour. Is Mr Bastable at home?'

'Ivor? Yes . . . I imagine so. He lives at the cottage down by the fishponds.'

'We're very keen to have a word with him. Can you get him on the telephone?'

'I'm afraid not. You'll have to walk down through the wood. What's it all about?'

'There's been a fire, Madam. You'll be acquainted with Mr Horace Birt, your next-door neighbour. His barn has been burned to the ground. We have reason to believe that Mr Bastable may be able to help us with our inquiries.'

CHAPTER 18

Something was holding my head in a ring of iron. I gasped and opened my eyes. Daylight pierced my eyeballs with lances of fire. I lay amid the shattered remnants of my dreams, which after the interruption by HM Constabulary had ceased to be cheerful escapades but had degenerated to images of horror telescoping into each other. They had filled me with sensations of terror as the children had fallen continuously into bottomless lakes and tumbled from mountainous walls, stretched themselves out in front of approaching express trains and been pursued by madmen with axes.

I sat up. I was safe in my own room, enfolded by linen sheets and woollen blankets beneath a silk eiderdown and hung round with curtains of the prettiest faded chintz printed with roses and foxgloves. I stared at the spotted throats and the furled petals for some time until I was convinced that the children were safe in their beds and the world was a tolerable place in which to live.

'Hello, Mum. I'm feeling a bit rough.' James put his head round my door. 'Got any aspirin?'

'Bathroom cupboard. Bring me some, will you?'

James brought the bottle and sat on the edge of my bed. We shared a glass of water.

'Terrific party. But I had the bloodiest dreams. Perhaps I'm overdoing the work.'

'I don't think it was that. Someone – I'm certain it was Sebastian and Florian – put something in the... Oh my God! Ivor!'

'If you're going to scream like that I'm going back to bed,' protested James, clutching his ears with his hands. 'What about Ivor?'

'He's in prison!'

'What?'

It was my turn to protest.

'Sorry. But, for God's sake, tell me!'

I explained what had happened after he had gone to bed. 'I must ring Leslie Mould. What's the time? Eight thirty. He's bound to be up by now.'

He wasn't, and sounded extremely annoyed to be hauled out of bed on Boxing Day. I explained about Ivor and he sounded a little less fed-up. It wasn't often that his clients got themselves arrested, and a charge of arson was much more interesting than the usual divorce case. I arranged to meet him in one hour. I bathed and dressed and breakfasted in a hurry and, at the appointed time, was sitting in a room at Marshgate police station with

James beside me. Leslie Mould was there a few minutes later, his piglet eyes full of self-importance.

When Ivor was brought in his face was bloodless. 'I'm sorry to have you involved in this sordid imbroglio, Miranda. I don't suppose you'll believe it, but I had nothing to do with that fire.'

'That'll do for the minute, Bastable.' Leslie Mould was peremptory. 'Let's hear the case against Mr Bastable, if you please.' He addressed the police sergeant in charge.

It seemed that at ten o'clock on the night of 25 December Horace Birt had looked out of his bedroom window and seen that his hay barn was on fire. He had telephoned for the fire brigade. At twelve thirty an anonymous caller had telephoned the police to tell them that the fire at Birt's farm had been deliberately started by Ivor Bastable. Given Ivor's previous convictions, they had acted on information received and taken him into custody.

When I was asked to testify to the whereabouts of Ivor between the hours of eight and midnight the evening before, I could only tell them that there had been a large party of people in the house and the lights had been out for some of the time, making it impossible to say where any particular person was at any moment. Then I remembered that Ivor had stormed out of the house just after Janòs's telephone call, which must have been at about half past seven. I decided not to tell them this. After some discussion it was arranged that Ivor would appear before the magistrates the following day with an application for bail.

'Oh, my head!' Maurice was sitting in the kitchen, dressed but unshaven, his hair in disarray. 'It hurts too much to comb it. Oh, for the cup that cheers but not inebriates. The kettle is on, my darlings. A splendid party but I fear I drank more than was good for me.'

I made some tea and told him my suspicions of Sebastian and Florian.

'So I have them to thank for some of the most horrid hours I've ever spent. Dreams to fright the reign of Chaos and Old Night. Bound hand and foot and suspended over a bath of acid by a character who I think, from his moustache, must have been Dr Crippen.'

'Oh, heavens, Rose!' I dashed upstairs, leaving James to tell Maurice about Ivor's arrest.

Rose seemed all right, three small glasses of the Cup having been enough to put her to sleep and out of harm's way. I helped her to dress and brought her downstairs. Stew Harker stood in the hall.

'Hello, Stewart. I suppose you've called for your Christmas box?'

I had given Stew a pound or two every Boxing Day for years. These days, he was a strapping youth of more than six feet, athletic-looking due to so much bicycling. I didn't like the hubristic swagger of his walk as he approached me. 'A word with you alone, Mrs Stowe.' He grinned, very unengagingly. 'Let's not stand on ceremony. You call me Stewart so how's about I call you Miranda?'

I was carefully composing a tactful but firm refusal to change our relationship as I took him into the library, but I had no chance to put it to him.

'I haven't never been in here before. Blimey, what a lot of books! Still, I didn't come here to discuss hinterior decorating. I was in the Magpie and Stump last night, just before closing time, and I sees the two FitzGerald lads at the table in the corner, laughing fit to piss themselves. I went over to the dartboard so as I could hear what they were laughing at. They was so cock-a-hoop they didn't notice me. Seb was telling Florry that he'd fixed something good and proper.'

'I'm surprised no one has told you that listening in to other people's conversations is very reprehensible. As is tale-bearing. What Sebastian and Florian did was very silly and might have had serious consequences but –'

'I haven't finished. I heard Seb tell Florry that he was goin' to make a phone call. He said something about a prison record and how the police would be sure to pick Bastable up straight away and he'd get a good long spell as arson was a serious offence.'

'You're sure he said that?' I was suddenly keenly interested in this rambling tale.

'Ent I telling you? Then Florry says, "Where's your hat?" and Seb says, "Shit, I must have left it there. Never mind it'll be a heap of ashes by now," and they bust into laughter again.'

I thought of gentle, sensitive Ivor and what these boys had done to him, and my head seemed to catch fire. 'You must come with me and tell everything that you heard to the police. I'll get my coat.' I was trembling with anger.

'Not so fast.' Stew put out a hand the size of a dinner plate to stop me. 'I ent so sure that I wants to split on a couple of village boys. They could make things very nasty for me if for any reason the cops didn't convict 'em. It'd be two against one, heven though Florry's a nance.'

'Oh, for God's sake!' I chafed at the delay. 'We'll tell the police that they mustn't reveal the source of their information.'

'Don't be daft. I'd have to give hevidence in court. No, I wants a little more than that to make it worth my while.' He stepped closer and put a hefty hand on my shoulder. 'From what I hear you likes a bit of fun – Ow! What jer do that for?'

Before I had thought what I was doing I had slapped him resoundingly across the face.

' "Suddenly she rages like the troubled main." What's happened?' said Maurice, seeing my face as I stalked into the kitchen.

'What's up, Mum?' James looked alarmed.

I told them about Sebastian and Florian, and everyone was properly furious.

'It's just about the most disgusting thing I've ever heard!' James was irate. 'I bet it's more Sebastian than Florian, though. He always was a sadistic little shit.'

'What I want to know is, why did Stew come to tell you about it instead of going to the police?' asked Maurice.

'You may well ask! He wanted to sell the information. The price was, well . . . How shall I put it? Sexual favours from me.'

'Bloody cheek!' James was whiter than ever with rage. 'Shall I go round and bash him up?'

'No! Let's not have a brawl and spread it all over the village. Anyway, I smacked his face before I'd thought what I was doing. I was in such a temper.'

' "They have ploughed wickedness and reaped iniquity," ' said Rose, screwing up her mouth and closing her eyes against such malfeasance. 'Those Harkers are a bad lot.'

'I've known him since he was a small spotty boy with braces on his teeth. I'm absolutely fed-up with every man within twenty miles thinking I'm fair game. It's too bad! Maurice, I absolutely forbid you to laugh!' I had to join in, though it made my head hurt as though knives were being driven into it.

'What are we going to do about Ivor?' I felt suddenly guilty to be laughing when he was in such dire circumstances. 'Naturally I shall tell the police what Stew has just told me. I feel dreadfully disloyal to Maeve, but there's no choice. Should I tell her first? I wonder. Will my word be enough, do you think, if Stew decides to deny everything? Could he just have made it up anyway?'

We debated this long and hard for the rest of the morning without coming to any very satisfactory conclusions. When I rang the police station I was told that I must wait to speak to the duty sergeant, who had been called out but would be back in the afternoon. After lunch I lay down on my bed for five minutes' rest as I was still feeling headachy. I was very worried about the effect of imprisonment on Ivor's state of nerves.

When I woke up it was six o'clock and already dark. I rushed downstairs. 'So sorry, everyone. I didn't mean to sleep so – Ivor!'

'Hello, Miranda.'

The kitchen was lit only by the table lamp next to Rose's chair and the crimson embers of the fire. The room was warm and smelt of drying washing from the racks that hung above the hearth and of wintersweet, which stood in a jar on the table. Ivor was sitting alone at the table holding a teacup in a hand that shook. A goose sandwich with a bite out of it lay at his left elbow. My instinct was to put my arms around him but there was a *noli me tangere* air about him that dissuaded me. 'Tell me what's been happening,' I pleaded, sitting down next to him and placing my hand gently on his arm.

'It seems that there wasn't enough evidence against me and they decided to let me go.'

Ivor started as Dinkie jumped up with a hiss on to a chair next to him. A quantity of tea spilled over the table. I fetched a cloth. 'I'm so glad. I know you didn't do it.'

'No. I didn't, as it happens. Thanks for the tea. I'm afraid I can't eat the sandwich. I'll go home now, I think.'

I would have liked some more answers from Ivor, but I could see that he was in a state of shock and didn't want to talk. Later, Maurice, who had bundled everyone into the library to play Strip Jack Naked so that Ivor could be alone, as he so clearly wanted to be, filled me in on the afternoon's events.

He and James had gone to see Stew Harker after lunch. Stew had resisted appeals to his sense of duty. James's threats to knock his block off had prompted the invitation to come and try it. Maurice had then tried blandishments.

'You mean you offered him *your* body to do with as he willed?'

'Artists are obliged to be seekers out of experience, you know. But I found that there was something other than dalliance with the lovely Mrs Stowe dear to his heart. He has long cherished an ambition, apparently, to obtain a Heavy Goods Vehicle licence. I was able to slip him the wherewithal for the training after he had been along to the police station to make a statement. It seems that the police already have in their possession a cap found at the scene of the fire, which Stew was able to identify as belonging to Sebastian FitzGerald. After that the police had to let Ivor go.'

'How can I thank you? How much was it?'

'I decline to answer that. It was a piffling sum. As I said before, I like to travel light and there's really an embarrassing amount of money accumulating in the Tremlow coffers. Whatever you do, don't tell Ivor. I couldn't stand the burden of gratitude. James had ideas of repaying me but I've managed to persuade him that I shall be deeply offended to be reimbursed by so much as a ha'penny.'

'It seems quite wrong that that little cur should come so well out of it.'

'Looking at the Harker household, it seems to me a kind of justice that Stew has had a lucky break. Harker *mère* is a harridan. I couldn't but compare poor Stew with James, the one a scruffy, ignorant lout doomed to a benighted existence within the circumference of lorry cab and pub, the other clever and good-looking, for whom the world will display its treasures for the picking.'

'Put like that, I can only agree. I suppose I'd better ring Maeve.'

There was no answer from the FitzGeralds' number. In fact, I didn't manage to get hold of her until the following day. Maeve was distraught and tearful. I knew that she had always refused to see her sons with any kind of objectivity. She was certainly not alone in this, nor did I blame her. I felt very sorry for the horrid shock she had received.

'I ought to be the one locked up. I'm a complete failure as a mother. I wanted everything to be so different from my own boring, bigoted childhood, and all I've done is produce a criminal!'

'Do remember that a stumble may prevent a fall, as Thomas Fuller said.'

'Who's he?'

'A seventeenth-century divine. He also said that he that hath no fools, knaves or beggars in his family was begot by a flash of lightning.'

'Sebastian seems to be a fool *and* a knave. If he goes on this way he'll soon be a beggar, too.'

'I didn't quite mean that. I was speaking more generally.'

'It doesn't matter. I'm too miserable to care what

anyone says anyway. They couldn't say worse things than I'm telling myself.'

Soon after this sombre conversation I had a discussion with Patience about Maeve. Maeve had persuaded her solicitor not to make an application for bail as she thought that a spell of imprisonment would do Sebastian more good than anything. There was every chance that he would get off with probation when the case came to court as he had no previous record.

'She's doing the right thing, I'm sure,' said Patience. 'Let's hope they're really nasty to him. It's all a bully like that understands. Should we have said something before, about what a little bastard he is? To Maeve, I mean.'

'I don't think so. Criticism of offspring is too hurtful, however accurate and well intentioned. That's a very attractive jersey. Is it new?'

I knew that it was but did not wish to underline the shortcomings of Patience's wardrobe.

'Yes.' Patience's smooth skin was delicately roseate. 'I bought it from the Oxfam shop. Is it really all right?'

'Lovely. And isn't there something different about your hair?'

'I've left out the kirby-grip. I'm thinking of cutting a sort of fringe. What do you think?'

'I imagine it should suit you very well.'

'The truth is,' Patience suddenly burst out, 'I'm fed-up with looking such a frump. I'm nearly forty and no man has ever even tried to kiss me.'

'Is the opportunity being thrown open to everyone, or have you someone specifically in mind?'

Patience looked down at her hands. Her fingers were strong and blunt, their skin roughened by continual needle-pricks. Her nails were cut short and square. They were capable hands, and I thought any man of sense would find them just as beautiful as the soft, white, unused hands and scarlet fingernails of a privileged society Parthenope.

'Actually, there *is* someone. I know I can trust you not to say anything.' I was warmed by this and made an immediate resolve that I would say nothing to anyone, not even Maurice. He and I shared an inexhaustible curiosity for other people's crotchets and idiosyncrasies. Our conversations usually ended in shameless gossip. 'I couldn't bear to be laughed at.'

'There isn't anything funny about falling in love. Not at the time, anyway.'

'No, but I mean laughed at because I've made a fool of myself. You see, I don't think he feels at all the same as I do. I'm terrified of becoming an embarrassment to him. Someone he's got to get rid of in the kindest way. I've heard you talk about the men who've made passes at you and you seem almost to despise them because they're a nuisance.'

'But we aren't talking about the same thing here. Those men are only interested in sex and their own egos. You're in love with Aubrey, aren't you?'

Patience looked at me, her blue eyes large with astonishment. 'Good God, is it that obvious? What have I done to give myself away? I thought I'd been completely circumspect.'

'It's just that I've known you a long time. It wouldn't be obvious to anyone else. It's equally clear to me that the feeling is returned with interest.'

'Really? You think so?' For a moment, her eyes were starry with hope. Then she shook her head and looked sorrowful. 'Much as I give you credit for remarkable observation, I think you must be wrong. He never attempts to detain me one second longer than the accounting requires. He always walks with me to the car, opens the door and waits politely until I've got in and then closes it and waves me off. He is generous with praise for my ability to add up but never pays me any other kind of compliment.'

'He said after you'd both been to supper here that you were – what was it? – as beautiful as you were clever, something like that. I should have mentioned it at the time, but I was afraid of making you self-conscious with him.'

'I *am* self-conscious with him. When we're together my mouth's dry and I'm so tense I can't speak or sit or walk naturally. We clear our throats and apologise for interrupting each other as though we're waiting to see the dentist. The atmosphere is electric with unease.'

'Mm. I wonder what's the best way to precipitate an alteration in the state of things.'

I was quiet for a minute, thinking. The difficulty was that neither Aubrey nor Patience had any aptitude for flirtation. With both of them I could see that the heart, having once been given, would be bestowed for life. They were both incapable of any kind of insincerity or volatility. It was one of the many things that made them peculiarly suited. But how to get them to the point of declaration was a thorny problem. I couldn't think of anything that might provoke an admission of love from Aubrey, except perhaps a touching bedside scene with Patience terminally consumptive. But I had seen how he looked at her throughout lunch on Christmas Day, with the tender gaze of adoration.

'You'll have to make a pass at him.'

'I've thought of it. I know how shy and modest he is. Last time I went to the vicarage I steeled myself to say something... you know... encouraging. I contemplated saying something all the way through tea, something about being lonely, perhaps. Not strictly true and disgustingly coy. Something about how I enjoyed our meetings? Too brazen. Aubrey would be terrified if I threw myself at his head. In the end, I just went cravenly away. Perhaps if it's meant to happen it will.' She looked at me hopefully.

I shook my head. 'Don't you remember that bit in Anna Karenina when Kitty's friend, Varenka, is walking in the woods with Kozneyshev, the man she longs to marry? He's decided that he's going to ask her. Tolstoy reveals all the workings of his mind, his appreciation of her suitability and her charm. Kozneyshev turns towards her. She's in an agony of anticipation, on the edge of finding her life transformed from monotonous drudgery into everything she has ever dreamed of. In her agitation and embarrassment she blurts out something about mushrooms. He's distracted, the moment passes, they return to the house together but everything is lost. Everyone understands that it isn't going to happen. And yet it might have, so easily. It's a delicate operation but someone, usually the man, has to advance love from being a figment of the imagination to something that has the reality of a declaration.'

'You've obviously been thinking a lot about it.'

'I've been reading myself a great many sermons lately and wondering what men and women might reasonably expect from each other.' I told her about the triangle of Maeve and Janòs with me making a reluctant third.

She was extremely indignant with them both. 'Never mind. I always knew in my heart of hearts that it wouldn't work. I just didn't want to listen.'

'I admire your common sense.'

'Actually I don't think it *is* common sense. More likely a phobia about sexual betrayal. I probably won't ever be able to have a love affair with a man again. I shall have to devote my life to good works when the children grow up.'

Patience gave a caustic and incredulous snort which, I must say, I found comforting.

Two days later Lissie called in. They had been staying with her hated parents-in-law since Boxing Day.

'When did you get back? Was Marjorie as ghastly as usual?' I addressed these questions to Lissie's elegant dove-grey-suited bottom as she dropped kisses on to Bridie's beaming countenance.

'Horrid. She asked me if I was putting on weight. What sort of thing is that to ask a girl? I could have stabbed out her eyes with my cocktail stick! We got home last night just before seven. Then we rushed out straight away to Hilary Scranton-Jones's drinks party. If I'd known that she wasn't going to ask you I would have turned her down flat. Lots of people wondered where you were.'

'She did ask me. I said I had a previous engagement. I didn't want to go.'

'What? But, darling, you and Jack always used to go. I admit she's an absolute bitch but her parties are terrific. Champagne positively streamed. You aren't becoming a hermit, are you?' She swivelled round from the crib and looked at me narrowly.

'Jack always had a cast-iron stomach for social occasions. However grim they were he could amuse himself by flirting with the prettiest woman in the room.' I remembered suddenly to whom I was talking, and bit back what I had been going to say about preferring to assent publicly to his liaisons rather than stay at home like a sulking wife. 'I have no such outlets. If there's a choice between scrubbing the larder floor or standing until my back hurts, sipping my way slowly to acute acidosis and yelling inanities to the Scranton-Jones coterie, give me the rubber gloves and Vim any day.'

'I know what you mean, and often I feel the same way, but one must make efforts.'

Lissie was the least self-disciplined person I had ever met but I let this pass.

'How is Alice?'

'Fine, thanks. It was a wonderful party, darling, and I haven't thanked you properly, but I'm afraid we overdid the Christmas cheer. We all had stinking hangovers afterwards.'

I explained about the Wassail Cup and Sebastian and Florian's latest exploit with fire-raising. I didn't mention Ivor's connection with the tale. Lissie was absolutely shocked. In some ways she is naïve but it adds to her charm.

'How is Elizabeth?' she asked, when we had discussed the FitzGerald boys *ad nauseam*.

'Oh, much better! I'm so pleased with her. Every day after Maurice has done his "purgatory on the plage", as he calls it – you know he's been commissioned for thousands of pounds to do a series of seascapes? – he goes out with Elizabeth in the pony carriage. He used to drive a horse and trap in Italy so he knows all about it. Luckily Puck turns out to be the ideal carriage pony, steady and stocky. Elizabeth loves it. She's forgotten all about being miserable. Oh, and the other thing she and Maurice are doing is making a shell grotto inside the old summerhouse. They spend hours sorting out different shapes and colours, and they've started making a pattern on the ceiling. She calls him Uncle Tremlow and he calls her Bessie.'

'I *am* pleased. I was worried about her at Christmas. She looked so gloomy.'

'Henry goes with them and is allowed to take the reins sometimes, and when they aren't doing that Maurice teaches him conjuring tricks. He's like the most marvellous nanny. Even James seeks him out for long, mysterious talks. I've no idea what about.'

'So they're all right.' Lissie lifted Bridie on to her knee and began to feed her tiny pieces of mashed banana, to which the baby had just graduated, with a disregard for her expensive shirt that I found touching. 'But I'm worried about you, darling. You're looking rather thin.'

I reassured her that I was quite well and perfectly content with my lot. This was, of course, a lie. I doubted whether I had ever been content in all my life. Is it even a desirable thing to be? Probably not. However, when I thought about the current state of my existence that night as I lay in bed, somnolent in the dying light of the fire, I realised that what worried me far more than the question of love and sex, which seemed to be bothering everyone else so much, was the problem of my future. By this I meant some kind of useful and stimulating employment. For too long I had been seduced by domestic pleasures. Some women would say that is an oxymoron, but a house as old and lovely as Westray rewards tenfold every effort made to preserve it. The paying guests were a stop-gap to pay the bills but I needed something more testing. I had to find out what I could really do.

I thought of Maeve, struggling gallantly with impossibly difficult children after two failed marriages. Then I thought of Patience, fearfully in love, labouring at work that made no use of her intelligence, a slave to an ingrate, and of Lissie, bored and guilty about being so, and I reflected that I had little to complain of. While I was looking for a chance to discover what I was really capable of, there were plenty of worthwhile things to get on with.

The next day I arranged sheets of paper on the writing table in my bedroom and filled my fountain pen with violet ink. When I was a little girl in London our cook, Fanny, had written regular letters to her fiancé, Leonard Binns, in violet ink and it had seemed to me the essence of romance. I used to admire the envelopes addressed to him in Fanny's good, firm hand with pangs of vicarious excitement. This feeling swelled to intoxicating sensations after Leonard Binns was run over by a butcher's van and had to have his leg cut off. Fanny married him soon after. I always liked to hold the bottle up to the light and watch the gentian blotches floating across my page, staining my hand amethyst. Fabia condemned coloured inks as vulgar. The purchase of my first bottle of violet ink, at the age of thirteen, with some money my aunt Nancy had given me, was the beginning of open rebellion against my mother.

I wrote 'Westray Manor: A History 1465–1974', and underlined it twice.

CHAPTER 19

January and February passed in a manner that was almost tranquil compared with what had gone before. The children went back to school and seemed, on the surface anyway, to be thriving. There was, locally, a general consensus that I should put aside my black crape and consort with the world in a fever of partying. Requests to lunch, dine, drink and dance were legion, and quite a few were from people who had not hitherto favoured me with invitations. I expect much of it was simple kindness. This is what I told myself, though the suspicion that I had acquired a notoriety which demanded that curiosity be satisfied at the cost of entertaining me could not be dismissed.

I went to Lissie's party because she would have been hurt if I had refused. It was, like all her parties, a masterpiece of planning, with generous quantities of champagne, lovely things to eat and beautiful flowers. Her house is red-brick William and Mary, charmingly decorated, and there was no justification for the feeling I had on getting home afterwards that I never wanted to go to a party ever again. I felt like a piece of fruit on a market stall, bruised with too much handling. All the women, as well as the men, had given me extra squeezes as they kissed me in greeting, and I was patted and stroked and fingered throughout the evening.

And my mind felt similarly bruised. I knew that everyone was thinking about Jack when they spoke to me and yet no one mentioned him. I tried bringing his name into the conversation myself, but the feeling of tension and alarm this created, as everyone made superhuman efforts to be tactful and sympathetic, seemed to dampen spirits so immediately that I pretty soon avoided the topic myself.

Probably a lot of this was in my imagination. Though a few months had passed, my feelings of responsibility and guilt had not diminished. I was happy only with intimates whom I trusted, or complete strangers. After a while I stopped accepting invitations.

More paying guests came, and I began to feel confident that I knew what I was doing as chatelaine of Westray Manor. Some of our guests were delightful. They ate whatever they were given and praised it lavishly, loved the house and the surrounding countryside and never left wet towels on the bed. We had one or two really horrible ones, who asked for obscure items of diet, like arrowroot or maraschino, long after the shops had shut, who complained about allergies to Jasper and Dinkie, who left taps running and lights on and then wanted a discount on their bill because it had rained throughout their stay.

Quite a few came to worship at the shrine of Christopher Chough. They were reluctant to believe that he had not lived in the house. My grandfather, hanging on to the coat-tails of William Morris, had extolled the values of the medieval world and Westray was its rural embodiment. They were wonderfully reverential and went mad not only about the bits of Chough memorabilia I had about the house but also about things like the lead-lined sinks in the scullery and the old jakes and the le Bec letters.

With Maurice and James's help I made a small Christopher Chough museum in what had once been the brew-house. This was in the oldest part of Westray. In one corner of the brew-house were the remains of the old furnace and a copper, which had boiled the water and hops, and a mash tun, which was like a large shallow barrel. The liquid from the copper used to be tapped off into this and left to mash for several hours while the starch changed into sugar. We swept and dusted and scrubbed and brought in spare pieces of furniture on which to display my grandfather's effects.

Beatrice, on hearing of the project in the course of one of our telephone conversations, sent us two large packages of things like Christopher Chough's spectacles, evening pumps, hairbrush and inkwell. Even Fabia sent a plaster cast of the great poet's hand. It made a heavy parcel and, as my mother had failed to put the correct stamps on it, was an expensive addition to the museum but it set off handsomely the rather nasty Arts and Crafts desk he had used, which had always looked wrong wherever I put it in the house. My handwriting is untidy and Maurice said his was illegible so James made neat labels, describing the articles and dating them where possible.

Patience had the brilliant idea of restoring the laundry and the dairy to a state worthy of inspection by visitors. We spent several days slinging out bent bicycles and broken bedsteads. Ivor whitewashed the laundry and rubbed the rust off an old mangle, which had stood in the corner for at least a hundred years. We cleaned out the great copper, filled the hole under it with logs and put my small collection of flat irons and goffering irons on display.

The dairy had been built in its present style in the early nineteenth century but by the time we bought Westray it had become a game larder. It was a very pretty room, lined with green and white ivy-patterned tiles and I had often planned to restore it. The visitors' interest gave me the impetus I needed, so Maurice and I spent a day scrubbing down the marble slabs and the gullied floor. We had only an old butter churn and some little bats for moulding butter, called 'Scotch hands', to put in the dairy.

Lissie saw an advertisement for a country-house sale, which listed, in small print down at the bottom, miscellaneous items, among which was a butter-worker 'of interest to collectors of domestic bygones'. We were thoroughly successful at the sale as none of the last-mentioned were there. We picked up the butter-worker for two pounds. This was a fascinating piece of equipment – like a large wooden tray on legs, across which a fluted roller was pushed back and forth to press moisture out of the butter and salt into it. We also bought flat ceramic milk pans, used for skimming off the cream.

At the same sale there was an iron-heating stove, which I longed to get for the laundry. The bidding went higher than the modest amount I felt I could afford, but Lissie insisted on buying it and then gave it to me to 'look after' as she had nowhere to put it. After that she was always coming in with bits and pieces she had picked up from sales and antique shops, like tin cheese moulds and glove stretchers. She said it gave her something really enjoyable to do, now that Alice was at boarding school and time was so abundant. Our small domestic museum gave us quite as much pleasure as it gave the visitors.

Maurice was almost always at Westray, which was wonderful: far from *being* work he was an alleviation of it and we spent happy evenings doing the washing-up together, comparing notes about his seascapes and my little history for the pageant. The latter project was going well. I rediscovered the pleasure that writing and researching gave me, and already the booklet was expanding to at least twenty thousand words.

A few weeks after Christmas, the rest of Maurice's present to me arrived, in the shape of a swarm of bees. We had already put the hive in the cherry orchard at his suggestion as cherries have excellent nectar and pollen. The entrance to the hive was four feet from a hedge so that the bees would not be blown about when trying to fly back in. We put on our overalls, veiled hats and gloves – mine were part of my Christmas present, new and very stiff – and like spacemen, moving with large slow steps, staggered out to the garden. Jasper was moved to fury by our eccentric appearance and howled and foamed at the mouth, which made Bridie scream. After this the cherry orchard seemed like a Virgilian evocation of rustic bliss and we declared ourselves to be *Arcades ambo*, in mutual harmony with each other and nature.

'I chose the Italian strain of bee for you,' explained Maurice, 'as they're better-tempered, and your climate's comparatively mild. See, they have two yellow bands round them.' I peered into the ventilated box, which seethed with annoyed buzzing. 'This is called a nucleus. We'll put the box right on the hive so that they'll always come back to this spot. Now open that little door. They'll fly about and settle down after their journey. This evening we'll move the frames into the hive with the help of a smoker.'

Late that afternoon, armed with a smoker stuffed with smouldering dried grass, we crept round the hive, being careful not to disturb the bees by the vibrations of our footfalls, and Maurice wafted a little smoke through the ventilation holes. 'This will make the bees gorge themselves on honey. A full bee is much more docile. Now a little more smoke... and we should be able to move the combs with the bees on them into the hive.'

I watched as he did this, carefully and patiently, and

looked at the latest additions to Westray with tender indulgence, imagining our first jar of transparent amber honey, perhaps in July. It was not only greediness that inspired my thoughts but also a pleasant idea that now, when I worked in the garden, Westray bees would be buzzing companionably about my favourite plants and working with me for greater fruitfulness. Maurice pointed out the queen and began to talk of supers and crowns and dummies, egg-laying rates and brood patterns until my head was spinning. 'You'll get the hang of it as we go along, don't worry. The marvellous thing about bee-keeping is that it can be quite simple or very complicated, depending on whether you want to rear your own queens and so on. Every year is different with different problems and I've always found it fascinating.'

We went in, very cold but in a satisfying state of anticipation, and talked apiculture throughout supper until Elizabeth said she realised that if she wanted to get attention from either of us in the future she would have to learn to secrete wax from her abdomen.

We had argued for some time about Maurice's financial contribution to the household. I wanted to charge him less than the going rate because of everything he did for us. He was firm that he would stick to the original terms, cash on the nail. In fact, he decided to pay for his room on a monthly basis so that even when he was in London he had, he said, the comfort of knowing that there was a room at Westray waiting for him.

I was grateful for his help. Now that she was growing older, Bridie naturally slept less and wanted more entertaining. Jenny was keen to let Rose do this but the baby was getting too heavy for Rose's increasingly feeble limbs. Jenny worked doubly hard when she had any spare time from the baby, but I realised that I must have more help. I put another advertisement into the post-office window, hoping that by now there would be another hapless pivot for gossip apart from me.

The only applicant was Mrs Harker, Stew's mother. She was a huge woman, strong as a water-buffalo and perfectly able to scrub the house from top to bottom in a morning without feeling the slightest bit fagged. My objection to her was that she was loud and aggressive and of doubtful honesty, coming from an enormous family all of whom dodged the law with a species of foxy adroitness which, if turned to honest purposes, could not have failed to make them millionaires. As it was, they crammed into a row of council houses and everyone in the village was terrified of the Harker gang. In other words, she was thoroughly unsuitable. I engaged her on the spot.

'I'm ever so sorry, Miranda.' Jenny was tearful after the departure of the mountainous Winnie Harker. 'I know you've had such a lot to do lately, with me being so tied up with the baby. I were wondering, like, would I be putting Bridie into a nursery now?'

'Oh, no!' The words were out before I could even pretend to consider what was to me a shocking idea. 'That is, of course she's your baby, Jenny, but think what you'd be doing! She needs you, not some stranger, however well meaning. Think how little attention she'd get by comparison with all the love she has here. And think what you'd miss, too.'

'I know.' Jenny was crying in earnest now. 'But I got to earn my keep. You didn't take me in, ever so good of you as it was, for me to loll about the place taking up room.'

'Nor did I ask you to live here because I wanted to kill you with overwork or make you give up your baby. I expect we'll get used to Mrs Harker.'

'She's like a Jabberwock, Mum,' said Henry, who was at home with a bad cold.

'I think you mean a Juggernaut, darling. She certainly made the chair creak when she sat down, didn't she? I had visions of a pile of matchwood every time she crossed her legs.'

'I wrote to Father Declan saying how good I were doing. What shall I tell him now?'

'Tell him how much we value you. No one can fry eggs and bacon so nicely as you do, and your rice pudding's unbeatable. We want you to stay with us as long as you like. And Mrs Partridge would throw herself off Beachy Head if you took Bridie away.'

Jenny giggled a little at this and seemed comforted. 'The thing is... Father Declan wrote me back to say he'd like to call in here to see me.' She blushed deeply. 'After a conference in Guildford.'

'I've always wanted to see a Catholic priest close to,' remarked Henry. 'Will he be wearing a lambretta?'

'Guildford's miles away. Won't he want to stay the night?'

'No, he's taking the late train back to Sheffield.'

I wondered about the blush. I had always had deep suspicions about Father Declan. These were confirmed when he arrived a week later. He was much younger than I had expected and extraordinarily hirsute. Black hair crept down over the backs of his hands and poked up round his neck. Thick waves clustered round his large damson-coloured ears but his teeth were very white and his smile was dashing. I could see a resemblance to Bridie, especially in the shape of the nose. 'You'll be the wonderful Mrs Stowe.' He grasped my hand, pressing my rings painfully into my fingers. 'We all want to thank ye for all you've done for our little Jenny!'

Jenny simpered and crimsoned, and wrung her hands. She could hardly have been more overcome if he had arrived in a chariot of fire rather than on the number twenty-two bus from Canterbury. I wasn't at all happy about the way he put his arms round Jenny and hugged her at intervals. 'Will you look at that now!' he cried, staring into the crib at Bridie, who woke and began to scream. 'And there's a lusty little creature, the spitting image of her mother!'

I tried to be polite but I couldn't quite keep disapproval from my voice as I asked him if he would like lunch. 'I'll not be troublin' ye but for a cup of tea and a nice chat, and then I'll away. Father Barnabas will be by in half an hour with the car. He's been visiting a dying priest at Herne Bay so it's all worked out right and tight!'

Father Declan was quite irrepressible and talked nonstop with an exclamation mark at the end of every sentence. By the time he went I felt exhausted. Jenny, though, was in transports. 'Think of him coming all the way to see me! When he left he asked me if I'd been saying me prayers and I had to admit that sometimes I forget. "God won't forget you, my child," he said, "and neither will I. I shall pray for you tonight and thank the Lord for finding you such a grand home." Wasn't it good of him?'

I forbore to remark that I thought it was what a priest was for. I couldn't bring myself to spoil the happiness wreathing Jenny's lovely face.

At the end of February, the inquest on Jack's death came before the coroner. I had been dreading it. In the event it couldn't have been simpler or less terrifying. Sir Humphrey Bessinger had telephoned me the day before to tell me not to worry. He had seen that it was due to come up and had had a quiet word with the coroner. I would find that it would all go smoothly. I put this down to showing-off on Sir Humphrey's part. I couldn't imagine that the coroner would be swayed from the path of justice, even though he and Sir Humphrey had, for decades, spent every Thursday night dressed in aprons and rolled-down socks, brandishing trowels at each other.

The coroner looked exactly like Robert Donat with white hair. He had the same soft voice and confiding manner. He was anxious to save me any distress and frequently asked me if I would like to sit down, have a glass of water, take a five-minute break or have the window opened. I said no to all of these things, and we got through the evidence pretty quickly. Ivor gave his testimony, after me, of how we found the body.

These days Ivor wasn't looking too good. He looked more like an early Plantagenet than ever, strained and tired and depressed. He was working very hard at rebuilding the coach-house and was doing it beautifully. We were all as kind to him as we possibly could be, but he was withdrawn and abstracted and I don't think he heard much of what anyone said. I felt sad when every day I looked from my bedroom window across the woods to his cottage and saw that drifts of heathery smoke no longer rose from his chimney. We had wanted to put electricity and central heating into the cottage for Ivor when he first came, but he had been reared in chilly aristocratic discomfort and preferred the simplicity of open fires and oil lamps. It must have been very dismal by the blank, cold hearth.

Dr McCleod gave evidence after Ivor. I hadn't seen him since he had come to take out Elizabeth's stitches before Christmas. Then he had been very friendly with Elizabeth but markedly cool with me.

Dr McCleod's evidence was confirmed by the policeman, who had come out in response to his call. The pathologist spoke for the longest time. As I had a chair with wooden arms I was able to cup my good ear in the palm of my hand and shut out almost everything that he said. I suppose this was cowardly. Afterwards the coroner asked me, in the sugared tones I always involuntarily adopt when talking to small furred or feathered things, if I knew of any reason why Jack should have wished to take his own life. I explained that he was considering divorce proceedings on the grounds of my having refused to share a bedroom with him for four years. I knew Leslie Mould would spill the beans if I didn't.

'Do I take it, Mrs Stowe, that you were happy to continue with things as they were?'

'Yes.'

'There was no question of any third person being involved?'

'No.'

There was no point in bringing Jack's girlfriends into it. Dr McCleod had turned his head sharply to look at me. I kept my eyes fixed on the coroner but I could see from the corner of my eye that Dr McCleod continued to stare. After more exchanges with the pathologist, the coroner recorded an open verdict, saying that it was clear that Jack had been responsible for his own death but that there was not sufficient evidence for a verdict of suicide. He expressed the sympathy of the court for the family of the deceased, gave me one last compassionate smile and then we were free to go. Ivor went to get the car while I waited outside on the steps.

'Well, that went very nicely.' Leslie Mould's tiny eyes were screwed to pinpoints with smiling. 'We'll be able to apply for probate now. I'll see that we get it through as fast as possible.' I knew that this was solicitor-speak for doing absolutely nothing for six months, followed by a couple of hours' hasty work for which there would be an exorbitant bill. 'Any time you want legal advice don't hesitate,' Leslie went on. 'Perhaps we could get together for a drink.' He looked at me speculatively. I pretended that I had not heard him.

'That must have been an ordeal for you.' Dr McCleod was at my elbow.

'Well, it could have been much worse. But I'm very glad it's over. I haven't thanked you for what you did for Elizabeth.'

'I'm paid to look after my patients. It's my job.' He looked rather fierce – the identical twin of Marcus Curtius. I had forgotten that he hated to be thanked.

I saw Leslie walk away with an expression of pique on his porcine features. I didn't care. I knew his wife fairly well and had always liked her.

'That's not quite true. You came to see her on your day off, I remember. And you made us laugh . . . saved us from going stir-crazy.'

He smiled. 'There's a punitive climate in hospitals, as though equating sickness and sin.'

'I was nearly driven to rebellion by those notices. I thirsted to untidy the sluice room. When I was leaving with Elizabeth I thought, just for the hell of it, I'd go and pinch their bloody old bung that they made such a fuss about. But it wasn't there. Someone had already taken it.'

I was delighted that he found this as ridiculous as I did. When he laughed he looked quite different. 'Why don't we . . .' he began to say, when a black Daimler swooshed up and Sir Humphrey stuck his head out of the window.

'Miranda! I was hoping to catch you. Allow me to give you a lift home.'

Sir Humphrey's driver leaped smartly out and held open the door for me.

'Thank you, but Ivor has gone to get the car.'

'I met your man in the car park and told him that I'd bring you back.'

I was silent for a moment as I contemplated Sir Humphrey's enormous cheek in arranging my affairs without consulting me and also in talking about Ivor as though he were a vassal to be ordered about. Sir Humphrey had telephoned me several times since our return from the hospital, and I had found plenty of reasons to refuse his invitations to dinner as I really had been busy. I expect he must have seen something of my indignation for he looked rather apologetic and added with less of his usual assurance, 'It was bold of me, I know. But you're always so busy and there's something I particularly want to say to you. Get in, there's a good girl.'

Sir Humphrey's driver stood rigidly to attention, his expression unreadable beneath his peaked cap. I turned to Dr McCleod, hoping for assistance, only to see him disappearing down the side street that led to the car park. There was nothing for it. I slid into the back of the Daimler next to Sir Humphrey. The car smelt strongly of leather and brandy. I wondered if Sir Humphrey had been giving himself Dutch courage before his attempt at kidnap. The door closed with an expensive clunk. The Count of Monte Cristo must have heard the hollow clang of his cell door with comparable dread as he began his lengthy term of incarceration.

Sir Humphrey shut the glass partition between us and the driver as we drew out into the Bosworth traffic. 'This is cosy, isn't it? I've been so looking forward to the chance of a little talk with you.'

He patted my hand. His touch was like being brushed with seed-pods, dry and rustling. I have no prejudice against age. Maurice was if anything older than Sir

Humphrey and, next to my own family, Maurice was as dear to me as anyone. But Maurice behaved like a man of seventy. He never tried to fool himself or anyone else that he was younger than he was. He was never remotely flirtatious. Sir Humphrey rolled back his lips in a smile like a death's head, showing the edges of his pink plastic gums. 'I had a quick word with Julius, the coroner, you know, while you were getting your coat. He seemed to think it had all gone off very well. An open verdict was the best you could hope for, he said. I hope it won't mean losing a great deal of money – from the insurance people, I mean.'

'Jack cashed in his life-insurance policy a few years ago. I had no idea. My bank manager told me. I think he bought the Aston Martin out of it. So it doesn't matter.'

'That's my brave woman! I expect Julius was won over by the vision of loveliness before him. What man wouldn't be?'

I resisted the temptation to say that the due process of the law might have had something to do with it. I was pretty certain that Sir Humphrey would attempt to gather his withered old haunches into a spring. I tried not look actually sulky but my mood of resentment was strong. By now we were gliding through the suburbs of Bosworth and picking up speed. 'I think your driver's made a mistake,' I said, as we turned right by the level crossing and plunged immediately into wooded countryside. 'It's much the most direct route to keep to the main road.'

Sir Humphrey seemed a little embarrassed. 'I told him to go the long way round so that we wouldn't be interrupted.'

I'm sure at this point that I must have looked absolutely fed-up, if not actually annoyed, for he began to talk very fast and rather nervously for a man who hitherto had displayed the sensitivity and excitability of a yoked ox.

'That was excellent advice you gave me about Matron. It worked a treat. Now she's very brisk. Never telephones but writes me memos. From what I hear from the powers-that-be she won't be doing her job much longer. This is terribly confidential, of course.'

It was on the tip of my tongue to ask him why, in that case, he was telling me, a virtual stranger.

'She didn't seem to me to be any worse than anyone else there,' I said. 'In fact, I should say that she had pretty high standards and was quite efficient, though I didn't personally like her.'

'Well, it's all to do with administration. I won't bore you. I don't want to waste these precious moments in your company talking about dull old work.'

He beamed at me, but I pretended not to see and looked out of the window. It was just beginning to grow dark. The woods were lovely in the last glow of afternoon light, still bare of leaf but filled with the soft shadows of the criss-crossing branches. Some creature scuttled away into the undergrowth. Was it a large fox or a small deer? A muntjak, perhaps. A large bird – could it be an owl out so early in the evening? – flitted across a clearing. I was envious of its power of flight. I longed to be out of this purring, overheated machine and to be by myself. Sir Humphrey was still talking. He was telling me about the voluntary helpers at the hospital, how much excellent work this charitable body did and what difficulty they were having in replacing Lady Alice Vavasour, who was retiring from the post of chairman. With a sensation of stunned relief I realised that Sir Humphrey had abducted me in this high-handed way because he wanted to ask me to take Lady Alice's place.

'I'm very flattered that you thought of me,' I said, smiling at him properly for the first time. 'But I must say no at once. I'm sorry. I know it must be hell trying to find people to do it. But I'm really rather forgetful and not terribly well organised. And I absolutely hate telling other people what to do. You must have someone who enjoys that sort of thing. What about Hilary Scranton-Jones? She'd be very efficient, I imagine.'

'I don't think she'd do.' Sir Humphrey looked disappointed. 'For one thing, I hear on the grapevine that she's very unpopular. And for another she hasn't quite got the status we need in a chairman.'

'Well, I haven't got any status at all,' I said quickly. 'I don't cut any ice socially.'

'You underestimate yourself, my dear. You're held in more respect than you probably realise. And as mistress of Westray Manor –'

'Oh, no, please, Sir Humphrey! I really hate that kind of snobbery . . . No, it's not to be thought of. I'm no good at charity work. But thank you for thinking of me.' I spoke firmly but gave him my kindest smile in an attempt to soften the blow.

In the obscurity of the car interior I saw him looking at me with unusual solemnity. 'There is one thing we could do to change that.' He spoke slowly and deliberately, in a quite different manner from his usual bluster. 'I can't agree with you that you don't have sufficient status for the job, but if you became Lady Bessinger, I flatter myself that that particular objection would be swept quite away. No,' he held up a hand to stop me, 'just hear me out, Miranda, for a moment. I can't offer you romance and excitement, I know that. I'm sixty-nine. I've got grown-up children . . . grandchildren, even. But there's something to be said for an old chap who's sown his wild oats. You need looking after, my dear, and I'd feel enormously privileged if you'd allow me to do that. I realised when you wouldn't come out to dinner with me that you weren't attracted to me. But there is another kind of love, isn't there? Based on friendship, respect and all that? I expect you think I'm a silly old dotard.' I felt very guilty at this point. 'I've made up for not being particularly bright by working hard all my life and, above all, by not letting people down. I don't think I've done too badly by the family name, though my father always told me I was an idiot. Well, that's all past, now.' There was something in Sir Humphrey's voice that made me feel very certain that the memory still hurt him. 'When we had that lunch before Christmas – you remember, at the Six Jolly Porters – it struck me that I hadn't enjoyed anything so much since my wife died. It's been four years now, but I still miss her sorely. You see, I'm being quite honest with you. But when we had that nice little talk over lunch I found I'd quite forgotten Helen. You were so sweet and lovely, and so intelligent. I was bowled over. And I haven't been able to get you out of my mind since. At my time of life to fall in love again is something of a shock.' He made an attempt to laugh, which wasn't convincing. 'I could give you financial security and try to be something of a father to your children. I'd like that very much. Naturally I wouldn't expect anything... in the bedroom line... until you'd grown to care for me.'

The feelings of resentment with which I had begun this journey had quite evaporated now and I listened to this awkward but affecting speech with such a weight of dismay on my heart that I felt close to tears. 'I'm very sorry, Humphrey. It's quite impossible – oh, but very kind of you. I don't think I could consider marrying anyone at the moment. I haven't come to terms with Jack's death, you see. And anyway...'

'Of course, I quite understand that. I hope you don't think me insensitive for rushing my fences. The thing is, I'm scared some other fellow will cut me out.' He laughed again, mirthlessly. 'I wanted to show you how serious I am. I really do love you.'

He took my hand. His felt very thin and trembly.

'Thank you, Humphrey. But if I do marry again it won't be for protection. I do appreciate all that you offer me.'

'You don't think you could come to love me? Perhaps I could ask you again in a few months' time?'

'It wouldn't be any good. I'm so sorry.'

I knew I was hurting him, and I felt distressed and ridiculously guilty. He patted my hand and then let it go. There was a long silence. I recognised the outskirts of Westray village through the gloom.

'I hope I haven't embarrassed you,' said Humphrey, at length. 'Old people become very selfish. I'm afraid I was carried away... One doesn't expect to feel...' His voice trailed away.

'Not a bit,' I said, with assumed heartiness.

'Here we are, then,' he said, as we turned in at the bottom of the drive.

'Won't you come in and have a drink?'

'I don't think so, my dear. Another day, perhaps. We must see if we can't get you on to one of our committees in some capacity. Now, you must be tired after your ordeal at the inquest. Run along in and don't worry about me.'

'Goodbye. Thank you for the lift.'

In the light that came on as the driver opened the door for me, I saw that Humphrey's face was crumpled with emotion. I suppose it was sorrow.

'Let's have that dinner some time soon,' I said, as an afterthought, bending down to look at him. I knew the moment I said it that it was silly of me. Neither of us had a hope of enjoying such an occasion after what had passed. He gave me a little smile and shook his head.

The first evening star shone with bright indifference above Humphrey's car as it went away down the drive. How Jack would have laughed at this proposal from a lonely widower with dyed hair, old enough to be my father. I saw Jack's face again, arrogant and contemptuous, as he banished those poor wretches who were unfortunate enough to love him. In this, at least, we could not have been more unlike. I began to shiver. The beauty and antiquity of the house closed around me with a reassurance of stability and promise of sanctuary for which I had never been more grateful.

'You look rather sad,' said Maurice, the next morning over breakfast.

'I was thinking about poor old Humphrey.'

'I've got some news here that will cheer you up.' He handed me a letter.

'Oh, gosh, I am cheered! He'll be in in a minute. How marvellous!'

'What's marvellous?' Ivor came in, stamping his feet and blowing on his hands. There was a particularly raw wind blowing from the east. I handed him the letter.

'What? I don't get it. Who is this man?'

'A friend of mine,' Maurice explained. 'Miranda showed me some of your poems and I thought they were good. This man's a literary agent, and the long and short of it is that he's found a publisher for them.'

'Think of it, Ivor,' I said, coaxingly, as he stood with folded brow, not looking at all pleased. 'You'll be in print and all sorts of people will be able to read your work.'

'I am aware of the consequences of publishing, Miranda.' Ivor's voice was chilly. 'Those poems were private... They were love letters to you. They are not for public consumption.' He stuffed the letter into his pocket and marched out.

'Oh, damn, oh, blast! I *am* disappointed.'

'Me, too,' admitted Maurice. 'He's perfectly entitled to feel like that, of course. I should have asked him first. It's just that I can never resist the chance to surprise people. It makes me feel like a magician. A frustrated power complex, probably. Well, it's a great pity but we must put it out of our minds. I'll go and help Elizabeth with the shell grotto. It's too cold for the beach today. The wind's roaring like a bull of Bashan.'

An hour later Ivor found me mending a pillow-case by the library fire. I looked at him nervously when he came in.

'I'm a complete lunatic,' he said, bending down and taking hold of the hand that held the needle. 'Of course I want my poems to be published! It was just that, for a moment, I was terrified of the idea of any kind of success. I've lived so long with the idea of myself as a failure that I couldn't bear to let go of it... like a foul-smelling, ragged garment that has sheltered one through many a storm and which has moulded itself to one's form. I felt insecure at the idea of exposing myself to the world without it.' He kissed my hand and pricked himself painfully on the lip. 'Never mind.' He dabbed at the blood with an earthy handkerchief. 'I don't mind about anything now. I feel regenerated. "O brave new world!"'

'Good. I should find Maurice and tell him. He was rather upset and it's he who's done it all.'

'I already have.' Ivor's habitually solemn expression was alight with the prospect before him of recognition, perhaps even fame. 'How much I owe him! You'll think differently about me now, Miranda, won't you?'

'Well, yes,' I said, cautious after yesterday's experience. 'But essentially you haven't changed as far as I'm concerned. I've always thought your poems were good.'

'A poet! Good God, the man's a crazy genius,' exclaimed Maeve, when I told her over tea about Ivor's literary *coup*. 'You'll soon be able to set up an artist's commune at this rate, with Maurice's painting, Ivor's poetry and Janòs's playing.'

'Now, now. You know that's finished.'

'Yep. I just feel a bit guilty, that's all.'

'How's Sebastian getting on?'

Much to everyone's surprise, he had been sentenced to six months in an approved school.

'He doesn't write very often, except to ask for things. What do you think he asked for last time?'

'A rope ladder? A sheath knife? Poker dice?'

'He wants me to send him rose-hip syrup as he's getting mouth ulcers and thinks it's the poor diet. Oh, and some arnica as he's always being beaten up.'

'Maeve! That sounds terrible!' For the first time a glimmer of sympathy crept into my thoughts of Sebastian.

'Do him all the good in the world. You're too soft, that's your trouble. Bloody hell, what's that?'

A sudden explosion of sound had made the cups rattle.

'Only Winnie Harker going home and slamming the door behind her. Didn't you hear her thundering downstairs? I'm always reminded of the gun salute in Hyde Park for the Queen's birthday. All the windows shake in their frames. But she's a hard worker and always cleans up the broken china and smashed furniture as she goes.'

'She's got a very good-looking son, hasn't she? I nearly

ran into him in the car yesterday. He was driving the school bus. I thought he looked quite like George Chakiris in *West Side Story*. Sort of mean and moody and Latinate.'

'He's mean, all right. I must say, Maeve, I think your tastes are somewhat degraded.'

'You're just a terrible old snob. I think there's something rather exciting about untamed man.'

'Stew is well tamed by his mother. When he came here the other day to fetch her, she boxed his ears so hard for not wiping his shoes on the mat that I expected to see his head spinning across the kitchen floor.'

'Mm.' Maeve was silent for a moment, no doubt contemplating the uncouth and virile charioteer of schoolchildren. 'I saw Dr McCleod the other day. He was in his car with that attractive woman I saw him with before. They were heading out to open country with what looked like a substantial picnic basket in the back.'

'Really? A little cold for picnicking, isn't it?' I wondered why there was a slight chill in my voice.

'I hadn't thought of that. Perhaps it was just his laundry, come to think of it.'

I couldn't help laughing. 'You are an incorrigible weaver of intrigues. Why are you interested in him? I wouldn't have thought he was your type. Too dour and strait-laced. Though he looks quite different when he laughs.'

'Does he, though?' Maeve looked at me sharply. 'Well, you're right. He's not my mug of cha. Too ascetic and clean-looking. But I couldn't help being just a little fascinated when he asked me the other day – I met him coming out of Mrs Mulligan's, she's just had her fifth, you know, and let's hope it's not as plain as the other four – whether Janòs was coming over to play at the next Titchmarsh Music Festival.'

'Well, what about it? He likes music, I suppose.'

'Yes, but he followed this up swiftly by asking me if I had known Jack well before he died. I said that I could hardly have known him afterwards.'

'I expect he was just trying to think of something to say.'

'Could be. I don't think so, though. He might have said something about the weather, after all.'

'I don't think he stoops to small-talk.'

'*You* seem to know quite a lot about him. You did say how much you disliked him not long ago. I'm always interested in relationships that start off at daggers drawn. It seems to me to suggest intense involvement not far from attraction. Like falling in hate at first sight.'

'It's all this psychotherapy you've been having. You imagine things.'

'Actually, I've just been reading something by a marvellous man called Malcolm Mutt about how we all emit coloured light-waves according to our mood and how well we're integrating spiritually with the world. Green and blue are the best and any of the colours near them. Yellow and orange are worrying, red is pretty sinister and black is, of course, the worst possible. Would you like me to divine your aura?'

'Love it. Mind if I finish these Brussels sprouts first? I shouldn't like the smell of brassicas to interfere with an accurate reading.'

'Ooh, you're so cynical you'll end up a crusty old recluse with cats, if you're not careful.'

'I can think of worse fates. I happen to like cats. I even like Dinkie, and if that isn't a test I don't know what is.'

It was true. I could think of worse fates. To be married to a man addicted to adultery, for example. The minute I thought this, I realised that I was relieved that Jack was dead.

'What are you doing, you clot?' cried Maeve. 'You've cut yourself.'

'Damn!' I mopped at the crimson beads oozing from my thumb. 'Serves me bloody well right.'

CHAPTER 20

'I could murder Hilary Scranton-Jones.'

Patience spoke in a low voice so as not to wake Wacko, who was fast asleep in the only comfortable chair with his feet on the fender, effectively blocking what little heat there was from the rest of the room.

'What's she done?'

I was having lunch with the Wakeham-Tutts. It was an ordeal for all three of us – for Wacko because he hated having to put himself out in the smallest way for anyone, for Patience because she felt acutely the shortcomings of her domestic arrangements, and for me because the house was freezing cold and the food horrible, despite Patience's best efforts. It had to be gone through, however, in order that Patience could feel happy about accepting hospitality from me. I understood and respected this.

'She's decided to appoint an official treasurer for Westray church. Now the accounts are in order she's persuaded Harold Pandy to do them. It's because she wants to be secretary and Harold Pandy's been secretary for years. It was the only way she could get him out of the way. Now all my chances with Aubrey are gone.'

She sank her head on to one hand and pushed her food around the plate with her fork. Wacko snored very loudly suddenly, and we both turned to look at him across the gloomy room. Years ago he had sold off all the land that belonged to the huge, ugly Edwardian house, and his neighbours had planted Leyland cypresses along their boundary to block out the sight of the Wakeham-Tutts. The hedge, ten feet from the front door, was now twenty feet high and cast the entire south-facing façade and all the principal rooms into a green twilight. It was like being in an aquarium. I always had a mad impulse to make strange movements with my arms as I breasted the swimming light. The odd ray of sun that found its way through the dense branches made green blots on the tablecloth.

I looked with dismay at the very large amount there was left to eat up. Patience was a good plain cook, but had to practise economies that would have defied the skill of Brillat-Savarin. Wacko insisted that all food, apart from porridge, should contain meat so Patience bought parts of animals that Jasper would have disdained. I prodded doubtfully at something white and tubular that had turned up in the sauce.

'Do you know? I think I'm getting Henry's cold. I do hope not. He was away from school for several days and still has a cough. I hope you won't mind if I leave a little.'

'Not at all. What about a biscuit with your coffee?'

'That would be lovely.'

Patience went over to the heated trolley to spoon some instant coffee into two cups from the giant catering-size tin of chicory-laced granules. I watched Wacko as he slumbered, his chest rising and falling beneath a yellow waistcoat stained a dirty khaki by the green light. He had gobbled down his food while denouncing the Labour Party, iniquitous taxation, and youth today, risen from the table before either of us had had more than a few mouthfuls and staggered to his chair and his newspaper. A whisky glass stood empty beside him. His daily whisky represented furlongs of curtain hemming.

'Here we are.' Patience put down a plate beside me. Every single biscuit was broken and I remembered the large square box at the end of the counter in Mead's, which contained broken biscuits for a few pence a quarter. A rich tea or a bourbon tastes just the same entire or in part but I realised that, despite my sudden ejection into comparative poverty, I still took whole biscuits for granted. Patience's life must be made happier, if it could not be more prosperous, and Aubrey was the man to do it.

'Don't despair. I've finished the first part of my history of Westray. You can take it to Aubrey for me so that he can start typesetting. I'd be very grateful if you would.'

We arranged that Patience would come the next day to

pick it up. I tiptoed away, noticing as I passed the burbling Wacko that all the bits of biscuit with chocolate on were on a plate by his chair. He would be something of a hindrance to a love affair between Patience and Aubrey, but I was determined that his tyranny should be overthrown. Emerging from the drive I was dazzled by the brilliancy of the cold clear day. On an impulse I decided to visit Aubrey.

I found him in the vicarage kitchen, wrestling with an ironing board. 'How good to see you, Miranda. I shall willingly abandon this hateful business until later.'

Aubrey seemed unconscious of his naked hairless chest beneath his coat.

'Just a minute. Let me help you. What's happened to the cover?'

'I don't think it ever had one.' Aubrey was vague.

'But, Aubrey, all ironing boards do. You can't possibly iron things straight on the metal.'

Aubrey gave his gentle, self-deprecating smile. 'I'm afraid I always have. That's just how I found it in the cupboard.'

'I'll get you a cover next time I go to Mead's. For now, see if you can find a clean blanket.'

While Aubrey was searching for one I tackled the iron, the plate of which was dark brown. Steel wool made some improvement, and when he returned with an old grey Army blanket I was able to make an impression on the shirt. 'What I really wanted to see you about was my history of Westray. I've finished the first part. It's expanded to cover more than just the house. In fact, the early part couldn't be written without including a history of the village as people's lives then were so much more interdependent.'

'Excellent! I hesitated to put too much of a burden on you but that's just what I wanted.'

'Will you be ready for it tomorrow? I've arranged for Patience to drop it in, actually, as I've got visitors. She's calling on me after work.'

'I'm sorry that our accounting sessions have been so

rudely curtailed. I have to confess that I very much looked forward to Mondays.'

Aubrey blinked and looked rather self-conscious as I incautiously glanced at him. I gave the points of his shirt collar extra attention as I said, as casually as possible, 'How interesting. Patience said very much the same thing.'

'She did?' Aubrey's golden eyes, slightly protuberant, looked fearfully alert, like a rabbit's when it spots a shadow moving along a hedge. He cleared his throat several times. 'Do you think, Miranda . . .'

I waited, iron poised.

'Do you think we'll have rain later on?' he said, in a rush, and I knew that the moment for confession had passed. I had said as much as I dared. I sighed and handed him the shirt. 'The wind is getting up. It *might* rain. I must go. Expect the history tomorrow. Telephone me if there are any changes you'd like to make.'

'I would not be so temerarious. I have a thorough respect for your intellect. I look forward very much to reading it.'

When I got home I found that the fire in the kitchen was beginning to smoke. Poor Rose had been driven from her chair to the library. It only does that when the wind comes from the south-east, which is rare. I thought there was a good chance of a storm. By the time I'd finished my Wednesday letter to Henry, the wind was beginning to roar in the chimney and rain was making the fire hiss as well as smoke. Then the electricity went off, which was a wretched nuisance though I knew my visitors would love it as Westray looks marvellously romantic by candlelight. Luckily the Aga keeps on going at a low temperature without electricity. I put the duck into a braising pan, with bacon, shallots, garlic, plenty of thyme and rosemary and a pinch of nutmeg. I added equal quantities of wine and water and a glass of brandy. After long, slow cooking for three or four hours, with a little deglazing of the sauce at the end, this dish is fit for the most exacting palate, especially when served with baked potatoes and aïoli.

I was busy peeling and quartering apples for pudding when Maeve came in, her hair in spikes and a quantity of water trickling from her mackintosh.

'I thought I'd pop in see if you were all right without electricity. Actually, what a liar I am. I was hoping you'd give me some tea and talk. It's unbelievably lonely at home now Florian's away on his school trip.'

'Where's he gone?'

'Rock-climbing at an outward-bound centre in Scotland. Poor lamb! He tried so hard to get out of it. He hates heights and is terrified of ruining his hands and getting broken veins. I could only feel that I had fallen down somewhat on my duty as a mother when I saw the other boys waiting at the station in anoraks and giant boots and rucksacks. Florian took my old crocodile suitcase and was wearing my long black velvet coat with a tussore silk scarf. He looked marvellous, I must say. Oh, good, is that seed-cake? My favourite!'

'That's what you always say. I don't know how you stay so slim.'

'Because I don't bother to eat when I'm on my own. And when I'm working on my jewellery I don't notice whether I'm hungry or not.'

'I wish I didn't,' said Maurice, coming in. 'As soon as I get down to the beach I have to eat my sandwiches immediately or I can't think about anything else. I need some more candles for the library, Miranda. I'm doing a sketch of it. Rose and Jenny are playing peek-a-boo and animal noises with Bridie. It's the most charming domestic scene. Oh, that cake does look good!'

I cut several slices and put them on a plate for him to take back with him.

Maurice went to fetch candles from the candle-box and teacups from the dresser. 'Little Bridie's face is beginning to take shape. I think she's going to be rather good-looking. She's growing some golden eyebrows and there's hint of a point to the chin now. She's got her mother's long face.'

'Let's hope she doesn't resemble her father,' I said, without thinking.

'Oh, do we know who the father is?' Maeve was on to it at once.

Since her last indiscretion, which was to tell her sons about Ivor's fire-raising bent, I had determined to watch what I said to her in future. It wasn't so much that I didn't trust her but that she wasn't very good at judging what might cause difficulties for other people. 'It's just a guess. And I'm not going to say, so don't try to prise it out of me. Jenny will tell us, or not, if she wants to.'

'Leonardo da Vinci used to rule his notebook into columns headed fox, wolf, bear and monkey, and make notes about human faces by ticking them off under these headings.' Maurice paused to consider us. 'You, Maeve, I would say, have predominantly a monkey face with foxy eyes. Whereas Miranda has the forehead and eyes of a wolf and the nose and jaws of a fox.'

'Now don't try and wheedle your way into my good graces with flattery,' I retorted, putting the silver teapot on to the tray. 'See if Mr and Mrs Smythe are back yet, will you? They went off this morning to trawl the antique shops in Brighton. They must be drenched and freezing by now.'

'Now, why can't I meet a man like that?' said Maeve, as Maurice went out bearing the tray. 'Clever, talented and interesting, but also kind, considerate and affectionate. I wish he was thirty years younger. I'd snap him up like a shot.'

'I agree he's in all ways the masculine ideal. Of course, there's always got to be something else, hasn't there? Something indefinable but irresistible.'

'Screwability, you mean? Well, I think I could fancy anyone who wasn't actively unpleasant. You're more romantic than I am.'

When I thought of Maeve's previous marriages I wasn't at all surprised that she now placed good nature above good looks. I had never thought of myself as being particularly romantic.

'I must take Henry's letter to the post. Damn!' I looked at my watch. 'I suppose Ivor's already put the car away. I'll get soaked before I get down to the coach-house.'

A violent gust of rain threw itself against the windows as I spoke.

'Don't bother. I'll stick it in the letter-box on the way past.'

'Would you? That would be kind. You mustn't forget. Henry relies on getting a letter midweek.'

'There you go again! So over-protective. Still I suppose, looking at Sebastian, I'm not the world's greatest mother so I ought to keep my mouth shut.'

While I put the buttered apples on to bake, Maeve and I had a very interesting discussion about how we would bring up children if we could start all over again. It was six thirty before she left. I had to rush about like a mad thing to put more wood on all the fires and lay the table, help Elizabeth with her French prep and feed Rose, Dinkie and Jasper. Rose generally went to bed early, these days, as she said that simply sitting and breathing wore her out.

Mr and Mrs Smythe looked like otters when they returned, sleek, dark and dripping. Mrs Smythe, who was an American, asked me to call her Ella. I liked her. She was warm and funny and intelligent. Her husband was English and rather dull.

'Look, Miranda!' cried Ella. 'We had a great day, and see what we found for your laundry!' Her husband was dragging something large, about four feet in diameter behind him into the kitchen. 'It's a buck! Not a bucket, mind you. A bucket is a little buck. It's for mixing lye in and I bet you don't know what lye is.'

'Tell me.' I tried to look expectant, but Ella was too bright to be deceived.

'Oh, all right, you do know. But you haven't got a buck in your laundry room.'

'No, and I'm thrilled to have it.'

There followed the usual wrangle about paying for it, but Ella was absolutely insistent on making us a present.

'What is a lye?' asked Jenny, who was giving Bridie her last bottle of the day.

'Not *a* lye, sweetie.' Ella was dying to impart her new knowledge. 'Lye is stuff that you washed clothes with in olden days. You take the whitest wood-ash you can possibly find and dilute it with water until the water runs clean. Then you sloosh it over the clothes and *zowee!*, all the dirt falls out!'

'It's because it's an alkali,' I explained. 'Other sorts of alkali were used, including hen dung and urine. Of course, you rinsed the clothes well afterwards.'

Jenny looked at me as if I had taken leave of my senses. I was getting used to that look. I had tried quite hard since Christmas to start her on the road to some kind of education but she found it all mind-numbingly dull and the first page of *Pride and Prejudice* defeated her. I tried her on light modern fiction, but she never managed to get beyond a couple of chapters. She explained that she couldn't hold the names of the characters in her head for more than a few lines so if there was a passage of description she was immediately lost. I didn't know whether it was nature or nurture, but I understood that Jenny's talents were practical rather than intellectual. Soon we allowed the studies to slip quietly away.

We had an enjoyable evening over the duck *en daube* by candlelight, and no one made a fuss about the bedrooms being very cold. The external temperature dropped dramatically with the howling, bitter wind. I had always believed until that evening that the central heating made only a minimal difference to the warmth of the house and that I continued to have the boiler fed with oil from a sentimental reluctance to see a boiler starve, but in fact, once it was off, the house slid into the kind of permafrost described in *Doctor Zhivago*.

I awoke the next morning to find exquisite ice ferns on my bedroom windows, and my breath turned instantly into clouds. Maurice took the Smythes to see the famous art collection at Brocklebank House. By the time they came back, electricity was restored and lunch was ready. I asked Peter Smythe about the paintings, but all he could say was that Brocklebank House had been very warm. I gave Patience the first part of my history to take to Aubrey, before setting off with Maurice, Jasper and the Smythes for a brisk walk round the village to get the smoke from the fires out of our lungs.

A hired limousine came after tea to take our visitors back to London. At the last moment Ella was inclined to put off their return to town because she said she couldn't bear to leave Westray and us, but Peter was firm. I imagine he was looking forward to taking off his overcoat. I put a bacon and egg pie into the oven for a family supper in the kitchen, and found I had half an hour to do with as I wished. Rose had gone early to bed, Jenny was bathing Bridie, and Elizabeth and Maurice were shell-sorting in the library. I sank down into Rose's chair by the fire with my book. Despite its fascination, for it was a well-written account by Eileen Power of the life of Thomas Betson, a fifteenth-century wool-merchant, I must have dozed for a minute or two. I awoke to find Patience standing before me. Her right hand was tied up in a large, inky and bloody handkerchief.

'Oh, I'm sorry to wake you!' she said. 'I was just about to creep out again.'

I sat up and rubbed my eyes. 'Don't go! I didn't mean to fall asleep. What have you done to your hand?'

'It was my own silly fault. I was trying to pull a piece of paper straight that had got fed into the press at an angle. There was a lot of blood but it didn't really hurt at all. I can't feel a thing now.'

As I began to emerge properly from sleep I saw that Patience seemed to be in a state of mind where she would not have felt it if she had been hanged, eviscerated and chopped into small pieces. I waited for her to speak.

'Oh, Miranda!' Patience's beautiful eyes were solemn with awe. 'I never thought . . . I never imagined that it was possible to feel like this. Do you know, I realise now that I've never been happy before. At least, not since I was a small child and used to lie in the field with Dusty, our old pony, and eat apples. Before my mother died. But this is different. It's like those visions of paradise I used to have at school when I went through a religious phase. I've got a sort of warm, light feeling as though at any moment I might float up to the ceiling. I feel both extraordinarily calm and tremendously excited by turns.'

'While I rebandage that hand, tell me what's happened. If you want to, that is.'

'I'm longing to tell you. That's why I came. Aubrey bandaged it for me. It does seem a pity – No, that's ridiculous – it's going to fall off before I get home.'

We sat together on the sofa. I found a fresh bandage and gave her Aubrey's bloody handkerchief. She folded it reverently and clutched it in her undamaged hand.

'We were standing in the dining room and Aubrey said that he'd see me to the car before starting up the press. He looked so delighted at the idea of getting on with the printing. You know how his eyes get huge if he's pleased about something.' I hadn't noticed but, then, I was not in love with him. 'I felt really miserable. It seemed as though he wanted me out of the house so that he could get on. I asked him if I could see the press working. He started it up and went into all sorts of technical explanations. I was convinced by then that he wasn't in the least bit interested in me.'

'It's because men can only think about one thing at a time. Annoying for women, but a serious handicap for men I should have thought. Anyway, go on.'

'Well, as I said, I was standing there, my heart if not actually in my boots then at least somewhere in the region of my knees, and I saw that the paper was going in crooked. I put out my hand just as Aubrey shouted not to touch it and suddenly there was blood everywhere. Aubrey went as white as chalk, grabbed an antimacassar and started dabbing at my hand. The bleeding wouldn't stop at first and he went frantic, wanting to telephone for an ambulance. I started to laugh. The fuss was out of all proportion. Then he looked at me very seriously – I shall never in all my life forget that look – and said, "I can't laugh. This little hand is the most precious thing in the world to me." Then he started to shake all over. I could honestly hear something high and strange ringing in my ears, like a heavenly choir or something soppy. I expect it was blood pressure. We stood for ages looking at each other. I thought, How odd. This man will be my whole life from now on. Sorry to be so unutterably slushy.'

'I don't think it's slushy.' Patience's eyes were very bright and I'm sure mine were too. 'What happened then?'

'Aubrey said, "Could you consider, dearest Patience, becoming my wife?" I just said, "Yes." Then he kissed me, very gently, on the lips. I thought I might faint. Oh, Miranda, the joy of it!'

I put my arms around Patience and hugged her, with a careless disregard for her hand. 'I know you'll be happy. You're absolutely right for each other.'

Later, when Lissie rang me to say that she had had a telephone call from Patience to inform her of the marvellous event, we agreed that it must be rare nowadays for a couple to become engaged before they had even kissed each other. 'It must make it so much more exciting,' said Lissie. 'These days, people have to resort to lurid underwear and smearing each other with yoghurt to get a thrill before they've even got up to the altar.'

'Yoghurt? That doesn't seem very sexy. I think you mean chocolate or honey. Yoghurt's too healthy.'

'You know what I mean. Anyway, I think they'll be happy together. It would be terrible if it all fell apart in bed. I shouldn't think either of them has the least experience.'

'I'm certain they'll be all right. Because they'll both think more about each other's happiness than their own, that's why. And that'll work in bed as well. Just as the advice columns say in magazines.'

'That kind of unselfishness I find awe-inspiring. I'm afraid I'm not up to it.'

'Nor am I. I don't believe many people are. But it's better to know oneself.'

I got a great deal of pleasure out of Patience's happiness as, I think, did everyone who knew her. Rose roused herself over her bedtime milk and whisky to say that it was the best thing she had heard in ages, and that Aubrey was one of the few men she did not absolutely despise.

'Now, Miranda my girl, you fix yourself up as well as she's done and I can go in peace.'

'Oh, Rose, you know I hate it when you talk about going. I'm quite all right as I am, anyway. You've led an independent life and been happy. Why shouldn't I?'

'Happy? No. I've had satisfactions but that's different. I've been at the beck and call of fools too much for my own good. And you and I are not the same. I'm prickly, I know I am. I *feel* prickly. You'll always be soft with men. As for dying, it's God's will that we can lay down our burdens at the end.'

I pressed my face to her cheek. 'I don't want to let you go.'

'You see? Just as I say. A man's what you need, girl, and not a worn-out old woman. God forgive me.' But she looked pleased and held my hand until she fell quickly and lightly asleep.

The telephone lines were down the next day, due to the high winds that continued to rage. Maurice could not paint as the wind blew away his easel so he worked on his own in the shell grotto while Elizabeth was at school. I began the second half of my history, and covered almost all of the eighteenth century in one go. It was wonderfully peaceful with no guests and no telephone. I thought how lovely it must have been to live at Westray when it was a priory. I could imagine working in the garden in good weather, being madly fruitful, and in bad weather copying manuscripts in an exquisite hand.

The telephone engineers came out very early next morning and repaired the line. It began to ring immediately. I picked it up, thinking that it was probably Patience wanting to talk about Aubrey.

'Mrs Stowe! Thank goodness! I've been trying to get you on the telephone since ten thirty last night. This is John Cotteloe speaking.'

My hand tightened on the receiver. John Cotteloe was Henry's headmaster.

'I have some disturbing news, Mrs Stowe. Late lights were conducted as usual at ten last night and Henry was not in his bed. There was an unconvincing pillow arrangement beneath the sheets, which fortunately alerted Matron at once. I instituted a search of the school grounds and rang the police immediately. We tried to get hold of you but your telephone has been out of order. Your local police should be with you very soon. Of course, the business with his father last term will have something to do with this. I'm sure the school is not in any way to blame. I'm so glad I managed to get through to you to break the news myself.'

I couldn't think why this made any difference. My mind immediately defected. I heard the sound of a car coming up the drive. Henry was missing. Henry had run away from school and was somewhere alone, perhaps lost, frightened and hungry. Thirty miles of countryside lay between him and home. I let out a high squeak of terror.

'Mrs Stowe? Are you all right?' Mr Cotteloe's voice was anxious. 'I'm sorry to be the bearer of bad news.'

I wanted to tell him to get off the telephone in case Henry was trying to ring me and, at the same time, to ask him what kind of school he ran that it let small boys wander off on their own. How dare he talk about the school not being to blame?

'I see.' I tried to sound calm. 'Thank you, Mr Cotteloe. I'll let you know at once as soon as there is any news of him.'

'Do so, Mrs Stowe, and please believe that we share your anxiety . . .'

Without thinking what I was doing I put the telephone back on the rest while he was still talking. I heard the front door-bell ring. I opened it. A fat policeman stood on the doorstep. 'You'll have heard, then, Mrs Stowe.' I suppose he could tell from the expression on my face. 'We come out as soon as we could but the station lines have been down. Can you give me a description of your son?'

I let him stand on the doorstep while the wind blew through the house.

'About five feet tall. Bright red hair. Green eyes. Freckles. A broad nose...'

'That'll do to be going on with, thanks. Can you think of anywhere he might be making for, if he wasn't set on coming home?'

Not coming home? Of course he was coming home. I frowned and tried to think.

'Any family quarrels you can remember, Mrs Stowe? I'm sorry to have to ask you but sometimes teenagers take these things hard.'

'No, nothing. We hadn't quarrelled.' My voice sounded odd. My mouth was so dry that my lips were sticking together.

'All right. Not to worry, then. We'll get on to it. All the stations between here and...' he consulted his notebook '...Noddlecats have been alerted. Don't you worry. Nine times out of ten the youngster's found safe and well.'

'Nethercoat's,' I said, automatically. Nine times out of ten! What was the man saying? Were the odds really so fearfully high? A one in ten chance that Henry might have been run over, drowned, absconded with... murdered?

'Best sit down quietly, madam, and have a cup of tea. Is there someone else in the house with you?' I nodded, and Jenny came into the hall at that moment. 'I'll be off, then.' The policeman sounded relieved. 'Never fear. It'll turn out all right. Little perisher, giving us all a scare!'

'Whatever is it, Miranda?' Jenny put her hand on my arm. 'My, you look queer! Here sit down.' She pulled me over to the hall chair.

'Mum!' Elizabeth's voice from upstairs was strident. 'Have you seen my clean jersey? I'm going to miss the school bus if someone doesn't help me find it.'

'It's in the linen cupboard,' I said, but I was in such a state of fright that I couldn't raise my voice.

'Linen cupboard!' bawled Jenny. 'Landsakes, Miranda! You're giving me a turn looking like that!'

'Henry's run away from school. He's been out all night.' I turned my eyes on to Jenny's face, hoping she would tell me it wasn't true and that I had been dreaming.

'Oh, law! He hasn't gone and run away! I don't believe it!' We stared at one another, each seeking reassurance that it was not, in fact, the case. I felt very sick. I could think only of Henry's face as I had last seen it. We always had to kiss each other goodbye before we turned in at the school gates so that his friends wouldn't see. I had said something about making sure to do some work as well as acting. Had I been placing unbearable pressure on the child? Supposing he was not trying to come home? Was Westray too hard to bear without his beloved father? Had he only seemed to be getting over it when really he had been feeling worse and worse inside? Had I in some way let him down?

Elizabeth came springing down the stairs and rushed along to the kitchen to get breakfast. I continued to sit on the hall chair and think of Henry's childhood. It was true that it had taken me longer to . . . what was that ghastly phrase people were always using about breastfeeding, these days? . . . bond, that was it. Well, I hadn't been able to breastfeed him because I'd been too ill. Had Henry felt somehow that I didn't love him as much as the other two? When I thought of his face, always upturned seeking confirmation and praise, I felt ready to tear out my hair at the idea that I had failed to show him how very much I loved him. I had thought that he had Jack's temperament, needing to be the star, the centre of everything, when in reality the child had been the victim of . . . what was that other horrible expression? . . . a refrigerator mother. Oh, dear, darling, beloved Henry! I was ready to get on my knees to beg his forgiveness for whatever wrongs I might have done him, if only I got the chance. 'Dear God!' I said. 'Please let him be safe! Let him be safe!'

Elizabeth ran past me to go upstairs again. 'What are you sitting there for? I'm going to miss the sodding bus and none of you gives a damn that I'll get a house mark. I wish *I* could sit mooning around all day.' I didn't say anything. I was too frightened to speak. 'Mum?' Elizabeth's voice came querulously down the stairs. 'What on earth is Henry doing on the bridge? Isn't he supposed to be at school?'

I was at the front door in one bound. I flung it wide and flew on wings to the gatehouse. The bridge seemed a mile long. Henry stood at the other end of it, his red hair raised by the wind like a macaw's crest.

'Mum!' His voice sounded pleased. 'I think you're going to suffocate me! You're making me all wet! Don't women cry a lot! I'm glad I'm a man. What I *really* want is a bacon sandwich.'

CHAPTER 21

'I was worried when I didn't get a letter.' Henry sat by the fire with a blanket round his shoulders, eating his bacon sandwich. He was very dirty and smelt strongly of cow dung. Jenny had gone to run him a bath. 'So I tried to ring you up but there wasn't any answer. Just a sort of buzz. I thought – I don't know – perhaps there'd been a fire or . . . something. I just wanted to see that you were all right.'

'Darling, the chances of anything happening to me are terribly small. I didn't realise that you worried about me. You must try not to.' I was sitting next to him on the sofa with my arm round his shoulders.

'I like that!' Henry was indignant. 'When you're always in a leather with worry about me! You'd be upset if suddenly you didn't get a letter when I'd *promised* and the school wasn't answering the phone.'

'Lather, I think you mean. Yes, I certainly would. I see your point. But it was a mistake to run away without telling anyone where you were going.'

'You don't think old Cutlets would have let me go? Perhaps you think he'd have helped me pack my bag and driven me to the station?' Henry's tone was withering. 'He'd have given me a jaw and then told me to shut up and do my prep.'

'Anyway, I did write to you. And I posted it on Tuesday just as I always – Oh, no! There was a storm, wasn't there? What an idiot I am! I gave the letter to Maeve.'

'Well, that was as good as chucking it behind the hedge! Honestly, Mum! Anyone less able to stick an oblong bit of paper into an oblong hole than Maeve I've yet to meet!'

'You're right, and it's absolutely my fault. I know she's unreliable. Oh dear! And when I think of what might have happened to you! I am a criminally negligent parent!'

'Never mind. Don't go on about it because I'm tired. I spent the night in a barn with hundreds of cows. I got used to the smell but they fidgeted all the time and mooed a hell of a lot. Every time I got comfortable against one it would get up and walk off the minute I fell asleep. I had to get under the straw to keep warm but it was very wet by morning.'

'My darling Henry, you've had an adventure that you'll remember all your life. You'll be able to entertain your children and your grandchildren with the story. But never do it again. I was so frightened that something had happened to you. I love you so much, you know . . .' I stopped talking as Henry's eyes were closed and the grimy hand holding the crust of the sandwich was slowly relaxing. I pulled his legs up on to the sofa and covered them with the blanket. I kissed his face, despite the reek of cow. For quite a long time I sat looking at him as he slept.

'How did he find his way?' Maurice spoke in a low voice, as he bent over the sleeping child.

'He caught the bus from the village near Nethercoat's. He once did the journey from here to school on the bus with Rose, when Jack and Ivor were away and I had a migraine and couldn't drive. That's how he knew what to do. You have to change at Burnt Askam. Unluckily that happened to be the last bus. It hadn't occurred to him that buses don't run all night. Apparently he wandered about Burnt Askam for a while until he came to a farm on the outskirts of the town. He spent the night in one of the barns.'

'It must have been very frightening for him.'

'I get the impression that it was an ordeal though he's very... defiant isn't quite the right word, defensive perhaps is better.'

'You haven't been angry with him?'

'What do you think? I can hardly bear the thought of letting him out of my sight ever again. It could scarcely have been longer than half an hour between knowing that he was missing and him turning up here but I've never been so terrified in my life. You don't reckon your love for other people until they might be lost to you.'

Maurice sighed. 'I happen to know how true that is. Well, what next? Have you rung his headmaster?'

'Good God! I completely forgot! And the police. They're squandering tax-payers' money looking for him at this minute.'

'Let me do it. You look fagged with shock and worry.'

I gave him the telephone numbers. All day I dithered about, starting jobs and then moving on to begin something else before I had finished the first. I couldn't concentrate on anything and I was in a state of exhaustion. Fortunately no guests were expected for several days.

Henry woke up just before lunch and complained that his head ached and his throat was sore. I ran him a fresh bath and after that he went without protest to bed. By evening he had a temperature. He drank pints of lemonade, which was the only thing he wanted, swallowed aspirins under protest and refused to eat anything. His skin was pale and clammy and his eyes were bloodshot. I had the usual agonising debate with myself, so familiar to mothers, about calling the doctor outside surgery hours. I told myself firmly to be sensible and wait until morning.

'I'm dreadfully sorry,' I said, showing Dr McCleod to Henry's room. It was seven o'clock and already dark. Dr McCleod had answered the telephone and cut short my apologies by saying that he would be at Westray in twenty minutes and putting the telephone down. 'I expect I'm panicking because of the shock. He ran away from school last night and for a while, you see, I didn't know where he was. But I can't help feeling that he might have caught something dangerous from those cows . . .'

Dr McCleod stared at me in disbelief. 'Just a minute. Start from the beginning and speak slowly. I can't understand you when you gabble.'

He pushed his hair back from his face with his free hand and I noticed how very tired he looked.

'I'm so sorry,' I said humbly. 'I didn't mean to gabble.'

'And do stop saying you're sorry.' He smiled suddenly. His face changed dramatically when the frown-lines between his eyebrows disappeared. 'Don't encourage me to bully you. I suspect I'm all too inclined to tyranny. Now tell me where these cows come in.'

I explained about Henry's flit.

'There are zoonoses – illnesses – caught from cows, of course. Brucellosis and Q fever are the obvious ones. But they need longer to incubate. You say he started to feel ill this morning? I think we can safely rule out the bovine factor. I'll have a look at him.'

He was very thorough in his examination, though Henry complained volubly about having spatulas stuck down his throat, lights flashed in his eyes and his stomach prodded. 'You'll be all right in a day or two, Henry,' he said, at last. 'You've got a touch of flu. Any flu at school?'

'The sanatorium's full. Matron said that if any more boys got it they'd start sending them home. We all exchanged toothbrushes in our dorm last week to make sure we'd get it.'

'There you are, then. A reward for cleaning your teeth for once.'

'Yes, but I needn't have done it. I hadn't decided then to come home on my own. Blast!'

Dr McCleod raised his eyebrows at me, looking amused. We left Henry, who was still grumbling.

'Call me if you're worried. But I'm pretty confident that it's a strain of flu that's stampeding about the country at the moment. It can be quite punishing, though. Don't be surprised if he's quite unwell for several days. I wouldn't let Miss Ingrams anywhere near him.'

He paused and patted his pockets. 'I've left my thermometer... No, I think I put it in my bag.' He put it on the chest on the landing and rummaged through it. He smelt of something familiar and agreeable, something outdoors that I couldn't define. His skin was pale, his nose long and thin, with strong lines down to the corners of his mouth. He looked up. 'Found it. Must be the tenth time I've lost it today.'

This reminded me that it must be the end of a very long, hard-working day. 'I'm not allowed to say sorry or to thank you, but I could give you a drink. Please. It's frustrating not to be able to express one's gratitude. Haven't you ever felt that?'

He looked surprised. 'No, I don't think I have. I can't remember ever feeling particularly grateful. Perhaps I'm a selfish bastard who takes everything for granted.'

'No doubt that's the explanation.' I was pleased to see him smile at this. 'But it's unfortunate for your patients. You can't understand how they feel.'

'I suppose I don't like being thanked because... I think because it reminds me of how little a physician can really do. Laymen have such unbounded faith in us, and I'm only too aware that we're still groping in the dark. We prescribe and hope for the best.'

'So what about the drink?'

'All right. Thank you.'

As we walked downstairs I was thinking fast. I could take him into the drawing room, where we would be alone, or into the kitchen, where there would be Elizabeth, Jenny, Maurice and Rose. I thought he might feel happier in the kitchen but on the other hand I wouldn't get a chance to know him any better. Not that it mattered. I chose the kitchen.

I saw him relax at once in the warmth and untidiness. Maurice's painting things were at one end of the table and Elizabeth's homework at the other. Ivor had called in to say that he would be away the next day, having lunch with his publishers. He had brought his latest poem to read to Maurice. Rose was nodding in her chair but she opened her eyes to see who had come in and shot Dr McCleod a penetrating glance. 'It's you,' she said, and closed her eyes again.

'Hello, Miss Ingrams, how are you?'

Rose kept her eyes closed and pressed her lips together. Dr McCleod smiled. I introduced him to Maurice.

'That's a good strong Scots face, Dr McCleod.' Maurice shook his hand. 'Bear for the top half and wolf for the lower part.'

'Maurice is a painter, and he's currently categorising faces according to the Leonardo da Vinci method,' I explained.

'It sounds more agreeable than defining people by diseases. My name is Rory, by the way. How do you do? Hello, Jenny.'

Jenny smiled and blushed, holding Bridie in her arms. The baby was just drifting into sleep after her bottle, her mouth still pursed and making little sucking movements. I thought how well Rory suited him. Rory... wild, Highland, roaring. I drew myself up short. I seemed to have a bad case of Walter Scott. I handed him a drink.

'Thanks. I'll wash my hands first. We must be careful about carrying germs from the sick room to the baby.'

I fetched a clean towel and, conscious of the implied reproof, washed mine, too.

Elizabeth looked pleased to see him. She was looking particularly fetching in – damn it – my favourite white jersey. 'Have you been to see Henry? He's shamming, isn't he, to get out of being sent back to school?'

'No, I'm afraid not. He really is sick. Nothing too serious, but stay away from him for a couple of days.'

'Am I allowed to call you Rory, too?'

'If you'd like to.' He smiled at her and sipped his wine, one hand in his trouser pocket, looking very much at his ease.

'I'll take Henry something to drink,' I said. I already felt rather light-headed after one glass. No doubt it was the anxiety of the preceding hours.

When I came downstairs again, Maurice, Rory and Ivor were in the middle of an argument about the existence of God. It was already growing heated and I could tell that Maurice was enjoying himself. Having lived for so long in Italy, he confessed that he now found the English rather cold-blooded. 'It seems to me,' he said, 'that there are moments in everyone's life when something occurs so fortuitously, so auspiciously, that it suggests some benign influence... what is called grace. Things have happened to me that have caused me to shiver from head to toe because of their peculiar aptness and felicity. It all sounds rather woolly but –'

'It does indeed,' interrupted Rory. 'What you are talking about is merely the ability the human brain has for sorting and organising sense impressions in order to make a governable world.'

'But what of the numinous experience? What of beauty, for example, that lifts the heart to something higher than we ordinarily recognise, to an acknowledgement of goodness as opposed to utility?'

'Let's not forget that the heart is an organ that pumps blood around the body.' Rory tossed back the remains of his wine and did not seem to notice when Maurice refilled his glass.

'I stand properly corrected. What I should say is that, in all contemplation of the *au delà*, we should not be alarmed by the lack of intellectual and rational proofs because it is the very nature of belief to be expressed in intimations of passion and sensibility. I maintain that there are different kinds of truth besides what is demonstrably true because we can eat it or prod the fire with it.'

'Aha!' said Ivor, who had been listening with interest. 'And what about the moral imperative? As Kant said, it hardly matters whether God exists or not since we are morally strengthened by believing in him.'

I longed to join in with this interesting discussion but I was unable to get a word in. I went up to see if Henry wanted anything more and to turn out his light. When I returned, they had moved on to the subject of Marxism and from there to definitions of Utopia. Voices were raised by the time I got out the chicken and potatoes I had roasted for supper.

'Good God! Is that the time? I must go.' Rory looked mortified. 'No, really, thank you. I've stayed too long already. I always used to have cracking good rows with my father and I've missed it since he died. My mother used to put cotton wool in her ears. She hated it when we argued but really it was the only way we could communicate.'

'Come round again,' said Maurice. 'I like a good rip-roaring argument.'

I showed Rory to the door. The stars were out already and it was bitterly cold.

'Beautiful, isn't it?' He took several deep breaths, looking up at the scintillating sky. Then he turned to me. 'Thank you. That was fun. It's rather sad, staying with the Kentons. Watching a good mind disintegrate. She's very patient and brave but it's hard for them both.'

'As soon as Henry's better, I'll go round and see them.'

'Would you? That would be very kind. People are avoiding them ... out of embarrassment, I think. But I'm keeping you on the doorstep in the cold.' He looked away from me and back up to the stars. 'I suppose you wouldn't – Oh, that's your telephone ringing. I'll go. Goodnight.'

He was already nothing more than a black shape disappearing beneath the arch that led to the bridge before I closed the door.

It was Maeve. 'What's this I hear about Henry having

run away from school? Mrs Veal got it from her cousin who cleans at the Marshgate police station. *Do* say it isn't true!'

'Yes, he did. But he got home all right and is safe in bed. Unfortunately he's got flu but I think he would have got it anyway.' I couldn't keep a little coldness out of my voice.

'But why? I thought he was happy at school?'

'Well . . .' I hadn't had time to think what I was going to say to Maeve about the unposted letter. My first instinct that morning had been to drive straight to Maeve's cottage and tell her just what I thought of her. But now all I wanted was to go to bed. 'He was worried about me. It's all right now.'

'Miranda? What's wrong? Is he really all right? It isn't like Henry, is it, to panic?'

'He's not as confident as he appears. Look, I'm tired. It's been a long day. I'll ring you tomorrow.'

'All right. Give him my love. Goodnight, then.'

I thought that Maeve might have sensed the chill that I had tried to conceal. I was too tired to worry about it. I went into the kitchen. Maurice held up a piece of paper. 'Recognise him?' It was a sketch of Rory McCleod. It was instantly recognisable, with dark brows drawn together in a frown and a fierce look in the eyes. 'A very interesting man. Unusual type. I think I've caught a likeness.'

'It's very good. Why don't you do portraits for the pageant? It would be terrifically popular. Everyone would want to be drawn in costume.'

'Well, I was rather hoping to be offered a part. I do love acting.'

'I never thought of that. You'd be a wonderful Henry the Eighth.'

'Because of my *embonpoint*, you mean? Tactless girl. I shall begin banting tomorrow.' Maurice was writing something beneath the sketch of Rory. 'There we are. *Saeva indignatio*. It's the man's presiding spirit. You know Swift's epitaph? "*Ubi saeva indignatio ulterius cor lacerare nequit*. Where fierce indignation can no longer tear his heart." '

'He has an expression just like Marcus Curtius leaping into the ravine to save Rome. On fire with conviction. I bought a postcard of the painting when I was in Venice.'

Maurice looked up at me sharply from beneath flocculent brows. He began to carve the chicken and didn't say anything more, but I could see that he was thinking.

That night I woke several times with a violent start and each time had to get up to see for myself that Henry was all right. He slept deeply, sometimes shivering with cold and sometimes fretful with heat. But in the morning, though he complained of a pain in every part of him, I knew that he really was going to be all right and I recognised, thankfully, that I had regained my equilibrium.

I spent all day running up and downstairs tending the invalid. Ivor said he absolutely never caught colds or flu and offered to read to Henry before supper so that I could go downstairs and have a drink with Lissie. She had come specifically to look after Bridie while Jenny went to tea with her new friend, Mrs Harker. This friendship surprised me but perhaps it shouldn't have done. Despite Mrs Harker's violent ways with my cups and saucers she had a grain of rough kindness, and Jenny's situation spoke volumes to her as she had, so she told us, 'fallen for me first at sixteen'. Mrs Harker had mothered seven more since then and didn't mind adding Jenny to the throng, particularly as Jenny was quite ready to behave towards her with the same subservience that she offered all her elders.

'Ivor seems on good form, these days,' said Lissie, as we sat by the fire in the library while Bridie wriggled on her stomach on the rug in yet another beautiful and expensive romper suit that Lissie had presented her with, in the guise of a cast-off from Alice. We had already discussed every possible aspect of Henry's flight and subsequent illness. 'He was quite jovial this evening. Usually he's rather quiet with me and we can't think of anything to say.'

'Oh, haven't I told you about his poems being published? At least, they're going to be. August, I think. It's made all the difference to him. I hadn't realised before how much he smarted under a painful sense of failure. He walks about whistling snatches from *The Tales of Hoffmann* now. It's beginning to get on my nerves but it does make a change from *Don Giovanni*. He hasn't given me a single poem since he got the letter. Now all his poems are too precious to be bandied about. So much for romance.'

Lissie laughed at this. 'And Patience, too,' she went on. 'Isn't it just marvellous to hear her talk about Aubrey? No one deserves to be happy more than she does. Her life's been pretty crummy. I don't know what she's going to do about Wacko, though.'

'That's all arranged. When Patience told him she was going to marry Aubrey and live at the vicarage but that Wacko was welcome to join them there, he said at once that he'd been considering for a long time going into a residential home for retired Army officers. He hadn't wanted to leave Patience on her own or he'd have done it sooner.'

'Well! The old devil! As though her life wouldn't have been infinitely better without having to slave about after him. Pretending to be considering her!'

'I don't know,' I said slowly. 'I can see that it might have seemed to him that it was his duty to stay with Patience. He doesn't see himself as a predacious drain on mind and energy, naturally. She said he's been restored to something resembling good humour at the prospect of joining his old chums for uninterrupted reminiscence. I begin to see him in a new light.'

'Darling, you are becoming tolerant!'

'What does that mean, exactly?'

'Now, you're not to be cross with me. It's just that I've noticed a little withdrawing on your part since Jack's death that worried me. As though you'd gone off the human race. Jessica Buxton told me she'd asked you to dinner three times since Christmas and each time you've been busy. She said she feels she can't ask you again because it seems too pushy.'

'Good. She's a perfectly decent woman but I've nothing in common with her or her friends. I haven't got to bear my part as the supporting wife any more so I can do as I please about my social life. Anyway I *am* busy.'

'Don't say you're hurt! It's only that you're my very best friend and it matters to me whether you're happy or not.'

'No, I'm not hurt. I just hope it isn't true. I don't want to be a psychological case. Jack's death must change all of us in a way, mustn't it? But I'm very reluctant to be categorised by language that is nothing more than high-sounding generalisations. All that stuff Maeve goes in for shouldn't be taken too seriously. Giving something a name doesn't solve the problem.'

'Maeve told me that you seemed rather reserved with her yesterday, as it happens.'

I told Lissie about the unposted letter. 'But it was stupid of me to be angry with her. I know perfectly well that the telephone lines being down was what made Henry decide to run away. The letter was just a part of it. And I *know* Maeve is disorganised and forgetful. She didn't mean to cause trouble. I must make it up with her as soon as I have a free minute.'

But the moment never came. Two days after Henry's return I began to feel a heaviness in my limbs and a scratchiness in my throat. My head started to throb and I found I was shivering. I kept going as long as I could, but soon a feeling of horrible malaise made me long to lie down on my bed. I sent Elizabeth down to Ivor's cottage with a message asking him to come and look after Henry, if he would be so kind, and to do the cooking. Elizabeth returned to say that Ivor's temperature was, according to him, 106 degrees and he feared that he had acquired some rare and possibly fatal malady. Despite a sensation that I was being seared on heated coals this struck me as funny. I asked Elizabeth to invite Ivor up to the house so that he could be warm and looked after properly.

I fretted myself into a state of invalidish irascibility over the question of who was to look after what and whom, and every plan that I put forward seemed to have insuperable obstacles to it. I was anxious that Rose, Jenny and Bridie particularly, and Maurice as well, if possible, be barred from all sources of infection, but it was like getting the fox, the goose and the sack of corn across the river. By nightfall I had retired into a solipsistic existence as I rode a bone-rattling roller-coaster from smelting foundry to ice plant and back again at decreasing intervals.

For three days I was helpless, able to do nothing more than croak, 'Sorry to be such a nuisance,' as people, predominantly Mrs Harker and Lissie, brought me soup and tea and aspirins. Mrs Harker's tread across the room figured in my waking dreams as the man beating the gong at the beginning of J. Arthur Rank films. My pillows were lambasted until feathers whirled like snow about my pulsing head. Her style of conversation was gloomy. She had read in the *Daily Banner* that this particular strain of flu was carrying off weak and strong alike.

'You're a very bad colour, Mrs S,' she said, on the third morning, looking down at me with a pessimistic air and folding her arms like crossed hams over her capacious bosom. 'Ent seen anyone so poorly lookin' since me auntie Glad was carried off with the pewmonia.' She clucked like a clopping horse and went out, slamming the door so hard that a trickle of dust fell down from the rafters.

Inquiries about Henry and Ivor to Lissie elicited cheerful answers as to their progress. At the end of three days I was able to see for myself. I crept downstairs in dressing gown and slippers to hear from the gun room the noise of the television accompanied by chortles from Henry. He looked pale but held a packet of crisps in one hand and something that looked like a slice of pizza in the other. He waved them at me in a friendly manner as he transferred his eyes to my face for a second before gluing them back to the screen.

In the kitchen, a reassuringly domestic if disorderly scene met my eyes. Rose and Bridie slumbered together by the fire while Maurice and Jenny, their faces and arms white with flour like two circus clowns, stretched, kneaded and pummelled a piece of dough.

'Pizza and pasta. It's the only cooking I know,' explained Maurice, while Jenny kindly brought me tea and tucked a cushion behind my back. 'Jenny's bacon and eggs and rice pudding are first class, but not three times a day. Lucia taught me a few local dishes and they're coming in very useful. I'm enjoying myself no end. How are you feeling, you poor girl?'

'Much better, thank you. Temperature gone. Just a wobbly feeling in the legs and a desire to lay down my head on every available surface. It's only weakness. A few more days and I'll be fine. How's Ivor?'

'Still convinced it's rheumatic fever or consumption. Flu isn't romantic enough for poets. He's been composing his last words for days.'

'Hello, Mum!' Elizabeth came in, flinging her boots into one corner and her school bag into the other. 'Are you feeling better? Uncle Tremlow's the most amazing cook!' Unexpectedly she came over and dropped a kiss on my cheek. 'It's nice to see you up.'

'Thank you, darling,' I said, taking her cool hand for a moment in my hot, dry one. 'How are you? No signs of flu, I hope?'

'Heavens, no! I shan't get it.'

As it happened, her confidence was proved right and she didn't. But the day after my first sortie into the world, Jenny complained of a headache and a few hours later was confined to her bed, delirious with fever. I was very worried at this turn of events. Not only because Jenny seemed to be sicker than the rest of us had been – though Ivor was to contend hotly ever after that if flu was what he had had then it was a unique and particularly virulent strain – but because I felt so anxious about Bridie. Every hour I scanned her for signs of infection and, sure enough, by the evening of the same day, she was fretful and pale and her temperature was raised. I got out my old manuals of child-rearing, and Lissie and I sponged her down with cool water and read and reread the section about infantile convulsions. For a while, Bridie grizzled with misery as the thermometer crept up by degrees, but then she became inert and pale and sticky with perspiration, which was just as worrying. Lissie was almost beside herself with anxiety.

'You'll wear that baby out if you take her temperature every five minutes,' said Rose severely to Lissie. 'Let the poor wee thing sleep. Hovering'll do no good.' I had tried to banish Rose to the library and away from the source of infection, but she was obstinate. 'If I'm going to get it I'll have caught it by now. Bridie's scarcely been off my knee these last days.' The common sense of this shut me up.

Poor Jenny was the most uncomplaining person I had ever nursed. I think she would have preferred to lie in solitary neglect than have people fussing over her and waiting on her. She didn't even murmur when Mrs Harker gave her a wash that looked to me more like dermabrasion.

'I've called Dr McCleod,' Lissie announced defiantly. 'I take full responsibility. Don't be cross. I couldn't stand it a minute longer.'

'I'm not cross.' I said. 'I'm as anxious as you. I just hate calling him out at ten o'clock at night when I know that he's very overworked as it is.'

Rory did look extremely tired. He examined Bridie and listened to her chest. 'Her lungs are clear so far. You're keeping her temperature down as much as possible with sponge baths? Good. Give her this suspension of paracetamol, not more than four times a day. I don't want to give her antibiotics unless I have to. I'll call in again first thing in the morning.' Then he glanced at me. 'You don't look very well.'

'I'm just getting over it. I'm miles better than I was. Stay and have a drink.'

The library looked particularly inviting, I thought. The scent from a bowl of early narcissi mingled with the smell of woodsmoke and the dim lights made fulvous pools on the tables and desk.

'I remember this room.' Rory looked about him. 'It's a beautiful house.'

I gave him a tumbler of whisky. Lissie and I finished a bottle of wine, which had been opened before supper. Maurice, Elizabeth and Rose had already gone to bed so the house was unusually quiet. We talked quietly about the epidemic and Dr Kenton. I asked Rory about his plans to move back to Glasgow.

'I'm not much further forward. I had to turn down the offer of a post at Glasgow Infirmary. It wasn't what I wanted but it would have got me back there. The real difficulty is that I can't find anyone to take over the position of locum here, probably because of the practice being in the Kentons' house. In a short while, perhaps even a few months, he won't know where he is and Mary Kenton will be able to take him somewhere else. But at the moment he only feels secure in his own bed. It would be cruel to ask them to move.'

We discussed the problem for another five minutes, then Lissie said that she must go. She thanked Rory fulsomely for coming out, and I noticed with amusement as well as chagrin that he was very polite and said that it had been quite right to call him if she was worried. He got up when she did but made no move to follow her.

'You see,' he said, after she had gone, 'I thought about what you said and made a resolve not to snap people's heads off.'

'I'm astonished. I never expected to have any influence.' I spoke lightly.

He looked at me and then began to wander about the room, picking up books that were lying around and examining the bindings in an absent kind of way.

'I never intended that you should have any,' he said, at last. 'I'm generally on my guard with people, particularly when I –' He stopped.

'Why did you come to Kent?' I asked, to fill the pause.

'It so obviously isn't the sort of medicine you want to practise.'

'Philip Kenton wrote and asked me to. He realised that there was something wrong with him a long time before the diagnosis was made. Have you ever read Trollope's tales of Barsetshire clergy?'

I nodded.

'Well, do you remember the story of a relationship between two men who are friends at university, Dr Arabin and Mr Crawley? One rises to become a rich and successful dean and the other remains a poverty-stricken curate. Philip Kenton was like Dr Arabin. When my parents were very poor he used to give my mother secret presents of money to help us out of debt. My father was too bitter and too proud to accept kindness. I didn't tell you before that my father's life was blighted by an accusation of improper conduct. It was thrown out of court eventually, but he had to retire early. The strain wore him out. I've always felt enormously grateful to Philip. He was one of the few people who believed in my father's innocence from the start. I think he kept my father sane. I didn't feel I could refuse him.'

'I see that you couldn't.' I don't know if Rory heard me. He was still pacing up and down and I don't think he noticed when I refilled his tumbler.

He picked it up from the table, tossed the contents back and put it down again without comment. 'Ever since I was a small boy,' he went on, 'I intended to follow my father into medicine. I took my degree at Edinburgh and right to the last year never had any doubts that it was what I should do. But the minute I began to practise I found that I had one vital qualification lacking. I suppose you might call it the ability to empathise. I'm intolerant. People make me angry. I can't always keep my temper. A doctor ought to have self-control. Like a priest, he should be concerned only with the suffering of humanity.'

Rory finished his peroration by coming to stand with his back to the fire, his hands plunged deep in the pockets of his tweed coat. He was staring down into the carpet, his eyes full of brooding, his lower lip folded slightly over the upper one in an attitude of melancholy reflection. The collar of his shirt was unbuttoned and the knot of his tie had slipped down, as though he had been tugging it impatiently throughout the day.

'I don't think there's any one way for people to be, whatever vocation they choose.' I leaned back in my chair and struggled to express my thoughts. 'There are plenty of people who wouldn't be helped by a benign, uncritical "great soul". Me, for one. I can think of few things more irritating than having to parade my physical or psychological weaknesses before a saintly mahatma, dispensing impartial goodwill. I prefer to engage with someone, however abrasively. Dr Kenton was a wonderful man, but he was frequently bad-tempered, forgot things, and sometimes was plain wrong. I liked him because he gave me confidence that I could deal with whatever disasters came my way. No doubt other people liked him for wholly different reasons. You shouldn't mind your patients discovering that you're human, you know. If you don't want people to treat you as a demi-god with all the answers, you'd better stop thinking that that's just what you ought to be.'

Rory frowned dangerously, and his eyes looked very cold. 'That's the second time you've accused me of arrogance.'

I ordered my thoughts as well as I could, considering the lateness of the hour, my debilitated health and the several glasses of wine I had drunk. 'Is it? Sorry. I'm afraid I'm becoming very dull and repetitious. What was it Dostoevsky said about the second half of life being made up of the habits acquired during the first half?'

To my relief, he began to smile and then to laugh. 'You always surprise me.'

'That must mean that you have a quite mistaken view of me.'

'The truth is that a large glass of whisky on an empty stomach threw me into self-indulgent introspection. I do feel rather drunk. I'm sorry to have made a fool of myself.'

'You haven't eaten? Why didn't you say?' I walked into the kitchen, ignoring his protests and began to cut bread. 'As a doctor you should know better than anyone how bad it is to go for long periods without eating,' I said severely, as I chopped tomatoes and cucumber to go with the cold chicken left over from supper. 'Don't make such a fuss about a few old-sandwiches. Look, they're made now and you'll have to eat them so as not to hurt my feelings.'

'You have feelings? I was beginning to think you quite invulnerable.'

I smiled and got out the seed-cake. He demolished the sandwiches with speed.

'Didn't you have any lunch either?'

'I can't remember. Anyway, I forbid you to scold. You aren't my mother.'

'God forbid!'

'God forbid, indeed! That would be a hideous situation. Will you stop fetching me glasses of milk and my school satchel and sit down next to me for one minute?' He was smiling up at me, his grey eyes pleading, but there was a look in them that put me on the defensive. I suspected that he really was quite drunk.

'I'll just stick these things in the sink while you finish that last bit of cake.'

'Damn it, leave those things alone, Miranda!' He leaned forward to take my hand but before he could touch it a sinuous black paw shot from beneath the tablecloth and raked five scarlet lines down the back of Rory's hand.

'For heaven's sake, don't be such a baby,' I said as I bathed his hand in water and Dettol.

'Thank you for your sympathy. It happens to be very painful. Ouch! You've put the plaster on too tight.'

'Nonsense. It would fall off if it was any looser.'

'No doubt I'll shall get cat-scratch fever and my arm will be a balloon by morning.'

‘If it does I shall drive you to the hospital myself. Sister Tugg will be able to administer a large and painful injection.’

‘I’d like to know what’s so amusing.’

‘Perhaps one day I’ll tell you. I’m so sorry. Dinkie’s a very bad cat.’

‘Bad isn’t the adjective I’d use. Thank you for the food and the whisky. Where’s my bag?’

‘Here on the hall chair. Shh! You’ll wake the house up. Will you be all right to drive?’

‘Sorry. Clumsy of me. Bit tired. Of course I can drive! See you tomorrow. Good night, Miranda.’

‘Good night.’

CHAPTER 22

‘Are you sure you want to risk catching flu?’ I said the next morning, as I hugged the telephone to my ear, the better to hear what my mother was saying on a fitfully crackling line.

I raised my eyebrows and mouthed, ‘Hello,’ at Rory, as Lissie let him in through the front door. I noticed that his hand still bore its plaster.

‘Well, it *is* extremely inconvenient.’ Fabia’s tones were reproachful. ‘But Waldo’s exhibition in Bond Street starts tomorrow, and after catching him naked with that woman I’m certainly not letting him out of my sight.’

‘Which woman?’ I was getting confused.

‘Gilda Tallow. The singer, Miranda, don’t be obtuse. I told you all about her. I remember distinctly. She came to stay when she was singing at Verona. She insists on doing her morning singing practice stark naked. She says that it allows her to *breathe*. Well, I happened to pop into her room to see if she wanted to come into Florence with me and there she was, all cellulite, *quite* revolting, and there was Waldo standing beside her, also without a stitch on.

Their explanation was that they'd been about to try a duet but I wasn't quite convinced. What do you think? Miranda? Are you there?'

'Well...' I was having trouble suppressing laughter. 'Did you look at the music? That would have told you quite a lot.'

'Damn! It never occurred to me.' A slight pause. 'That was quick of you, Miranda. I suppose, living with Jack, you must have become adept in these matters.'

That was to pay me out for laughing.

'If you want to keep tabs on Waldo, shouldn't you be staying with him?'

'I would, but Waldo says that he's obliged to accept the invitation of this reviewer who's going to give him a terrifically good write-up. Apparently it's a very small flat. I think it all sounds very fishy. I thought I'd come over secretly and pop up to town and see what was what. I've been supporting Waldo for the last two years. I don't want to find that I've paid for his aeroplane ticket so that he can creep off and canoodle with his mistress at the Royal Berkshire. I happen to know that's where Gilda always stays in London.'

'We're still pretty infectious. There's a sick baby here. You know how you dislike babies. What about putting up in an hotel?'

'Don't you want to see your own mother? Well, after *all* the sacrifices I've made, I must say Shakespeare was spot on when he said –'

'All right,' I put in hastily. My mother was notoriously mean about paying for hotels when she could stay with someone and coax five-star service out of them for nothing. 'But don't blame me if you get a bad dose of flu.'

Fabia rang off, and I went along to the kitchen to hear what Rory had to say about Bridie. I had come down several times in the night to check her, and each time she had been flushed and hot and breathing noisily. This morning she had woken early. I could hear her crying from my bedroom, which was directly over the kitchen. I had had great difficulty in getting more than a teaspoon of water down her. The sticky solution of paracetamol had oozed out of the corner of her mouth and I had no idea how much she had swallowed. Despite having had three children of my own I felt pretty inadequate, and it had occurred to me once or twice, as I stood shivering in the dim light of dawn, that this was what Rory might feel when others depended on him to make everything all right.

Rory was bending over her, listening carefully to her chest. 'I'm not entirely happy about her lungs. If she hasn't picked up by tonight I'll consider antibiotics. Keep giving her as much fluid as she'll take.'

He stood up. He looked even more tired than usual. I took him to the front door.

'By the size of my hangover I think I must have been drunk last night.'

'Only a little.'

'I'm sorry.'

'Don't be. How's the hand?'

'Agony. Not that you care.' We both laughed, and the slight feeling of awkwardness was dispelled. 'You're looking exhausted. Did the baby get you up?'

'I went down to see her a few times.'

'I'll come back this evening to look at her. Meanwhile, be sure to leave a message at the surgery if you want me. Try to get some rest yourself.'

I peered at my face in the hall looking-glass after he had gone. Flu had made my skin very dry and my hair was lank and mousy. I felt vaguely depressed, the sort of feeling that in the old days, I'm ashamed to say, would have driven me straight to the shops. These days, there was no possibility of that. Fortunately I still felt too ill to make inroads on the chocolate digestives, which was the alternative.

'My mother's coming to stay,' I told Maurice, putting my head round the library door. He was sitting at the desk, reading. 'Let's hope she doesn't fall ill. She's perfectly exhausting when well.'

'Oh, good! I look forward to meeting her. When's she coming?'

'Tomorrow evening for three days.'

'Oh, no! How very disappointing! I'm going to London tomorrow and I'll be away for at least a week. I was just about to tell you. That *is* a blow! You'll have to treasure up bits of conversation to report.' By now I had thrown discretion and family loyalty to the winds, and Maurice and I had had a great many giggles at my mother's expense.

'It *is* a pity. I could have done with your help, actually. My flaccid sinews refuse to stiffen and I can't seem to summon up a single red blood cell.'

Maurice gave a mock scream and covered his ears. 'Please, not even a jesting mention of *Henry the Fifth*! It's wonderful that dear Henry is better but I've already heard that speech ten times this morning. I'm beginning to know just what Shakespeare meant by hard-favoured rage and a terrible aspect in the eye. It's what comes over me when Henry approaches and asks me to hear him all the way through from Act One.'

'Well, you're a darling to be so patient with him. But a cad for creeping off just when I need you. Thank goodness I cancelled my next batch of guests.'

'I'll send you supportive telegrams. You know I'm chained to the treadmill of commerce these days. How's little Bridie?'

'Not too bright. Jenny seems a bit better this morning.'

'And Ivor?'

'Just able to work his way through four slices of toast and marmalade. He says that a poem, which is possibly quite, quite brilliant, came to him in his delirium. He's sitting up in bed scribbling frantically before he forgets it. It's all very Samuel Taylor Coleridge.'

'It strikes me as amusing that, despite all your reservations, here you are surrounded by artists.'

'I think I'm getting over my early formative experiences.'

'I hope so, my dear girl. I very much hope so.'

I spent the day tending the sick and trying to stop the gradual erosion of domestic order, which always happens after a few days of my being out of action. Mrs Harker had put several of Bridie's beautiful and expensive dresses, given by Lissie, into a boil wash with Henry's black woollen school socks. I regretfully threw them all away and ordered more socks to be sent from the outfitters.

I cleared out the larder and the fridge, and took a bag full of pasta and stale bread to the hens. They seemed delighted and ran about squawking with strands trailing from their beaks, their speckled feathers fluffed against the sharp March wind. I changed their water, collected the eggs and rushed indoors again, feeling perished to the bone and in need of a week's sleep. Instead I made some gingerbread, and prepared a large pan of soup for the invalids. Rose sat in the kitchen with me, and tried to give Bridie little sips of water from a teaspoon. It was very hard for her to hold the spoon and rather a lot went over the baby's chin and down her neck.

I was just changing Bridie's damp nightdress for a dry one when I looked up to see Maeve standing in the kitchen. I had entirely forgotten about telephoning her, and when I saw the expression on her face I was very sorry indeed about this omission. She held a large basket in one hand and a crumpled envelope, addressed in my writing, in the other.

'I found this in my mac pocket yesterday. I was frightened to ring you up. I thought it would be better to come and face you. I'm so very, very sorry.' Her voice grew unsteady. 'That was why Henry ran away, wasn't it? Because he didn't get your letter. I really am useless. I can't look after my own children and now I've done injury to yours.'

'Hold on,' I said. 'It wasn't only the letter. The telephone wasn't working when he tried to ring.'

'But I should have been more responsible. Naturally, after Jack dying, Henry's bound to worry that you might suddenly disappear too. It was appallingly thoughtless and careless of me.'

I went up and put my arm round her. 'Honestly,

Maeve, it was just an unfortunate combination of things. Don't be so hard on yourself. I know quite well you would never do anything to hurt my children.'

Maeve's eyes were filled with tears. 'I hope you believe that. I wouldn't ever!'

'Of course not! Now, do come and have some tea and forget about it. Really, I'm not in the least angry.'

'I've brought you something to make up. It's in this basket.' Maeve's *gamin* face looked hopeful.

'How kind of you. I'm really not cross but it was dear of you to think of it.'

'Open it.'

I put the basket, which was very heavy, on the table and opened the lid. Two brilliant carnelian eyes stared up at me. I probably gasped. I was certainly surprised. With tremendous grace a large cat with long grey fur leaped from the basket and stood waving its tail and looking around.

'Isn't she beautiful?' Maeve spoke anxiously. 'She's a Blue Smoke Persian, you know. Terribly valuable. Her name's Sukie.'

I could think of nothing to say for a moment, as Sukie gave me an appraising stare and then resumed her examination of the unfamiliar room in which she found herself. 'Darling Maeve, she's wonderful! But wasn't she awfully expensive? I can't allow you to –'

'Oh, no. I got her for almost nothing from a friend of mine who breeds them. Sukie doesn't like being shown and won't allow the toms to go near her so my friend wanted a good home.'

'Well . . .' I was still at a loss for words as I watched Sukie twitch her flat little nose and then jump to the floor and glide like an elastic-hipped starlet in the direction of Dinkie's dish. 'It's utterly charming of you to think of it, Maeve, and she's perfectly beautiful but I'm rather worried about –'

I broke off as the cat-door banged behind a fast-moving Dinkie intent on sustenance. When his incredulous gaze fell on Sukie, he juddered to a standstill and his green eyes started in their sockets. Every hair on his body grew as erect as his tail, his claws became scythes and his face was contorted into a hideous growl. Sukie began calmly to eat Dinkie's chicken. Dinkie gave a howl of fury and advanced to within striking distance. Sukie immediately shot out a paw and smacked him sharply on the nose. Dinkie retreated.

'My friend said it would be all right. Sukie's very dominant, apparently.'

Sukie continued to nibble the chicken with tranquil enjoyment. Dinkie sat down to watch, as though spell-bound.

'Well, I'm astonished. I'm dumbfounded!'

'You do love her, don't you? I know how much you like cats. I thought you'd like to have one you could stroke and who'd sit on your knee.'

Maeve's face wore the same excited hope the children's do when giving me a present. I suppressed all my misgivings about having yet another being in my life whose creature comforts had to be considered and provided for, and looked as pleased as I possibly could. 'It's a most thoughtful and generous present. Thank you!' I kissed her warmly.

After I had made tea for Maeve and Rose and we were sitting by the fire drinking it, Sukie came over and looked at each of us coolly. Then she leaped up on to the sofa, strolled on to my knee and began to knead my skirt. Maeve was thrilled. Sukie gave me a casual glance, brimful of Confucian sagacity, and began to purr.

By six o'clock Bridie was sleeping more comfortably and I thought she was less feverish. As soon as Maeve went home, I started on my hospital rounds, accompanied by Sukie, who seemed to consider me her equerry, guiding her through the evening's duties. Jenny was able to sit up and drink nearly an entire bowl of soup. Sukie jumped on her bed and condescended to have her fur stroked. Ivor was enchanted by Sukie and insisted on feeding her some of his scrambled egg, which made a mess on the blankets. He managed two bowls of soup, the aforementioned eggs, two slices of toast and a piece of gingerbread, and declared his poem finished. 'It's quite the best thing I've done. I shall send it at once to my agent for inclusion in the collection. I think I'll get up tomorrow. I'm beginning to feel almost my old self.'

'I'm so glad,' I said, gathering all his plates and cups on to a tray and staggering over to the door with it while Sukie wound round my legs.

'You've been an angel. There's never been another woman for me and there never will be. "Admir'd Miranda, so perfect and so peerless".'

'Thank you. Do be careful with that tea. We haven't any clean sheets until the laundry comes back tomorrow.' I made my escape as quickly as I could, for once Ivor starts quoting Shakespeare he can go on for ever and the tray was heavy.

'I think she is a little better,' said Lissie, lifting Bridie tenderly into her arms.

Lissie had been to London to take Alice to the orthodontist and was looking very elegant. I caught sight of myself in the looking-glass. I had a splodge of soup on my sleeve, my hair hung in greasy hanks and my nose was red from much blowing. I asked Lissie to watch the potatoes, which were boiling for supper, and listen for the door-bell and Rory. I washed and dried my hair, changed into a black wool dress and made up my face. I looked so much better that when I returned to the kitchen everyone commented on my appearance.

'Are you going out, Mum?' asked Elizabeth. She had Sukie on her knee and was plaiting her fur into tiny braids. Sukie seemed quite happy to lend herself to this. She balked at nothing, even having her fur licked the wrong way by a dribbling Jasper, who was reduced to an excited jelly at finding a cat who did not try to hook out his eyes.

'No. I just thought I ought to make a bit of an effort.'

'That's more than a bit,' said Henry. 'It's a transportation.'

'Goodness! I must have looked terrible before.'

‘You looked what you were,’ Rose said firmly. ‘A sick woman with too much on her hands.’

‘Well, I’m going to do the supper,’ said Maurice, ‘so that you can sit and look beautiful. I’m sorry so much pulchritude is to be wasted on such a limited audience. Aha! Here is the Young Lochinvar. What a happy chance!’

Rory looked at Bridie carefully and pronounced her definitely improved.

‘You’ve got to have a drink and celebrate with us,’ said Maurice, who had tied an apron over his elegant olive-coloured waistcoat.

‘No, thanks, really. It’s good of you, but I ought to get back and see if there are any more calls.’

Everyone but me pressed him so hard to stay that, in the end, he gave way and went to give our number to Mrs Kenton, who was in charge of emergency calls. After he had had a glass or two of wine, he accepted an invitation to stay to supper. Elizabeth and Henry laid the kitchen table while I put Rose to bed. During supper I was content to sit back and let the others do the talking. I was at that point of tiredness when it was torture just to keep my eyes open. But though quite often I lost the thread of the conversation as my mind wandered, I did notice that when Elizabeth thought Rory wasn’t looking she stared at him with peculiar intensity. When he spoke to her she looked very self-conscious, almost embarrassed. Her manner was quite different from the flaunting challenge she had thrown at Janòs but I suspected that she was strongly attracted.

I watched Rory as he argued with Maurice about the merits and demerits of Fabianism. He often ran his hands impatiently through his hair and it always flopped forward at once. It was dark brown, slightly wavy and very thick. He was just the sort of young man I would have chosen for Elizabeth if only he had been twenty years younger. Intelligent, hard-working, good-looking... all those obvious things but also something more than that. He was... what was the word? Not vulnerable

– that would have made him seem weak, which he wasn't – more like undefended.

Most men I had had anything to do with were impregnable by virtue of their maleness . . . a sort of fellowship, the rules of which they had learned from their fathers, from school, from their friends, from books, from acculturation. In two important areas they were vulnerable: they might fail at work, they might be rejected by women – but the failures could be explained in male terms. The jobs were too commercial, too competitive, too mundane. The women were too greedy, too dull, too sexy, too frigid.

Jack had been cryptic and indecipherable. Whatever his real feelings might have been he cloaked them in dash and an air of invincibility. Nothing mattered more than that he should seem to be in command of himself. Janòs, though trading in romantic sensibility, still operated essentially in the arena of display and control. I felt that Maurice had deliberately thrown off this masculine conspiracy to embrace something he felt to be more worthwhile. He allowed himself to be assailable. Ivor was so conspicuous an apostate that he had suffered cruelly from a tender age. Rory, though superficially a member of the cabal, had been prohibited by the very core of his temperament from truly belonging.

'You're falling asleep, darling,' said Lissie, patting my arm.

'No, yes, I was thinking.'

'What about?'

'Too complicated to say. Already I can't remember. I *am* tired. I'll go to bed. Sorry to leave the washing-up. I've fed Jasper and the cats.'

'I must go home too.' Rory stood up politely when I did. 'I hope Dinkie's been generously fed. He's been eyeing me in a way I don't care for – as though I might be a delicious savoury.'

'His nose is very much out of joint.' I pointed to Sukie's recumbent shape on Rose's chair. 'Only time will tell what it does to his temper.'

Rory was adamant about leaving, though everyone tried to persuade him to stay. We stood alone in the hall. I was yawning so hard that my eyes watered.

'You *are* absolutely worn out. I'm not surprised. You have so much responsibility.'

'How strange. I was thinking just the same about you earlier today.'

He was silent for a moment. 'Perhaps we are the kind of people who find reassurance in a weight of responsibility. Or we are temperamentally incapable of arranging things to suit ourselves. That would be more flattering. Goodnight. Thank you. Call me if you think anything's wrong with the baby. I expect she'll be all right now.'

'Goodbye.'

I put out my hand and he took it and held it.

'Bridie's fast asleep,' said Lissie, pulling on her coat as she came into the hall. 'She's a much better colour. I'm so thankful she's turned the corner. Goodnight, darling.'

She kissed my cheek, and she and Rory went off together into the night.

Lissie rang me at nine o'clock the next morning and told me in a voice of despair that she had woken feeling quite terrible and, though she felt completely rat-like deserting me in my hour of need, she was certain that she was coming down with flu. I reassured her that I was very much better after a night's rest and could manage perfectly well. I promised to telephone her later to see how she was.

After I had put down the receiver I sat on the hall chair in a cloud of post-flu gloom. James was coming home for the weekend, which was lovely but it meant three children, two sick adults (Ivor had come down for breakfast but gone back to bed afterwards saying that his legs were weaker than vermicelli), Rose, my mother and Bridie to look after. Mrs Harker never came at weekends. James was always willing to help, but his domestic skills were limited. Besides, I knew he would want to work. While I was wondering in a depressed way how I was going to manage without Maurice, who had already left for London on the early train, the telephone rang. It was Beatrice.

'You dear thing!' I said, embracing her in person at six o'clock that evening. 'I hope Roger didn't mind?'

'He seemed disconcertingly eager for me to come.' I didn't like the sound of this. Beatrice was, if anything, plumper than ever, and her appearance was not helped by the strange garment she was wearing, a sort of hand-knitted coat trimmed with bobbles like those fluffy balls you make for babies if you really have absolutely nothing better to do. 'Oh, don't worry,' she went on, evidently seeing my dismay. 'He's much too idle to have an affair. He was pleased about me going because he won't have to get out of bed until eleven o'clock, that's all. Oh, what a heavenly pussycat!'

By the time a mute and grim-faced Freddy deposited my mother at the door, we had everything beautifully under control. Beatrice had taken over the cooking. She explained that she was hopeless at housework and even worse at tending the sick. The only thing she was good at was cooking so, for the few days she was at Westray, she would make herself entirely responsible for the grub – only she couldn't cook meat. Having been a vegetarian for so long, she had forgotten how. I put the chicken and sirloin of beef into the deep freeze and looked forward to sampling the various unusual-looking substances that were gurgling and plopping away in pots and roasting pans.

'One forgets about the *arctic* winds you have in this part of the world,' said Fabia, as I kissed her cheek. 'Be careful!' she added sharply to Freddy, who was carrying her suitcases into the house. 'I suppose these people cannot distinguish leather from plastic.' She addressed this aside to me in her loudest tones. 'Give him something, Miranda. I must do my best to get the blood flowing in my hands once more. Is there a fire in the drawing room?'

I explained that we were using the library at the moment as it was smaller and cosier.

'Cosier?' Fabia's mouth broadened into an expression

of disgust. 'I have never wanted to be "cosy" in my life. Marrying into the lower-middle classes has coarsened you, I think. I suppose you will be wearing slippers and watching television next.'

'Beatrice is in the kitchen. She has come to help me. Isn't it kind of her?'

'Beatrice is a born drudge. I shall go and see her.'

Supper was a trying occasion in many ways. Fabia found fault with everything, starting with the children, who were reeking of cheap scent (Elizabeth) and talking with their mouths full (Henry). Beatrice had made a gratin of vegetables, which tasted delicious though the inclusion of so many mushrooms had coloured the whole dish an extraordinarily unappetising colour of battleship grey.

'This tastes really nice, Aunt Beatrice,' said Henry. 'It looks exactly like the stuff we dredge up from the bottom of the moat but luckily it smells quite different.'

'"Nice" is not a word educated people use, Henry.' Fabia was poking about on her plate with a fork. 'Are you quite certain there are no mushrooms in this, Beatrice? Please try to remember that one *single* mushroom is enough to keep me in bed for a week.'

Luckily as my mother had never in her life done anything so useful as boiling an egg she was quite unable to distinguish the ingredients of anything she ate. I was banking on her allergy to mushrooms being a figment of her imagination. I did not want anyone else confined to bed, and certainly not my mother.

'That is a singularly ill-favoured child,' said Fabia, looking severely at Bridie, who was sitting propped up by cushions in her cot and playing with something rubbery and squeaky that Lissie had brought her.

Bridie, who, with the resilience common to all little children, had recovered much quicker than the rest of us, laughed and held out her arms to me as I went past with the empty plates. I had to stop and kiss her.

'I think she's going to be very pretty.'

'The working classes *always* put too many clothes on

their children.' My mother had never held a feeding bottle or changed a nappy, yet felt herself to be something of an authority on babies. 'That child needs to be out in the fresh air. Why is it wearing a cap indoors?'

'Really, Fabia, it's completely dark outside! And bitterly cold. Jenny likes her to keep her bonnet on because she's susceptible to ear infections.'

'Exactly! Working-class babies are always puny, delicate things. If you'll take *my* advice you'll put the pram out first thing in the morning and feed it charcoal biscuits.'

I was pleased to see Elizabeth stoop over the cot when she thought no one was observing her and give Bridie a pat on the cheek, murmuring, 'You're a little darling, that's what. Don't listen to a word she says.'

Rory came in unexpectedly as Beatrice and I were washing up. I was pleased to see him but I was aware that I hadn't combed my hair since seven o'clock that morning. I introduced him to Fabia and Beatrice. Beatrice shook his hand but my mother merely bowed her head stiffly and walked off to the library. After Rory had confirmed that Bridie was definitely on the mend, I asked him to join us for coffee and drinks.

'Oh, *please* do,' said Beatrice, with all the unconscious charm that made me love her. 'I know my mother's going to lecture me and she won't be able to if you're there.'

'What's she going to lecture you about?' asked Rory, smiling.

'She'll begin by telling me I'm too fat. Then she'll ask me about my husband's work and she'll tell me how much artists need their wives' support. She adores artists, you see, and thinks that it's the duty of the artistically unproductive to arrange exhibitions, chat up reviewers, and generally whip up a creative froth. She thinks I ought to make sure that Roger – that's my husband and he makes pots – has absolute peace and quiet to work in and no worries about taps needing new washers or the bank threatening to call in the overdraft. The trouble is that even if I did all this Roger would only be able to exhibit about five rather small egg-cups. He's lost all enthusiasm. If only he'd get a proper job!'

'I thought your mother looked at me rather coolly when we were introduced, but if you think it will help I'll come for a short while.' He glanced at me and smiled.

'If I were *you*, Beatrice, I should leave those chocolates alone.' Fabia looked sternly at Beatrice as she put down the tray on the table in the library. 'What is Roger working on these days? I can introduce him to Dame Loïs Brie, if it would be of any help. You know, she has acquired an international reputation now. She might be able to give him a few tips. I'm *sure* it would be inspiring.'

While Beatrice stumbled her way through some kind of elaborate exordium, leading up to saying that Roger was thinking of giving up potting altogether, I saw that Rory was aware that my mother was deliberately ignoring him and that he was amused by it. Beatrice constantly tried to bring him into the conversation and Fabia swiftly cut him out of it. Elizabeth sat eating all the chocolates, and looking at him with a dreamy expression on her face.

'You mustn't encourage these people,' said Fabia, after Rory had gone.

'What people?' asked Elizabeth, coming in and overhearing this remark. She had insisted on showing Rory to the door herself because, she said kindly, I looked so tired. I was beginning to resent this continual harping by everyone on my diminished looks. But, of course, I let her go with him and I prayed that he would be kinder than Janòs to adolescent crushes.

'Country neighbours. They're all very well in their way but once you let the barriers down you can never put them up again. They never know when to go home. I am surprised at you, Miranda, asking the village doctor into the library just as though he were a friend. I hope you're not becoming a Bolshevik? There's a distinct timbre to his voice, I noticed. I don't suppose his family is anything. He has an insolent, presuming manner. I should discourage him.'

'I think he's one of the nicest people I know.' Elizabeth's voice trembled slightly. 'He isn't insolent or presuming. What horrible words to use about anyone! Actually he's very kind and much cleverer than anyone I've ever met. I don't happen to know his family but I'd bet anything they're a lot nicer than ours. And his voice is lovely. Of course it's a bit Scotch because he was born in Scotland –'

'That's it, exactly. The upper classes don't have accents –'

'I don't want to listen! You don't know him and it's stupid to pretend you do!'

'I've heard enough, I think.' Fabia picked up her book. 'If this is typical of your children's behaviour, Miranda, I can only say that you are failing in your duties as a parent.'

I saw Elizabeth's face go bright red, and I got up and took her out of the room before she could say anything more.

'All right. I know. She's a silly old snob. But she doesn't know any better. Rory didn't mind, honestly. I could see he thought it was funny.'

Elizabeth's eyes were full of tears. 'You really think he didn't mind? I *hate* it when grown-ups talk like that. As though anyone can help who their parents were.'

I hugged her. 'Go to bed, darling. You're quite right and Fabia's wrong. That ought to be enough for you. She's going up to London tomorrow and back to Italy on Monday. Just keep out of her way.'

Poor Fabia. It seemed that everyone was trying to avoid her. Even Sukie, generally so gracious in the bestowal of her favours, chose to ignore her. Fabia arrived back from London just before supper the next day in a mood of unusual taciturnity. She kept on her dark glasses and retained also the black turban, which had been her disguise for the entrapping of Waldo. She reminded me of an allegorical figure from a Cocteau film, perhaps Woe or Acedia. I told her that she was looking exceptionally elegant, which was true, but she made a *moue* of indifference and sat drooping over her plate of Crunchy Cabbage Medley, which was Beatrice's *pièce de résistance*. She tried a few mouthfuls, then laid down her fork and lit a cigarette.

'Honestly, Fabia,' said James, who was sitting next to her, 'I think you might wait until we've finished. Beatrice has been working for hours, chopping and shredding and whatever, and I can hardly see my plate for smoke.'

Fabia glared round at us – at least, her mouth seemed to glare. She got up and walked out of the room without another word. As soon as I had eaten as much cabbage as my jaws could munch I joined her in the library.

'Of course I was suspicious.' Fabia spoke in tones of umbrage. 'No one can say that I allowed the wool to be pulled over my eyes. But somehow I was unprepared to catch them at it.'

'What! You don't mean –'

'Oh, they weren't fornicating in the writing room or anything like that. I spent a *hideous* morning sitting behind a palm-tree in the Royal Berkshire drinking putrid coffee – they have never heard of espresso, can you imagine? – and waiting for Gilda to come down. In the end I felt I had to go as this stupid waiter kept asking if I wanted a table in the dining room for lunch. He might have realised that I was trying to conceal myself. Hotel staff these days are *hopelessly* badly trained. So I went and stood outside on the opposite pavement. Then it began to rain. It was a beastly day. Actually hail! The weather in this country has deteriorated a great deal since I went to Italy. There was a newspaper kiosk nearby so I paid the man ten pounds to remove himself and let me shelter inside.'

'Poor man! Wasn't there room for both of you?'

'No, there wasn't. Besides, he smelt strongly of beer. Ten pounds is probably more than he earns in a single day. I sometimes wonder if you are quite in sympathy with me, Miranda. It seems that *anyone*'s feelings – even those of someone you've never met – are more important than mine.'

'Sorry. Go on.'

'Well, just as I was deciding to give up the whole wretched business and go home, out of the hotel entrance came Gilda. And hanging on her arm was that rat, Waldo. She was wearing a white fur coat. You never saw *anything* so vulgar! I crouched down under the counter. I heard Waldo say something to the news vendor about being outside in such weather. He always prides himself on having the common touch. It will certainly come in useful with Gilda. Then *she* said, "Don't let's stand about, darling, I'm freezing to death." As though the *rest* of us weren't. Then he said, in that treacly voice he always uses when he wants to be particularly winning, "Oh, darling, let's rush back inside and make glorious love all over again." The *treachery*!'

'I was *very* tempted to stand up and let them see me. But I wasn't perfectly sure that I could carry it off. I might as well admit that I felt extremely wounded.' I noticed a tear slip from under her dark glasses and trickle down my mother's cheek. She lit another cigarette and continued in a voice that was slightly unsteady. 'When I think of *all* I've done for that man. He's an ungrateful *brute*. I'm not having anything more to do with men. They're selfish and greedy and besotted with sex. From now on, I shall keep them at arm's length and concentrate on improving my mind. "Art alone enduring stays to us: The Bust outlasts the throne . . . the Coin, Tiberius." How wise Longfellow was!'

'I don't think it was Longfellow who said that.'

'Well, at the moment I don't much care. You're becoming rather too keen on finding fault with everyone, Miranda.'

'Sorry. Have another drink. It's very upsetting to be let down by someone you trusted. You must feel miserable. Waldo's an idiot. You were wasting yourself on him.'

'You don't think I'm beginning to look just a tiny bit . . . old?'

'Good heavens, no! No one would ever think you were nearly . . . fifty-three.' I had paused to work out my mother's real age and then deduct ten years. I was perfectly prepared to sacrifice truth in the interests of a reasonable weekend.

'What do you think about a face-lift?'

'Oh, Fabia! Your skin is lovely. Don't mess about with it, for goodness sake! Those wonderful bones would make you a good-looking woman if you live to be a hundred. And you've kept your figure beautifully. I don't believe you've put on an ounce since you were a girl.'

'Well...' Fabia removed the spectacles and the turban and smoothed her skirt over her hips. 'Perhaps the *merest* smidgen. Not more than a few pounds. I've always been careful about what I ate. Come to think of it, I *am* a little hungry. Something to eat would cheer me up, I expect. I really can't manage these great coarse peasant dishes Beatrice is so fond of. Do you know what I'd like? A piece of white fish – any kind, I'm not in the *least* fussy – baked with a touch of really good olive oil, some peeled tomatoes, garlic and basil. Perhaps a few simple grilled vegetables to go with it?'

While I was peeling tomatoes and thawing a piece of cod I had bought for Dinkie, which was all the fish I had, the telephone rang. It was Diana Milne, who had come so providentially to my rescue on the day of Jack's funeral. I told her, with perfect truth, that I was delighted to hear her voice, but I would not be able to talk for long as I was preparing a dish of some complication for my mother who was staying.

'Heavens, *plus ça change*! I won't keep you long. Rollo's aunt has asked us to a dance near you. It's her granddaughter's twenty-first. It sounds pretty awful but Rollo says we ought to go as the invitation is something of an olive branch. She – the aunt, that is – quarrelled with Rollo's father years ago because she didn't approve of him marrying his housemaid. I suppose she's getting on a bit and is softening up. Anyway, I hoped we might make the thing more enjoyable by seeing you. I suppose you don't know the Vavasours of Titchmarsh Hall? Perhaps you've been asked?'

'Yes . . . no . . . that is, yes, I do know them slightly and no, I haven't . . . Hang on, here's today's post, which I haven't had time to look at.' A large envelope lay on the hall table, addressed to me in an unfamiliar hand. I cupped the receiver beneath my chin and tore it open. It informed me that Lady Alice Vavasour was At Home to celebrate the coming of age of Candida Vavasour. My name and Elizabeth's and James's were scrawled at the top. With the invitation was a note from Lady Alice. 'Dear Mrs Stowe,' it read, 'My husband asked me to say that he very much hopes that you will be able to join us on this occasion. A.V.'

There was something so cold in this little note that I thought it would have been better left out. I reminded myself that I must not allow myself to become tiresomely over-sensitive.

'Do come with us,' pleaded Diana. 'We won't know a soul otherwise.'

'Let me think about it. Anyway, you must come and stay here whether I go or not. Really, I insist.'

We left it that I would telephone her later in the week to let her know what I had decided.

'Absolutely not,' said James, when I showed him the invitation. 'I know just what it will be like. Filthy food, dreadful band, guests exhumed by courtesy of the fox-hunting brigade, freezing cold. No, not even to please you, Mum, will I give up a perfectly good Saturday night to endure the torments of Tophet and Gehenna.'

'Darling, you're really becoming frighteningly well educated. It isn't for another month. It won't be cold by the end of April.'

'No.'

I admired James's firmness of mind even more than his erudition. I knew that he was quite right and that the evening would be a combination of everything I most disliked. As I went to bed that night, a brief perusal of the sky, blazing with stars above the bare branches whitening with fast-falling frost, reassured me that everything I needed was here at Westray. Here was beauty in abundance. I had occupation, more than enough, and companionship that satisfied me. I decided to send a polite refusal. I was old enough now to choose to do only those things I considered beneficial, profitable or enjoyable. As I got into bed I found it was already warm. Sukie gave me a brief flash from her eyes before closing them and starting to snore.

CHAPTER 23

The car, driven by Rollo, nosed its way between the lines of grotesquely knotted, once-pollarded limes in the motor procession leading up to Titchmarsh Hall.

'I always regret having accepted an invitation at this point,' said Diana's voice, from the darkness of the back seat. 'However old I get, I shall never conquer pre-party nerves. Something to do with childhood. Those parties when I was always wearing the wrong thing ... the only child in a cotton frock and big brown sandals when all the other little girls were in pink organza and bronze kid pumps. Being tall as well – Oh, the agony of self-consciousness!'

I was surprised and touched by this confession. Diana seemed almost frighteningly self-possessed. 'You need have no fears this evening,' I said. 'You look ravishing.'

It was true. She was wearing a slim column of dark blue velvet, with sparkling diamanté straps, which plunged to a V at the back. Rollo had said, when she came downstairs in it, that she looked like the embodiment of Night. The expression on his face made me smile involuntarily. Here was a man helplessly in love with his wife. I was glad to see it.

'You all look so entrancing that I feel extremely proud.' Rollo braked as the ancient Bentley in front of us stalled and had to be restarted. 'Every man in the room is going to feel the stirring of base envy when I take you all in.'

Elizabeth was sitting next to Diana and it was largely her fault that I was embarking on an evening that, despite the company of Rollo and Diana, had the potential for real misery. Elizabeth had declared that she was certainly going to go as Johnny had threatened to commit suicide if she didn't.

'Well, darling,' I had said, 'in that case I do see that you must. But you don't need me to come with you. You can go with Diana and Rollo.'

'Oh, do come with me! I've never been to a grown-up party before. Not with dancing and everything. I shall feel much less nervous if you're there. Please?'

I was so flattered by this fervent desire for my company that I allowed myself to hesitate and the damage was done. Elizabeth fetched pen and paper and stood over me while I wrote an acceptance for us and expressions of regret for James. Then came the problem of what to wear.

'Actually I tried on your black dress the other day and I thought it looked rather good on me.' Elizabeth's tone was coaxing.

'I'm sure it does, but if you wear it what can I wear? I suppose there's my old green silk. I could send it to London to be cleaned and it will look all right.'

'Let's go and look in your wardrobe and try things on.'

Elizabeth was anxious to be helpful. I tried on several long dresses that Elizabeth said looked dated beyond belief and must go straight to Oxfam. I could only agree with her, and we bagged them up straight away. The choice was narrowed to a very tight, low-cut silver handkerchief dress and the stalwart green silk. Elizabeth favoured the former but I decided against it on the grounds that it was murder to wear, prohibiting any kind of relaxation, even sitting down, and was really suitable for someone much younger.

'That green thing's really dull,' grumbled Elizabeth. 'I want you to look marvellous.'

'I think it's still quite elegant,' I persisted, 'but I'm

worried that the mark on the front won't come out even with cleaning. I could wear a shawl and hold it over the front, I suppose.'

'Too Josephine March for words.' Elizabeth was contemptuous. 'No, if you can't do better than that you must wear the black and I'll put together something wacky like Dad's dress shirt over black tights or something.'

'I know,' exclaimed Lissie, who had come in on the end of this discussion. It was her first day out of bed and she had, she said, rushed round to see us before she died of boredom and being fussed over by George. He had been an absolute darling and was really much too good for her but she had been driven mad by his insistence on tiptoeing about the room as though her life hung by a thread. 'I bought a wonderful dress a few weeks ago and you'll look stunning in it, Miranda. It'll be shorter on you, of course, but that won't matter. Ankle-length is all the rage these days.'

'But won't you want to wear it?' I had been enormously cheered to discover that Lissie and George were also going to the Titchmarsh party. George, it turned out, knew John Vavasour quite well, having sat on several local committees with him.

'To be truthful it was too tight when I bought it but I loved it so much that I convinced myself that by buying it I'd spur myself on to lose weight. Well, it's still too tight so I'm going to wear my black taffeta. I should be so pleased if you'd wear it, really I would.'

Lissie insisted on driving straight home to get it. It was a beautiful dress and I could see at once why she had found it irresistible. It was made from stiff white cotton jacquard, very slender and straight with tiny sleeves and a scalloped neck. It was the cut and the simplicity that gave it its supreme chic. I put it on. It fitted as though it had been made for me.

'Lovely, perfectly lovely,' breathed Lissie, walking round and round looking at it. 'It's absolutely you.'

'You really wouldn't mind?'

'I'd be thrilled.'

'You're the most generous friend anyone could have.' I kissed her. 'I promise I'll be careful. In fact, I think I'll just spend the evening standing up in a corner by myself so as not to get it dirty.'

As it happened, that was just how the evening began. Johnny, looking charmingly raffish with hair flattened like a Choctaw and a dinner jacket two sizes too large for him, was waiting by the front door for Elizabeth. He whisked her away. During the party I caught glimpses of the back of her head and occasionally an arm as they danced in their own corner and ignored everyone else. She had no need of me, after all.

Diana and I took off our coats in Lady Alice's bedroom, which was simply enormous and decorated in a horrible shade of yellowish-brown, like congealed mustard. There was a stately bed, very high with a little wooden step to get into it, with a corona and counterpane of dark green satin, very slippery-looking, as though to repel all boarders. I tried to see my reflection in the looking-glass of her dressing table but it was so blotched with age that I saw only the sketchiest suggestion of a face, like an incomplete jigsaw.

By the door of the ballroom Lady Alice and her husband were receiving their guests. I introduced Diana to Lady Alice, who at once presented Diana to a woman standing nearby. She had the same high-bridged nose and cold protuberant eyes, so I guessed that she was a member of the family. This woman immediately engaged Diana in earnest, low-toned conversation in which I was not invited to take part. Lady Alice gave me a slight thinning of the lips, which was her notion of a smile, and turned to greet the next guest so I walked by myself into the ballroom. I saw Rollo on the far side, talking with a group of men, none of whom I recognised. I looked for Lissie and George in vain. I knew that, before long, Rollo would see me and come to the rescue so I stayed where I was and tried to absorb the details of the scene, in order to describe it faithfully to Maurice when I got home.

The room was a little more cheerful than on the night of Janòs's concert. The full complement of chandeliers was lit and reflected in the pier glasses between the windows. The curtains, once red, now a shade of plummy chocolate, hung in rips and festoons. Several dark full-length portraits of earlier Vavasours decorated the wall opposite the windows, and there was a massive fireplace heavily allegorical in marmoreal relief. At the opposite end from the double doors the band were getting out their instruments and tuning up. I suspected that they were musical friends of John Vavasour, all being white-haired and several having a struggle to climb on to the dais.

The atmosphere was thick with the smell of camphor drifting from fur stoles and dinner jackets. There were innumerable stern-looking dowagers, with thin, freckled chests encased in the ruched strapless bodices of pre-war ballgowns. A lot of the men teetered on shrunken shanks and held glasses in hands that trembled with age. There was an air of nostalgic gallantry in the effort to keep going and maintain the old standards which I could not but admire. I saw Wacko and Sir Humphrey Bessinger in conversation. Patience had been asked but had declined. When her father went out, she was able to spend the evening alone with Aubrey. I could see in her eyes, when she spoke of it, that this was purest bliss.

I tried not to feel self-conscious as I made my way from the door to the table where drinks were being served. The great consolation for being alone was that I no longer had the prospect of seeing Jack cutting swathes through the younger and prettier women until he had homed in on his quarry for the night. As I sipped a glass of tepid wine I amused myself by selecting the girl who would have been his final choice. I knew his taste exactly. Though I thought Diana – still standing patiently listening to the female counterpart of the Ancient Mariner – by far the most beautiful woman there, I was certain that Jack would have not have chosen her. She was too cool, too inaccessible. I quickly saw just the type that Jack admired. She was about thirty, still quite girlish and very animated, flashing her large eyes about a circle of younger men, her hair straight and blonde, her figure very good, her slender arms bright with bracelets, her dress a red splash against the muted shades of the dowagers' robes. As I watched her, amused by her coquetry, a man bearing two glasses of wine came up to her and she slipped her hand at once into the crook of his elbow and bent her charms on him, ignoring the others. It was Rory McCleod.

I had not seen him since the evening of my mother's arrival. I had been busy working in the garden and finishing the history of Westray in my spare time and had scarcely been further than the post-box. He had been, no doubt, occupied by the remnants of the flu epidemic. Though Maurice had asked me once why I did not invite him for supper, since he obviously enjoyed coming to the house, I had not done so.

As I watched Rory with his girlfriend – for I imagined that this was the girl Maeve had described seeing him with on several occasions – I thought how attractive they were together. His dark good looks complemented her blonde prettiness. She was laughing up into his face and, as the band began to play, she put her arms at once about his neck and began to sway in time to the music.

'Miranda! I'm sorry to have left you alone so long.' Rollo was at my side. 'I got stuck with a great bore of a relation, who wanted to trace our connection through an absolute forest of second cousins three times removed.'

'Miranda! You're looking perfectly gorgeous.' Humphrey had seen me and sped across the floor at a surprising rate. 'What a treat that you're here tonight!' He wrinkled his nose and snorted.

'Now, Humphrey, you old goat, stop monopolising all the best-looking women. Introduce me!'

A tall, middle-aged man with hair streaked black and silver, and an impressive manner of self-consequence, planted himself squarely before me and managed to take up the space of three men simply by the impact of his presence. His eyes had yellowing pouches beneath them, and a few broken veins proclaimed the beginning of a drinker's nose, but he carried himself like a matinée idol. He bent and kissed my outstretched hand and muttered something through white bared teeth, which sounded like 'yum-yum'. I thought Humphrey looked a little sick.

'This is Crispin Carter-Brown, our Member for East Sussex. This is Mrs Stowe.'

'Call me Crispin.' The lips that had kissed a thousand infant cheeks were taut with smiling. 'May I have this one?'

Before I could answer he had caught me in his arms and was waltzing me away into the middle of the floor.

'How come our paths have never crossed, Mrs Stowe? Of course, I don't get out this way as often as I'd like – outside my constituency. But John's a great mucker and I shall certainly see to it from now on that I spend a great deal more time in this charming neck of the woods.' He gave me a squeeze and looked excited. 'That's a very lovely dress you're wearing. My goodness, this is fun, isn't it? Hello, Quentin, old man, isn't this fun?' he called out to man slowly circling past us, clamped in the arms of a large woman with iron-grey hair in a pudding-basin cut.

'Super,' a grim-visaged Quentin returned, without the smallest enthusiasm.

'Crispin! Good to see you!' A young man steered his partner over to us with enormous strides so that the poor woman had to scurry to keep up. He grinned sycophantically at Crispin as they cantered alongside. '*Must* have words with you about that business we mentioned last week. Some important developments.'

'Not if I know it,' muttered Crispin into my ear, as we chasséd briskly away. 'Ass wants me to put him on the board of one of my companies. Sooner have my hunter on the team. Twice as many brains.' He threw back his head and laughed at this sally. I smiled politely. 'I say, this *is* fun, you know.'

I heard the last few bars of 'Smoke Gets In Your Eyes' with relief and prepared to thank him and move away, but Crispin held me tighter and bobbed on the spot until the band struck up again.

'What, I wonder, could be the name of this beautiful, mysterious stranger?'

I began, helpfully, to cast my eyes around until I realised he meant me. I was out of practice with this kind of heavy-handed courtship.

'No, don't tell me. Let me guess. You look like – let me think a moment... Olivia. Or Juliet. Something very romantic and Shakespearean.'

I felt unreasonably annoyed that he was so nearly right. He beamed down into my face, screwing up his eyes with self-satisfaction, the bags beneath them crumpling into sallow reticules. 'I'm getting there, aren't I?'

'It's Miranda,' I admitted, reluctantly.

He gave a crow of satisfaction, which made everyone in our part of the room stare at us.

'You see! Is Crispin Carter-Brown brilliant or is he not?' Emphatically not, I longed to say but lacked the courage. 'And which one of these chaps is the astonishingly fortunate *Mr* Stowe?'

I tried not to look cross but the strain of so much cheerfulness was beginning to tell. 'None of them. My husband died last year.'

Crispin's face crumpled into practised sympathy, the sort of face he habitually wore for his weekend surgery. 'That *is* rotten luck.' We managed several circuits in regretful silence.

'That's my wife over there.' He fluttered his fingers into a corner, where a disgruntled-looking woman sat in a petrol-blue dress. She lifted her hand. For a moment I was convinced she had raised two fingers in the traditional gesture of dismissal but then I realised that I must be mistaken. MPs' wives do not do that sort of thing at county balls.

'Which is Candida Vavasour?' I asked, in an effort to be less cross. 'I expected her to be in the receiving line.'

'Poor little Candida. That's her. The one with the appalling frock. Plain little thing, isn't she?'

I looked in the direction of his pointing finger. Candida appeared much younger than twenty-one. She wore her mousy hair in a pony-tail and her bony shoulders were encased in a dress of a most unbecoming shade of brown, terribly old-fashioned and much too big. She looked miserable. No one was talking to her. 'Why don't you introduce me?' I tried to steer Crispin in Candida's direction but he resisted me.

'No fear! She's got no conversation. If you want to meet a young Vavasour here's one that's much more worthwhile. Hello, Annabel.'

We had almost collided with another couple.

'Hello, Crispin. You're looking disgustingly well. Living off the backs of everyone else suits you.' Annabel turned to her partner. 'Darling, this is Crispin Carter-Brown. MP for God knows where – not this patch anyway.'

'How do you do?' said Rory.

'You're a shocking little madam.' Crispin patted Annabel's bottom fondly, and then grabbed two glasses of wine from a passing waiter. 'Drink up, sweetheart.' He gave one glass to me. 'This is Miranda Stowe. A new discovery of mine. Gorgeous, isn't she?'

'Miranda and I have already met.' Rory's face was impassive. 'How are you?'

'Very well, thank you.'

'Of course you are,' said Annabel. 'Crispin doesn't allow people he's taken a fancy to to be under the weather. It's not the Carter-Brown way. Everything's always got to be tickety-boo for Crispin, hasn't it, darling?'

I was surprised by this sharpness on Annabel's part. I had set her down as a pretty, empty-headed noodle, but it was evident that she was not. I was unaccountably irritated by this discovery.

'Is this the personable young quack I've heard so much about from your mother, Annabel?' Crispin's face was creased with merriment at this *bon mot*. I saw Rory's face darken. 'Don't mind my little joke, Dr McCleod. We

Parliamentarians have to keep our spirits up. Running the country's a serious business. Heard all about you from Annabel's mother and I like what I've heard. Put it here, sir.'

Crispin held out a large, brown hand and Rory, after a moment's hesitation, held out his own. I detected a fraction of a smile about his mouth.

'This is Rory, yes. Isn't he wonderful?' Annabel looked up at Rory, with suddenly moist eyes. She certainly was keen. It was hard to find fault with her appearance. Her face was rather hard, even brazen, but this was the sort of thing that, in my experience, men never notice. Jack would have loved her.

'When are you going to pop the question, old chap? Annabel's mother's already chosen her mother-of-the-bride outfit, you know.'

Crispin had drunk his glass of wine in one gulp and was exchanging it for another full one. I recognised the sort of man who can stay more or less steady on vast amounts of alcohol simply because they are never really sober, but I could see that he was losing his habitual caution. Rory looked annoyed and I didn't blame him.

'Now, Crispin,' Annabel pushed him firmly away, 'you go and mind your own business,' she gave me a patronising look, 'and I'll mind mine. Rory's very honourable and industrious – not at all like you – and he's going to do important work among the disadvantaged. I've got to prove to him that there's a serious side to my nature or he won't have me. Come on, darling.' She put her arms round Rory again. 'Let's not waste time talking when we could be dancing.'

'I think I'll sit this one out,' I said, as the band began to play 'As Time Goes By' and Crispin clutched me purposefully. I tore myself away.

He followed, protesting that I was a spoilsport, to where George and Lissie were standing with Rollo. I made signals of desperation with my eyebrows as I approached, and Rollo kindly took me into his arms, saying, 'You promised this one to me, Miranda.'

In a moment we were whirling about the floor. Rollo was a much better dancer than Crispin and for a while we danced in silence.

'He looks a dreadful bore, that fellow.'

'You've got it in one. Where's Diana?'

'She's talking to that poor little girl this party's ostensibly for. Of course, it's really an excuse for my aunt to pay off all her social debts.'

'How kind of Diana. I thought how sad and lonely the child looked.'

'Diana is the kindest person I've ever met.' Rollo sighed out of a full heart and, not wishing to be outdone in kindness, I invited him to expand on his wife's virtues.

I really liked Diana but, none the less, voluble praise of another woman isn't quite what one wants to hear when dancing in the arms of an attractive man, even when you know quite well he is out of bounds. But I put up with it with as much grace as I could conjure up and added some sincere praise of my own.

Supper was announced. I saw Humphrey walking towards me with the light of intent in his eye. 'Please don't leave me,' I begged Rollo. 'Can we fetch Diana and Candida and have supper together?'

'Just what I was about to suggest.'

In these circumstances we managed to have quite a reasonable time though the food was terrible, as James had predicted – stringy chicken and coleslaw and horrible new potatoes from a tin. Humphrey joined us, and because I felt safe I was able to be kind to him. Lissie sat on his other side and was utterly charming. George put himself out to amuse Candida and soon made her laugh. George's chief social accomplishment was that he could convey the impression that though you were the cleverest, nicest, prettiest woman he had ever met he would never presume to offer anything but the incense of a happily married man. We made up for the shortfall in food by drinking more than usual. I saw Rory and Annabel sitting with Crispin and his wife. Annabel was a perfect blur of animation while Rory was staring down at the remains of his chicken as though trying to divine the future from its entrails.

My heart sank rather as the band began to play again. I tried to look pleased as Humphrey led me on to the floor. He made an allusion to blighted hopes, not for the first time that evening, and I wilfully misunderstood him and spoke of his hospital work, my garden, and the fall of Saigon.

'You are a very beautiful woman, Miranda.' Humphrey's smile was lopsided with sentiment and alcohol.

'Thank you. What do you think of Harold Wilson?'

'I don't trust him. Has anyone ever told you that your hair is like spun gold?'

'I don't believe so. Thank goodness Greece has got rid of those dreadful colonels.'

'A lot of that was propaganda. Just holding you in my arms makes me feel young again.'

'Oh, good. Wasn't Watergate fascinating? Do you think England would ever do its dirty washing so publicly?'

'Our politicians are nothing like as corrupt. Your eyes are like dark pansies . . . so soft and large I could drown in them.'

And so the conversation went on, and very tiring it was, too.

'Ladies and gentlemen!' bellowed the band-leader. 'We will now have a Paul Jones!' Usually this sort of gaucherie makes me grind my teeth but for once I thought it a good idea. 'Ladies form a circle in the middle now. No cheating! Keep going till the music stops!'

Everyone started shuffling slowly round, holding hands and trying to disguise the fact that they felt like absolute idiots. I noticed that Rollo, passing me in the opposite direction wore a 'good sport' expression, which was wholly unconvincing but made me laugh. To my horror I saw Crispin approaching. He was skipping playfully and attempting a larky, boyish grin, which made him look demented. If he had been carrying a sharp knife I would have been very frightened.

'*Isn't* this fun?' he called out to me, as he approached, pulling his neighbours' arms in an effort to get in front of me.

The music stopped and I schooled my face to remain agreeable.

'This is ours, I think.' Rory put his arm round my waist and took hold of my right hand. I saw Crispin's eyes widen in indignation and then we were away, dancing towards the other side of the room.

'Frightful party, isn't it?'

'Dreadful!'

Then we both laughed.

'What are we doing here?'

'I came because Elizabeth begged me to lend her moral support. But she hasn't needed it. I could have stayed at home.'

'Annabel wanted the same thing. But, as far as I can see, she knows everyone here.'

'She's very pretty.'

'Yes.' A pause. 'How's your mother?'

'Oh, she went back to Italy a few days later. Rather miserable because she found her lover more or less in the arms of another woman. But when she telephoned last week she sounded much more cheerful. Apparently she's met a ballet dancer who's defected from Russia and needs patronage. He sounds ideal in every way, except he's a little too young. Well, thirty-five years too young, in fact. But she assures me that Sergei only finds sexual fulfilment with experienced women as he has an Oedipus complex. One has to admire such pragmatism.'

'It must have hurt her, though, finding that her lover was unfaithful.'

'Oh, yes, no doubt.'

'What about Maurice? Maeve told me he's a very good painter.'

'I didn't know you knew Maeve?'

'I've just done a report on her son's state of mental health. He seems to be having some sort of nervous breakdown in the detention centre. We're trying to get his sentence shortened.'

'Poor Sebastian! There's a certain justice, though. He was nearly responsible for driving a dear friend to absolute madness.'

'You mean Ivor. Is that all he is? A dear friend? Oh, sorry, I shouldn't have asked that. It isn't any of my business. I'd thought he seemed rather in love with you, that's all.'

'That's just the poet in him. He's a very good poet and I'm his muse. He likes to hold my hand and kiss my marble brow.'

'I bet he does.'

'To answer your other question, Maurice has been commissioned to paint a giant seascape by a man who's a film director in Hollywood. He could spend the rest of his life in luxury on what he's being paid for doing it. It's to be ten feet by six so he's going to take over the coach-house as his studio. I'm so pleased that he's going to spend the summer at Westray. Not only for my own sake. When he got back from London, though he'd only been away a few days, his hands were very shaky and he kept almost bursting into tears. Luckily he and my sister Beatrice took to each other like long-parted lovers, and spent hours talking together and discussing Life, pottery and dieting. Beatrice says he's exactly the man she wishes she'd married. I'm talking much too much, aren't I? Gabbling you'd call it.'

'Oh, don't stop. I was just thinking how brilliantly well you gabble. Now when *I*'m nervous I become terribly quiet.'

'What makes you think I'm nervous?'

'Well... I suppose because *I* am. You were too busy gabbling to notice.'

I became aware of my hand in his as we danced, of the proximity of his chin somewhere above my head and a feeling that I very much didn't want to have again, ever, in my life suddenly weakened my knees. I admonished myself sternly. I was a woman of nearly forty with three children and various other dependants. I had decided that my life was filled to overflowing and I must not allow the romantic rubbish that was peddled by people of little brain and no sensible occupation to interfere with the admirable projection of my life which I had constructed.

'What's the matter?' Rory's voice was somewhere near my ear. 'You've suddenly become stiff.'

Whatever answer I might have made was pre-empted by a call from the band-leader to form circles for another Paul Jones.

'Oh, this is intolerable!' said Rory. 'I saw someone opening the french windows over there. Will you be cold if we go outside?'

We stood on the terrace, looking down at the moonlit garden. Behind us the music drifted into the darkness as the band continued to grind out a cheerful, nondescript tune.

Rory leaned on the balustrade. I was mindful of Lissie's dress and remained upright, though I longed to lean, too, and close my eyes, the better to breathe in the delicious scent of narcissi and daphne that rose on the cool air. For a time we were silent, though I wanted to say something to break the mounting tension, which, I told myself, could do no good.

'Tell me about Annabel,' I said at last, making an effort to conjure her image on to the terrace with us.

'Annabel? I met her on the train going up to London the first weekend after starting work here. It sounds ridiculous, I suppose – I'm too old for such nonsense – but I was lonely. I thought I'd go to a concert, perhaps look up some friends. Anyway, I wanted to get away from the country. I've lived in towns all my life and I was finding the silence and softness completely unnerving. Annabel was coming back from a visit to her uncle. She said she hated the country, too. She asked me to go with her to a party that night. It was somewhere in Notting Hill. Lots of painters and musicians, a wonderful contrast to the gloom of the Kenton household and the head-colds of stockbrokers' wives. She took me back to her flat afterwards. It was a pig-sty in Fulham. I was amazed when she took me to meet her parents in Eaton Square. They were enormously welcoming. Annabel's been very wild, by her own account. Her parents are thankful to see her with someone who isn't shooting heroin and who's got a job. She's an amusing girl, very confident, very accommodating of my moods.'

'Very pretty, too.'

'You said that before.'

'It's clear that she's very much in love with you.'

'Oh, I don't know. She's someone who's always extreme in whatever she does. I suppose she's always had everything she wanted.'

'You're sounding a little envious.'

'You mean I've a chip on my shoulder?'

'Perhaps I did mean that, yes. You weren't exactly bowled over by us at Westray when you first came. I rather gathered you thought me, well . . . spoilt, worthless, dangerous, even.'

'I did think just that. I didn't realise it showed. I was a fool. On the first two counts anyway.'

He stood up straight and took a step so that he was standing very close to me. 'On the last count I was right. You are dangerous . . . very.'

'Rory, I –' I stopped as he bent his head to mine.

'There you are, Rory!' Annabel had flung open both doors and light poured on to the terrace. 'I've been looking everywhere for you. Come quickly! Uncle John's about to make an important announcement.'

The band stopped playing in response to a word from John Vavasour who clambered on to the dais. 'My dear friends!' He spread his arms wide. 'I must interrupt your revels for a moment to make an announcement. My very dear niece – Where are you, Annabel? – Ah, there you are – has just told me that she is engaged to be married to Dr Rory McCleod. I'm sure you will all want to join me in wishing them a long life together and every happiness.'

Everybody turned to the french windows where the

three of us stood. There was much clapping and a few cheers from the drunker men.

'Dance with me, Rory,' pleaded Annabel, looking up at him. 'You don't mind, darling, do you? I decided you needed a lesson in making up your mind.' She laughed boldly, but I detected anxiety in her voice. 'Kiss me, darling.'

'Go on, Young Galen. Give her a smacker.' Crispin had come up, rubbing his meaty hands together. 'If you won't I will. Ha, ha!'

Rory looked at him and then at Annabel's upturned face, alight with hope. He bent his head and kissed her on the mouth.

'That's the ticket! Young love, marvellous stuff! Ah, Miranda, I wondered where you were. Let's do a circuit together. Isn't this *terrific* fun? Come on, darling.'

He took me round the waist and propelled me away. I caught a glimpse of his face, suffused with alcohol and shining with sweat before he pressed me so closely to him that my view was limited to a few inches of boiled shirt-front. His hands were roaming over my back and sliding down to my bottom. I was worried about Lissie's dress.

'I'm very tired. I wonder where my guests are?' I turned my head to try to find Rollo and Diana, accidentally giving Crispin's nose what must have been a painful knock as he attempted a discreet kiss. 'Oh, don't let's be silly,' I said, in the voice I used to quell the children.

'You're lovely when you're roused.'

'Well, actually, *you*'re rather horrible!' My temper had finally snapped.

'It will do you absolutely no good, you know.' Crispin's wife was standing beside us, her face mottled with rage and drink. She swayed slightly, and her head nodded as she tried to focus. 'The great joke is that my husband can't get it up. He's absolutely im-po-tent.' Her eyes swivelled unseeingly across the group of faces around us, as people froze in fascination and horror. 'It's like being in bed with a great pet seal, thirteen stones of weeping blubber, and it's all quite useless. Intopent!' She laughed savagely and tried again. 'Immo – you know what I mean. Can't get an –'

'Come along, my dear.' John Vavasour was leading her firmly away. 'Time to go home.'

'What a very unhappy woman,' said Diana, as Rollo turned the car on to the main road.

'Wretched,' I agreed. She was not the only one, I reflected, as I sighed in the darkness.

CHAPTER 24

I was weeding in Temenos, so aptly nicknamed the Jealousy Garden, on the afternoon following the Vavasour dance. Diana and Rollo had left for Oxford after lunch, having made arrangements to come and stay during August with their little boys. They insisted that they would be paying guests, which was incredibly kind of them as I wanted them to stay for nothing. They were marvellously easy to entertain. Diana even made friends with Rose, who pronounced her a capable and thoughtful young woman.

Ivor was mulching the places I had weeded with farmyard manure. The hellebores always needed their dead leaves stripped off at this time of year. It was a simple job, with satisfying results. The April sun made attractive shadows on the grass and warmed my back. The tips of *Galtonia candicans*, a tall, greenish-white, late-summer hyacinth, were pushing up through the soil, rich with last year's leaf mould. Sukie lay on her back and warmed her stomach. Birds sang and leaves whispered in this horticultural paradise. My mood was one of Cimmerian gloom.

'You seem a little depressed, Miranda,' said Ivor. 'Not a good party?'

'No.'

'I expect you're liverish.'

'I probably am.'

'I know what will cheer you up. I'll fetch the eclogues I'm working on and read you little bits. I think they're coming on nicely.'

'Thank you.' In my current state of mind, pastoral dialogues would be as good as anything to console me for the collective madness of the human race. The eclogues turned out, in fact, to be both good and interesting, and I did feel better after hearing them if only because my mind was diverted from the tiresome spiral it had been climbing and descending for the last twelve hours.

'What did you say those poems were called?' asked Henry, who was at home for the Easter holidays. 'Eclairs? Because they're rather mushy? All those bits about love make me feel as though I'd eaten too much treacle tart.'

'Eclogues. And there weren't any love bits in them.' Ivor ruffled Henry's hair affectionately with a manure-impregnated hand. 'At least, not the kind you mean. There was something about the love of men for each other in battle, intellectual communion . . . sodality and so forth.'

'Father Ardal says that's sinful. He gives us long jaws about how it will bring us out in pustules.'

'I think you're confusing sodality with sodomy.'

Ivor entered into a long and bewildering explanation, while I allowed my mind to drift back to that moment on the terrace with Rory. I had been under a spell cast by the scented night air and the presence of a handsome man. I had wanted him to kiss me because I had had too little to eat and too much to drink. It was fortunate that we had been interrupted.

Annabel had been very high-handed. Perhaps she had seen us walk out on to the terrace together and lost her nerve. But unquestionably she would make a suitable wife for Rory. I dug viciously at a creeping buttercup.

What absurd maggots are hatched in the brain! It was certainly nothing to me whomever he married. I decided to think no more about either of them. There was a gap in the border just there. I must find something May-flowering to fill it. More Solomon's Seal, perhaps? Annabel was rich, independent, pretty, and deeply in love with him. She was young enough to have his children. Good. I was delighted that things had worked out so satisfactorily. I snapped the top off a sow thistle and swore as a speck of dirt flew into my eye.

'What's up, Mum?' Henry was kindly offering me his handkerchief. 'Are you sad or have you hurt yourself?'

'Just a bit of grit. Thank you, darling. That's better, I think. What on earth have you been doing with this hanky?'

'I was trying to clean some of the grease off my bike chain. If you're not enjoying doing that, might you possibly think of taking me into Marshgate? Aunt Nancy sent me a pound for Easter so I can get that air pistol from Braithwaite's now.'

There was a serious (on my part) and indignant (on Henry's) exchange about what targets were suitable for air pistols, that is, nothing alive and capable of being hurt. On Henry's assuring me that he wouldn't even fire at a spider, I agreed to take him into Marshgate. Ivor said he would carry on with the weeding.

After I had removed most of the bicycle grease from my face with some of Maurice's turpentine, which stung and made my face red, we set off in the car. I was horrified to see, as we approached the crossroads at the outskirts of the village, a car coming the other way that I easily identified as Rory's. I hoped that I could wave and carry on, as though in a hurry, but Rory had already slowed to a standstill and wound down his window as I drew alongside.

'Hello, Miranda.'

'Hello.'

'Recovered from last night?'

'More or less. Have you?'

'I'm still in shock, I think. What's that strange smell?'

'It must be the turps on my face.'

'I suppose it's cheaper than Elizabeth Arden.'

'Very funny. It stings, actually.'

'You're a very mysterious woman. I was hoping we might meet. There's something I must say to you. Alone.'

'I haven't congratulated you on your engagement. I'm so delighted. Annabel is absolutely the right girl for you. I'm really pleased about it.'

'Are you?'

'Yes. Now, if you'll forgive me, I must get to Braithwaite's before they shut. Goodbye.'

I wound up the window and drove off before he could say anything else.

'Mum,' said Henry, after a few miles, 'I don't think that bike grease did your eyes any good. They look very watery.'

Braithwaite's was filled with mothers and children searching for dresses, games shorts, bathing suits and all the other things demanded by schools for the summer term. The assistants were telling them in tones of satisfaction that there had been such an unexpected run on these items that they had sold out weeks ago and wouldn't be able to reorder until Christmas. I went upstairs to soft furnishings and bought twelve yards of the cheapest black fabric they had to make monks' habits for the pageant. I was walking back through the baby-wear department, on my way to meet Henry in the restaurant, where he would be gloating over his purchase and eating his customary chocolate and banana sundae, when I saw Lissie. She was looking wistfully at a doll-sized nightdress embroidered with a rabbit.

'Hello, darling.' She kissed me and then recoiled. 'What *is* that ghastly smell?'

'Turps and bicycle grease. Sorry.'

'Never mind. What did you think about the party last night?'

'Somewhere between purgatory and hell.'

'You seemed to be dancing a lot. Didn't you have any nice partners?' Lissie looked distracted and her voice was vague. Her attention was on the nightdress. 'Isn't it pretty? Hand-embroidered, I think.'

'Charming. But much too small for Bridie. And I think

Jenny actually likes these Babygro things better. I suppose they don't need to be ironed –'

'It isn't for Bridie!' Lissie turned swimming eyes on me. 'I've been to London this morning. I went to see Mr Nash, my gynaecologist, because I was worried and – Oh, Miranda, you're the first person I've told! George doesn't even know yet! I never guessed. I didn't think after all these years it was possible.'

'Lissie!'

'Yes, it's true!' Tears were falling now. 'I'm going to have a baby!'

I cried, too, not caring that we were driving embarrassed mothers from the department and causing shop assistants to mutter behind the counter. I knew what it meant to Lissie. Despite the turps she clung to me and sobbed with happiness.

When she was calmer I led her off to the restaurant. Henry was very disapproving of our tear-stained faces and took Lissie's news with cool detachment. 'It's lucky you're pleased about it. I remember that row Mum had with Dad when he wanted her to have another baby. Mum said it would be the very last thing on earth she wanted, didn't you, Mum?'

'Oh, well, our circumstances were rather different, darling. We already had three children anyway. And how did you hear all that? I don't remember arguing about it in front of you children.'

'I happened to be passing,' said Henry, cryptically.

'Yes, well, never mind. How are you feeling now, Lissie? Now I think about it, you have that bloom about you. I ought to have noticed.'

'Of course it wouldn't occur to anyone. I missed four periods and I just thought it must be premature menopause or something. After all, I'm forty!'

'I think I'll go downstairs to the toy department,' said Henry, getting up. 'This is not the sort of conversation I enjoy.'

'Goodness!' I said, after Henry had departed. 'I'd forgotten you're a year older than I am. But so what!

Forty's nothing, these days. And, after all, Fanny Burney was forty-four when she had her *first* baby.'

'Do I know her?'

'She wrote novels and a wonderful diary in the reign of George the Third. Think of obstetrics in those days.' We both shuddered. 'What did Mr Nash say?'

'He took ages examining me, and then he told me to put my clothes back on and to come back into his office. He made a joke to his nurse that I didn't understand. I thought he was trying to make me feel better. I was sick with nerves. I was convinced it must be something quite terrible. Then, when I walked into his consulting room, he was smiling like mad and said, "Well, Mrs Partridge, it seems that congratulations are in order!" I honestly couldn't think what he meant at first but he was so twinkly and jolly that I knew it couldn't be cancer. It came into my mind very slowly what he must mean, and then I felt all the blood swooshing very fast round my body and for a minute I couldn't see or hear anything. Even now I can hardly believe it!'

'I'm so pleased about it.' I took her hand across the table. 'And what a lucky little baby it's going to be.'

'Thank you. What's specially good is that I've got through the tricky time at twelve weeks – when I had those two miscarriages, you know – without knowing anything about it. I'm twenty weeks' pregnant and Mr Nash says it's all going very nicely and there shouldn't be any problems. No wonder none of my clothes would fit me!'

'Let's celebrate by going to buy something for the baby right now. It will make it seem more real.'

We had a lovely time choosing things. Lissie bought the nightdress with the rabbit on and I bought a pretty pink, white and yellow check blanket for the pram.

'I feel so privileged to be the first to be told. Is it to be a secret?'

'No. I want everyone to know. I'll ring Patience and Maeve this evening. Oh, I just thought! Perhaps Patience and Aubrey will have babies. Then mine will have someone to play with. Wouldn't that be lovely?'

'Perfect. She hasn't said anything about it but I hope they will.'

'And you'll be godmother, won't you? I wish you could have a beautiful baby with someone. It would help you get over Jack.'

'Thank you, darling, but it isn't quite what I want right now. I shall enjoy yours.'

Patience came round at lunch-time the following day to discuss the news.

'It's exactly the thing she most wanted. I bet George is pleased, too. He loves looking after people. I do feel happy about it.'

'Yes, I'm thrilled to bits.'

'Of course, she's already had one baby so she knows what it'll be like.' My antennae were alerted by the tone in which this was said. I knew it behoved me to choose my words carefully. 'It won't be a more difficult birth, will it, because she's older?'

'Well, of course, I'm not an obstetrician but I'd say it will make no difference.'

'I've never even seen a calf born. I could hardly be more ignorant.' There was a pause. 'Is it absolute agony?'

'Mm . . . I don't think you can generalise. Every birth is different. And every woman probably feels different things about it. It can be painful, yes, but it's a relatively short time. James hardly hurt at all because I was so full of drugs I was almost unconscious. Elizabeth happened so quickly I didn't have time to think about it. Henry was rather worse because he wasn't in the right position. One thing you can be sure of. It will be nothing like what you've worried about and anticipated for all those months. There's a momentum that carries you through it. And these days, now that the father is allowed in, it must be so much better.'

'Aubrey's dying to have children. He wants two girls and a boy. Perhaps because he's always been an outsider he wants a proper family. He didn't get on with his mother, and his father died when Aubrey was twelve. He was an only child. At school he was hopeless at games and brainy so the other boys despised him. He never had any confidence with girls. I'm very lucky. I feel he belongs to me, every bit of him. Before he asked me to marry him, we felt awfully constrained. Now we can't stop talking. We've made each other feel like *in*siders.'

'You'll be very happy together, children or not.'

'I think we will. Well, I'd better rush back. We're making three sets of the most terrible lilac-coloured festoon blinds with tassels on the bottom. It's torture. By the way, as I drove past Maeve's cottage I had to manoeuvre past the school bus, which was parked right outside. A man on a tractor was cursing like anything because he had to go the long way round. What do you think it's doing there?'

'Goodness knows! Perhaps it's broken down.'

When I walked past Maeve's cottage an hour later with Maurice, Elizabeth and Jasper to take some eggs to an old lady who was bedridden, I was surprised to see that the bus was still parked outside. A car was squeezing past with two wheels up on the bank.

'What do you think it's doing there?' asked Elizabeth, on our return journey, as we walked past a small queue of tractors and cars. I kept my surmises to myself. 'Wasn't Miss Boswell sad? I felt really guilty, when she was so pleased to see me, that I hadn't been to visit her before. She's so lonely and the house is so dark and dull. And she was so kind to us when she taught us in primary school.'

'Let's take her something next time that will cheer her up,' said Maurice. 'I don't mean presents. That would embarrass her. Wild flowers or that old long-tit's nest we found in the ivy the other day. Ordinary things that she can't get out to see any longer. What about some frog spawn in a jar?'

'That's a good idea. All schoolmistresses are loopy on nature. She was more pleased to see Jasper than any of us.'

'I'll make a cake and you can take her a piece,' I said, pleased by evidence of Elizabeth's dawning awareness of the existence of other people. 'I don't think she eats enough.'

'Shall we stop off in the churchyard and see Dad's grave?'

'That's a good idea.'

We stood, the three of us, round the place headed by a wooden cross that bore Jack's name. Six months after his death the mound was slowly subsiding. Jasper had to be deterred from trying to dig up the most recent burial.

'Whose flowers are these? Aren't they ugly?' said Elizabeth, pointing to a lividly pink spray of roses.

'Miss Horne has a standing order once a month. She told me about it when I rang her up the other day. She says she'll be able to visit the grave soon, but at present it would upset her too much.'

'Well, I like that! She wasn't even his family.' Elizabeth was resentful of this claim to grief.

'She really loved him, though, all the same.'

'Ugh! I've had enough of miserable people for one day.' Elizabeth spoke with all the insouciance of youth. 'I'm glad I came. I didn't want to come on my own. But I won't be frightened now.'

'Frightened, darling?'

'I thought I might have dark and horrible feelings that I wouldn't be able to forget. The fact is that Dad isn't here, is he? He really has gone away. I wasn't sure before. But now I know.' She looked down again at the mound. 'Are those your flowers, Mum?'

'No. I never bring flowers. Jack didn't like them. I don't remember him ever admiring so much as a buttercup.' I looked at the bundle of dog violets and lady's smock. 'I think they must be Ivor's.'

'I should have thought he was too busy these days, writing poetry,' said Maurice. 'He's a great deal brisker and less wrapped up in the numinous.'

When we got home I telephoned Maeve. I had to let it ring a long time.

'Hello? Oh, it's you, Miranda. Mind if I ring you back later? I'm a little tied up.'

'Just look out of your window, Maeve.'

'What? Have you been drinking? Oh, all right, anything to please.' There was a brief pause as she went away from the telephone. 'Oh, Christ! What an idiot that boy is! That'll teach me to cradle-snatch! He might as well have put up a printed sign. Oh, bloody hell! Thanks. I'll speak to you later.'

We carried tea out to the summerhouse. The shell interior was one third finished. It was a terribly slow job but already I could see that it was going to be beautiful.

'You look tired, Bessie,' said Maurice, as Elizabeth yawned. 'Still recovering from the party, I expect.'

'Oh, no!' said Henry. 'Not that wretched party again! I've heard of nothing else for the last two days.'

'Really?' I was surprised, as Elizabeth had hardly mentioned it to me.

'Oh, yes, jawing on and on about that gooey doctor.'

'Shut up before I stuff this razor-shell down your silly gob,' said Elizabeth, blushing furiously.

'But I thought you had such a nice time with Johnny, darling.'

'Johnny's just a boy. I like him but that's all. Rory fetched me a drink while Johnny went to the lav and then we danced a little. It was a pity that the music stopped quite soon afterwards.'

'I didn't see you.'

'You were prancing about with that fat oaf with the stripy hair. I saw you dance with Rory, though. Did he say anything about me?'

'I don't think so.' I frowned. 'I'm glad you enjoyed it. It's a good thing to have friends of all ages.'

'Elizabeth doesn't want him as a friend,' sniggered Henry. 'I found a poem she's written. All about his eyes and his stethoscope. And she's got those little bits of stitch all saved up in a special box! Yuck!'

'Henry!' Elizabeth got up, upsetting her plate and grabbed him by the hair. 'If you don't stop I'll chuck your air pistol into the moat and cement your pellets into this wall. You pig! Sneaking about in other people's business!'

'That'll do,' I interrupted, crossly. 'You've spilt Maurice's tea. Henry, you shouldn't read things not intended for your eyes.'

'How do I know whether they're intended for my eyes until I've read them?' retorted Henry triumphantly, and not altogether unreasonably.

'Well, we'll argue about that later.' I was worried about this crush of Elizabeth's, which seemed to be getting out of proportion. Though perhaps exaggeration is part of the definition of a crush. 'You mustn't let yourself get hurt, darling. It's quite natural for girls of your age to fall in love with an older man. I was hopelessly in love with Gregory Peck when I was fourteen.'

'That isn't at all the same thing.' Elizabeth was very angry and I realised that I had been tactless. 'This isn't a silly pash on someone I've never met!'

'But, sweetheart, you heard Johnny's grandfather make the announcement, didn't you? About Rory being engaged to his niece?'

'What *are* you talking about?'

'Darling, just before we left.' I remembered suddenly that we had found Elizabeth and Johnny playing billiards as they had tired of dancing. She would not have been in the ballroom when the announcement was made. I said gently, 'He's going to marry Annabel Vavasour.'

'Johnny's cousin? That girl in the red dress? I don't believe it!'

'I'm afraid it's true.'

'I can hardly believe it myself,' said Maurice, who had sat quietly observing this troubled conversation. 'Young Lochinvar seems to have got himself into a mess.'

'I think I'll go in,' said Elizabeth, looking pale. 'And I wish you wouldn't call him Young Lochinvar. Grown-ups have very stupid ideas of what's funny.'

She walked away quickly, back to the house. I apologised to Maurice.

'Oh, the poor darling thing.' Maurice was all sympathy.

'She's got it bad. I'm so sorry for her. Alas, alack! So that's the cloud that's been hanging over the house for the last two days! My dear girl.' He reached out and patted me kindly on the hand. I looked at him suspiciously but his expression was inscrutable.

'Well,' said Henry, in tones of disgust, 'if everyone's finished blabbing about love and engagements and boring things like that, perhaps someone'll hear my lines from Act Three?'

Elizabeth ate hardly anything for supper. I could see that she was trying to behave as though nothing had happened, but it was obvious that she had been crying. At last Maurice persuaded her to go out driving with him in the governess cart and they went off with Henry and Jasper to catch Puck. There had been a sense of strain throughout the evening and I was very pleased to see Maeve, who arrived rather hot from an uphill bicycle ride in time to have some coffee and pudding.

'Did you make this, Jenny? Oh, it's delicious!' Maeve helped herself to remains of the rice pudding and two tablespoonfuls of the scented, dark-red quince jelly.

'Miranda made the jelly.' Jenny was sitting at the table with Bridie on her knee, giving her some teaspoons of rice pudding, which the baby ate very slowly, wearing an expression of intense thoughtfulness. 'I haven't never made preserves. We always had jam out of a jar at home. I thought it *had* to be made in a factory. I've learned ever so much since I've been here. Me mum couldn't cook at all, except sausages and chips.'

'Miranda has always been an example to us all in the domestic arts. I've never made so much as a lavender bag in all my life and I don't intend to start now.'

'That's a great pity,' I said, as I heated Rose's milk on the Aga, 'because I'm going to cut out the monks' habits tonight and I thought you might help me. We've only got seven weeks until the pageant on Midsummer's Eve and there's loads to do.'

'Of course I'll help. I probably won't be any good, though. You'll have to look over my shoulder. I owe you a favour, anyway, for your telephone call this afternoon. God, I feel really humiliated at the thought of what the village is saying! What a fool that boy is!'

'I thought you were above caring what other people say.'

'Well, in theory I am. But that was a bit much. And I'm twice his age. I shouldn't have done it, I know. But he's very appealing in a hunky sort of way. And there's always the thrill of rough trade.'

'What's that?' asked Jenny, absently licking Bridie's spoon.

Maeve looked a little embarrassed 'It's . . . well, making love with . . . someone different from you.'

'You mean someone of a lower class?' Jenny was ignorant, but she was not a fool.

'Well, it does sound a silly expression, now I come to think of it. And Stew Harker's a perfectly nice bloke beneath the tattoos and crew-cut.'

'You mean you and Stew –' Jenny looked very red suddenly, and got up from her chair with a violence that made Bridie whimper and Jasper bark.

'Oh, well, I . . . you know how it is. He asked me and I thought why not and –'

'I know how it is, all right.' Jenny's voice was bitter. 'You haven't got nothing to lose. If you want an abortion you've got the money to pay for it. The likes of me have to be careful and say no because there isn't anybody going to bail us out of trouble. I suppose it don't mean nothing to you to turn a young boy's head with yer fancy ways so that the rest of us haven't got a chance. And Stew's a decent man – or would be, if women like you'd keep your hands off him. Can't you find no one of yer own sort?' Jenny was crying now, as Maeve and I stared at her in absolute astonishment.

'I'm sorry. I didn't realise . . . Goodness, I've been incredibly tactless but I didn't know –'

'I'm ever so sorry, Miranda.' Jenny rubbed her eyes with the knuckles of one hand while holding a protesting Bridie around the middle with the other. 'You've been goodness itself to me and all, but it fair makes me mad to listen to such carryings-on. You've always had everything and you don't think what folks like us might feel like. I only let a man do it to me once and look what happened to me!' She gave Bridie a savage little shake that made her yell.

'Let me hold the baby while you calm down,' I said, taking Bridie from her. 'Now sit still, Jenny, and listen to me.' Jenny obeyed, looking sullen and sniffing hard. 'That sort of talk about them and us isn't very helpful. I know you've had a hard time but you've got a chance now to make things better. When Bridie's bigger you can get some proper training in whatever you'd like to do, perhaps cooking or typing or something, and you know I'll always help you. As for getting pregnant the first time, that's absolutely nothing to do with class. Remember Elizabeth?' Jenny began to look rather ashamed. 'It's always a dreadful thing for any young girl. Maeve's entitled to go to bed with whomever she pleases, and because she's older and more experienced she takes proper precautions. Class has nothing whatever to do with it.'

'Maybe there's something in that,' Jenny admitted reluctantly. 'But what you don't see is how a woman with lah-de-dah ways can do anything with a bloke like Stew. Then she drops him because she wants something better, and he don't want someone like me any more.'

'That's nonsense, Jenny.' Maeve spoke a little impatiently. 'You've got far more to offer him than I have. I'm nearly forty, for heaven's sake! You're young and very attractive.'

'I know Stew likes what he calls a bit of classy twat.'

'All young men like to talk big,' I said, suppressing a laugh. 'And that's a very vulgar expression. I don't think you should use it.'

'Is it? I didn't know.' Jenny was silent for a moment, thinking. 'Would it be all the same to you if I went and had it out with him? I won't get no sleep with this on me mind.'

'By all means go, if you think it will help. You can leave Bridie with me. I'll put her to bed.'

'Thanks.' She faced Maeve. 'I'll say I'm sorry if I've been rude. But you wouldn't like it if someone went to bed with your feller.'

'That's all right, Jenny. I'm so sorry I upset you. It certainly won't happen again.'

Jenny sniffed disbelievingly and left us.

'Well!' said Maeve. 'That was a thunderstorm and no mistake! I had absolutely no idea she was his girlfriend.'

'Nor had I. I thought she was still getting over James. This house is positively pullulating with star-crossed love.' I told her about Elizabeth and Rory.

'Oh, poor little things!' Maeve was sympathetic. 'Who'd be young again? Not me! Though I must say I'm beginning to tire of the life of a single, nearly-middle-aged woman.'

'I thought you liked being free.'

'I did. But recently – perhaps it has something to do with contemplating Patience and Aubrey's unalloyed bliss... and there's Lissie so excited and fulfilled. My own life seems a mite empty. I suppose that's why I agreed to go to bed with Stew. Fancy being thought of as classy twat! Serves me right.'

'Do my ears deceive me?' asked Maurice, who had come into the kitchen unobserved. 'Is this a sample of the dirty talk women indulge in when they're on their own? There's something boiling over on the Aga.'

'Damn! It's Rose's milk. Oh, Sukie! You'll be sick.' Sukie was crouching over a now empty dish, which had been three-quarters full of rice pudding. She gave me a look from her mandarin eyes and began to wash her ears. I got up, took away the dish and put the milk pan under the tap where it hissed and gave off a nasty smell of burning. I began all over again with a fresh saucepan as I explained the small drama that had just occurred.

'"Twat" is an interesting piece of historical slang.' Maurice poured himself a glass of his favourite *grappa*, with which he always kept the house supplied. 'In fact, it was used by Robert Browning, who was actually rather a prissy man, in his poem "Pippa Passes". He mistook its meaning and presumably his publishers were all innocent souls, so it remains as possibly the worst literary brick of all time. Now, let me hold the baby, Miranda, while you see to Rose or we'll have burnt milk again. Elizabeth and Henry are practising driving in a perfect circle beside the coach-house. They'll manage on their own.'

Rose drank most of her milk but was too tired to talk. She seemed satisfied to lie with half-open eyes while I told her what everyone was doing, and was asleep before I had finished describing the visit to Miss Boswell. Maurice insisted on helping me with the monks' habits and proved to be better at cutting out than I was. He denied this, modestly, but admitted to experience as a sail-maker. 'It's all in the eye. Close the scissors completely and then pause, align your eye. Don't saw at it, Maeve. No, look, that isn't right, you've got to get the line straight – No, stop! Too late!'

'God, I'm sorry!' said Maeve, as Maurice held up the severed end of the beautiful panne velvet scarf that he wore knotted about his neck.

'I'll hem the cut end,' I said, 'and it will just be a bit shorter.'

'Wait until I've strangled Maeve with it first. Look, my girl, put those scissors down and make us some very strong black coffee. We've a long night ahead of us.'

It was nearly eleven before we had finished the cutting out. Patience was going to help me stitch up the sides of the habits on one of the industrial sewing machines that she used for work. Maeve had left at ten, having given moral support in the form of reading 'Pippa Passes' aloud as we snipped. Maurice staggered to bed the minute we had got all the potential habits folded into a neat pile, saying that his entire body had seized up from kneeling on the floor and he would have to lie all night screwed up in the shape of the letter Z. Jenny had not returned. I felt anxious about her, but there was nothing I could do.

I fed Dinkie, who had been a perfect nuisance all evening by insisting on lying on any bit of fabric we were working on and suddenly shooting out his paw between the blades of the scissors and making us scream with fright. Jasper had already had his supper and gone to bed with Elizabeth. Of Sukie there was no sign. I suspected she had slipped up to my bedroom to sleep off the rice pudding.

I checked the fire and had a last look at Bridie, who had fallen asleep hours earlier. She lay on her back, her pale lashes fluttering as she dreamed, her mouth a little open showing the white gleam of her first tooth. I touched her face gently. She seemed very hot. I undid the strings of her bonnet. Her head was sticky with perspiration so I removed the bonnet altogether. Something caught my attention and I looked closer. Then I fetched the lamp that always stood by Rose's chair and carried it to the full length of its flex so that I could see Bridie better. The baby stirred a little as the light fell on her face. Her skull was covered with the finest down, half an inch long. Her hair was bright red.

CHAPTER 25

'Why didn't you tell me?' I asked Jenny, in a voice that would not be calm, however much I tried to make it so.

She still had her coat on, having returned from the Harkers' just as the others were finishing breakfast. I had waited until everyone had gone away to get on with their various ploys before saying to Jenny, 'Sit down a minute. We've got to have a talk.' Jenny had gone fearfully white and had sunk into a chair with her frightened eyes on my face. 'Bridie is Jack's child, isn't she?'

Jenny burst into tears. 'I did pray ever so hard that she'd have hair like mine. But when I saw the red hair coming I knew it were only a matter of time afore you'd guess. I'm sorry!'

I waited a minute while she sobbed, and then I spoke, this time more gently. 'Why didn't you tell me? I feel such a fool! I thought we were friends and that you trusted me.'

'Oh, it weren't like that!' Jenny looked earnestly up at me with agonised eyes. 'I never meant to deceive you. I did mean to tell you but I were afraid. You was so good to me and I were so desperate for someone to help me! I was so on me own, like, and you were the answer to a prayer. I thought mebbe it would be for just a bit and then I'd find somewhere else to live and you needn't ever know and be made unhappy. I didn't want to hurt you by saying that your husband were dallying, like, with other women.'

'I can understand that. But I do wish you'd decided to trust me. That's what hurts.'

'I thought mebbe you'd kick me out of the house at once and I'd have nowhere to go! I were so happy here and everything were so nice. Where would I go? I'd be on me own with Bridie, and she were so well looked after here. I couldn't make things so good for her on me own.'

'Yes, I do see.' And I did. The girl had been desperate. And her experience so far was not such as to give her any reliance on adult probity.

'Where did you meet Jack?'

'He were staying in the hotel where I were chambermaid. He stayed there quite a bit.' I remembered that Jack had negotiated some loans for an Indian bank, which had an office in Sheffield. 'He were always very nice to me. Sort of joking, while his eyes said summat else. He said I were very beautiful... He made me feel I were someone special. I thought he were the most handsome man I ever did see. I couldn't refuse him when he asked me. I thought I were in love with him. It were only the one time.'

'Did he know about the baby?'

'No. I looked up his address in the hotel register. But I were afraid he'd be angry. I knew he'd likely be married. It were Father Declan that persuaded me to come. He were the only one that knew who Bridie's dad was. He said Jack had a right to see his child and perhaps he'd give me some money. I didn't want to. I thought he'd hate me if I turned up with a baby. Then, when Father Declan showed me the advert he'd cut out of the *Weekly Furrow* for Mr Birt's housekeeper it seemed to me like Our Lady were telling me to come. I wanted to see Jack . . . to see his fine handsome face just to cheer me up, like. I were that low. I didn't know whether I'd tell him or not. I couldn't make up me mind. And the day I got here Mr Birt told me that Jack were dead.' Jenny put her head on to her arms and cried with great sobs like a child.

I put my arm around her and stroked her hair. 'Don't cry, Jenny. I'm not angry any more. I see how it all happened. You've had a bad time. Never mind. It's over now. I know you didn't mean to hurt me.'

'Oh, no, I didn't! I never meant that! Of course he didn't love me. I see that now. I were nothing to him – just a bit of skirt to spend the night with. The minute I saw you coming out of church after the funeral I knew that. You were so beautiful and smart. And then when I got to know you, you wasn't the sort of woman I'd thought, only caring about yer hair and staying in grand places. You were better to me than me own mum. I felt really bad about deceiving you, Miranda. It fair tore me up! Father Declan told me when he came here that the Lord had put me in your path when I were so desperate, and that it were God's way of showing me that He'd forgiven my sin. I don't know. Could that be right?' She looked at me, full of perplexity and hope.

'If I could answer that, Jenny, I'd be a religious seer. There *is* a peculiar aptness in your being here, I suppose. But you don't stand in need of forgiveness from me or God or anyone else. I wish I could make you see that.'

I saw that she longed to believe it. Jenny cried some more while I kept my arms about her and tried to soothe her. My own feelings were elusive. I had lain awake for some hours the night before, trying to be honest with myself about what the discovery of Bridie's paternity meant to me. I had felt wounded by the deception. Perhaps all the time Jenny had been secretly laughing at me, scorning my attempts at philanthropy, if so instinctive an impulse to protect could be described as that. Might she have been gloating over the opportunity I had given her to exact some kind of revenge on Jack? Once I had entertained these thoughts and matched them against what I knew of Jenny's character I dismissed them all as so much speculative paranoia.

When I thought about Jack, a cold rage made me feel physically sick. I pressed my good ear into the pillow and tried to blank out the world and the image of him lying in the gun room, which filtered into my mind as soon as I began to drift towards sleep. Eventually I took two sleeping pills left over from the supply Rory had given me when Jack shot himself.

I had woken at six when the alarm went and stumbled down to the kitchen in dressing gown and slippers. Jenny's bed had not been slept in. A momentary irritation at her irresponsibility was quelled by reminding myself of what I had been like at eighteen. She saw me as some kind of parent figure, no doubt, and had been sure that I would look after Bridie. The baby was just waking as I bent over her cot. Without opening her eyes she made little grizzling sounds and her fists flew to her mouth. By the time I had made a bottle for her she was beginning to yell. I sat in Rose's chair by the embers of the fire, still sparking red among the snowy ashes, and held the solid little body in my arms. Her mouth fastened swiftly on the teat and she sucked with absolute concentration. Her eyes, now losing their slaty-brown colour and turning green, were fixed unseeing on my face.

When she turned her head away from the teat and lay in my arms, still gazing up at me, I stroked her cheek and smiled. Her face broke at once into a broad beam. This innocent generosity was like a balm laid upon the tired confusion that disordered my thoughts. I kissed her hands and then her cheeks and told her that I loved her, and she laughed as though everything in the world was the most tremendous joke. 'Bridie,' I said, holding her up so that her toes dangled on to my knees, 'we all make fools of ourselves, so enjoy your dignity while you have it.'

Bridie chuckled with pleasure.

'Now,' I said to Jenny, three hours later, 'that's enough unhappiness for one day. You needn't worry about it. I need a little time to think about what I'm going to say to the children. But between you and me all's square. All right?'

Jenny looked at me from swollen eyes and nodded, sniffing hard. Then she suddenly burst out into a final paroxysm of tears.

'Jenny, Jenny! No more! I swear to you I'm as fond of you as ever!'

'It isn't that, quite. I were just thinking what a lovely man he were and how I loved him! So you must've loved him ever so much more and I'm so sorry for you to have lost him!'

'Yes. It's very good of you to think of me. Now, dry your eyes and tell me about Stew. That is, if you want to.'

Jenny blushed. 'I were very angry with him at first and he was so sorry and loving. Then, I thought, I can't blame him for going with other women if I won't let him . . . you know. So I did.'

I made a mental note to have a word with Jenny about contraception when the emotional temperature was cooler. We did the washing-up together and I showed her how to make choux pastry, which was a calming sort of occupation.

'Those'll not puff up,' said Mrs Harker, with satisfaction, when she arrived and saw the shiny yellow blobs of pastry on the tray. But choux pastry being the easiest kind to make, of course they did. 'What d'you call 'em? Toffee rolls?'

'Profiteroles. You fill them with cream or custard and pour a chocolate sauce over them.'

Mrs Harker's look was scathing. 'I like a nice butterscotch Instant Whip myself.' She held up a duster to examine it for cleanness, shook it over the pastry, then stuffed it back in her pocket. 'I hope you know what you're doing, young lady.' She looked severely at Jenny. 'There's six of us in our house and one outside privy and we don't want a little basket, do we? You make our Stew use a rubber.' Then she went crashing away, swinging the vacuum cleaner like a censer and denting the door jambs as she went.

I spent the morning with Patience in the converted barn where the curtain-making went on. As it was Saturday we had the place to ourselves and were able to talk freely as we stitched the sleeves and side seams of the monks' robes.

'I can hardly believe it, even of Jack,' said Patience, when I told her. 'Bugger! I've just stitched my finger with shock. Oh don't worry, it quite often happens. I've grown extra thick skin on my fingertips with use and I can't feel a thing. It's like a horny layer. But to sleep with a child of seventeen without taking precautions, and then just clear off without another word! He really was a complete bastard!'

'I'm afraid that sort of thing happens pretty often. Not that that excuses Jack.'

'What do you feel about the baby now? And Jenny?'

'I can't be angry with her. As you say, she's a child and I can imagine that to someone so starved of love Jack must have seemed like some kind of god. She's as free from stratagem as anyone her age could be. As for Bridie . . . I suppose it's just made me love her more, in an odd way. Because I have some small claim to her as the mother of her half-sister and brothers, perhaps. And she has the look of James about her. Poor little thing . . . What ill-starred origins.'

'What will happen now?'

'I've got to tell the children. As soon as Bridie grows a bit more hair, people will start to talk and I want them to hear it first from me. I don't want to say anything in front of Jenny. She's going to the Harkers' for tea this afternoon so perhaps I'll do it then.'

'I'll take these down to Aubrey,' said Patience, folding the finished habits into a pile. 'I'm going to cook supper for him as it's my father's regimental dinner. Will you come to the first rehearsal of the pageant tomorrow? Aubrey wants to consult you about the script. He's so knocked for six by the excellence of your history of Westray. He says you ought to be a writer.'

'That's kind. But I shrink, rather, from the thought of invention on the blank page. I enjoy making something of past incidents and using my imagination strictly as a bridge between facts.'

'Well, you've got a chance in the next few years to make something of your talents and not bury them as I've done mine.'

I sighed.

Over tea in the library, which included Rose and Maurice as well as the three children, I said, as casually as I could, 'I've got something very interesting to tell you all. I hope everyone will be pleased.'

'You're not going to have Sir Humphrey Bessinger's baby?' said Elizabeth, in tones of horror.

'You've won the pools!' shouted Henry.

'No, there isn't the least possibility of either, even if they were desirable outcomes.'

'I know what it is,' said Rose. But, when pressed, she refused to open her mouth again, except to put in another piece of walnut cake.

'That's cheating!' Henry was indignant. 'We could all say that! Write it down on a piece of paper now and then we'll believe you.'

'Do hush!' I interrupted. 'It's this. Bridie is your half-sister.' The children's faces looked so blank that I added, by way of explanation, 'Daddy was Bridie's father.'

No one moved or spoke for quite five seconds while they digested this.

'Well, I never!' said Maurice. 'How extraordinary life is! Well, well! I congratulate you three on the acquisition of a most charming sibling.'

'Do you mean to say,' Elizabeth spoke slowly, 'that

Dad and Jenny . . . I think it's the most disgusting thing I ever heard.' She got up and walked out of the room.

'Oh, Mum.' James's face was grave. 'That's a bit of a facer for you.' He thought for a minute and then added, 'I must say Dad was a fool. You were much too good for him.' He looked at me with his father's green eyes. 'You know that, I hope?'

'Thank you, darling. I don't suppose it's true but thank you anyway.'

' "Let us do evil that good may come," ' said Rose. 'St Paul's letter to the Romans.'

'Are we allowed to be pleased, really?' asked Henry. 'Everyone seems to be mad as hornets. I expect Dad felt sorry for Jenny because she was poor and didn't have a boyfriend. I always thought Bridie liked me specially. I shall enjoy having a little sister. I don't like being the youngest. Perhaps she'll tidy my bedroom for me and clean my bike.'

'Don't you hate her, Mum?' asked James. 'Jenny, I mean.'

'Not a bit. And it will please me very much if you don't let this make any difference to the way you treat Jenny. She's very young and she was in love with your father. She didn't mean to do us any harm.'

'But it must have changed the way you feel about Dad.'

'I suppose it has . . . a little. But that's my problem.' I saw that James looked hurt. 'Oh, darling, I didn't mean to shut you out. It's just that there are some things that absolutely no one can help one get over. You have to do it by yourself. But having you here . . . just looking at you is the most cheering thing I can think of.'

'More cheering than looking at me?' demanded Henry.

'No, clot! All my children are the most important thing in my life, and if you're all all right, then nothing else matters too terribly much.'

'You seem to have taken it like a trooper,' Maurice said to me that night, as we washed up together alone in the kitchen.

Rose had gone to bed and the children were watching

television. Jenny had not yet come back from the Harkers'.

'Well, I know how I *ought* to react to it and that's been a great help. I love Bridie and nothing could change that. Anyway, of all of us, she is blessedly sinless. Jenny is only guilty of loving unwisely. Perhaps even Jack is not quite as black as he appears to be. I refused to make love with him. He was bound to look elsewhere.'

'But not necessarily to a defenceless child, who didn't know what she was doing.'

'Jack always felt that everyone had to learn to fight for themselves. He was without an ounce of sentiment. But I must admit that there is a sensation in my stomach like a large, cold stone. I've had it before and I know I'll get over it. Action's the thing. I just don't want any more painful revelations for a bit.'

'You know how fond of you I am.' Something in Maurice's tone made me turn to look at him. His brown eyes were shining with tears and he twisted the drying-up cloth in his hand into a rope as he pressed his lips hard together to prevent them from trembling. 'I should so very much like to have the right to protect you from hurt.'

He swayed slightly, his large bulk encased in a black velvet coat, the folds of his neck girded by a Paisley bow-tie. On his small feet were the embroidered slippers I had given him for Christmas. His white hair stood ruffled at the crown. He was not a romantic figure but I thought, as I looked at his intelligent, anxious face, that I loved him quite as much as I had ever loved any man. 'I can't tell you what a help you've been to me... in more ways than I could ever have the time to list. Please always think of Westray as your home.'

'Thank you, dear girl. I will as long as you can put up with me.' He cleared his throat. 'Now I've a good idea. Enough of this delving the deeps. I bought a Duke Ellington record in Marshgate this morning. Let's go and listen to it while I finish that drawing of you I promised to give your sister.'

*

The first rehearsal of the Westray pageant, which took place in the vicarage drawing room the following afternoon, was not an auspicious beginning. Aubrey had decided to begin with a tribute to Hengist and Horsa as the fifth-century Saxon mercenaries and sequestrators of Kent.

'I'm afraid it was rather a fiasco,' I said to Maurice later that day, as I was stuffing profiteroles with *crème patissière* for supper that night. 'Aubrey's script was hopelessly high-flown and rhetorical, and there was no chance that anyone was going to be able to understand what they were supposed to be saying, let alone memorise it. I've brought it home with me to try to get it into plain English. Ivor was completely miscast as Hengist. Aubrey asked him to extemporise his speeches to give a feeling of authenticity. You'd have thought he and Mr Marjoribanks, the bank manager – he's playing Vortigern – were planning a painting holiday together in Provence, rather than threatening to hack each other to pieces. Patience and I had to go out of the room so that we didn't disgrace ourselves by laughing. We've persuaded Aubrey to give Ivor the part of the Abbot of Westray. He'll be perfect as the conscience-torn martyr.'

'I long to be in it myself. I've been starved of English Pastoral.'

'I've asked Patience and Aubrey to come to lunch tomorrow, as soon as the paying guests have gone, to discuss the alterations in the script. Let's ask them if you can have a walk-on part. All the speaking parts have been allotted to the villagers, of course, but there's no reason why you shouldn't be a man of Kent and help carry green boughs to meet William the Conqueror.'

'It doesn't sound the kind of thing that gives much scope for dramatic expression. However, if that is all I am offered I shall accept it gratefully. Let me practise now.'

He skipped about the kitchen, waving imaginary branches, while Jasper barked and Rose told him that he was making her dizzy. 'There never was such a gaby as you, unless it's Ivor Bastable. Mind you, unlike most men you give as well as take. I can see that. You've made my girl happy. Now don't blub, man, for pity's sake. Tst! Bridie's got more self-control than you.'

'Unkind, Rose. There was only what is called a "suspicious moisture". My lachrymal ducts are infected by years of living in Italy where people laugh and cry like breathing. And very pleasant it is too. You Scots are like your landscape, rugged and silent. But your good opinion of me is warming.'

'I wouldn't go so far as that,' replied Rose, tersely.

I was rather pleased to see the guests off the next morning. The husband was a golfer and keen to describe every inch of the round he had played at the Marshgate golf club. His wife despised the game and told him that he was an utter bore at least every five minutes. She had a superior taste for poetry, and after dinner had held me in literary talk until my eyes were stinging with the effort to keep them open after a long and busy day. I think if she could have persuaded me to part with the inner soles of my grandfather's boots she would have been a happy woman ever after. As it was, she cradled his boots in her well-manicured fingers, muttering, 'Flanders mud! What did he say? "The precious earth now turned to mud/ Scorched by death and seamed with blood." Wonderful lines!'

I thought she was going to kiss the toe-caps. I didn't like to tell her after this that the boots were the pair he had been wearing when he died, walking his dog, and that the mud was sacred only to Hampstead Heath.

Over lunch with Patience and Aubrey, Maurice confessed his longing for a part in the pageant. Aubrey was delighted. 'There may even be a small speaking part for you. I'm having a job to persuade people that they're capable of learning even a handful of lines. Now I come to think of it, you could be the Bishop of London who consecrates the spring that rises up on the spot of St Wolberga's martyrdom. He has a long and quite complex speech. It's a pity that my original idea of having people extemporise the talk between the ceremonial bits doesn't seem to work, quite. I never realised how much there is to putting on a show. Luckily Maeve is wonderful as the Holy Maid of Kent. She has real acting ability.'

'I've asked her to come round as soon as she gets back from visiting Sebastian in the detention centre,' I said, as I made coffee and got out the box of chocolates given me by the grateful departed guests. 'Ivor's coming up, too, to rehearse his part. I'm sure you did the right thing, Aubrey, to change his role. He didn't have quite the *brio* for Hengist.'

Though it had been Patience's idea to put Ivor in another part it was instinctive to both of us to support Aubrey's waning confidence with a tactful obfuscation of the truth.

'I hope it won't be awkward,' I added. 'They haven't met since the business of Mr Birt's hay barn.'

Maeve, when she arrived, was in high spirits. She and Ivor went through their scene of impassioned resistance to the Reformation like repertory pros, and drew spontaneous applause from all of us when they made their last speeches of defiance before being arrested and taken away to be hanged at Tyburn. 'Can't we have the hanging bit as well?' asked Maeve. 'The villagers would love it!'

'I do think it would make a fine punctuation mark for the medieval section,' said Ivor. He had begun the rehearsal with an air of extreme reserve, ignoring Maeve's attempts to be friendly. But the emotion of the scene, as together they defied Henry VIII's determination to be *rex et sacerdos*, broke down all barriers. By the end, when Maeve was prophesying doom and death for Henry, Ivor, kneeling at her feet in worship, looked almost like a lover.

'Quite brilliant!' were his words of approval. 'You managed to get a splendid mingling of utter conviction and madness.'

'I'm not at all sure the Holy Maid was mad,' said Maeve. 'I believe firmly in divine inspiration. It's just that I haven't been able to quite define what else I believe, which accounts for the very large number of faiths I've adopted and abandoned.'

'Oho!' said Ivor, or words to that effect. To a devout Roman Catholic, this was a silver hook. I was quite certain that Maeve knew exactly what she was doing but I wasn't at all sure why.

'I've just read this riveting book,' she continued, 'about pyromancy. You know, divination by fire. It's very complicated. I had a go last night but it's awfully difficult to pinpoint the relevant shapes as the flames flicker so much. But one of my great-aunts was a pyromantic. She lived in a tiny village in Ireland with nothing else to do but stare at smouldering peat turves. Apparently Great-aunt Deirdre foretold the sinking of the *Titanic*.'

While Maurice made tea for everyone and I gave Bridie her scrambled egg, Ivor and Maeve sat next to each other on the sofa and continued to discuss this recondite subject.

'I can't stand this. I shall go and sit in the library,' said Rose, getting to her feet with the aid of the two sticks she now used. ' "What meaneth then this bleating of sheep in mine ears?" First Book of Samuel. I never heard such twaddle!'

After tea we all, including the children and Jasper, went for a walk. The weather being warmer and drier, it meant that the ancient right of way through the woods, which all winter was churned up by Mr Birt's cows walking down to be milked, was no longer miry so we were able to follow the bounds of the Manor and end up on the ridge of the hill behind Westray, looking down on the house. This was my favourite view of it. The central courtyard lay square amid the roofs and turrets, surrounded by the shining moat. It reminded me of a toy fort.

'Lovely, isn't it?' Maurice stood beside me, gazing down.

'I know. I'm lucky to have it. I'd stuff a good many more profiteroles to keep it.'

'I'd like to be able to save you all that work.' Maurice's glance was tender. His hat was fastened on against the wind by a scarf and had taken on the shape of a Quaker bonnet. I loved this combination in him of vanity and eccentricity. 'I suppose there aren't any circumstances you can think of in which you could accept a substantial sum of money from me?'

I put my arm through his. 'None, darling. But don't think I'm not tremendously grateful. It would be a pity, wouldn't it, to change things when they're so perfect as they are? It would be dreadful to run the risk of money coming between us.'

Maurice seemed to be about to say something, and then he changed his mind. We stood a little longer in silence and then he said, 'What a terrible idiot I am!'

I didn't know what to make of this, but as he began at once to talk to Elizabeth no answer was necessary.

Elizabeth had come into my room that morning as I was brushing my hair and had taken the brush from my hand and continued the task herself. 'Do you remember how I used to love doing this when I was little?'

'Yes. What a dear little thing you were. And infinitely dear now.' Her eyes met mine in the looking-glass. 'I'm sorry you're upset about the baby, darling.'

'The trouble is that I loved Dad. And I still love him. It hurts like anything to know that he could do that. There's something so horrible . . . I can't bear to think about it.'

I turned round and took her hand in mine. 'Then don't think about it for a while unless you've got to. Keep busy, ride Puck, drive the carriage, do the shell grotto with Maurice, watch television, anything to be occupied. Then gradually, when the first shock is over, you'll feel much calmer about it and it won't hurt so much. And when a good bit of time has gone by, you'll be able to think about it clearly.'

'You've had to do that a lot, haven't you?'

'Yes. I've got quite good at it. But that's all over now. I want you to remember two things. One, that Jenny had no intention of hurting anybody. And, two, your father really loved you.'

'He loved you, too, Mum.'

Her eyes in the mirror were earnest.

'Mm, well, perhaps he did. Those other women were

supposed to be as well as me, not instead. Perhaps I shouldn't have minded so much.'

'Don't be silly. Anyone would mind.' She bent over my shoulder and kissed my cheek and then went away, leaving me comforted.

Now, as she and Maurice discussed aerial perspective and James and Henry ran down the hill with their arms out, pretending to be Sopwith Camels which they had done ever since Henry had been old enough to run, I thought that, considering everything, my children looked reasonably well adjusted and happy. As long as there were no further surprises in store, we were probably set to enjoy a period of relative calm.

Maeve and Ivor, I noticed, were lagging behind the rest of us, deep in conversation. I couldn't hear what they were saying. Then I saw Ivor pull a piece of paper from his pocket. While he read, Maeve assumed an expression of rapt attention. She really was a contriving minx. I would be furious with her if she made him unhappy.

Over drinks, we discussed more of the costumes in greater detail and tried to work out a budget. Maurice promised to go to a shop he knew in Camden Town, where they sold off bolts of discontinued fabric. He made a list of the colours we wanted and approximate yardage. Then we moved on to props.

'We want a sword for Charles the Second to knight Harold Wychford,' said Aubrey, sucking his pen thoughtfully.

'Ink, Aubrey,' said Patience. 'You're making your mouth black. Father will lend us his regimental sword, I'm sure. Or what about yours, Miranda? It would look more authentic.'

'Actually, it's only nineteenth century. But we can see which looks better.'

'Bishop's mitre for the consecration of St Wolberga's Well,' continued Aubrey, putting the pen back in his mouth.

'I'll have a go at that, if you like,' said Maurice. 'With

some stiff cardboard and gorgeous fabric it shouldn't be too hard.'

'Bishop's staff?' Aubrey looked round the table for ideas.

'I've got a shepherd's crook,' said Ivor. 'We could wrap it in silver foil.'

'Excellent,' said Patience. 'Pen, darling! It's leaking like anything. What shall we do about a well-head? All the fountains are much too large and magnificent, besides being in the wrong place.'

'We want something like the *pozzi* in Venice,' said Maurice. 'Squat and rugged. What about something in cardboard again, painted in shades of grey to look like stone? It's got to be light enough to bring on and carry off.'

Soon after this, Patience and Aubrey got up to go. I pressed them to stay for supper but Patience had to go and feed Wacko and help him with his packing. 'He's really keen to go to this retired Army home. He's in such a good mood all the time. I had no idea how much of a sacrifice he was making. I feel quite guilty.'

'You're the very last person who should feel guilty, my dear,' said Aubrey gently, stooping to kiss her cheek. Despite the black imprint his lips left on her face, like a dark and exotic butterfly, it was a tender sight that brought a lump to my throat.

'Has everyone got their lists of what they have to find and do?' I asked, gathering up all the bits of paper that had somehow become scattered about the table. 'Here you are, Patience,' I said, as I recognised her tiny, neat script. 'And this is yours, Aubrey.' There were several black thumbprints round the edges. 'And this must be . . .' I stopped as I looked at the piece of paper I held in my hand. 'Quantity of cheap fabric. Red, blue and yellow. Cardboard (lots),' it began and, 'Well-head. Suitable fabric for Bish.' I stared at the paper.

'Miranda! What's the matter?' cried Patience. 'You look dreadful!'

I continued to hold the paper in front of my eyes with a

hand that shook so much that I could hear the piece of paper rustling, though no other sounds in the kitchen registered on my consciousness. Everything else had shrunk away to an immense distance. I continued to gaze at the paper. I knew that writing better than my own. The Ts were like spears and the Ys were like whips. Into my mind's eye flashed the picture of the world as an apple-pie and the sea as black, boiling ink.

The blood began to roar in my ears. I lifted my eyes. The room was wavering but I saw that Maurice had become deadly pale.

I felt Patience's hand on my arm and was aware that she had said something to me but I couldn't understand what it was. The thing was impossible. I knew it was. But yet... the writing was there. I saw again the frontispiece of the book beside my bed. *To my darling daughter, Miranda, on her fourth birthday, with all my love, Daddy.* I stared round the kitchen, whose walls had receded to an impossible distance. Then I turned my eyes slowly back to him.

'Oh, my darling,' said Maurice, tears streaming, his hands held out towards me. 'I'm so ashamed! So dreadfully ashamed!'

CHAPTER 26

The memory of what happened immediately after I realised that Maurice was my father has vanished. The shock was so immense that I seemed for a while to be divorced from anything I could recognise, including myself. I know I cried a great deal.

At first I started to cry in sympathy with Maurice, who was so distraught that he wept like a baby. I put my arms round him to comfort him, but then found that he was comforting me. I cried not only with the shock of discovery but for all the things that had made me so unbearably sad in the past and which I now dared to acknowledge. I cried for the painful dissolution of my marriage and for Jack's death. I cried for the children losing their father and for Bridie never knowing him. I cried for everyone whose sadness I knew anything about. It was a cathartic breaching of accumulated reservoirs of pain, which had been stored up, I suppose, because I had been afraid that I might not recover from the expression of such sorrow. Now I knew that I could. I tried to explain some of this to Maurice, who must have thought that he was solely responsible for this paroxysm of grief.

'I feel better now, really,' I assured him, when the weeping began to abate and I could speak. 'I needed to do that. But it took a huge shock to force it out of me.' I tried to laugh. 'I think I'd better sit down. My legs seem to have gone rubbery.'

Then I found that I was sitting on a chair by the kitchen table with a *grappa* in my hand. Everyone else had tactfully left the room.

Maurice sat next to me, holding the bottle. 'You poor sweet, your face *is* wet. Have my handkerchief.'

We sat in silence and drained our glasses, looking at each other.

'I won't blame you for being angry,' said Maurice at last. 'Or hating me. I can't make any excuses. It was sheer selfishness.'

'At the moment I don't think I can take it in. I've got to try and believe it properly. I keep thinking it can't be true. But it is, isn't it? You are my father? You are Michael Trebor?'

'I'm ashamed to say I am. That is, I'm very proud to be your father but I'm only too bitterly aware that I don't deserve you.'

In answer I put out my hand and took hold of his. We sat like that for some time.

'Mum?' Henry put his head round the door. 'Is there going to be any supper? What's the matter with your face?'

'I've been crying, that's all. But everything's all right.

Just go and fetch the other two, darling, straight away, will you? I want to talk to you all.'

'You're not going to tell us that Bridie isn't our sister?' Henry looked disappointed.

'No. It isn't anything to do with Bridie or Daddy. Hurry up.'

The children took the news much more calmly than I had expected. I suppose they were becoming inured to shocks. They looked pleased, but became suddenly shy and clearly didn't know what to say. As soon as they could they went away.

'We shall all be better when we've had a little while to grow used to it,' Maurice said, getting up and fetching some potatoes from the larder. 'Now it's time to be practical. You're too tired to talk and I'm in a bit of a tizzy myself. Let's do something mundane and reassuring. Shall I peel these?'

We made supper together. I don't think we said much. I felt completely exhausted. My face was tight from all the crying and my body ached. The children were summoned to lay the table. While we ate, everyone made huge efforts to behave normally.

'I'm really glad you're my grandfather,' said Henry. 'Having only one grandfather up to now hasn't been much fun. Donald only ever sends me a lousy fifty pence for Christmas. When he was here last, for Dad's funeral, he told me about the measly old stocking presents he had as a child. Lumps of coal and oranges and apples and nuts and things. Can *I* help it if his parents were misers?'

'It's good that we all got to know you and like you without having to because you were our grandfather,' said Elizabeth. 'I mean, if you'd told us when you arrived it would have been impossible to know what we really felt. Is that why you didn't say?'

'I didn't say who I was because I wanted to help your mother – and all of you if I could – to try and make up a little for having deserted her for all those years. I was afraid that if your mother knew, she might justifiably want to give me the bum's rush.'

This expression was new to Henry and delighted him.

'But do you mean to say that you were never going to tell us?' asked James, thoughtfully. 'Wasn't that a little... unkind? Even dishonest?'

'I thought, perhaps wrongly, that it was more important to do what I could to help. I couldn't make up for the past. Though there have been many times in the last few weeks when I was sorely tempted. As it is, I've got a lot of explaining to do.'

'It isn't going to make much difference, is it?' asked Henry. 'Since you practically live here and we already like you a million times better than Donald.'

'I hope it won't, except in good ways.'

'I was so afraid you'd be terribly angry with me,' explained Maurice, as we sat together on the sofa by the fire late that night. The children and Rose were in bed but for me, exhausted though I was, sleep was impossible. I leaned my head against his arm, which was around my shoulder. 'You see, I couldn't think of one single reason why you might be prepared to forgive me for deserting you and Beatrice all those years ago. And your mother, of course. I still can't, now. For thirty years I've told myself every day that I was a coward and a brute. It hurt me very much to know that you were growing up without me. Do believe that, at least.'

'How did it happen that my mother was told you'd been killed at Anzio? She was sent your medals and your watch and photographs of us. They're all displayed in her house in Italy, in the room with your paintings.'

'Oh, those paintings!' Maurice groaned. 'Well, it was very simple, really. My platoon was in a trench quite a way from Company Headquarters. We were picked off by a German rifle grenade. I got a graze on the knee but I could still walk. Lance-Corporal Tremlow was hit in the shoulder. Everyone else in the trench was killed. We lay without moving until nightfall so that the Germans should think we were all dead. We decided we'd make a run for it back to HQ under cover of darkness.

'Tremlow trod on a mine. He was a mess. I never found his head. During those long hours while we'd been waiting we'd talked in whispers to keep our spirits up. He'd commented on the fact that we had the same initials, M. T. He was a simple man, a nice man. I thought of that again when I looked at him lying in several pieces in the moonlight. It was the coincidence of our initials that made me think of changing places with him. No better reason. But you don't think clearly when you've been under that sort of barrage. All I knew was that I couldn't take any more. All my friends were dead. Some died so horribly... Well, you don't want to hear that. It was the same for everyone. I emptied the contents of my pockets and shoved them into the bits of gory matter that were once Tremlow. I took his watch and threw it into a bush at the bottom of the wadi. That's a sort of dry valley – they run all about the grassy plains behind Anzio. He'd told me that both his parents were dead. I just hoped there wasn't someone who would have been comforted by that watch.'

'Then I started to walk away... out of the valley, out of the fighting... out of my life as Michael Trebor. I didn't really know what I was doing. I only knew I couldn't stand it any more. One of my best friends had shot himself the day before. His nerve had gone. I buried him. You never saw anything so silly as a war. Failure of communications. Stupid decisions. A nightmare of destruction and waste. It never stopped you see, the Spandau-ripple, the Bren-crackle, the mortar-rattle, the screech of tracer bullets. It got so that I couldn't stand the din. Even now I dream that I'm back there...' Maurice's hands had begun to shake as he talked.

I put one of mine over both of his and said, 'It's all right. I can imagine.'

'I walked for days. I didn't bother to hide from the Jerries. It wasn't death I was running from. I thought, If I'm shot or blown up that will settle everything. I walked until the sounds were faint and the sky was dark and then I lay down and slept the first decent sleep I'd had for months. The sun was high in the sky when I woke up and I was desperate with thirst. There was a muddy trickle of a stream nearby and I knelt down and drank from it like a dog. When I looked up I got a shock. A German soldier, helmetless and with a bandaged head, was standing on the other side of the stream gaping at me in terror. He said something, which I didn't understand, and put his hands in the air. Then I saw that he had no gun. Perhaps he had fallen off the back of a transport lorry . . . I'll never know. He fell on his knees and wept. I looked at him for a bit and then I threw my rifle over the stream. It landed at his side. I said something like, "It's yours, I've killed my last human being. Good luck to you." Then I turned my back on him and walked off. I expected him to shoot me. He looked crazy with fright. But I never looked round and I never heard a shot.

'I carried on moving south. The Italians had got rid of Mussolini by then and come on to our side. They hated the Germans so much they were pleased to help me. They gave me lifts and food and clothing. I was tanned by the sun. I could pass in a crowd for an Italian peasant. After eight days the landscape started to take on the burnt look of the South. I told myself I was a deserter but I felt no shame. I'd fought because of my comrades in the battalion. When they were dead I had nothing left to fight for. England meant nothing to me. It had no reality at all.

'When I got to Calabria I thought I'd try to find some work and stay there for a bit. I didn't want to – couldn't – think further ahead. It was then that I saw Lucia with her goats and I fell in love with her, I think, at first sight. I told her soon after we met about Fabia and you girls. I did a lot of crying then.

'When the war ended, a year later, I knew I ought to get a message through to Fabia. Technically speaking, I was a deserter but in the mental state I was still in at that time I didn't think I'd be sent to prison. I meant to, but the months passed and I did nothing about it. I was a coward. I knew she'd be disgusted by my desertion. Fabia had imbibed all that heroic claptrap from her father.'

'I do see. Poor Fabia. How angry she'd be if she knew! And dreadfully humiliated. Are you going to tell her?'

'I don't know. Honesty bids me confess but kindness is, perhaps, a better thing than honesty. I can't think that she'd be very pleased.'

'You wouldn't want to live with each other again. From what I know of the two of you it would be a disaster. And at the moment she seems quite happy. I don't know either. But what was it, for heaven's sake, that brought you here to Westray?'

'After the war finished I wrote to my brother, your uncle Oliver. I hoped he might have survived the fighting and be back in Wiltshire, where he and your aunt Nancy had had a house before the war. As you know, he went down with his ship. But that letter was forwarded to Virginia where Nancy, who had just married for the second time, was living. She wrote to me at once – a letter of the greatest sympathy and kindness. She warned me that Fabia had virtually canonised me.'

'That's quite true. But I don't think you need feel too guilty about that. Fabia has tremendously enjoyed her role as the widow of the greatest painter the world was never privileged to know.'

'Oh, yes. I can imagine.' Maurice paused. 'I don't want to run your mother down. I've behaved *very* badly to her. But a major part of my difficulty about recalling myself to life, as it were, was the question of my painting. Your mother felt keenly that painters who had no intellectual message to impart, and no revolutionary technique with which to impart it, were mere illustrators, unworthy of the name of artist. The truth is that I like figurative landscapes and seascapes. I'm simply not an innovator. I can paint competently and my paintings are, I hope, attractive, perhaps even interesting, to look at. That's all. I detested those things that I painted under Fabia's influence. They were sham bravura... mere pretension. Whenever I thought of going back and battling out the issue of what I ought to be painting with Fabia, it made me start to shake and sweat and I just couldn't do it. I couldn't stand conflict of any kind. Lucia knew that and protected me. By the time I'd got myself into a more sensible frame of mind, it was four or five years later and it just seemed better to stay where I was and continue with my present life.'

'And, of course, you loved her. Lucia, I mean. You didn't want to leave her.'

'Yes, I loved her. And no, I very much didn't want to leave her.'

I sat silent for some time after this, trying to put myself into everybody's state of mind and then finally exploring my own. I saw that the truth of it was that he had come to dislike Fabia, perhaps even to hate her. I knew from my own experience how terrible it was to hate the person to whom you were bound by marriage, children and society. 'I understand why you didn't come home. I know you didn't intend to reject Beatrice and me.'

Maurice lifted my hand to his lips and kissed it. 'Thank you for that. Nancy and I kept in touch. She sent me photographs of you both... as babies, schoolgirls, students and, later, married women with your husbands and your children. I've still got the poem you copied out for her, when you won the school poetry competition, do you remember? She sent me every scrap about you girls that she could lay her hands on. Then, when Jack died, she wrote to tell me how worried she was about you. You had so much responsibility to bear. She sounded frantic. I knew when I got Nancy's letter that I must come and see for myself whether I could be of help. I couldn't bear the thought that all the men in your life had let you down so very badly. When I walked through the front door that first evening and saw you standing there – my own dear girl – I very nearly broke down and confessed it all then and there. But I was too frightened. And then I found, to my amazement, that not only could I be useful in some small degree but that here was everything I wanted. It hardly seems right that I should be in such a blessed position after being such a... scoundrel.'

'Oh, let's try to forgive ourselves! If you knew how

guilty *I* feel about Jack! Let's agree not to allow past mistakes to spoil the rest of our lives. It can't be undone, after all.'

'Shakespeare said, "To mourn a mischief that is past and gone / Is the next way to draw new mischief on." We can make a bold attempt, anyway. I don't want anything to spoil the happiness of having found you again. My darling daughter.'

I slept profoundly and dreamlessly that night, and when I awoke I felt happier and more at peace than I had for years. The first thing I did was run downstairs and telephone Beatrice. I told her that something wonderful had happened but that she must come herself to hear what it was. I wanted Maurice to tell her himself. She said she would leave at once and that she had some good news, too. Roger was away so the timing was excellent. She sounded excited.

When I told Rose she was extraordinarily calm. 'So that was it. "Lord shew us the Father and it sufficeth us." St John, fourteen, eight. Not quite what was meant. A deserter, eh?' Rose laughed suddenly. 'Your mother would be mad as fire if she knew.' I left her to drink her tea.

When I came back half an hour later to dress her she said that she was too tired to get up. 'The Lord giveth and the Lord taketh away,' she said, fixing me with her eyes. 'You've got your man now, though it wasn't what I thought.'

When I asked her if she wanted to see Maurice, she said that she had had enough of men.

'But wouldn't it be a good idea if I asked Rory McCleod to call? He might be able to prescribe something to make you feel stronger. Perhaps you've got an infection?'

But Rose refused to see him either. Maurice said that, in his opinion, I ought to respect her wishes. I told myself that this was a temporary tiredness, natural in one of eighty-six, and that in a few days she would be up again and sitting in her chair.

Beatrice stayed with us for nearly two weeks. As soon as she arrived, in the early afternoon, I sent her into the library where Maurice was waiting for her. The door remained closed for two hours. I hoped that the explanations were easier for Maurice the second time. I knew my sister well enough to be confident that her gentle nature would immediately find grounds to exonerate him.

We went, the three of us, for a long walk by the sea. Maurice strode along between us and we each held an arm. We had already told him so much about our lives before we knew that he was our father that further explanations seemed unnecessary. Instead we talked about trivial things, made jokes, teased each other. The wind was strong and playful, whipping the waves into slippery sequins of platinum. Maurice stopped suddenly, struck, he told us, by a new colour in the water he had never noticed before, a slinky silver jade like a mermaid's tail.

'"Sabrina fair / Listen where thou art sitting..."' he began.

'"Under the glassy, cool, translucent wave..."' Beatrice and I joined in, and the three of us solemnly chanted the invocation to the wild, incurious sea, and the years of absence were, for the time, blown by the wind out of existence.

After tea Maurice, the children and I worked on the shell grotto, while Beatrice sat with Rose. As I stood on the step-ladder, pushing scallop shells into wet concrete over the door lintel, I wished very much that things could stay just as they were. But, of course, they didn't.

Three days after my sister's arrival I sat down with her in the kitchen to sew name-tapes on to new summer shirts for Henry. Sukie lay on my knee, purring and trying to chew off the buttons.

'I think Rose is dying,' I said, pushing the needle through the thick Aertex.

'I'm afraid she is, darling.' Beatrice put her hand across the table to rest it on mine. 'I know it will be hard for you. Oh, don't think that I don't love her too, but I wasn't so dependent on her. For one thing, I had a big sister five years older. You always took such good care of me. And then I was closer to Fabia than you were. You mustn't mind my saying that.'

I didn't mind. It was perfectly true. Beatrice's nature was much more compliant than mine, and when we were young Fabia had been proud of the pretty younger daughter. Once Beatrice had put on weight in her early twenties she had joined the common throng in being the butt of constant criticism of the most negative kind, but Beatrice was endlessly forgiving.

'Of course we can't be certain that she is dying as she won't see a doctor. Perhaps,' I looked over at her empty chair, 'she may rally. There isn't anything really wrong with her, apart from tiredness.'

'Perhaps she will.'

But Rose never came downstairs again.

After this conversation I telephoned the surgery and hired a night nurse for her. During the day, Beatrice, Jenny, the children and I took it in turns to sit with her. James and Henry, though male, were acceptable to Rose. Often we read aloud to her from her beloved Bible. She drank and ate a little less each day, but she never complained of pain. On the seventh night of her decline I was aroused by a tapping on my door. The nurse told me that Miss Ingrams was asking for me.

I sat by her, holding her hand. The other hand smoothed and pleated and plucked at the sheet folded across her. Her eyes were open. I had noticed the day before that they had become very large and almost blue. She fixed them on my face and, after a minute, the expression of bafflement cleared. 'Miranda!' she said, with an inflection of pleasure, as though I had just returned after a long journey although I had, in fact, kissed her goodnight less than two hours ago.

'Yes, darling, I'm here.'

'I must tell you . . .' She looked bewildered again. 'Your father . . . No, not that. It isn't the children . . . Ah, I remember. That man.'

'Yes, Rose? Which man?'

'You know.' She looked at me with fierce eyes. 'Him.'

'Jack?'

Rose nodded and closed her eyes with a sigh of exhaustion. After five minutes had passed without her stirring I got up to go back to bed, thinking she had fallen asleep. Rose's eyes opened. 'Jack. Must tell you.'

'Yes, Rose? What about him?' I leaned my good ear close to her mouth so that she need not raise her voice.

'I don't know... Oh, yes, Jack... "When the wicked man... turneth away from his... wickedness that he hath committed and doeth... that which is lawful... and right..."' She paused, panting, exhausted by the struggle to speak. I waited and at last the words came. ' "He shall save his soul alive." '

I leaned forward again. 'Are you saying that God has forgiven Jack?'

'No.' Rose shook her head slowly from side to side and frowned. 'He... has... forgiven... me.' For some time she moved her lips but I could not hear what she was saying.

'Of course He has,' I said, stroking her thin arm, which lay on the coverlet. 'You've lived a better life than anyone. Dearest Rose. What would I or Beatrice have done without you?'

Again Rose frowned. 'No. God... forgive... me! I wanted... He was going to... ruin your life...'

I began to have a terrible fear of what Rose was going to say. She moved her lips and I thought I saw her form the word 'cartridge', but it may have been my imagination. She stared at me with her large, filmy eyes and smiled then closed them. I sat with her until dawn, but she was now so deeply asleep that the nurse said she was in a coma.

We sent for Rory now that her dignity was beyond being wounded. He lifted her eyelids and felt her pulse. 'It may be any time. One can't say. It will be very peaceful.'

He went away. I had scarcely spoken to him, except to say hello and goodbye.

For two days Rose lay in profound sleep, her breaths coming at longer and longer intervals. Then at dawn, on the tenth day, I noticed a different sound at the end of every breath. A sort of dry rasping. I sat, listening to the increasingly laboured sighings, and watched her face intently. The expression of habitual severity had gone. She looked younger, defenceless as she had never looked in life. Her eyelids began to flicker. I bent over her. 'Rose, darling, I'm here,' I said, very low.

She turned her head slightly towards me and opened her mouth very wide. I took hold of her face between my hands and in one moment the colour fled from it like a racing tide, and she was gone.

CHAPTER 27

Rose's funeral was so different from Jack's that we were spared many painful recollections. For one thing the weather was glorious, the first really hot day of the year. The congregation was small, consisting of all of us from the house, as well as Patience, Lissie and Maeve, and a few of the village people who remembered the charitable acts of Rose's younger days. Rose had not wanted a large circle of acquaintance. She had not the confiding spirit essential for the making of women friends.

That Rose had died peacefully at a great age made this funeral distinctly unlike the other. There was a sense of fitness in her passing. Though I missed her, of course, she had been withdrawing from me slowly over several months. Her willingness to go and the easy way in which she had slipped out of life were the greatest consolation. I could not feel that her dying was a sorrow to her. She was buried next to Jack. Wherever she now was, in heaven or oblivion, it could no longer matter to her that he had been a much hated man.

I never spoke to anyone about our last conversation. Rose might have been deluded or I might have misunderstood her. It would not help the children to believe that Rose had murdered their father. Though at the time of Jack's death I had worried obsessively about the cause and manner of it, I realised now that, as absolutely nothing could change the fact that he was dead, our energies were better spent on living as well as we could in the circumstances in which we found ourselves.

After the funeral the children made the grave beautiful with armfuls of roses from the garden. I talked about her with Maurice and Beatrice, digging in the past for every scrap of Rose that lingered in my mind and I hope that we did justice to her memory.

Soon afterwards Beatrice went home. Roger had been given a job at the local comprehensive teaching handicrafts. Now it had the loftier title of Craft and Design. Beatrice said that one of the things she was most looking forward to was buying a loaf of bread instead of making it herself.

'But you make it so beautifully!' I protested. 'And it's much better bread than anything you could buy!'

'I'm just fed-up with spending so much thought and time on boring old survival. I want to go to the supermarket and have it all done in an hour so that I can think about other things. I've been making four loaves a week for years. I want a washing-machine. It takes me three hours every week to wash our clothes by hand. The sheets drip everywhere. I'm sick of it. Of course, I know I can't have everything at once. We'll still be hard up but it won't be the absolute bread-line poverty it's been up to now, when I had to think whether we could afford to buy a bar of beastly carbolic soap. I'm going to put aside so much a week for the washing-machine.'

This gave me a great deal to think about. As I had only ever been once to Beatrice's house, I had had no idea that things had been so difficult, though I knew that Beatrice's share of the Christopher Chough money had run out several years ago. I didn't go there because there wasn't room for everybody, and I hadn't wanted to leave Rose with the responsibility of running the house as well as looking after the children. Also, Roger was touchy and difficult, and resentful of what he sneeringly called Beatty's grand relations. I had tried hard to make friends with him, but he was determined that we could have no common ground. Fabia had put his grumpy hostility down to the sensitivity of the artistic temperament because it never occurred to her that anyone might not want her patronage. As we waved Beatrice goodbye, watching her van crawl lopsidedly down the drive, Maurice turned to me and said, 'Let's play fairy godmothers! Come with me into Marshgate and help me choose a washing-machine!'

Which is what we did. The man in the electrical-goods department of Braithwaite's promised to have the model we chose sent to Devon immediately. I bought a box of really good soap from the cosmetics counter and posted it to Beatrice myself later that day. Maurice bought crabs and turbot and brown shrimps from the little fish stall near the pier, while I bought a large piece of *dolcelatte* from the new Italian delicatessen and, with asparagus and lettuce from the garden, we assembled a delectable supper, which helped to distract me from the diminution of our family circle. After supper we listened to Henry's speeches while we made props for the pageant, and Dinkie and Sukie crunched noisily through the shrimp heads. James wrapped Ivor's crook in foil, Elizabeth and I made pilgrims' hats out of felt and scallop shells, and Maurice struggled with the Bishop's mitre. The finished result was magnificent, very tall and shaped like the prow of a ship, gorgeous in silver lamé and gold braid. When he tried it on for effect, he was disconcerted by the immediate explosion of mirth it provoked. 'I don't want the entire audience laughing fit to bust at the solemn moment of the blessing of the well. Perhaps I'd better make it smaller.'

We reassured him that it was only the juxtaposition of mitre and pink bow-tie that made it look ridiculous. I think also it was the strain of the past few days that made us closer to either laughter or tears.

The pageant proved to be an absolute godsend. Work makes a callus to grief as someone – I think it was Cicero – said a very long time ago. In my role as wardrobe mistress I had more to do than I could possibly manage, even with the capable help of Patience. Though Lissie had a role as the Fair Maid of Kent, her part was short, requiring her to simper up at the Black Prince, look gratified by his manly attentions, and prate about her maiden modesty... rather implausibly, I pointed out, as this was her second marriage, but Aubrey said that another change to the script might well see the departure of what little remained of his reason and would I mind keeping this piece of information to myself.

So Lissie lent us a competent hand, and we spent many hours stitching and gossiping about Patience's forthcoming marriage and Lissie's baby. Stew Harker was the Black Prince, to be clad in cunningly painted corrugated cardboard. He was, Lissie said, embarrassingly uxorious. I warned her not to tell Jenny, who seemed rather silent and tense, these days, and not in a fit state to see the joke.

I had given a lot of thought to the problem of Jenny. She now went to the Harkers' as often as she could, leaving Bridie with us. Mrs Harker – put out, I imagine, to find her own charms overlooked in favour of Stew's sexual attractions – commented on this frequently and unfavourably, chiefly because of the strain it put on the privy, which was already oversubscribed. I loved Bridie, but I found that I was scarcely able to run the house, shop, cook, look after guests, make costumes and take care of a baby as well. I came to the conclusion that we should offer Jenny a permanent home with us. If she felt more settled she might be willing to devote more time to Bridie. I consulted Maurice, and he agreed that if I was sure I wouldn't regret the decision it would be the best thing for Bridie. He offered to set up a trust for her so that she would have the same education as my own children.

I told Jenny this one afternoon, on one of the few occasions she was with us, helping to dye yards of white fabric suitably dark shades to represent fustian. I had thought she would be overwhelmed by this generosity on Maurice's part, and at the chance of being adopted by the Stowe household. But she appeared to be anything but enraptured with the idea. She promised to think about it, then slipped away as soon as she could without saying anything more. I did feel a little hurt and disappointed, but I told myself not to be childish.

For several days Jenny was very quiet and I wondered if she had forgotten all about the proposition. But one afternoon, when I was sitting alone in the drawing room, she came in, followed by Stew. I had been arranging flowers and was overwhelmed by a sudden feeling of tiredness. I sat down opposite the window that looked down to the sea. Staring at the bright, white sunlight on the watery horizon had brought me near to sleep. I opened my eyes with a jerk to see them standing before me, hand in hand, full of portent.

'Sorry if we woke you,' began Jenny, 'but we thought it were only fair to let you know as soon as we'd made up our minds.'

'What?' I said feebly, hopelessly disorientated.

'Stew and me, we've applied for a house.'

'A house?' I shook myself properly awake. I was being dreadfully stupid.

'Yes. Them new council houses at the end of the village. As a couple with a baby we get priority.'

'You're going to move into a council house?'

'That's right,' said Stew, with a suggestion of belligerence. He was a natural bully, I thought, looking at him with his chin stuck out and his arm possessively about Jenny's shoulder.

'But...' I tried to pull my thoughts together. 'What about Bridie?'

'She'll have a home with her mum and her step-father. Stew and me's going to get married at Christmas. No need to worry about her.'

I wondered quite why I was picking up a faint degree of hostility from Jenny. Maurice said afterwards that it was only because Jenny herself had doubts about whether she was doing the best thing for the child. I expect he was right.

'You don't think Bridie might be... happier with her brothers and sister?'

'She'll have them soon enough, I dare say.' Jenny blushed. 'Anyways, she's too young for your children. They'll be grown up by the time Bridie can play properly.'

I couldn't deny this. What I really felt was that by living with us Bridie would have all the advantages of education, money and privilege, but naturally it was impossible to say this. At least, I found it impossible. It sounded so appallingly snobbish and unkind that I couldn't even begin to hint it.

'She'll have all the love she could want and that's what matters,' said Jenny, as though sensing everything I could not bring myself to say. 'I thank you kindly for everything you've given us and for offering to keep us both, but when all's said and done I don't want to be beholden and nor do I want to live all me life with folks who are cleverer and smarter than me. I'll be bound you'd want Bridie to do everything your way, like, sooner or later. And I should hate for to find that Bridie looked down on me when she grew up. What's she to think if you've give her a posh education and then she has to come home to me? She'd be right ashamed of me.'

'Oh, Jenny!' This all seemed so sad and so senseless that I felt tears of disappointment come into my eyes.

'Don't think I don't feel your goodness.' Jenny's tone was softer. 'I know right well what I owe you. But it isn't comfortable to be grateful all the time.'

'Oh, but you've helped me so much!' I cried, ashamed that I had made this poor girl feel so burdened. 'I needed you just as much as you needed me. You've worked so hard!'

'I done me best. But if I worked all day and all night, too, I shouldn't feel right. Every stitch Bridie and me's got on comes from you or Mrs Partridge. I want a proper job so as I can buy me own things. Oh, I wish I could make you see!'

The sudden desperation in her voice made me realise how Jenny was divided. I got up and, despite the lowering presence of Stew, hugged her. 'I do understand and I think I'd probably feel just the same. It's a very proper pride and I respect you for it. If we've been insensitive, please try to forgive us. Now, whatever you decide, I want you to feel that we *are* your friends.'

For a moment Jenny clung to me. I knew it would not be long before Stew had worn away this good feeling between us with more bitter doctrine of the 'us and them' kind.

'She'll be packing up and leaving today.' Stew's voice was chilly. I could see he was enjoying himself in the role of twentieth-century Sea Green Incorruptible. 'Me brother's gone up north on a job for six weeks so Ma says we can have his room till the council house is ready.'

On the strength of the previous moment's good understanding, I persuaded Jenny to stay with us until after the weekend so that she would have time to buy a second-hand cot and bedclothes for Bridie. I wanted to lend her ours but she was adamant that she didn't want them. 'All that embroidery and stuff, them things is too fine. I should worry about spoiling them in the wash.'

'You'll take the clothes Mrs Partridge gave you? I think she'd be terribly hurt if you didn't.'

'Well, I wouldn't want to hurt her feelings. All right, I'll take them.'

'Good. Well, that's settled, then.' I attempted to lighten the atmosphere. 'How exciting for you to have your own house. I hope you'll let me come and visit you.'

'You can come if you want,' said Stew, with the face of a tumbrel driver. 'It's a free country. I dare say you won't want to come too often.'

'Stew! That isn't very hospitable! Course you can come, Miranda, and right welcome, too.'

Afterwards, discussing it with Maurice, we agreed that

gratitude was a heavy weight to bear unless there was love on both sides. Our anxiety on Bridie's behalf would have to be endured with resignation and discretion. Mrs Harker had raised six children without actual mishap. Probably for a little while there would be a struggle between Jenny's ideas, as instigated by us, and Stew's own notion of what was right, culled from his childhood experiences. I did not doubt that the Harker method would prevail.

Lissie was horrified when I told her of Jenny's plans. 'Surely you can do something! They'll smack her and shout at her and smoke all over her and give her chips instead of a bottle!'

'Darling, apart from the chips, perhaps, you could be describing any household of any social group in the land. It isn't only the poor who smoke and smack. And if that's all she has to put up with it won't be so bad. It will be what's familiar. Jenny's her mother and she has every right to bring her up as she chooses.'

'I can't bear it!' Lissie burst into tears. 'My little darling with those . . . criminals!'

'I wouldn't worry,' said Elizabeth, scornfully, who happened to be within earshot of this conversation. 'Stew Harker will soon get tired of nappies and broken nights. He'll get Jenny pregnant again and then push off with someone else.'

When I thought about it, I came to the conclusion that Elizabeth was probably right.

I bade Jenny a sorrowful farewell on Monday morning. When it came to getting into Stew's rusting Ford Capri, her stern little face broke into tears, much to Stew's evident annoyance. I reminded her several times that she was only moving to the opposite end of the village and could come back to see us at any time. I was very near to crying myself as I kissed Bridie goodbye but remembered that this must be seen, for Jenny's sake, as an exciting venture into maturity. I finished my breakfast alone in the kitchen, which seemed almost frighteningly silent. Rose's empty chair and Bridie's empty cot brought my spirits low. I reminded myself that my three children and my father were upstairs, and that I was surrounded by those most dear to me.

Ivor came in just as I was reflectively crunching up the last crust of toast.

'Hello, my sugarplum. You look sad,' he said, pouring himself a cup of tea from the pot that stood on the warming plate of the Aga.

He, on the other hand, looked happier than I had ever seen him. His hair was brushed, which was unusual, and his clothes reeked of incense.

'I was feeling a little glum. For no good reason. How good it is to see you! We haven't had a proper talk for weeks.'

'No. We've both been busy and the house always has so many people in it.'

'Suddenly it feels a bit empty. And no guests for a while. I've stopped taking bookings until after the pageant. There's too much to do. Maurice suggested that I should give it up altogether as he wants to give Beatrice and me a present of money. To make up, he says, for all the years when he didn't support us. I don't think he'll ever stop feeling guilty.'

'Perhaps not,' said Ivor, in a rather absent tone. I wondered whether he had a poem coming on. These days he was very consciously the Artist. 'Actually, there was something I wanted to talk to you about. I've fallen in love.' He looked at me and assumed an expression that some might have called soppy. I certainly felt the temptation. His vision seemed to be filled with bright circling stars.

'Ivor! How wonderful!'

It would have been unkind to point out that he had told me at least once a week for the last fifteen years that he was in love with me. Ivor seemed to recall this as I sat, looking, I hoped, encouraging.

'For me, you will always be a beautiful dream that could never become real. You never returned my love. But Maeve has shown me what a man and a woman can feel for each other. I've written a poem about it. It's my longest so far.' He handed me a thick roll of paper.

'Thank you. Goodness, it is long! I'll read it later, when I'm a little more awake.'

'I must say, I was terrified at first. Maeve is a very powerful woman. I've been celibate for twenty years. But she persuaded me that I needed to experience physical love in order to be able to write truly organic poetry. It was a revelation! You don't mind me confiding in you about these things?'

'Not a bit.' This was more or less true.

'I realise now that I've been asleep all these years. Maeve has brought me to life. What an extraordinary intelligence! Truly synoptic! We were talking last night about forming a kind of pantisocracy, along the lines described by Coleridge. You remember?'

'Dimly. Everyone to be boss. A sort of Communism without the police state. I see the system breaking down rather badly when it becomes time to empty the latrines.'

'We thought we might go somewhere wilder. Kent is a little too tame. Wales, perhaps.'

'You may find Wales rather more crowded, these days,' I murmured.

'Well, that's in the future. But for now, what I wanted to tell you was this. Maeve has asked me to move in with her. I've been so grateful to have my lovely cottage all these years, Miranda, my darling. You've saved my sanity, you know that, don't you?' He leaned forward and took my hand. 'But now I want to explore a different way of life. Oh, I'd like to go on working here for the time being, if you still want me. I don't expect to make much money from my poetry yet.'

'Of course I want you to stay working here. I'll never find anyone half as good to replace you. And, anyway, I should miss you terribly. We've been good friends for such a long time.'

'Oh, haven't we!' he agreed, but I could see that his mind was not entirely on the conversation.

'Good morning, Miranda, Ivor.' Maurice saw our

clasped hands and politely averted his eyes. He filled a cup with coffee and cut some bread for toast.

'I must be off.' Ivor stood up. 'There's a poem here you might care to cast your eye over, Maurice. You know how I value your opinion.'

'It will be a pleasure,' said Maurice, bowing from the waist, very stately in his dressing gown and pyjamas. 'That seemed a conversation infused with emotion,' he remarked, after Ivor had gone. 'Shall I keep my long nose out of it?'

'Oh, no. It was only that he wanted to tell me that he's going to live with Maeve. He seems terrifically happy.' I paused. 'It's just the thing for him, actually. He's been sadly short of female companionship, apart from me, all these years.' I paused again and Maurice, with a slice of toast in one hand and a plate in the other, looked at me and raised one eyebrow. 'The cottage will always be there if he needs it. If they fall out or anything.'

'Very kind and wise. So why the march-to-the-scaffold expression?'

'Was I looking like that? Well, it's mean and selfish but I slightly had the feeling that all the people I used to rely on, and who used to rely on me, have found someone else. I'm ashamed to admit to a feeling of redundancy. It seems very petty of me and, of course, in one way I'm absolutely delighted. Patience will have Aubrey, Lissie will have her new baby, and Maeve and Ivor will have each other. Rose has God, and Jenny and Bridie have... oh dear, the Harkers.' I got up and embraced him. 'Do you know, if I didn't have you, I should be in despair. The children will, very properly, grow up and go away with other people, who will be much more important to them than I am. I'm sorry to be so egocentric, but if it weren't for you I think I'd be very depressed. But we can be very happy together, can't we?'

'Well, I'm glad to be of use. Now, sit down, darling, and compose yourself while I make some more toast. This piece is covered with fluff from your jersey.' He cut more bread and made fresh tea, while I sat obediently and tried not to look mopish. 'Now, my love, listen to me. I hope that you and I will spend much of however many years remain to me in each other's company. But you are still a young woman and there's to be no question of you tying yourself to me. At my age I'm quite content to stand in the wings and hold the towel. You must and will find someone your own age to make a proper life with.'

'Oh, no! That isn't what I want at all!'

Maurice held up his forefinger. 'I don't want filial disobedience. My mind is made up.'

'Well,' I couldn't help laughing, 'we'll see.'

'Good. Now we must prepare ourselves for a visitation. No less a personage than the great film director Presley O. Powlburger has written saying that he wants to see how his commissioned seascape is coming on. He'll be in England in two weeks' time. What do you think? Should we ask him to stay here or recommend the Magpie and Stump?'

'Two weeks? That'll be the time of the pageant. Still, if there's only one of him that ought to be all right. He isn't bringing a retinue?'

'No. His wife is visiting relatives in London.'

We agreed that Maurice should send him a letter of invitation to stay at Westray. Later, as it was a lovely day of the balmiest kind, we took a picnic lunch to the beach while Maurice made some painterly notes for the great work. It was relaxing to sit eating hard-boiled eggs, cold chicken and tomatoes with the customary seasoning of sand while the wind blew salt from the sea into our faces. I watched the children running into the waves with the usual shrill screams of those in the embrace of the North Sea. James, after swimming so far out that my eyes watered trying to keep track of his head in the glittering liquid silver, flopped beside me on the rug and towelled himself vigorously.

'I feel better for that. I don't know why you don't swim every day. You'd be so fit.'

'It probably has something to do with the fact that it's

icy cold, full of jellyfish and dangerous currents, probably sewage as well, and I'm too busy.'

'When these exams are over I think I'll get a job doing something outdoors. Felling trees or building dry-stone walls. I won't want to look at a book for months.'

'Have you changed your mind about staying on for a seventh term and trying for Oxford?'

'I don't know. Is that fruit cake? Yes, please. It all depends on how well I do.'

'But you've worked so hard! Of course you'll do well!'

'That's it, you see. The expectation is that I'll succeed. But it's all in the doing. All the work I've done doesn't mean a thing unless during those hours of the examination I get it all out on to paper. It's perfectly possible that my mind might suddenly go blank.'

'It won't do that, darling. I have every confidence in you.'

'That's what makes it so bloody terrifying.'

'Oh, James! I see what you mean. That was silly of me –' But he'd already got up and gone down to the sea's edge where Henry was trying to throw pebbles to make them bounce on the water. While Maurice sketched and the children swam or read, I dozed uncomfortably beneath the sandy, damp picnic rug with a vague sense of disquiet hovering about my dreams. I awoke to hear the triumphant shouts of the children as the tide crept into the moat of a magnificent sandcastle James had helped Henry to build. It was turreted and crenellated and garrisoned with razor shells for soldiers. Maurice had contributed three painted paper banners, which flew from sticks, and even Elizabeth had roused herself from sunbathing to gather seaweed and shells for decoration. I joined them to watch the scum-flecked brown water lick the sides of the moat and nibble at the base of bridges and dams.

'Henry, it's the best castle you've ever made,' I said, enthusiastically. 'I wish I'd brought my camera. This barbican's brilliant!'

'James did that,' said Henry, with something of a sulky note. 'I only wanted to make something small and simple but everyone insisted on helping me, pretending it was for my sake but really because they were enjoying it.'

'Shall I throw you on top of it then?' James picked him up over his shoulder. 'We'll squash it flat, shall we?'

'Ow! No! You're tickling me! Stop!' giggled Henry. 'Don't! No!'

'Say you're grateful to us for helping you, then.'

A fight developed, which Henry adored. He and Jack used constantly to have mock fights. I was glad to see that James was old enough to take his father's place with Henry. James lacked Jack's sadistic humour, though. Jack thought morality was hypocrisy. I saw that James would be a better guide. We left the beach as it began to grow cold, a flock of seagulls falling on the remains of the chicken and bread which we had spread on a rock above the incoming tide.

'You look very cheerful, Elizabeth,' I said, as she stood at the sink, washing her hands before supper.

'I had a nice ride with Puck. He went really well today. He is getting rather small for me, though. What a good thing we can keep him fit driving. I couldn't bear to sell him.'

At the time, I accepted this as the explanation for Elizabeth's remarkably high spirits that evening. She was looking particularly pretty and rather grown-up, with her flaxen hair in a single plait and a reasonable amount of makeup. She wore a new dress, which Maurice had bought for her. It was scarlet, a colour I had never seen her wear before but which suited her.

'By the way,' she said a little later, cutting with her spoon into the pot of egg custard on her plate, 'I met Mrs Scranton-Jones as I rode back through the village this evening. She asked me how you were getting on and said how sorry she was to hear about Rose. She wanted to know what Rose had died from. I said it was tiredness.'

'That woman is an appalling gossip-monger,' I said. 'It really is indecent.'

'She asked if Rory had looked after her. According to

her, he's got a new job. She didn't say where. And he's broken off his engagement to Annabel Vavasour.'

CHAPTER 28

'Maurice, this is terrific!' Presley O. Powlburger scrutinised the enormous seascape. 'You've got it! The violence! The implacability! Shakespeare's rough, rude sea! I knew I wasn't mistaken in you! This is passion!'

Maurice and I stood a little behind the film director as he strode up and down the floor of the coach-house, arms spread wide, cigar in mouth, head thrown back. Presley, as he had told us to call him, was scarcely five feet tall, with a balding cranium edged with black curly hair and a long, fat nose, a bulging stomach and ridiculously short legs. But when you saw his eyes, keen, dark and intelligent, you forgot to think him a figure of fun.

'When I saw those little paintings of yours, Maurice, in that gallery in Albemarle Street, I said to myself, "This guy's got more to give." Accomplished they were, passionate they were not! I thought, What this guy needs is scope! Make it big! Make it audacious! Give this guy a chance to loosen up. Movement. Yep! Was I right?'

'Well, I'm glad you like it...' Maurice began diffidently.

'Like it! I don't *like* it, Maurice! No, that's not a word in my vocabulary. I'm crazy about it! If I'm not crazy about something, it goes out! There's no time for liking and so forth. A thing's got to speak to me here!' He thumped his chest with a violence that might have disrupted the heart rhythms of a lesser man. 'Or I'm not interested!'

'Of course, it isn't finished.'

'Finished? A work of art is never finished, Maurice. You don't need me to tell you that! We send our children into the world half naked. But that's all we *can* do. When I've worked nine months on a film, I start telling myself it's time to stop. Of course I want to go on – to make it more beautiful, to make it the most perfect little film ever conceived! But I know that I'm losing something every day after that. I'm working on the surface. I'm obscuring the heart of the piece. I'm tinkering with cosmetics. The spirit of the thing is formed, inchoate as it is, and there comes a time when you have to let go. You have to say, "Go forth and be judged. *Mea culpa.*"' Presley took his cigar from his lips and stood for a moment with bowed head.

'I agree with you, Presley,' said Maurice, seizing this gap in the conversation, 'but I should like to work a little more on the –'

'Maurice, I'm not telling you your job. You go on with it. It ain't my painting yet. Not till I give you the money do I have the right to any say-so. But remember this. Any hack can paint a wave. You've got something else here – there's rage and *malocchio* here. Yes, baby, that sea's a brute!'

Over tea in the drawing room, Presley filled us in on his itinerary. While his wife, Loelia, was visiting her English cousins, which she did every year, he always made a pilgrimage to Stratford to do homage to Shakespeare. 'I believe in God because for me the words of Shakespeare are divinely inspired. Folks go on about wanting proof of the existence of another world. I tell them, "Read Shakespeare. There's your proof. No mortal wrote that poetry without help from above." I'm a simple man, Mrs Stowe, and when I see proof writ in great big letters a mile high, I'm inclined to believe it.'

'I don't believe that for a moment, Presley – that you're a simple man, I mean. Please call me Miranda.'

'Thanks for the compliment. I will. Say, this room is . . .' he kissed the tips of his little fat fingers and flung out his hand '. . . pure grace. Everything that man has to offer that's good is here in this one room. There's beauty, there's craftsmanship, there's endurance, there's comfort, there's respect. All here! I've seen some beautiful rooms in my time but generally I find they have things that ain't so good – vanity, display, artifice. What do you say, Miranda?'

'Well,' I looked round, 'I couldn't have put it better myself. There is an integrity –'

'Integrity!' Presley smote his knee. 'Is this girl a wordsmith? Spot on! And this is excellent cake! You know that?'

This gives some idea of what being with Presley was like. It was exhausting in that he subjected every small detail of his experience to intense scrutiny and evaluation in the most extravagant terms. If it was not to his liking he cast it aside and never deigned to think of it again. But his enthusiasm was unbounded, and as he was properly discriminating one felt buoyed up by his approval. He loved Westray with the sort of transports I considered quite appropriate. He was generous in praise of Elizabeth's beauty, Maurice's talent, Jasper's fidelity, Dinkie's independence, Sukie's seductive elegance and my cooking. The effect on us all was that we blossomed beneath his critical eye and made new efforts. It was exhilarating.

When Presley met Ivor in the garden on the afternoon of his arrival, it took him two minutes to extract the information that Ivor was not just a horny-handed son of toil but a great poet in the making. He made Ivor bring his collection of poetry to the house and spent two hours in the library, sipping brandy and puffing at cigars, reading it. When Ivor appeared with the logs the next morning Presley made him sit down and go through each poem line by line to make sure that he had correctly grasped the gist and to praise the felicity of Ivor's expression, or question whether it was quite what he had meant to say.

I was worried at first that Ivor might be offended by Presley's criticisms but Ivor was so pleased to find someone both patient and energetic enough to discuss his work in infinitesimal detail that he became wildly excited. Together they worried and teased phrases until they were confident that they had defined their meaning as nearly as they could.

'Say, Miranda,' said Presley, as I gave them both a glass of wine before lunch. 'This is one hell of a brain here. You know that? A classical education's hard to beat. I never had one but when I get back to the States I'm going to start with Virgil. Ivor thinks I'll find that the most accessible. I've learned something today! Wait till I tell Loelia! She's always on at me to read something else besides Shakespeare. But the trouble is I have to read all those goddamn scripts. Oh, boy! It's like eating crap. Beg your pardon, Miranda, but if you saw what stuff they turn out!'

'Will you stay to lunch, Ivor?' I asked, deciding to say nothing about the staking of the herbaceous border that had been his allotted job for the morning. None knew better than I that the muse must be coaxed and could not be commanded. 'It's early today because of the dress rehearsal this afternoon.'

Presley was on to this like a terrier on to a rat. 'You got a play on here?'

'It's a pageant. The history of Kent, with special emphasis on events that took place in this village.'

'No! By all that's wonderful! My next film's historical. Maybe I can pick up something from your pageant. What's the difference between a pageant and a play?'

'I suppose a pageant is just a representation of historical events. It has no social or philosophical argument.'

'Say, I love the way this girl talks! I get it. Mind if I come along?'

'We'd be delighted.'

I was a little anxious during lunch about what might be Aubrey's reaction to Presley's style of communication. Over the last few days Aubrey had become something of a mental wreck with the strain of production, and only Patience's support had prevented his collapse. I had not taken into account Presley's intelligence and tact. When I introduced Aubrey to Presley the former was inclined to be defensive, almost defiant about his love-child.

Presley cut short his apologies and explanations with one hand raised, like a policeman in Piccadilly Circus. 'Say no more, Aubrey. We'll just let it roll. A performance is animate. I'll just sit quietly here and enjoy this excellent cigar.' He looked around him at the blanched stone basins of the fountains, in which gigantic horses were frozen in mid-plunge and fabulous sea-creatures wallowed in air. 'You ought to restore these, you know? They were built to be enjoyed in spate. You English don't value what you've got. I guess it's because you've got so much of it.'

'I think it's money, probably,' I said, sitting down next to him with the script in my hand. Though I had rewritten the entire thing and made it easier for the cast, there were still those who could not remember a whole speech so, having more or less completed my work as wardrobe mistress, I had become Prompt.

Aubrey waved his hand as the signal to begin the pageant. Linda Mayhew, who ran the local riding school, cantered in on her white horse. She was clad in luminous yellow.

'I'm afraid the dye was rather too strong,' I murmured apologetically to Presley. He had his cigar between his teeth and his eyes narrowed against the sun, watching intently as Linda galloped a full circle and then came to a stop just in front of us.

'Dear friends!' she panted. 'Imagine, if you will, this green sward as the battlefields of Kent, this charred and hollow ruin now filled with light and life as we lay before you scenes of treachery, tragedy and glory. Here lies the foaming sea.' Linda gasped, and made a sweeping gesture in front of her that made her horse shy.

'Just a minute, Linda,' called Aubrey. 'Perhaps if you just trot in it would be better. You wouldn't be so out of breath.'

'Rather a derivative script, I'm afraid,' I said to Presley.

'*Au contraire*. I think it's very interesting.'

Linda burbled on, stumbling so many times over the word 'internecine' that I scored it from the script and told her to say 'bloody' instead.

'That'll be the third "bloody" in four lines,' she protested.

'So it will. Oh dear! Say "savage", then.' The pageant proceeded so slowly, with constant interruptions from Aubrey and me, that I forgot that Presley was there, so quiet and attentive was he to the spectacle. Three hours later George Partridge, as Charles II, knighted a kneeling Horace Birt as Sir William Wychford, and the cast lined up to take their applause.

Presley clapped louder than anyone. 'Bravo, bravo!' he called, to the delight of everyone involved. 'You people have really got something here. I don't mind telling you, I'm impressed!'

'You really liked it?' Aubrey was glowing.

'Yep! It gets my vote! There were one or two little things but I don't know if you want to pay any attention to an old Hollywood journeyman...'

'Please!' said Aubrey, eagerly.

'Right. Well, I'll have my little say-so and then you can just send me about my business.' Presley stretched up to place an avuncular arm round Aubrey's neck for a moment before stubbing out his cigar and flexing his arm muscles.

'Right,' he bellowed. 'Everyone hear me? Good. Now, everyone except the aristos dirty up. You gotta remember that there ain't no such thing as a bathroom. You stink, you crawl with lice, you never brush your teeth. There ain't no dry-cleaners. Your houses are dirty, you're cold, often hungry, you're lucky to reach forty. Most of your babies die. You kids, off with your shoes. You men, no glasses or watches.'

I was interested to see that everyone rushed to do as they were told. When I had tentatively suggested that Frank Causeman might remove his tweed cap to lend greater verisimilitude to his portrayal of Sir Thomas Wyatt, his wife had told me with cold severity that Frank was prone to chills in the head. I had pointed out that Patience had made him a perfectly warm velvet hat, complete with feather, to go with his slashed doublet and hose, but she informed me with satisfaction that the velvet had brought up his forehead in a nasty rash. Now the flat cap was gone, as were Betty Higgs's spectacles with the diamanté-speckled upswept wings and various other anachronisms that their owners had clung to with maddening intransigence.

'Now we'll start at the end and work backwards,' said Presley, striding up and down before the bedimmed crowd now gathered before him, hanging on his every word. 'That'll shake us up, make us rethink. You've got a peach of a script. Wish I had this kind of material! Right, you.' He pointed a finger at George, who was peering mournfully out between the ears of his long curly black wig, reminding me of the cartoon character, Goofy. 'That was a good King Charles. Very gentlemanly. But you ain't stepped ashore to play a round of golf. You want these folk to love you, right? Your pa has had his head lopped off! The stakes are high! You gotta appeal to the people. Hold up your head, throw out your chest. Look pleased to see 'em! And, you folks, this is your king. He's a mighty powerful man. Some of you ain't too sure about the past. You maybe had some Puritan shenanigans. Let him know whose side you're on. We don't want a bashful titter, we want a cheer! Take it away, Your Majesty!'

George drew himself up and stepped from the imaginary prow of the boat.

'Hold it! Props!' Patience ran forward. 'Now this man's got to descend with royal dignity. Stands to reason he's got to have something to descend from! It's a great moment. Get the guy a boat.'

'Boat', wrote Patience obediently on her list.

'Now, you people. Let's hear it for the future King of England!'

A cheer went up. Presley shook his head. 'You sound like a ladies' literary social. Show this man you care! You want him to love you! He can give you an earldom or have your tongue cut out! Get those heads back! Let's have it!'

A bellow rose from the crowd.

'That's more like it! Now, you're all too static. I know! We want animals! Everyone who's got a dog bring it. Unless it's a clipped poodle. Never mind if they fight. Medieval times were bloody. Anyone got a donkey? Great! Bring that. What about geese?'

It was nearly sunset before Presley had finished drilling the actors, when the children were yawning and the grown-ups inclined to be quarrelsome.

'Okay. Cut!' yelled Presley. 'That's it, folks, for today. You've done good things. I begin to think we'll see something like a show tomorrow.' Presley clapped his hands together with satisfaction. 'Now remember, everybody, acting happens in the guts! You gotta *feel* it. Say, Aub! I've just had a great idea! I want to give a party for these good people after the show. What do you think?'

'Well, it sounds a very kind and generous –'

'Great! The treat's on me! We'll have beer and wine. Champagne! Why not? I'll consult my hostess, Miranda, as to the best place to order the comestibles.'

The exhausted troupe of actors began to cheer up at the mention of free drinks.

'Excuse me, Mr Powlburger,' said Mrs Higgs, who was president of the WI and accustomed to taking the lead. 'Seeing as you're so kind as to stand us the wine and what-not, besides giving us so much of your valuable experience, I think *we* ought to supply the food. What do you say, ladies? Finger buffet, it had better be. Hands up, savouries. Now hands up, puddings.'

Thus the question of food was swiftly and expertly dealt with.

'If you'd like to have it up at the house,' I said rather diffidently, 'you'd all be very welcome.'

'Miranda, baby, that's one hell of an idea! What do you say, folks? Ain't that the nicest invitation?'

I could see that one or two of the cast, like Mrs Veal, resplendent in magenta bodice and kirtle, were torn between curiosity and hostility, but generally people seemed to be pleased by the idea.

'Hope it won't be a lot of work, Miranda,' said Presley,

as we restored our aching bodies with a bottle of Chambertin in the library before dinner. 'Maurice and I'll do the dishes after the party, won't we?'

'Don't worry,' I said, kicking off my shoes and curling up on the sofa. 'Mrs Higgs will dragoon relays of WI members to do it. I expect the house will be the cleanest it's ever been. Presley, you've geed the whole pageant up so much I'm feeling really excited about tomorrow. Imagine all those animals!'

'It'll give the whole thing zip! Free 'em up. They weren't bad, though, for amateurs, and that friend of yours, the Holy Maid was good! That girl can act!'

'I agree. She was marvellous today. I never knew she could. Do you think she could make a living at it?'

Presley laughed and shook his head. 'If I had a dollar for every time I've been asked that! The thing is that pretty girls who can act some are ten a dime. But in the movies there has to be something else... something that makes you want to go on looking at someone on the screen. And that's not good looks so much as interesting looks. You can't tell till they're on celluloid. And then even if you've got that quality you gotta have loadsa luck as well. It ain't something I'd want my best friend to go in for. No, sir!'

'I'm sorry Lissie couldn't be there today. She's the Fair Maid of Kent, very pretty and just right for the part. She had to go to London today to see her obstetrician. She's having a baby in October.'

'Loelia and I couldn't have kids. I never minded. Loelia said to me when we got told the news, "Pop" – that's what she calls me, they're my initials, see – "Pop, if you ever get glum about a little thing like that I'm going to be real mad with you. We got each other and we have a good time. It's wicked to grumble about what you can't have. We won't waste time on it." She's a girl in a million. But when I see you two, just what father and daughter ought to be, I do feel kinda envious.'

'Do remember that not every man is as lucky as I am,' said Maurice, pursing his lips and screwing up his eyes as he made a sketch of Presley. 'I've got two wonderful daughters and I don't deserve them one bit.'

Presley was on to this at once but Maurice only smiled, shook his head and wouldn't be drawn. We had decided that, in fairness to Fabia, the fewer people who knew our secret, the better. So far, only the children and Lissie had been told. Aubrey, Patience, Maeve and Ivor had, of course, been present at the *dénouement*.

'Well, if you won't talk I'll read this little book before dinner. I picked it up in the church. *A History of Westray*. When I saw my hostess had written it, I knew it was a must!'

'Oh, that's very kind of you. It's really a trivial little piece.'

Presley merely smiled, lit a cigar and began to read, frowning with concentration. When dinner was ready, he was still reading. He ate in an abstracted way, and then resumed the book over coffee in the drawing room. I was rather flattered. Maurice continued to draw and I made some last-minute alterations to Linda Mayhew's dress. When I got up at ten to go to bed, Presley waved me back into my seat with a motion of his cigar. 'Miranda, honey, you can write. No, don't let's waste time with all that,' as I began to disclaim any such ability, 'take it from Pop. He knows. I spend nearly as much time reading as directing and I tell you that actresses tumble out of our ears but writers are as scarce as rain in the desert. You know your poet, Thomas Gray?' I nodded. 'Well, he said something about "thoughts that breathe and words that burn". You gotta be able to turn a sentence that scintillates. I can't do it myself but I know it when I see it. That script was good. I don't mean okay. I mean good! This is excellent! You got any experience apart from this?'

'No. I read history at Oxford but then I got married and had children straight away.'

'Uh-huh. Well, maybe that's to the good. There's a freshness allied to intelligence that sings to me here. I'm going to take a risk, Miranda. And when Pop takes a risk, he don't often regret it 'cause it's a calculated one. How d'you like to write me the script of my next film?'

'You're not serious?'

'Never was more so.'

'But I . . .' I was nearly speechless. 'I don't know how to go about it. I hardly ever go to the cinema, these days.'

'Excellent! I don't want any fashionable imitative stuff. I want it from the bowels. I want guts, sweat, ferocity.'

'But, Presley, I'm sure I couldn't provide that. I'm the mother of three children, not an artist cruelly spurned by society and full of *Angst*.'

'Now, Miranda, you gotta get rid of these stereotypes. I eat wholesome food, don't shoot up or make love to other men's wives. That don't mean I ain't an artist. You got feelings. I got feelings. That's all it takes. That, and the skill to put 'em over. "There's the rub," as Will would say. I tell you, you got that skill! Now listen to me. I'm going to make a film that'll hurl back the boundaries. There are great steps taking place in the art of cinematography. We got new wide-aperture lenses and super-fast film so we need less lighting for a shot. I'm going to make a film with natural lighting. It's going to be eighteenth-century, the Age of Elegance, all candlelight, it's going to be exquisite. There's this kid, Fanny Burney –'

'You mean the diarist?'

'You know about her?' Presley slapped his leg with delight. 'Of course, I should've guessed. A bright girl like you. You know her novel?'

'*Evelina*, you mean? Yes. That's her best, I think, but there are three others.'

'Oh, boy! Wait till I tell Loelia about you! My idea's this. I want to make a film of her life, as lived at court with poor old, mad old George Three and show the seeds of her creative life. Evelina, you remember, is a young girl who goes out into the world and has her personality shaped up by the folk she meets. We'll relate that to Fanny Burney herself, flashes of her imagination, as she gads about the court. We'll be telling two stories interwoven, showing the creative process. It's going to be subtle. We've had enough of cowboys and bank robbers being shot to hell in slow motion. I'm going to give 'em something to think about, knock their eyeballs for six with history that looks real! It'll be beautiful and dim and dirty – like life.'

'It sounds wonderful. But I'm sure I couldn't write it. Anyway, there are the children to look after and the house to run. I couldn't just leave everything and go to America.'

'You don't have to. It's all being shot on location. In England.' He paused a moment, drew on his cigar and, as he breathed the smoke out, he fixed me with large, bright eyes that tantalised, somewhere between bewitchery and bedevilment. 'I'll make it worth your while.' He named a sum that silenced me. It was enough to keep myself, the children and Westray for at least a year.

'That figure's negotiable,' said Presley, eyeing me with obvious enjoyment. 'Upwards, naturally. I'll be honest with you, four out of five scripts don't get to be filmed. But I've a hunch about you.' I still couldn't say anything. I looked at Maurice, who was smiling. 'Don't say anything now. You sleep on it. Chew it over with your papa.'

I discussed it with Maurice the next morning over breakfast. Presley was already up and gone, having arranged with Freddy to take him to see Chartwell. He had promised to be back in time for the pageant.

'It's a ridiculous idea.' I was gloomy at the impossibility of the thing. 'I've never even had the faintest idea of writing for films.'

'That doesn't make it impossible. There's a first time for every script-writer, after all. Presley can guide you through the particular exigencies of the trade. He's looking for a writer with the feel for period. You have that.'

'So do thousands of other people,' I objected.

'Yes, but they aren't entertaining Presley O. Powlburger. There's fortuity in everything, Miranda, and when good things happen to fall into your hand it's a sin and a shame not to close your fingers over them.'

'Suppose I'm no good at it?'

'Failure has as many valuable things to teach as success. Not to make the attempt is to refuse to learn. Besides, I don't think Presley often makes mistakes. The whole film might not catch the public imagination, of course, but I think you can give him what he's looking for.'

'You think I'd be a coward to refuse?'

'That's a cruel word. I understand why your confidence is low. But there's only one way out of that. You've got to take risks.'

Since the idea of trying and failing made me squirm with horror, I was forced to conclude that he was right and that I must seize the chance of a lifetime and be damned to the consequences. All morning I walked around in something of a daze. But the sensation of terror was coupled with a growing feeling of anticipation and excitement.

The pageant was due to begin at three o'clock and to end with a procession to the church and a short service of thanksgiving at five. By lunch-time the village was teeming with impatience and agitation as the outside-broadcast van of the local television station lumbered through the village and parked itself on the lawns by the ruins. This turned out to have been Presley's idea. By half past one, several reporters were in the Magpie and Stump canvassing the regulars for their views on the pageant, their Member of Parliament, and the proper age of consent for teenage sex.

I was just about to leave the house to drive to the vicarage, which was being used as the Green Room, when the telephone rang.

'Hello, Mum.'

'James, darling! How lovely to hear you! How are you? Did you get my good-luck card?'

'Yes, it came today, thanks. I'm all right.'

A pause.

'First exam this afternoon, isn't it? Keep calm, sweetheart, and all will be well.'

'I wanted to talk to you about something...'

'Yes, darling?'

'If I fail absolutely . . . if I can't write a single word . . .'

There was another more painful pause.

'Will it matter? No! Absolutely not! Not as far as I'm concerned, if that's what you mean.' I was speaking very emphatically to conceal my growing alarm. I could hear from James's voice that things were far from well. There was a tone of anguish, which was quite unfamiliar. I suspected that he was very near to tears. 'No, darling, if that should happen, that you can't write anything, ring me up and I'll arrange something with the headmaster. You can come home and forget the whole thing.'

'Really?'

'Certainly. Then, if you want to, you can take a year off. Or go to Bosworth High and do a resit. Whatever you want. It would be so marvellous to have you at home!'

'I've been thinking a lot about Dad. I wish I'd tried harder to – I didn't give him much of a chance the last couple of years.'

'It was his mistake, too, darling.'

'Yes. Well, I'd better go. It starts in half an hour.'

'Goodbye, darling. Ring me this evening. Let me know how you are.' I waited but James didn't say anything. 'I love you very much,' I said. Then I heard him put down the receiver.

I drove down to the vicarage with a horrible pain in the region of my diaphragm. Jack had been adamant that the children should go to boarding schools but I hated them being away. I know all the arguments in favour of the system, and perhaps they do make children more independent and all that stuff, but when your child is unhappy the separation is nigh on intolerable.

Had I been positive enough? Should I ring his housemaster and ask him to keep an eye on James? It might be a betrayal of confidence. Everyone has pre-examination nerves. It was the mention of Jack that frightened me. I could do nothing at the moment. I had better wait to see if James telephoned me. If I heard nothing, perhaps it would be a good idea to go to London in the morning. Was I being over-anxious? Whatever I did, the children were bound to be miserable from time to time. Nothing could prevent that. He knew that I loved him. I must wait and see and try not to get things out of proportion.

Despite my resolution the worry nagged at the back of my mind throughout the afternoon. Fortunately for my sanity there were so many distractions that, though I never lost the sense that something was wrong, the forefront of my mind was soon absorbed with trying to find Horsa's boots and Wat Tyler's hat. When everyone was dressed, Presley arrived.

'You look a sight for sore eyes, folks! I see a pair of earrings there that ain't right. Just a minute.' He adjusted the pinning of someone's cloak. There was no detail so small that it escaped his sharp eye. Aubrey's face, eau-de-Nil with nerves, appeared round the vicarage drawing room door. 'There's a huge crowd! The entire county's here! Linda's in the saddle. Good luck, everyone.' He withdrew then, as an afterthought, he stuck his head in again. 'Beginners, please.'

The players paled beneath their mud, and their eyes glittered with fright. Even Stew looked anxious.

'Give 'em what they've come for!' roared Presley. 'You're a filthy rabble wanting to tear each other's throats out! Hengist, baby, you and Horsa here are going to send those Britons to kingdom come! Britons, you're going to kick those filthy Saxons right where it hurts! Now, get out there and let me hear it!'

The actors for the first scene clumped out. Presley grabbed Maurice's arm. 'Come on! We're going to do a little cheer-leading!' Maurice, dazzling in gold-embroidered cope and the mitre, which looked entirely magnificent as part of the episcopal ensemble, stalked majestically from the room in Presley's wake, nearly colliding with Lissie.

'Lissie! Thank goodness you're here!' I picked up her blue robe and white girdle from the chair which was labelled 'Fair Maid of Kent'. 'George has just gone to ring you. He thought you must have fallen asleep.'

'Sorry, he always makes me lie down after lunch. It's his fault.'

'Never mind. Get those things off. You're in the third scene. Pity you missed the dress rehearsal. It was so good!'

'I can see things have gone from strength to strength. All those animals look wonderful! There's a great flock of geese wandering about, looking very well behaved. And the sweetest donkey!'

'I brought heaps of chicken corn and scattered it where we want the medieval fair to be. I was worried about the geese attacking the audience. Arms up!' I threw the blue dress over Lissie's head.

'Mind my hair. I've had it done specially. Oh, Lord!'

'What's the matter?'

'I can't do it up! I must have put more weight on!'

'Nonsense! I made it with plenty of room in case. Let me!' I struggled with the hooks and eyes. There was a gap of at least four inches, and no hope of fastening it. 'What are we going to do?'

'Monks, please!' shouted Aubrey, and was gone again before I could consult him.

'I can't go out in front of all those people with my bottom showing. Someone else will have to play the part. Damn! I was so looking forward to it!'

I looked round the Green Room. Everyone there was already in costume.

'You'll have to do it, Miranda! Come on! Get those clothes off. Don't be silly,' as I protested. 'You're the only one who knows the part.'

It was quite true. Reluctantly I undressed and pulled the blue robe over my head. It was too wide, which hardly mattered as I could gather in the excess with the girdle, and about a foot too short. I was wearing flat green strappy sandals, pretty but distinctly unfourteenth century. Lissie's black pumps were at least a size too small.

'Never mind! No one will notice. Here's the veil and prayer-book. Hurry up! You're on next!' Aubrey's face appeared round the door. 'Miranda's having to stand in for me because I couldn't get into my dress. Go on, darling, you'll be terrific! Good luck.' She kissed me and whispered in my ear, 'Whatever you do, keep your mouth shut when Stew kisses you.'

The next minute I was tripping across the grass in solemn procession with my ladies-in-waiting towards the Rose Arch, an inspired creation of crêpe paper, beneath which waited Edward, Duke of Kent, the great warrior Prince. As I got closer, I saw Stew begin to smile quite unpleasantly. The priest began his solemn address on the institution of marriage and then Edward pledged his allegiance to the people. As the eldest son of Edward III, he must have looked a good marriage prospect. I had always thought it a shame about the Black Prince.

Stew did his bit quite well, with a strong local accent that was probably pretty near the way the Prince would have spoken. He had a loud voice, which even those members of the audience who were standing on school benches at the back, to get a good view, must have heard with ease. Fortunately he lowered it to say, with a rakehellish leer, at the conclusion of the ceremony, 'Come on then, Miranda, let's be having you.' I took good care to follow Lissie's advice and was thankful for the chaperonage of at least five hundred people.

The performance continued to unfold with breathtaking rapidity. Now that my brief moment in the limelight was over I relaxed and, if it had not been for unhappy thoughts of James, I would have thoroughly enjoyed the rest of the pageant, which proceeded with scarcely a hitch. There was a moment when the donkey bit the Abbot and Ivor swore very loudly in an unchurchmanlike manner but he went on with admirable *sang-froid*, though he said afterwards that he had been in considerable pain.

When Charles II stepped from his boat – a quite convincing prow knocked up hastily by the local carpenter – Presley led the crowd in patriotic hurrahs, and William Wychford rose a knight, to ringing cheers. It seemed that the clapping would never stop but at last we formed a procession to lead the way to the church. Many of the audience, to Aubrey's great delight, wanted to come, too. We were packed into the pews while others stood in the side aisles and the porch. A goose somehow found itself in the congregation and hissed so fiercely that no one dared to shoo it out. Aubrey said a prayer of thanks for village life, for all the good things of the community and for the success of the pageant, which had raised an enormous sum of money for the restoration of the roof. I added a prayer of my own for James. Then we sang the doxology with tremendous fervour.

Afterwards Miss Potter played a masterly recessional from one of Handel's oratorios. I was tremendously struck, not only by the unprecedented absence of squeaks and wrong notes but also by the musicality of the playing. 'Has Miss Potter been taking lessons?' I whispered to Patience, who was standing next to me as we shuffled slowly down the aisle. 'I've never heard her play so well.'

'Miss Potter has a poisoned finger. She rang Aubrey this morning to say she couldn't possibly play. Poor Aubrey nearly had a brainstorm but luckily he remembered that he'd heard Rory McCleod playing in here once or twice. He rang him up and Rory very decently said he'd put off going to London for a day to play for us. He plays beautifully, doesn't he? It's a pity he's leaving. I like him.'

'Leaving?'

'Oh, yes, haven't you heard? He's been offered a job in Glasgow. Just what he wanted, apparently. He told us that he's found a locum for Westray and he's going to Scotland tomorrow for good.'

CHAPTER 29

I was delighted to see Miss Horne, Jack's former secretary, in the crowd outside the church.

'Oh, Mrs Stowe, I just had to wait to say goodbye to you! It was so good of you to write and suggest that I come to your lovely pageant. I don't know when I've enjoyed anything as much.' Her handkerchief was at her eyes and she didn't appear, despite her words, to be in the best of spirits. 'Only I couldn't help shedding a tear, remembering the last time I was here.'

I put my arm through hers. 'Let's go and look at Jack's grave together.' I admired the bouquet of lilies she had brought. Beside their scented glamour a small bunch of buttercups looked mournful.

'Isn't that sweet?' said Miss Horne, bending to put them straighter on the grave. 'The dear children, I suppose.'

I felt I could not tell her about Jenny. It would be a desecration of Miss Horne's shrine.

'I'm glad I came. I feel so much better. I do miss him so terribly. Well,' she smiled brightly, practised as she was at showing a brave face to the indifferent world, which had always been so unrewarding, 'I shouldn't mention my own grief to *you*. You're an example to us all.' She pressed my hand feelingly. 'Thank you, dear Mrs Stowe. I must put my skates on and run for the bus.'

'Don't go yet, Miss Horne. We're having a party up at the house. I shall be so disappointed if you don't join us.'

'I couldn't possibly!'

'Oh, please, do come! I'll arrange for you to be driven to the station for the ten o'clock train.'

Miss Horne clasped her hands together and hunched her shoulders in fright. 'But I shouldn't know anyone. I'm not very good at parties. I'm always frightened that I'm boring people.'

I saw Aubrey walking out of the church door. I waved and beckoned to him. 'Lovely service, Aubrey. The whole thing was a brilliant success! I want you to meet Miss Horne. Miss Horne was Jack's secretary. This is Aubrey Molebank, our vicar. Aubrey, I want you to help me to persuade Miss Horne to stay for the party.'

Aubrey took in the situation at a glance. Having spent so much of his life among the lonely and unloved of his congregation, he read the signs of privation. His large, gentle eyes were full of irresistible kindness. He kept hold of her hand, having shaken it and said, 'Now, Miss Horne, Miranda's quite right. You must stay and help us. It would be so good of you. I'm supposed to take round glasses of wine and I'm terribly clumsy. I can see that you've got a steady hand.'

'Well, if you think I could be *useful*.'

'I'm sure of it. Now, I particularly want to introduce you to Miss Wakeham-Tutt.' Retaining Miss Horne's hand, he drew her over to where Patience was standing in a group of others. I thought to myself what a satisfactory man Aubrey was.

The telephone was ringing as I entered the front door.

'Come in, everyone,' I said, to those who had walked up with me. 'Abbot, will you start uncorking the wine? Bishop, the fires, please, darling. I'll just answer this.'

It was James. 'Mum, it was all right! I thought I'd better ring and tell you as I made a fool of myself this morning on the telephone. I didn't want you to worry.'

'You didn't make a fool of yourself. We can surely be vulnerable without appearing idiotic.'

'Well, anyway, when I got in there it seemed different from what I'd imagined. There was a good question at the top of the paper and once I began to think about it the ideas poured in. Actually, I think it went not too badly.'

'I'm delighted, darling, for your sake. But it really wouldn't have been the end of the world if it hadn't.'

'I got this idea that I might not be able to make my brain move my hand to write. Does that sound mad?'

'No. It sounds like the idea of someone who's been working rather too hard and getting very tense. I'm prone to this kind of irrational anxiety when I'm tired. Even trivial things become important and I'm obsessed by fears that I can't do it.'

'I'm glad I'm not the only one. I'd better go. There's the supper bell. Don't worry, Mum, I'm feeling fine. I'll come home this Saturday, if that's okay.'

'You know you don't need to ask. Goodbye, darling.'

I stood for a moment by the telephone and felt a delicious sensation of relief rush over me.

The party needed no help from me to make it a success. Alcohol lifted the euphoria generated by the success of the pageant to yet greater heights. Maurice had been very efficient in distributing candles in all the downstairs rooms, and it was bizarre and delightful to see Westray filled with soft shadows and peopled by Saxons and Jutes and Tudors and Stuarts all at once. I was the only actor in a position to change out of my costume, which I did with relief, having felt ridiculous in it. I found a blue silk dress and brushed my hair and did things to my face quite at my leisure. It was the most relaxing way to be a hostess. I could probably have gone straight to bed and not been missed.

I wandered downstairs and found Maeve the centre of an admiring circle. She broke away from her disciples to ask me if I had seen Ivor. 'He went off to feed the pony and I haven't seen him since,' she said, resentfully. Maeve was wearing her Holy Maid costume, and looked romantic and provocative at the same time. I could see why Ivor had been going around looking as though he had been struck on the head.

'Oh, that was good of him,' I said. 'Couldn't Elizabeth have done it?'

'Ivor said Elizabeth was talking to Rory McCleod. She was looking so captivated he couldn't bring himself to interrupt.'

So Rory was here. I was annoyed to feel my heart-rate break into a canter. How treacherous the subconscious was! Well, it would give me the opportunity to say goodbye.

'That was understanding of Ivor. He's the most considerate of men. You won't let him get hurt, will you? He's awfully in love with you.'

'Actually, I'm pretty in love with *him*. You're a bit too inclined to think of everybody as though they're helpless creatures in need of your protection. I feel rather insulted on Ivor's behalf. He's a very good-looking, fantastically intelligent bit of crumpet. You might as well ask him not to hurt *me*.'

'Sorry.'

'What's more, he's a marvellous lover. You never wanted to go to bed with him yourself so you assumed that he's a sort of impotent eccentric. If anyone's hurt him, it's you. He's wasted a lot of years languishing hopelessly after you, making do with a crumb of kindness from time to time, and I intend to make it up to him.' With that, Maeve walked away.

These were strong words and I must admit that, though I knew Maeve had been drinking, they cut me to the quick. Miss Horne brought me a glass of wine. She said she couldn't stop to talk as she had promised to help Mrs Higgs put sausages on to sticks. I went into the library, where Presley was holding court. He gave me a wink when he saw me and continued with indiscretions about the famous names of Hollywood before a fascinated audience. I went to sit in the oriel window. The curtain was pulled half across and I was almost entirely hidden from view.

I stared out across the moat. The sun had set and dusk cast blue shades across the black water, quaking beneath a breathing wind. Darling Westray! It was mine, and in all probability it would remain so for some time to come. I thought about what Maeve had said. Was I only able to see people as dependants on whose weaknesses I could build my strengths? I drained my glass, depressed by the suspicion that she was right.

James was all right now. That was the important thing. I had meant every word I had said in our earlier conversation about not minding if he flunked this lot of exams. It was only for his sake that I dreaded the erosion of confidence, the fearful grind of resitting the examinations. Next week I was going to Nethercoat's to see Henry in his starring role. It was unlucky that Elizabeth had fallen in love with someone else who was hopeless, but perhaps an impossible love was what she was seeking after the disastrous experiment with Johnny. She would get over it, once Rory had gone away for good. I sighed deeply.

'That sounded rather sad.' Rory was standing beside me.

'Oh!' I was embarrassed. Luckily the light was too dim to reveal my discomfiture.

'Mind if I sit here? You haven't got anything to drink.' He poured half his wine into my glass. 'I think you'd better get that down. You're looking so miserable.'

'Oh, no! I'm not miserable at all. The pageant was such a success. Presley was marvellous! And you played so well! I had no idea that you were a musician.'

'I'm very much an amateur. There's a great deal we don't know about each other.'

'And now we never will.' My voice was fatuously cheerful. 'Patience tells me that you've got the job you always wanted.'

'Yes. I'm going to help set up a new health centre in the worst part of Glasgow. We intend to run it on quite different principles from a conventional surgery. It'll incorporate an addiction clinic. We're going to treat them in the community. We'll have regular clinics for women run by female doctors. So many of the women won't seek medical help until it's too late because they don't want an unsympathetic male burrowing in their insides.'

'It must be very satisfying to feel that you're going to do something really important that will make a huge difference to people's lives. I'm going to do something quite trivial and frivolous. But perhaps that's what I'm best fitted for.'

'What's that?'

'I'm going to write a film script for Presley. About Fanny Burney. And I'm going to be paid a ridiculous amount of money for doing it. It just shows that it's an insane world and it's no good trying to make sense of it.'

'It sounds terrific! What an opportunity! Why are you running it – and yourself – down? You can't think that I imagine everyone wants to be a doctor? What's happened to upset you?'

'Nothing. I'm not upset. I'm very happy. You're quite right, actually. I do want to write this script. I've got ideas already. It will be a challenge and that's just what I need. I just got a little depressed because a friend told me some unflattering home truths. She was rather too accurate and it hurt. I think I *am* inclined to see others in terms of their dependence on me. I suppose it's because I haven't got much self-confidence.'

'You astonish me. I've always thought you more self-assured and independent than almost anyone I know. I remember when we first met –'

'I was being sick, I think. Yes, well, don't let's talk about me. I'm absolutely fed-up with the subject.'

'So you were. You were the colour of grass. And you'll never believe what I wanted to do.'

'Walk right out of the house, I imagine. You seemed to hate us all on sight.'

'And you didn't have the gumption to recognise the phenomenon. What a simple girl you are, after all.'

'I think I must be.'

'I had the most inappropriate impulse. That's why I was angry.'

'I always have a desire to laugh when you're angry.'

'Do you, you wretch?'

'That's good. Be angry now. I need to be cheered up.'

'You've asked for it. Let me pull this curtain right across. Now no one can see me be angry with you. It's very dark. I can only just see you. We might be quite alone.'

'Yes.'

'But I don't feel angry any more.'

'No.'

'Instead I – Oh, Miranda!'

'Yes?'

'I want to do something else.'

We sat in silence, looking at each other. I could dimly see his face in the glimmering light. We had been in this situation once before. For a moment I smelt again the heady scent of the night, as though we were once more standing on the terrace at Vavasour Hall. Again his head bent slowly to mine, and this time there was no interruption.

After what might have been a second or a year or any time at all, we drew apart but that was unbearable so we kissed again and yet a third time.

'Oh, Miranda!' He held me close to him. 'My darling! What are we going to do?' I could hear the thumping of his heart.

'I don't know.'

I didn't want to think about the future. I wanted to stay just as I was, sitting on the window-seat with his arms around me, weak with an extraordinary floating sensation of something like violent joy.

'Too many people's lives are involved with yours. Clearly you can't bring your children to Glasgow.'

'Oh, Rory, I don't think I could! Schools and things. They've had so much adjustment to make already.'

'Well, there's only one of me so I'll have to make the change of plan.'

'You wouldn't! You couldn't! No. That can't be right.'

'It's the only solution.'

'You mean you'd give up the job you've always wanted?'

'Can you doubt that – after what happened just now? If you feel even half of what I feel, you must see that it's a foregone conclusion. I love you, Miranda. I fell in love with you at that horrible party. But I thought you didn't care about me. We met the next day, do you remember? You were colder than the Arctic Circle. It was yet another baffling encounter. From the day we first met, when your husband was lying dead in the next room, I've wanted to tear off your clothes and make love to you. But I was sailing in unknown waters with no pilot to guide me. I've never been able to decode your signals. You seemed very English, supremely confident of who and what you were. I put you down as a rich, spoilt, upper-class bitch. Then later you seemed so.. rackety. Always in the arms of some man or other. I felt sorry for your husband. I could quite see why he might have shot himself.'

'I'd like you to know that I've had two lovers in my whole life and one of them was Jack. In these days of sexual freedom I'm practically a nun.'

Rory laughed. 'So you are, my poor darling. How I long to add a notch to the tally!'

We kissed again. I was terrified by the agony of my longing for this man. Someone somewhere had begun to sing, 'For He's a Jolly Good Fellow'. It must have been for Presley.

'But what can we do?' I murmured, as I laid my head against his chest and felt his arms tight around me. Oh, the comfort, the happiness of it! 'You know you *have* to take that job. It's exactly what you've been looking for.'

'Yes, in a way that's true. But I have to confess that I'm no longer the dedicated urbanite I was. Don't you remember telling me that the people here needed medicine just as much as the city dwellers? You were extremely annoyed. I wanted to kiss you then, even though I hated you. Now I can, I will.'

He paused to carry out the threat. Oh, don't stop! Don't stop!

'Be serious, Rory. Think how you'd resent me for making you give up such an opportunity. I'd be selfish beyond description if I let you.'

'But I've abandoned all my prejudices about Kent being a beautiful garden filled with Fortune's darlings. This morning I delivered twins to a woman whose family have lived in the same farm cottage for generations. They've just had electricity put in. In Glasgow, every tenement has had electricity for fifty years. I was a fool. I didn't know what I was talking about. Things are hard if you're poor, wherever you live. Philip Kenton's practice hasn't kept pace with the times. There's so much that I can do here to improve things. There'll be some other leech with a mission dying to take on the Glasgow job. Damn it, I like it here!'

'You're just trying to make me feel better about it. But I know what would happen. After a few months you'd start feeling restless. You'd find excuses for going up to London and getting some soot into your lungs. Then you'd meet some lovely young girl who could give you babies and dedicate her life to furthering your career. And you'll explain to me very kindly, but with your eye on the door, how it is that you find that things aren't working out with me, after all. The last thing you need right now is an affair with a widow with three children and an enormous, demanding house who's about to start her own career. You'll be furious with yourself – and me – for having been such an idiot as to give up the job you've always wanted. And I'll be –' I could not finish what I was going to say for the sensation of pain that seized me as I thought of saying goodbye to Rory after I had allowed myself to love him.

'Bloody hell, Miranda!' Even in the gloaming I could see that his face was dark with indignation. 'What sort of man do you think I am? I'm not a philanderer. I love you. You make me sound like a – like a wolf on the make.'

'You should have married Annabel Vavasour!'

'So that's it. You're jealous!'

'Yes, I am, if you want to know! She's young and hasn't got anyone hanging on to her coat-tails.'

'I don't happen to be in love with Annabel Vavasour. I knew perfectly well by that time that I was in love with *you*. I only kissed her because I didn't want her to look a fool in front of all those people.'

'Very thoughtful of you.'

'Well, I suppose you don't want to marry an absolute shit! But perhaps you don't want to marry me at all. I begin to see that I've made a fool of myself. I thought the way you kissed me just now ... God, surely I didn't invent that. But you're always so bloody ... defensive. It's like trying to get behind barbed wire. Even now you're pushing me away.'

'I'm not! I don't mean to be! It's the very last thing I *want* to do! But I'm older than you! I know what happens when people fall in love and lose all judgement.'

'You're eleven months older than me.'

'How on earth do you know that?'

'Well, if you must know, I looked it up in your medical records. You're young enough to have plenty of children, if you want to.'

'What? Oh, that's ridiculous!'

'Anyone seen Miranda?' said Lissie's voice, from beyond the curtain. 'I must go home. My ankles are swelling like balloons. Give her my love, Presley. And tell her I'll ring in the morning. Marvellous party!' Her voice faded away.

'QED!' Rory stood up suddenly. 'What is it you do want, Miranda? Are we supposed to shake hands and utter a few words of polite regret about what might have been? Do you really want me to take that job and leave you?'

I was silent, trying to think... not what I wanted, I knew that... but what would be the rational, sensible thing to do? He put his head closer to me and I saw that he was angry. His eyes were glittering faintly in the reflected light from the house cast up by the surface of the water. I felt sick with misery at the sight.

'I'm beginning to think that what you really like is to have men fall in love with you so that you can make them dangle on a string after you. Is that what your friend meant? An enslavement... something you can soothe your vanity with? Well, that's not what *I* want!'

I stared up at him dumbly. He reminded me so vividly of Jack. He knew how to wound.

'All right! If you want me to go away just say so. I'm not going to stand around and be made a fool of. I'm sorry I misunderstood what you wanted.' He laughed, most unhappily. 'I'm just like all those other men. Wearying you with their attentions. I despised them then. Now I know just how they felt!'

I knew he was waiting for me to say something, to tell him that he must stay, that he was different from those others. But I could not believe in love on any terms. Those who do not remember the past are condemned to repeat it. Jack had made me believe that if I did not marry him his life would be a desolation to him. He had probably believed it himself at the time, just as Rory did now. I tried to find the words to explain my idea of a temperate love that was founded on mutuality of needs and circumstances. I could not think of a way to express this idea that did not sound unutterably cold and dreary, even to myself.

'I'm sorry –' I began.

Rory pushed the curtain aside and left me.

'There you are!' Patience came up to me. 'I've been looking for you. What's the matter with Rory? Have you had a row?' Then seeing my face, she said, 'You're in love with him, aren't you?' I shook my head, unable to speak in case I burst into tears. 'I'm sorry,' she went on. 'I had the feeling you were. But I'm so ignorant about these things. Anyway I'm glad you're not in love with him as he's going away.'

'Yes.' I swallowed. 'It would have been disastrous, wouldn't it?' It was annoying that my voice sounded quivery. 'I've been winged... I admit that, but it's recoverable. A few bad days and I'll be over it.'

'Poor Miranda.' She put her arm round me and I very nearly howled. 'It's a terrific party. Lots of people have been asking me where you were.'

'I'd better go and talk to them.'

Miss Horne was standing in the hall putting on her mackintosh and head scarf. 'I can't think when I've enjoyed myself so much, Miranda.' She looked excited, almost girlish. 'People have been very kind. It's rather lonely in Willesden. The only time I speak to my next-door neighbours is to find out when the rubbish collection is after a bank holiday. Mrs Higgs said why don't I move into the country?' She looked wistful. 'I expect a single woman is just as out of place here as in the suburbs. An embarrassment. People invent excuses to get away because they don't want to get stuck talking to me.'

'I'll send you details of cottages in the village,' I promised. 'Then you must come down and have a look at them.'

Miss Horne's round grey eyes looked at me through her thick spectacles. 'Wouldn't I be a nuisance? I'd hate you to feel you had to be nice to me, for Mr Stowe's sake.'

I kissed her cheek. 'For your own sake I'd be delighted if you came to live at Westray.'

'Come, Miss Horne, or we'll miss that train,' said Aubrey, taking her arm.

'Another dependant?' hissed Maeve, as she walked past into the drawing room.

'Darling, you look as though you've been run over by a steam-roller,' said Maurice. 'Hurt and disbelieving all at once. What's the matter?'

He was magnificent in his bishop's cope, Prospero restored to his dukedom, potent with spells, the cheap Christmas-tree braid from Braithwaite's transmuted to twinkling, talismanic gold by the candlelight.

'I was silly enough to get carried away by wine and tiredness, that's all. It was a romantic dream. But I'll get over it. I know what I've got is more than anyone could reasonably ask for. You and the children and Westray. And now something really exciting to get my teeth into.'

'Presley's script? I'm glad you've decided to do that. I should have known you to be seriously insane if you'd decided against it. As it is,' he shook his head, 'I still have my doubts.'

'What do you mean?'

'It's Young Lochinvar, isn't it? You've sent him packing? Child, I don't think you know what you're about!'

'It's extraordinary how sagacious everyone is. Except me, naturally.'

'Darling, you know perfectly well that none of us is fit to be allowed out on our own when it comes to matters of the heart. It's so easy to predict shipwreck for others and so impossible to chart the rocks in our own course. I speak from experience. I've made enough wrong decisions in my life to consider myself an authority on how best to make yourself thoroughly wretched and miserable.'

'I expect you're right.' I sighed. 'I really can't think properly. I'm too tired and confused. I'll go to bed. We'll talk in the morning.'

Elizabeth was sitting on the stairs with a boy I recognised as one of the young Scranton-Joneses.

'Night, Mum,' she said, briefly looking up at me as I passed. Her companion continued to glue his eyes to Elizabeth's face, with the fascination of one who might say, if he could command his voice, 'Behold, Kismet!'

Sukie moved over to let me into the bed and gave me a couple of generous licks and a five-second burst of purring before resuming sleep. I lay with my good ear pressed to the pillow to shut out the noise of the party downstairs. I was fortunate to be able to do this, I reflected. It was yet another benison in a life weighed down by good things. I couldn't even hear properly the sound of my own sobbing.

I was not at all surprised when I looked at my face in the mirror the next morning to see that tears had wrought havoc. I bathed my face with icy water until my eyelids began to lose their resemblance to buoyancy bags. I was sitting at the dressing table brushing my hair when I suddenly remembered that it was Saturday and, in the press of events of the day before, I had forgotten to take eggs to Miss Boswell. I swore aloud. It was quite unforgivable of me to have neglected her. It was only seven o'clock. I could walk down to her cottage and be back in time to make breakfast. I felt pretty certain that Miss Boswell's infirmities would prevent her from sleeping much after dawn.

I opened the door of Elizabeth's room, bent down and beckoned to Jasper. He came up, thoroughly mystified, to sniff my finger. I grabbed his collar and hauled him out. We went via the hen run so that I could give Miss Boswell the very freshest eggs in expiation. The hens ran out, cackling with pleasure, to eat their breakfast corn. There were half a dozen eggs still warm and clean in the nest boxes. I put them in the basket with a comb of honey that

Maurice had extracted from the hive a couple of days before.

The air was very clear and the sun warmed my bare arms as we walked down through the village. I met the milkman on his round and the newspaper boy steering his bike with one hand and picking his nose with the other. An early Marbled White butterfly swooped suddenly down on to the road in front of me to bask in the growing heat of the day. The hedges were bright with dog-roses and sweet-briar and the heady-scented elder, flowering above the yellow oat-grass and meadow fox-tail. Jasper trotted ahead, lifting his head occasionally to give a small bark of pleasure at a passing bird. All nature conspired to celebrate a perfect midsummer day. I attempted to put a spring into my step and to rid myself of the sensation that I was wearing deep-sea diver's boots.

Miss Boswell was sitting by her window and waved as she saw me coming up the path to her door. She cut short my apologies. 'Bless you, dear! I knew you wouldn't have time. Miss Wakeham-Tutt came in her car and drove me to the pageant. I had a ringside seat. Oh, I did enjoy myself! And she drove me home afterwards! She was so kind. A real lady! I said to Mr Molebank, "You've chosen wisely and well!" You were so good, dear, in your part! It was so good of them to think of taking me to see it!'

I felt overwhelmed by so much grateful cheerfulness. Poor Miss Boswell was in continual pain and almost always lonely. She had nothing to look forward to but the cessation of labour and pain in death, and yet she was thanking me for the eggs and exclaiming over the honey as though I had brought her great treasure. I stayed to talk to her for half an hour about the pageant, feeling that it was the very least I could do.

On my way back through the village I was hailed by Maeve. Remembering our conversation of the night before I wasn't at all pleased to see her, but she called my name so determinedly that I felt obliged to stop and wait for her as she came up the lane behind me.

'You're out very early,' she said, panting a little in her effort to catch me up.

'I might say the same to you.'

'With complete justification. I can't remember when I last got up at this hour. I've been down to the station to post Sebastian his Gestapo hat. He's got ringworm and they've shaved his head. The other boys are threatening to beat him up for being infectious. Hardly the place to learn to be a model citizen. Anyway, guess who I saw at the station?'

I began to be apprehensive. 'I hate those sort of guessing games.'

'Well, I'll tell you. Rory McCleod. He was waiting for the London train. He's agreed to sell me his old banger, by the way. I thought it might cheer Sebastian up when he comes out in a couple of weeks' time. Well, anyway, while he was standing on the platform I had a long talk with him and very interesting it proved to be.'

'Really?' I attempted to increase my pace but Maeve took hold of my sleeve and made me turn to face her.

'I don't know what you think you've been playing at, my girl, but it seems to me that you're making a very big mistake. It's obvious that he's completely nuts about you, and I don't believe that you're exactly indifferent.'

'I must say, everyone seems very concerned to mind my own business for me. I know what I'm doing.'

'I don't think so. You're in love with him, aren't you?'

I made no reply. I really felt angry at this intrusion, however well meant, into my feelings.

'I thought so. Allow me to tell you that you're a coward, Miranda Stowe! A coward and a fool!'

'Thank you.' I assumed a light tone, but I felt my face begin to burn.

'You think all men are bastards and so you won't allow yourself to have anything to do with them.'

'Not quite all men.' I laughed, attempting to hold my quarter, but Maeve was into her stride.

'You do! You're terrified that Rory's going to treat you as Jack did and have affairs with other women! I told

Rory all about it. That you've got a sort of phobia about men being unfaithful to you. You always say psychotherapy is all misleading humbug but actually you're scared witless! You daren't look inside yourself and see what you really feel!'

Now I was furious. 'How dare you talk about me with Rory!'

Maeve snorted. 'I dare to do a lot more than that when I see you behaving like an absolute chump. What the hell are you doing sending this man to the rightabout? All right, I grant you Janòs wasn't a good bet. Too devoted to himself. He'd never make any woman happy. You were right to get out of that when you did. I can see that now.'

I made a mock curtsy. 'I'm so glad to have your approval. I'll be sure to consult you any time I want to dispense with a lover.'

'No, but don't be sarcastic now. I'm serious. You're wrong about Rory. Can't you see that you've got to take risks if you want anything out of life? Things aren't going to float down from heaven into your lap. You used not to be such a faintheart. I always admired you because you were strong. I saw what Jack was doing to you and how you stood up to him. It was amazing, really. I couldn't have done it. I told Rory how cool you were about Jack's women, how you wouldn't let yourself get into fights with him or let him play games with you. Rory was shocked. He obviously had no idea about your marriage. Why didn't you tell him, you idiot? Why didn't you have the honest gumption to ask him to help you?'

'Maeve, I don't doubt that you mean well. Though there is scarcely a more damning phrase, is there? But it's time you realised that the rest of the world does not exist in the sort of mystic haze of love and sentiment and gush that you like to spoon about in. You, above all people, ought to have learned the dangers, to your sons if not to yourself, of taking risks!'

I stood still, breathing hard with indignation and then, because I hated to see the hurt look on Maeve's face, I turned and started to walk away very fast. I took large strides that almost split my skirt, in an effort to put the largest distance possible between me and her. I forgot altogether about Jasper and when I reached the top of the ridge above Westray I was surprised to see him come panting up, waving his tail, pleased to have found me.

'Jasper! Good boy! Here, boy!' I bent to stroke him. He licked away a stray tear that had unaccountably found its way on to my cheek. I was already regretting that allusion to Sebastian. It was thoroughly mean and I was ashamed of myself. God! Why couldn't everybody take their damn fingers out of my pie? What was it to them if I shrivelled up altogether for lack of male attention? Plenty of women led satisfactory lives without being beholden to men. Rose, Miss Horne, Miss Boswell... all exceptionally honourable and likeable women. The thought was depressing. When would they all understand that I knew what I was doing?

But it was hateful of me to have been unkind to Maeve. She had wanted, in her own misguided but kind-hearted way, to help me. As soon as I got home I would ring her up and tell her I was sorry. Perhaps I ought to go to her cottage now. I stood irresolute on the crest of the hill for a moment while warm tears slid easily down my face. Dear Maeve, she was a good friend, taken all in all.

But supposing what Maeve had said was true? Was I a coward? I picked my way carefully among the pot-holes made in the track through the upper woods. The cows' hoofs had gouged out small craters six to nine inches deep in places and now that the mud was hard and dry one's ankles had every chance of being turned and broken on the treacherously uneven ground.

Was there just the smallest chance that Maeve was right? I lifted my head and gazed thoughtfully at the distant strip of coruscating sea. Maurice had said that none of us can see our way clearly in affairs of the heart. Was the simple truth that I was frightened of being hurt? How had it come about that I had taught myself to believe that Rory was incapable of anything but vacillation and duplicity? I knew some men were capable of loving well ... imperfectly, perhaps, but with enough honesty and steadiness of purpose that made their affection worth having, that made it probably the greatest blessing of existence. As Maurice had loved Lucia, as George loved Lissie and Rollo loved Diana, as Aubrey would doubtless love Patience, so might Rory be capable of loving. Had I not decided for myself that his nature was open and candid, that he was unguarded?

Suppose Rory found the challenge that could satisfy him working here? Perhaps he had really meant what he had said about liking the countryside, after all. Might I allow myself to be happy ... really happy? Eventually the children might come round to the idea of my getting married again. Perhaps Elizabeth would discover that boys her own age were more satisfactory. As I allowed the possibility to take shape in my mind I felt a weakening of resolve.

Was it possible that I did not know what was best?

I stumbled on, thinking of all this, cursing the pot-holes, teetering on crumbling muddy pinnacles, daring myself to entertain the prospect of what it would be like to be really happy. Well? And why not? The future was undetermined. Anything could go wrong with one's life at any moment. There was always the possibility of earth-quake, shipwreck or tempest. Wasn't there a time when it was wise simply to trust in other people? Or God? Or one's own instincts? I stood still and took a deep breath of wonderfully mild, clean air smelling of brine.

Perhaps Maeve was right. There must be some tenable ground between her impetuosity and my cautious calculation. But Rory was already on the train going out of my life. No doubt he was horrified by what Maeve had told him. What man wants a woman so publicly humiliated by another man? I had not been enough for Jack, said the sneaking little voice that had tortured me with its stinging insinuations for so many years. Rory would be staring out of the window as the train sped north, thanking his lucky stars for a narrow escape. Mrs Kenton would, no doubt, have a forwarding address. Could I possibly ...? I *was* a coward! I didn't have the courage to go after him and call him back. I stood and wept at my own weakness.

I had reached the point from where you can see the best view of Westray. It was laid out below like a drawing from a history book of medieval England. The only movement was the slight waving of trees in the gardens, laid out neatly and diagrammatically around the house. The rose garden was a large square of pink, white and green dots. There was Temenos and the Quincunx Garden and the cherry orchard. The roofs of the pigeon tower and Ivor's cottage showed as patches of red and grey among the tree-tops . . . There was a car on the drive by the gatehouse. And someone was standing on the bridge looking down into the moat. A man with dark hair. I saw him push it back impatiently as he turned round to lean against the parapet and lift his face to warm in the early-morning sun. It was Rory.

Abandoning the preservation of my ankles to Fate, I broke into a run.